I…reach for the ties in my hair.

Once it's unbraided, tumbling down my back, I pause for a moment, holding a soft handful with my eyes shut tight. I wish for a mirror, so I could see it one last time, and so I could see what I'm about to do. But if I had one, I'm not sure I could force myself to go through with it.

My heart is in my throat as I lift the shears. I open them, take a shuddering breath, pull the hank of hair out straight, and aim.

With a tiny, inarticulate noise, I lower the shears again. I can't do this. I can't. Not my hair…

All it takes is another steadying breath, the memory of Jak calling me a trollop, remembering what he did. An uncaring fire burns through me, and this time, when I lift the shears, I don't hesitate before I snap them shut.

From **THE KING COMMANDS**

THE KING COMMANDS
Tales of the Borderlands · Book Two

Meg Burden

Brown Barn Books
Weston, Connecticut

Brown Barn Books
A division of Pictures of Record, Inc.
119 Kettle Creek Road, Weston, CT 06883, U.S.A.
www.brownbarnbooks.com

THE KING COMMANDS
Tales of the Borderlands, Book Two
Copyright © 2010, by Meg Burden
Original paperback edition

Library of Congress Control Number 2008940806
ISBN: 978-0-9798824-1-8
Burden, Meg
THE KING COMMANDS: Tales of the Borderlands, Book Two

Printed in the United States of America

For my parents, Brad and Diana Burden,
with all my love.

Acknowledgments

I couldn't have written this book without the support of my friends and family. Heartfelt gratitude to:

My husband, Nick. You're always looking out for me. I'd be lost without you, and I love you. Thanks for taking care of the cats while I was writing, too.

Mom and Dad, Matt and Annie, thank you for everything.

My extended family, the Daltons and the Burdens, thank you so much for your support and encouragement.

To my editor, Nancy Hammerslough, thank you for your unfailing patience and your belief in me. You're a joy to work with.

Rebecca Anderson, thank you for shining a light in the dark so many times, for encouragement and inspiration, hand-holding and friendship. I couldn't have done this without you.

Jo Graham, an inspiration to me and a true friend, thank you for your unfailing kindness and support.

Emma, parts of this are for you. Thank you for your enthusiasm and pep talks.

Jenna, thanks for the name I needed, and so much else.

Deepest gratitude to my friends for your encouragement and belief in me. You kept me going when I didn't think I could, poked me when I needed it, and distracted me when I needed that, too. Special thanks to Kim, Jody, Stephanie C., Dani, Stephanie G., Alice, and the Tabbert family.

A huge thank you to Christian Y. for my first fan letter about Northlander.

Thanks also to Eisley, whose music provided my writing soundtrack for this novel.

CHAPTER ONE

THEY SAY NORTHLANDERS and Southlings are different as winter and summer, stone and wood, the moon and the sun. But then, they say many things, most of them foolish. True, Northlanders are blond, Southlings red-haired, but we're not so different. I ought to know.

---∘∘∘-)◯(-∘∘∘---

We circle one another on the hard-packed dirt of the castle yard, beneath the bright midmorning sun. Even after months of practice, the sword feels awkward in my hand, and I grit my teeth as Coll guides me through the drill. High, then low; slide my blade from beneath his and disengage; shift forward to meet again. On to the next form, and the next, the same ones we've been doing for an hour. Frustrated, I try to increase the speed of my blows, try to break from the pattern for something different, but he lunges forward and disarms me with an effortless flick of his wrist.

My sword clatters to the ground, and I groan. "Damn it, Coll! Just once, can't you let me…"

"Let you what?" he rumbles, bending to retrieve the weapon. "Hurt yourself by being foolish? Push yourself beyond your skill?"

"My hand slipped!" I exclaim. "I wasn't holding tight enough. If you try that again, I won't make the same mistake."

He holds out my sword and gives me a doubtful look. "I've told you a hundred times, it's not your fingers, girl. Mind your wrists."

1

I breathe hard through my nose, still annoyed, but wrap my fingers around the hilt anyway. "It's not as if I forget every time," I mutter. "I'm not stupid. I'm just not good at it."

"No," Coll agrees, looking down the length of his blade as he tilts it, catching the sun. He might be fighting a smile behind his short, dark blond beard. "But you've stopped ducking. That's something."

"Oh, thanks kindly. That's very reassuring."

Coll opens his mouth as if to reply, then closes it again and gestures with a nod at the low wall nearby. I wait until he has settled his bulk onto the weathered stones before I sit, laying the practice sword across my apron. I concentrate on a clump of weeds growing between the stones, afraid to look at him for the lecture I know I'm going to get. I know it already, anyway. Coll Horse Master is a prince of the Northlands. He's busy with his own affairs and oughtn't be wasting his time teaching the castle's healer to play at swordfighting. At the very least, I should be gracious and grateful instead of cross and frustrated at my lack of skill. I brace myself.

"Ellin," he begins, and it's his use of my name as much as his uncharacteristically gentle tone that makes me look up, startled. For Coll to call me anything besides "girl" means it must be worse than I thought. He gives me a small shrug. "Has it occurred to you that perhaps Southlings—or at least healers—aren't meant to be fighters?"

"That's ridiculous! I have arms and legs and hands that work, don't I? Why couldn't I?"

"You don't have a knack for it," he says bluntly. "More importantly, I don't think you have the heart for it. And if you don't want to..."

"But, Coll, I do! I want to be able to defend myself and my friends! I want..." To be strong, I finish silently. To be able to take care of myself without being afraid. And I want to be as dangerous physically as I am with my mind. In the past year, I've learned to see the value of both.

He sets a hand on my shoulder and gives me a pitying look. It would be annoying if I weren't so upset. "Do you? You're small and ought to be light on your feet, relying on speed, not strength,

2

as the Sword Maidens up north do. Instead, you stand there like a stone and let me out-maneuver you. I'm a Rider for a reason, girl," he adds, referring to the fact that, in the Northlands army, only the biggest, strongest (and, frequently, slowest and fattest) men typically ride the enormous, furry-legged Northlands horses into battle. "And though I'm more experienced," he continues, "the least you should do is move your feet faster. But you don't."

"Maybe not yet, but I can learn," I reply, unsure which one of us I'm trying to convince. "Can't I?"

He shrugs again, looking doubtful. "I still don't see what value swordplay has for you anyway, when you can control people with your thoughts, and heal them, too. Surely those are greater skills than this." He pushes himself to his feet. "I've work to do," he says, gesturing with the point of his blade toward the stables, "but consider what I've said. You'll be better off if you content yourself with what you have."

Less than a year ago, I was content. I had a home in the Southland, and the most wonderful father in the world. I knew—had always known—that someday I would be a Healer like him. Master Rowan Fisher was renowned for being the best Healer in all the Southland. So well-known, in fact, that tales of his skill reached the cold, forbidding Northlands.

It was winter when Master Willem, Chief Physician of the Northlands College, came to the village of Harnon in the Southland. It was midmorning. I was kneading dough for bread, and my father had gone out to deliver a tincture to Thom Alder. When Father came home, Master Willem said that King Allard of the Northlands was ill, dying, beyond his or any of his colleagues' ability to treat. And Master Willem, who was old enough to remember a time when the Northlanders and Southlings were at peace, remembered the talents of Southling Healers. He begged my father to come to the Northlands with him and brew remedies for the king in secret, even though doing so would be illegal.

According to the laws of the Northlands, Southlings like my father and me were lesser people, forced to have papers stating their name, what their business was in the Northlands, when they had arrived, and when they planned to leave. Required to use the same gate into the walled city that was used for livestock, required to live on certain streets. Use of Healing powers was called witchcraft and was against the law, punishable by death.

My father didn't hesitate. He was a Healer, a good man, and it didn't matter a bit to him that King Allard's hair was blond instead of Southling red. It didn't matter to him that Master Willem had probably spat at a fair few Southlings in his day. Father nodded once, calmly, and told me to start packing my things.

The Northlands were even worse than I'd imagined. The winter was bitter, the Northlanders themselves colder still. But it wasn't until the night when King Allard was close to death, the night of the blizzard, that I realized how little my life meant to any Northlander. I'd been outside the city walls, gathering herbs for a medicine my father wanted to brew as a last resort, and I came to the gates at sundown, just as they were closing. Instead of waiting for my father to come escort me to the College, the guards locked me out. I would have died, and King Allard too, had one of the guards not taken pity on me and let me stay in the gatehouse.

It was lucky he did. A younger guard came to the gatehouse later, and I discovered that he was Garreth, youngest of the five princes. He helped me get into the city, to the castle. At the castle, for the first time, I used my Healing power, desperate to save the king's life. With my father's help, I succeeded, and for a time, my father and I were befriended by the princes: Alaric, Coll, Erik, Finn, and Garreth. When King Allard recovered and imprisoned my father and me instead of sentencing us to death, the princes helped us escape to the Southland.

I was the one who broke us free from our prison cells, however. When I healed the king, I accidentally awoke the forbidden mental abilities that some Southlings possess. At the time, I didn't know they were forbidden. All I knew was that I could "speak" with my mind to Erik and Finn, who somehow had the power, too.

Back home in the Southland, I soon wished I'd never discovered my powers. A mysterious organization called the Guardians sent some of their members to kill me, as they had executed many others with powers like mine. My father died protecting me. Orphaned, homeless, and banished from my newfound friends in the Northlands, I thought all hope was lost until I met Levachai Kinshield and his band of True Southlings…Southlings with gifts like mine, who wanted to live freely, without fear of persecution.

That wasn't all Lev and his men wanted, but I didn't find out until it was almost too late. I traveled with them to the Northlands, not knowing that their plan was to use their mental abilities to control the royal family's minds, to force them to invade the Southland with their army and defeat the Guardians.

The princes and I defeated the True Southlings, but the cost of the battle was high. Wielding my powers, I fought Lev, who was compelling the king. King Allard died as we struggled for control of his mind, and Lev nearly did. I didn't know my own strength, and I damaged his mind beyond repair.

Alaric was crowned king just as winter ended, and I became a permanent resident of the castle. But even now, though Alaric changed the laws and declared that Southlings are equal to Northlanders, no longer required to have papers or any of that rubbish, I still feel sometimes as if I don't truly belong.

That's why I've started wearing my hair in looped braids and bought a pair of heavy boots and poked at Coll until he agreed to teach me to use a sword. I may not be a Northlander, tall and blond, with eyes the color of the sky, but I'm not a Southling, either. Not anymore.

I'm Ellin Fisher, called Healer, and most days, that's enough.

———∘∘∘-)◦(-∘∘∘———

By the time I've fetched my basket and knife and made my way through the gates, the sun has nearly reached its peak. I pause a short way down the road and take a deep, contented breath.

Sometimes, the tall, pointed-roofed buildings and stone walls begin to feel like a cage, and it's a relief to be out in the open, with trees and dirt and grass.

When I first came to the Northlands, I thought it the most forbidding place I had ever seen. Blank snow, gray stones, whitish sky, dull black trees... I loathed its ugliness. Now, I marvel at the beauty before me. The grass here is as green as it is back home, and wildflowers speckle the meadows with blue and pink and yellow. I can find many of the plants here that I use most often in my work. I often make use of the castle's gardens, too, but I enjoy the solitude I find outside the city.

In no time, I've filled my basket with fragrant, dusty-soft wild lavender leaves and blossoms, the hairy inner bark of twisted elm, white verbena, and assorted parts of other useful plants. On my way back to the gate, I stop to cut several blossoms off the short-stemmed wild roses scattered along the sides of the road. They smell so wonderful that, were they white instead of pink, I'd thread them into my braids and enjoy their fragrance up close. Instead, I content myself with putting them on top of the lavender and promise myself I'll put them into a cup of water beside my bed.

Soon the wall looms in front of me, a blue-coated sentry at each of the open gates. The noon sun glints off the hair of the taller guard, at the smaller gate, like a beacon. I smile and veer off the main paved road onto the dirt track beside it, unable to resist the temptation to nettle him.

"Twenty-eight pigs," Garreth greets me, sounding pained. He waves the record book in his hand with a flourish. "All this morning! I hate market days."

"I see you've had plenty of cows, too," I reply, skirting a particularly big, fly-covered pile on the road. I can't blame him for hating to be assigned to keep records of the livestock being brought to market. The big gate requires a lot less work of the guard assigned to watch it, and involves far less mess. "And," I add, though it isn't really true, "you stink."

Garreth grimaces and wipes his forehead with the back of his hand, leaving a faint smear of dirt. "I'm not surprised. Thought I smelled something rank. Guess it was me."

I have to bite the inside of my lip to keep from laughing, but he doesn't seem to notice as he glances at my full basket. "Are you headed for home?"

I nod.

"Wait a moment, and I'll walk with you," he says. "I've been here since sunrise."

"All right." I follow him in and perch on the stone steps that lead to the top of the wall while he goes up to tell someone to replace him. He and another, older guard come down again a moment later, and Garreth and I set off.

"Whew," he says before we've gone ten paces, shrugging out of his limp coat and folding it over his arm. "It's warm."

"I like it." I tilt my face to the sun and smile. "I can almost forgive the Northlands her winters for this."

"Well, you haven't been herding runaway pigs and getting shoved around by cattle all morning."

It's difficult, but I manage not to gloat. The urge fades when I look over at him and notice that he's stepping gingerly, favoring his right leg. "What happened?" I ask.

"One of the damned cows stepped on my foot," he mutters. "It's nothing."

"It's not 'nothing' if you're limping like that."

"Didn't hurt so much when I was standing still."

"Well, I'll look at it when we get back to the castle."

He nods in reply, jaw set. I feel a little sorry for teasing him before. He is awfully sweaty, and both his hair and shirt are damp and wilted-looking.

"Would you like a drink?" I offer, as we pass through the crowded town square. "I'll get you a dipper at the well."

Garreth shakes his head. "Have one yourself, if you want. I'll wait."

I shake my head, too, and refrain from pointing out that I probably don't look like I need refreshment. Or a bath. Or both.

"What's all that for?" he asks a moment later, with a nod at my basket. "Medicines?"

"Mostly. Not the roses."

"Why'd you pick 'em, then?"

"Not that it's any of your concern, but because I like them. They smell lovely."

Garreth snorts. "Next you'll be curling your hair and learning to dance rather than to fight, won't you?"

"You know, it's a wonder to me that half the girls in town find you so..." Catching his sudden, interested look, I clear my throat. "Oh, never mind."

He laughs, sounding so smug that I'm positive he knows exactly how many girls wish and hope and sigh for a moment of his attention. "Roses. I'll remember that." Then his grin turns sly. "Though you know why the ones on that road grow so well, don't you? It's because of all the dung."

"Garreth! You're disgusting!"

"Says the Healer!"

———ooo‑◦◦◦———

At the castle, I shepherd Garreth straight to my workroom and unpack my basket as he takes a seat and bends to remove his boot. He doesn't make a sound, but it takes him longer than it should to peel off his sock, and when I turn, his face is tight with pain.

And no wonder, I think, getting my first look at his injured foot. The top of it is swollen, marred with a dark bluish bruise and, in the center of it, a curved red scrape where the edge of the cow's hoof must have borne down. It's not bleeding, but it looks ugly.

"Garreth!" I wince as I kneel in front of him. "You should have told me it was so bad. You shouldn't have walked on that."

He shrugs as if it's nothing, but I know better. "Is it broken?"

"I doubt it, but..." I gingerly take his foot in my hands and run my fingers over the bruise. He hisses, but holds still, and I look at him after a moment and shake my head. "Nothing's broken. You can soak it in cold water to help with the swelling, and after that, I'll bind it up."

Garreth nods, and I go to the cupboards for a basin. "Ellin?"

"Hmm?"

"Is there—would you use your power on it? To make it hurt less?"

I struggle not to flinch. "You want me to do a Healing on you? Garreth, it's not even bleeding."

"It's throbbing now that I'm looking at it," he mutters, clasping his hands tight on his lap.

He sounds about ten years old and looks it, too, all hunched and miserable. I know how delicate the bones in a foot are and can only guess how much it must hurt. Even so, I could make a tea to dull the pain, or tell him to wait and see if it feels better after he's soaked it, or...

He's looking at me strangely, head tilted, no doubt puzzled by a Healer hesitating over such a small request. I sigh. "Of course I will," I say quietly, kneeling again. I lower my head as I touch his foot, hoping he won't notice that my fingers are trembling.

Slowly, reluctantly, I call up my power and feel it wash through me. It doesn't take long, but when I've finished, I'm breathing hard, heart racing. "There," I say, false-brightly, rising quickly so he won't see the look on my face. "If you can hobble to the kitchen yourself, I'll be there in a moment with the basin. You can eat lunch while your foot soaks."

I separate the lavender from the verbena at the counter, picking at them and trying to seem busy, while he gathers his things. But when the door thumps shut, my palms splay open on the countertop, and I let my breath out in a whoosh. I'm still shivering.

What sort of Healer am I? I wonder, staring at the piles of herbs spread before me. The answer comes immediately, whispered from some dark corner of my mind.

Not a very good one, apparently.

Chapter Two

IN THE KITCHEN, I find Garreth at the table, already eating. "There you are," he says. "I was beginning to wonder if you were coming." But his expression isn't probing, and I can only assume, with relief, that he didn't notice anything odd about my behavior when I Healed him.

"Sorry." I bend to set the basin on the floor beside him. "Let me fetch some water for that."

After I've gotten a pitcher of icy well water and have Garreth, with some complaining, settled in for a soak, I see about finding myself something to eat.

Jana the Cook, coming in from the garden with a basket of greens, gives me a nod of her blue-kerchiefed head. "There's more pies, if you're wanting lunch," she says, gesturing at a cloth-covered tray.

I help myself, then grab a napkin from the laundered heap in a basket on the counter. I take a bite of the flaky pastry crust as I sit across from Garreth. The pie's filling is delicious, spicy gravy with chunks of meat and onions, and I close my eyes happily. "I didn't realize I was so hungry," I say when I've swallowed.

Garreth nods his agreement, mouth full. "Thought I wouldn't even want to look at food today, before you Healed me, but now it hardly hurts at all. Thank you."

I look down at the pastry in my hands, losing my appetite. "It was nothing." The next bite is so dry I can barely swallow it, and the crumbs stick like dust in my throat.

A light touch on my shoulder makes me jump, but when I turn, I smile, grateful for the interruption. *"What happened?"* Finn asks both of us, forming the words with his hands, then motioning to Garreth's foot.

"A cow stepped on it," Garreth replies darkly. Though Finn can read his lips, he signs the words as well. I don't speak the language as well as they do, but I'm sure he adds another word before 'cow,' and I think it's one of the ones they all refuse to teach me because it's not polite.

Finn peers critically into the basin as he sits, and ruffles his brother's hair. *"I think you'll live."*

"I got more sympathy from Ellin!"

Finn raises an eyebrow at me across the table, and I roll my eyes. "He was limping," I explain. "I told him I'll wrap it later. And he's to sit. All day," I add, fixing Garreth with a warning look.

"Did I say I wouldn't?"

"She knows you," Finn points out. He pinches off the corner of Garreth's second pie and pops it in his mouth. *"I was looking for you,"* he says to me. *"Do you want to bottle the wortroot extract this afternoon, or have a lesson? Or both?"*

I shake my head, though the extract does need tending to before it ferments, and I would love a lesson. Finn and Erik have taken it upon themselves to give me a 'proper' Northlands education, as they once received from their tutors, and so far, I've found the study of everything from history and geography to poetry to be fascinating. "I can't," I reply at last, reluctantly. "I have to—I have something else to do." I don't want to upset either of them by elaborating.

He looks disappointed. *"Later, then?"*

"Maybe." It depends on how terrible I feel afterward, though I don't voice this aloud or with my hands. "Does one of you want the rest of this?" I add, nodding to my half-finished pastry.

Finn shrugs and takes it, and I leave the boys to their meal.

——∘∘∘-)◯(-∘∘∘——

Walking down the narrow side-street, my heart and my feet feel as if they're made of lead. My stomach knots, making me regret my lunch, as I open the door of a squat, ugly stone building. The main room is plainly furnished and lit by a grimy lantern and a few narrow windows up near the ceiling. The lone guard, seated with his boots propped up on the table, cracks one eye open. "Time again already, hmm?" he rasps. His feet drop to the floor with a thump before he stands and picks up the lantern. "Come on, then."

I follow him down a flight of narrow, cobwebbed stairs, and then a hallway with cells on either side. I shudder, as I always do, remembering all too well what it was like to be kept prisoner here. We turn a corner, and the guard reaches for his ring of keys in order to unlock the door at the end of the hall, revealing an even darker stairway. I brace myself and follow him down.

The air is damp and musty, so far underground, and the stone walls seem to press in when we step out into the corridor. The guard's big nose casts a long shadow in the lantern light. "They'll let you in," he says, jerking his head at two others at the far end of the hall. "Tell Stan I said to bring you up when you've finished."

"All right," I murmur, though he has already turned to go. His unfriendliness doesn't surprise me. Nor does the fact that Stan the Unlucky, the younger of the guards on this level, doesn't bother to hide his flinch when I approach, my footsteps seeming too loud on the stones.

When my father and I were imprisoned, my powers allowed us to escape. When I first discovered my gifts, I thought that talking mentally with Erik and Finn was the extent of my abilities, but I couldn't have been more wrong.

I helped Coll's favorite mare birth her foal and found out in the process that I had the power to control her mind with mine; to compel her. That dark, terrible power came back tenfold when I tried to escape from this prison. Instead of using my Healing ability to put Stan the Unlucky to sleep, my mind became meshed with his in what I later learned was the first step of compelling a human. At that point, all I knew was that I was out of my depth, and terrified. I wrenched my mind away and knocked him unconscious in the process. For someone named Unlucky, he's fortunate I didn't accidentally kill him.

I apologized to him the first time I saw him here, after Alaric became king, but I didn't explain what had happened. I suppose I can't blame him for still being wary around me, knowing firsthand what I'm capable of. I'm afraid of myself.

I try to look as non-threatening as possible as I approach Stan and the other guard, Ivan Scarbrow. Ivan looks up only briefly from the chunk of wood he's whittling, leaving Stan to unlock the cell door for me and step back quickly, without a word. I wish there was something I could say to reassure him, but there isn't. I lower my head and give him a wide berth as I step inside so he can lock the door behind me.

The small windowless cell is illuminated by a single candle. The only furniture, besides a narrow bed with a thin, filthy mattress and an even thinner blanket, is a small, crudely made table and a rickety stool. The room reeks of mildew and human filth, stale urine and unwashed body. It is the figure on the bed, though, that draws my attention.

Pale as parchment and too still, the only sign that he is alive is the slow, shallow rise and fall of his chest. His hair, once worn roguishly long, has grown longer and snakes in lank tangles around his head, looking, in the dimness, dark and flat as dried blood. His hands rest beside his thighs, limp, fingernails as long as a fine lady's.

His lips, once so warm, are chalky and slightly parted. His eyes are closed, dark lashes caressing bluish, hollow circles.

He looks like a corpse. And I have done this to him.

I swallow, dry-mouthed, and force myself closer to the bed. For a moment, I merely look at him. I didn't used to look. I couldn't. Immediately after the battle with the True Southlings, I thought

Lev would surely die. When I tore my mind away from his, he fell to the floor, unconscious, bleeding from his nose and his ears. I thought I'd killed him.

When it became apparent that he wasn't going to die—at least, not immediately—I realized I had done him even greater harm. Not dead, no, but not alive, either. For days, he sat and stared, slack-jawed and drooling. I didn't think I could bear to see him again, but I couldn't bear the thought of him like that, either. I asked Alaric to let me drug him with the strongest narcotic brew I could make. I told him and Master Thorvald the Physician that I wanted to make sure Lev would never recover and try to harm anyone again, but I think they both knew that wasn't my true reason.

Lev was my friend, once. He kissed me once. And despite everything, I wanted to give him the only assistance in my power to give: oblivion. These visits to the most secure cell in the prison, these visits to the most dangerous criminal in the Northlands, have become my weekly punishment. At first, I averted my eyes and hurried, but now, I look. I linger. I did this to him. I *am doing* this to him. Such torture is the least I deserve.

Despite the guilt and the nagging beginnings of a headache, my hands are steady as I withdraw a tiny glass vial from my pocket and uncork it, careful not to get a single drop on my skin. Pinching the vial between the fingertips of my right hand, I lift Lev's head up with the other and gently urge his mouth open. Though he looks dead, his skin is hot and dry. I've wondered if this long-term use of the drug is killing him.

I don't falter as I tip the contents of the vial into his mouth, then massage his stubbled throat, urging him to swallow. I should go, I think, when I've set his head down. And yet, as always, instead of leaving, I turn back to the bed. The wooden frame digs into the backs of my thighs when I sit on the edge of the mattress. His hand, when I take it in mine, feels too soft. Too still.

I will never forgive Lev for what he tried to do to my friends. I don't blame him for hating the Guardians, and I know that he was desperate. But to turn to evil himself…there is no excuse for that.

My father would have agreed with me, I'm sure. He told me once that having abilities like mine isn't wrong or evil, but it matters, very much, what I choose to do with them. The only truly bad thing would be if I used them to harm others.

At the thought of my father, the inside of my nose burns, and my lips tremble, fighting tears. I've often wondered what he would think if he could see me now, using the skills he taught me to do this to Lev. No person was too bad or insignificant for Rowan Fisher to heal. He once tended Darin Blackwood's hand after Darin got stinking drunk and started a huge brawl at the inn and broke his fingers punching a wall. Others might have said he deserved the pain, but not my father. He'd heal those who were too poor to pay, and those so rich they treated him like a servant. He came without hesitation to help King Allard, simply because he was needed.

If my father were here now, I know he would say it is my duty to try to heal Lev. He would be appalled to see me using my talent as a Healer to keep someone from recovering…and that on top of the horror he would feel, knowing that I did this to Lev with my powers. There is nothing I could have done to make him more ashamed. My father was slow to anger and quick to forgive, but I don't know if he would forgive this. I don't think I would ask him to.

I am Ellin Fisher, called Healer, and yet it is a name I no longer deserve. I don't deserve to call myself my father's name, when I know he would turn his back on me for what I have become. And I certainly should not be called Healer. Not when the one I ought to heal is lying here, near death, because of the poison I give him.

I am ashamed.

At last, I take a slow breath and blink back tears with an effort. I let go of Lev's hand but can't resist reaching to push a stray piece of hair back from his face. When my fingertips brush his forehead, I jerk back, stumbling to my feet.

Burning. Skin hot like fire, nothing but blackness when I open my eyes. A red flower, falling. Drops of rain on white stone.

The images sear into my mind, sharp and vivid. The vision lasts only an instant, but it leaves me reeling. I know those things—the wet stone, the flower. I've seen them before, several times, in my dreams.

Gooseflesh shivers up my arms as I look wonderingly at Lev, lying motionless, outwardly peaceful. How...?

Surely not, I think a moment later. Seeing Lev always upsets me. It's no surprise that I would remember a strange nightmare when I'm already out of sorts. It's nothing. I'm sure of it.

Still, I practically trip over my own feet hurrying for the door, then pound on it until I hear Stan's key rattling in the lock. I suddenly, urgently need warm sunlight and fresh air, away from these close, cold walls and ghosts of my own making.

CHAPTER THREE

THOUGH THE LATE SUMMER days are balmy and
pleasant, the fire in the great hall of the castle
is still welcome at night, when the cool breeze drifting through the
windows brings the scents of pine and sweet grass to mingle with
the woodsmoke. I've come to love these lazy summer evenings
spent here, eating sweets dripping with fresh berries and talking.
I think at least part of the feeling is that we're all free to go if we
wish, free to step outside without so much as a thought for freezing
one's feet or fingers or catching a chill. Everyone who gathers does
so because they want to, not because there's nothing else to do.

I smile and sip my tea as I look around at my friends, sitting on
the low benches arranged around the hearth. This late, only the
brothers and I remain. Farthest from me is Alaric, seated with one
hand upon his knee, the other holding a glass of wine. At twenty-
six, he is the oldest of them, king of the Northlands. They call him
"the Golden," and not only for his hair and beard, which glint
with strands of deep bronze in the firelight. It has long been said
that he is unusually blessed, and it's easy to tell by looking at him
and speaking with him, that it is true. Tall, broad-shouldered, and
handsome, with a strong jaw and straight nose and eyes so dark
blue one could drown in them, he looks every bit the charismatic
leader that he is.

My smile deepens as I shift my gaze to Coll, beside Alaric. Two
years younger than Alaric, half a head shorter and something

like twice as heavy, it's easy to see why Coll is called "the Fat" in jest. After all, names in the Northlands are always true. But so is his real name, Coll Horse Master. Though his hands are meaty and callused, I've seen him caress his favorite mare's neck with a gentleness that would put any healer to shame. Not to mention plait horsehair into cord so deftly that most women would envy his skill. At first I disliked Coll, unable to see beyond his customary scowl and gruff way with words, but now I know better. I know to look for the glint of boyish mischief in his keen blue eyes, the way his mouth quirks down when he's fighting a smile. He's not an easy man to know, but he's well worth the effort.

Erik, though... I look at the boy sprawled inelegantly on the flagstones at Coll's feet and shake my head with private amusement. As easygoing as his posture would indicate, it's nearly impossible to resist liking Erik, even if you want to. Though possibly the homeliest of them all, he's also the friendliest. He's the shortest of the brothers and wiry, clean-shaven, with messy sandy hair and a long, thin nose, but his eyes, light blue and lively, and his wide, brilliant grin more than make up for his plainness.

As always, I marvel that Finn is so different from Erik. Both of them twenty years old, they are twins, though one would never know it. And one would never guess that Finn, so serious, is the younger of the two. Though, perhaps I can understand that difference in them. Erik, called Archer, is a surpassing skilled marksman and a force to be reckoned with using other weapons, a fast runner, a passable musician, and possessed with the greater gift of being easy with anyone he speaks to. He's as sure of himself as one might expect. For Finn, though, music and the rhythmic clash of steel have never had any appeal, and casual conversation with strangers is difficult. Deaf and unable to speak as well, while Erik followed in his older brothers' footsteps, Finn turned his attention to reading and study and, later, to the physicians' trade. He can ride as well as any Northlander, and fight, but his interests lie elsewhere. I don't think this would be different even if he could hear.

As tall as Alaric if not a fingersbreadth taller, Finn certainly doesn't look like Erik's twin. He's also sandy-haired, though his lies smoothly instead of looking like a bird's nest, and he's also slender and clean-shaven, but that's where the resemblance ends. Finn's eyes are gentle gray instead of vivid blue, his features fine but not sharp, and, unlike Erik, he has freckles. He has a scholar's rounded shoulders and a physician's stained fingertips, and his hands are every bit as expressive as his face.

Then there is Garreth the Youngest. Seventeen, a scant few months older than I am, and already nearly as tall as Alaric, Garreth is all knuckles and knees and big hands and feet, gawky rather than imposing. He looks a bit like Alaric, too, though beardless and much paler, white-blond hair and eyes the color of the winter sky. The problem with Garreth is that he is the youngest, and too conscious of it. Though he is a skilled enough swordsman and marksman, Alaric and Erik are better. Though he rides well, Coll is better. Alaric is more handsome, Finn is a better confidant, and Erik is more amusing. Erik told me once that they used to call him Garreth the Nuisance, and even now, when Garreth is reasonably close to being a man instead of a boy, I think he still wants to prove himself. It makes him haughty and prickly and frequently reckless, not to mention a show-off. But underneath all of that, he's a nice boy.

"Ellin!" Garreth's voice jerks me out of my thoughts.

"What?"

"Do you want to play, or sit there staring like a frog?"

Looking around at the others, I realize they're all watching me, and I feel my cheeks getting hot. "I was just thinking," I mutter. "What's the game?"

"Naming," Alaric says. "I'll judge this round."

"And I'll start," Coll adds. He takes a swig of his wine, then sets his cup down and looks at his brothers and me in turn, slowly. At last, he points a finger at Garreth, and I smile with anticipation. "I name you Garreth the Tall," he pronounces, speaking with his hands as well. "Not for your height, but for your tales."

When the laughter and groans have faded, Garreth, pink-cheeked, clears his throat and sits up straighter. He looks around at all of us, squinting slightly. Then he grins. "I name you Erik Keen-Eyed. Not for your skill at hitting the mark, but because you always ogle the prettiest girl in a room within seconds of entering it. And subtly, too," he finishes, snickering.

At that, we all laugh and nod our agreement again. Erik only shrugs—after all, it's true—and jumps to his feet, giving me a cocky grin. "I name you Ellin the Red," he says at once, so quickly I know he must have thought of it beforehand. "Not for your hair, but for your temper."

I squeeze my eyes shut, embarrassed, but I can't keep from giggling. Coll snorts, and even Finn is grinning broadly when I look. Erik bows, and then it's my turn.

I look at all of them, considering. Only Coll and Finn are left this round, and though I'm free to select either, I know I'm expected to choose Finn, so he can then Name Coll, and everyone will have a fair turn.

I fix my gaze on Finn and tilt my head in thought. He raises his eyebrows at me, smiling a challenge, and I look back wickedly, suddenly inspired. "I name you Finn the Cautious," I say, then hold up a hand. "And not because you measure even tea leaves three times for accuracy, but because..." I hold my hand up to my chin and adopt a mock-thoughtful pose, squinting into the distance, "you're very..." I turn the other way and scratch my head, pretending to be deep in thought. Erik snickers. Then I face Finn again and give him a cheeky grin. "...Deliberate."

He makes a face at me, but he's laughing in his strange-sounding way, and I know from his brothers' chuckles that my caricature of his thoughtful hesitance was on target. Then we all howl when, instead of starting immediately, he puts his chin in his hand, mimicking my mockery of him.

"I name you Coll the Valiant," he signs at last, and Erik speaks the words aloud since not all of us can see his hands clearly. *"And*

not for any battle won, but because it takes true bravery to trust Garreth with your tack."

They all applaud as if this was a good jibe, but I don't understand. Alaric looks across at me, grins, and takes a drink before explaining. "Years ago," he says, "when Garreth was a small boy, Coll let him help with the horses and, finally, said that Garreth could help clean his saddle. What he didn't know was that Garreth planned a gift for him and decided to clean the saddle himself one morning. So, imagine Coll's surprise when, instead of oiling the leather, Garreth used kitchen grease."

I gasp, torn between laughter and horror. "He didn't!"

"He did, and pounds of it," Coll says, cuffing Garreth lightly on the shoulder. "It was *years* before I let him near my things again."

Garreth crosses his arms, looking annoyed. "I call foul," he grumbles. "That wasn't aimed at Coll so much as me."

Finn shakes his head emphatically. *"No, it was at Coll. I think it takes a brave man—or a fool—to trust your little brother with your prize possessions."*

Laughing, Erik looks up. "Oh? I'll remember that. So will Coll and Alaric."

"I trust all of you with my life," Alaric says lightly. His mouth twitches, and he buries his smile in his cup before adding, "If not my sword, my favorite boots, my saddle, my books..." Though he's teasing them, he winks at me, and a flush of warmth that has nothing to do with the fire washes over me.

"And your heart?" I ask lightly, trying not to let on that my own seems to be fluttering in my chest like a caged bird. "Would you trust us with that, at least?"

I sense Finn flinch, next to me, and wonder if I've gone too far, if my attempt at teasing revealed what I'm sure they must already know. But then Alaric smiles again, easily, and gives me a slow nod. "You don't need to ask. You all already have it." Then he raises his cup to Erik. "This round to Erik," he says. "Do you all want to play another?"

CHAPTER FOUR

FINN BARELY NOTICES as the next round of the game begins. The wine in his mouth suddenly tastes sour, and he grimaces as he swallows. And though his eyes are on Garreth, sore foot apparently forgotten as he gives Coll a particularly rude name, doubled over with laughter, it is Ellin that he sees. Another time, in other circumstances, he would have cherished the image of her as she was a moment ago—eyes shining, lips slightly parted, spots of color staining her cheeks. The tilt of her head said clearly that she asked the question half in jest, and Alaric answered in kind, but Finn knows better. He has seen the way she straightens when his oldest brother comes into the room, the way her smile is brighter in his presence, her hands restless and nervous.

He first knew perhaps before Ellin herself did, when she and Garreth burst, dripping and shivering, into their da's sickroom, when her gaze swept over the room and landed, and remained, on Alaric. She has never spoken of it, but then, she doesn't need to. Though she would probably resent his saying so, her face speaks volumes, especially to anyone who watches her closely.

A sharp jab on his knee startles him, and Finn lifts his eyebrows at his twin. *"What?"*

"It's your turn! Are you deaf or something?" Erik teases, then nudges him again. *"What're you thinking about, so seriously? We're trying to play a game, in case you've forgotten."*

Finn looks at the others, watching him expectantly. Ellin's lips are pressed together, hiding her amusement, though when she catches his eyes, she puts a finger to her chin and adopts a pensive expression, imitating him again. Finn smiles at her, then shifts his gaze to Alaric, sobering.

He can't blame her for her choice. His brothers are all the best men he knows, and Alaric is the best of them. Finn takes another drink and sets his cup down slowly, careful not to meet Erik's eyes for what his twin might see. *"I forfeit."*

After Erik declares Coll the winner, Ellin rises and bids them all goodnight. And though it's Finn's shoulder that her fingertips brush in passing, the casual touch is like a sister's, and it is Alaric, of course, who draws her gaze.

When she goes up to her room, only the five of them are left, with the dying fire, a half-empty carafe, and a bowl of tart berries, picked in the morning and beginning to wilt. On the floor, Erik pulls off his boots and puts his sock-feet near the fire, wiggling his toes blissfully. After a moment, Alaric goes to sit beside Garreth, no doubt hearing all about the damned cow—again. Since morning, the beast has grown with every retelling of the tale, and now has sharp horns and a temper to match. Finn fully expects it to snort fire and have iron hooves by morning.

He smiles at the thought and looks to Coll, who meets his eyes steadily; as always, seeing more than most would expect. With a motion of his head, Coll indicates the space on the bench next to him. When Finn has settled into the seat Alaric recently vacated, he turns to Coll expectantly, but, as he should have known, his brother doesn't say a word. Instead, he leans over and bumps his shoulder against Finn's, before reaching for the wine to refill both their cups. After a few moments of sipping silently, staring into the fire, Coll sets aside his cup and nudges him again. *"Don't look so glum. You know I'd trust you with anything of mine, little brother."*

Finn has no choice but to laugh, which, he supposes, was probably the point. He lifts a hand to thank Coll but checks the motion when his brothers turn toward the door. Following their lead, his eyes widen at the sight of Lord Tomas striding in, posture tense, gray moustache practically bristling.

Alaric rises at once, with Coll, of course, at his heels. Their backs to him as they speak, Finn waits for Erik to join him on the bench, still bootless. *"What's wrong?"*

Erik's face darkens. *"More trouble with Southlings,"* he replies tersely.

"Here?"

"No. In Rannok," Erik says, naming the nearest town. He swallows visibly as he raises his eyes to Finn's. *"You know a lot of Southlings have settled there. Lord Tomas says there was a brawl at the tavern. A gang of young hotheads decided to give a Southling barmaid some trouble..."*

"And all the Southlings in the place had something to say about it?" Finn finishes, wincing.

"Sounds like." Erik's lips press together as he glances at the others. *"It's getting worse,"* he says, unnecessarily.

It seems like an age before Coll and Alaric rejoin them, and when they do, they sit heavily. Coll takes a deep drink of his wine, then passes the cup to Alaric, who drains it. At last, Alaric raises his eyes to them, the harsh shadows cast by the firelight making him look far older than his years. "You heard?"

Finn nods, and out of the corner of his eye, sees Erik and Garreth do the same. "What are you going to do?" Garreth asks, voicing the question for all of them.

Alaric's jaw tightens. "Lord Tomas said that the guards in Rannok broke up the fight. He merely wanted me to know about it."

"That's not what he meant," Erik says, and Alaric closes his eyes.

"I know. What do you suggest?"

"Make it illegal to mistreat Southlings," Garreth says at once. "That would solve the problem, wouldn't it?"

Alaric doesn't respond immediately, but Erik gives him a withering look. "That would certainly encourage the people who already think the king's mad—or worse—for letting Southlings live here in peace, without all of the old regulations."

"Besides, the worst of it is already illegal," Coll points out, "and it's impossible to change the way people think. That's the real trouble."

"I think the only option you have is to wait," Finn says. *"Be patient, and fair. Don't seem biased toward either the Northlanders or your Southling subjects. And in time..."* He trails off into a shrug.

Alaric gives him a wry look. "In time, maybe our people won't curse my name for changing things, and the Southlings won't hate me for not doing more on their behalf?" He shakes his head. "Sorry. You're right, and I know that's the only choice. I just don't like it."

"You never have," Coll says, cuffing him on the arm. "You're not called Alaric the Patient, are you?"

Alaric gives him the ghost of a smile, but sobers immediately when Erik speaks. "Are we going to tell Ellin this time?"

"No," he replies. "At least, I won't, and I hope you won't. If she hears about it from someone else, that can't be helped. But the new laws matter so much to her, and if she knew how tenuous this peace truly is... I'd like to shield her from that."

"And the wedding?" Finn has to ask, though the question makes his heart twist. *"When do you plan to speak to her?"*

"You've waited a long time," Erik adds. "Too long. You'd best talk to Ellin about *that* before she hears about it from someone else."

Alaric pushes his fingers through his hair, making it stand on end. He used to do that when he was studying, Finn remembers suddenly, hunched over books and parchment with ink stains on his fingers. It seems like far too little time has passed since then, far too few years between scribbled mathematics and the weight of a kingdom. He takes a sip of his wine, thankful, and not for the first time, that he isn't the eldest.

"Tomorrow," Alaric says at last, and he yawns as he stands. "I'll speak with her tomorrow."

CHAPTER FIVE

FIRE. MY SKIN BURNS. I can hear my heartbeat, fast and quiet and irregular, like the far-distant pounding of a frenzied drum. I open my eyes, and all I see is black.

I see a clearing, ringed with beeches and maples and oaks. A red leaf falls. The red leaf becomes a red flower, still falling. It spins in midair, blurred, and I can't discern its shape. Its shape is important, its type is important, but I don't know why. I strain to see it more clearly...

A drop of rain splashes down on a white rock.

And then darkness, again, as the fire consumes me.

I wake with a gasp, clawing my way out of the tangled sheets to sit bolt upright. The morning sunlight streaming through my window assaults me, far too bright after the all-consuming blackness of my nightmare. I squeeze my eyes closed against the pain, then realize, after blocking myself from the sun, that my head aches despite it. Not merely a headache, either. Stabbing agony at my temples, deep inside my skull...

I groan quietly, then lurch to my feet, clutching my head, and barely make it to my knees in front of the bucket in time.

When I've finished, the pain is much better, though now I feel shaky and weak. Not to mention thoroughly annoyed—and confused. After the first time I woke this way, I brought the bucket to my room in case of future emergencies. But I never imagined the next time would happen so soon, much less that starting the day by being sick would become a regular occurrence.

There's nothing physically wrong with me. Of that I'm certain. If a woman told me she'd been vomiting in the mornings, of course I'd think she was with child. But, of course, I'm not. And it's not some other sickness, either. I know it's the nightmares. The same ones have been coming frequently, more vivid and real than any others I've had in my life. The first time I woke from them, I nearly wept with relief to find that my skin wasn't blackened and blistered from the flame. In my sleep, I can smell the grass and fresh, outdoor air in the clearing. I can feel the breeze on my cheeks as the flower falls.

And each time when I wake, my mind feels bruised and fragile, the way it does after I've used my powers. I haven't told my friends. I'm afraid that discussing it would draw out the truth I can't bear to face. I think it's another power. My own body, my own mind, is betraying me. It must be that. Or else...

My hands pause on the ties of my apron, shocked to stillness as I remember what happened yesterday, with Lev. I saw the images from my dreams when I touched him! Perhaps, I think, feeling my heart start to pound fast and excited, perhaps this power isn't mine at all!

But then I drop with a soft thump onto the edge of the mattress, one boot on, the other dangling in my hand. If these nightmare visions are coming from Lev, it must mean that he really is alive in there. Conscious enough, if not for true mind-speech, to send this message. Maybe the dreams are some kind of plea for help.

"That's impossible," I murmur aloud, struggling with numb fingertips to lace my boots. Why would Lev send these dreams to me, of all people, intentionally? I shake my head, realizing how foolish the thought is. Maybe this is nothing more than what happens when a gifted Southling goes mad. Instead of speech and coherent thoughts, perhaps his mind just sends out memories and images and feelings. That makes much more sense. Still, the thought that it's Lev and not me fills me with a mixture of relief and unease, leaving me jittery and on edge as I braid my hair.

---·∘∘∘·)☖(·∘∘∘·---

"Thought you'd be out with Coll already," Erik greets me, when I join him and Finn for breakfast at the end of one of the tables in the great room.

"Not today." I help myself to a spoonful of eggs from the serving bowl. "I have a headache."

Finn looks at me sharply across the table. *"Again?"*

"It's nothing," I reply. I take a few bites of my breakfast before I realize that he's still staring at me, and I roll my eyes at his concerned look. "I'm all right, Prince Physician. You needn't worry, honestly."

"It isn't only that." Finn takes a drink of his tea and glances at Erik, who looks back significantly in silent communication that has nothing to do with their powers. At last, he sets his cup down and raises his eyes to me. *"Ellin, I wanted to tell you…"* Grimacing, he waves the words aside and starts again. *"It's just—It's not important."* He sighs, letting his hands drop to the table, then stands and takes his cup and plate without another word.

I turn to Erik, wide-eyed. "What was that about?"

"Hmm?" He shrugs and takes a big bite of bread, avoiding my gaze. "You know Finn," he mumbles, mouth full.

"That's why I'm bothered. Do you know if he's angry with me?"

"Angry?" His eyebrows climb. "No. As he said, it's nothing. Or if there *is* something, I'm sure he'll tell you another time. When he's ready."

"But what…?" I stab some eggs and shake my head as I chew. "I can't imagine he'd need time to…Do you know what it is?" I ask suddenly, looking at him with new interest.

He grins. "Curious, are you?"

"Like a cat, and you know it. Erik, what is it?" I plead. "Do you know?"

"No," he mutters, in a tone that clearly tells me he does. His red cheeks do nothing to help his lie. "And even if I did, do you really think I'd tell you?"

"Only if it suited you," I reply tartly, though I'm not really annoyed.

"Naturally." He gives me a wicked smile, and I sigh.

"Well, if you see him before I do, will you please ask him to tell me whatever it is?" I ask.

"That's what I have been telling him," he says quietly, surprising me with his serious tone. But before I can ask him what he means, he stands and takes his plate and says he has to go, leaving me alone, even more unsettled than before.

---∘∘∘-❧◈❧-∘∘∘---

At least there are some questions I can answer on my own, I think a little later, as I walk down the street to the prison. Though today is as warm as yesterday, sky the color of a robin's egg between mountainous white clouds, its beauty has no appeal for me. I'm too consumed with worry about what I plan to do.

By the time I reach the prison, my hands are trembling. The grizzled head guard looks up in surprise when I open the door, and I hope my apprehension doesn't show as he scrutinizes me. "Yes?" he rasps. "What're you doing back so soon?"

"I left my—I mean, I forgot to give him his second medicine," I stammer, and curse myself for being a terrible liar. "He's supposed to get two kinds, now, instead of just the one."

The crevasses on the guard's weathered face deepen. "I've not heard of this."

"Well, you're not a Healer, are you?" I ask, scarcely needing to feign indignation. "Why would you have been consulted?" I straighten my shoulders and try to remember how Alaric sounds when he's being particularly commanding. "Now, I must see the prisoner at once. Please." The last word slips out as an afterthought, unintentionally, and I mentally kick myself again.

The guard shrugs and pushes himself to his feet. "Well, remember better next time, girl. Come on."

And down we go again, through the corridors and stairways that set my teeth on edge. At least Stan the Unlucky isn't on duty this morning, I note with relief. I don't think I could bear frightening him two days in a row. His replacement is hardly better: a hook-nosed, hard-eyed guard I don't recognize, who watches me with deepest suspicion. I'm sure I don't imagine his loathing as he glances at my red hair.

It's almost a relief when the door of Lev's cell is locked behind me, leaving me alone with him. Almost, except that I know what I must do now. I know, too, that I don't have any time to waste.

At the side of the bed, I take his hand, closing my eyes as soon as my fingers wrap around his. I take a deep breath to calm myself and reach for my healing power, but instead of welling up inside of me as gently and naturally as a spring blossom unfolding, it feels distant, reluctant. Instead of summoning it easily, I stretch; reach it like wading through mud. At last, it comes, and I feel the familiar, soothing warmth tingle along my palms.

I have neither the time nor the skill for a complete, complicated Healing, and so instead I do the best I can for his mind. In truth, I don't know what exactly is wrong. I can sense that there is vast damage, something like the ruins of a once-great city, and all I can do is to repair what I can, and quickly.

When I withdraw, I look at him, exhausted. Though it has only been a matter of moments, it feels as if I've been laboring in there for days. And yet there is no change. Lev looks as much like a corpse as he did yesterday and every day before, skin still pale, breathing still shallow. My lips shake, and I turn away.

And then I swallow a scream as his fingers clench mine hard. With a gasp, I jerk my head to look at him. He gasps too, mouth wide, as his eyes snap open and dart wildly around the room.

Too shocked to speak, to move, to do anything except stare, I sit like stone with my fingers being crushed into dust.

"What is it?" he demands, and his voice, hoarse and barely above a whisper, is such a pale echo of himself that I could weep. I think I do, a little. "What is the flower?" He shakes my hand with urgent need. "Is it a rose? A rose is very soon, or most distant. I don't think it's soon, do you? Not so soon. Not with—no, much has to come before. A chrysanthemum makes more sense. The tulip would be better."

It takes me a moment, lips parted soundlessly, before I can answer. "What?" I whisper. But he doesn't seem to hear.

"No—no, no, no. Not the rose, though it's rain, not snow, isn't it? White snow. Red. Falling. Do you know what is it? Yellow would be too—too easy, wouldn't it? Tulip. Spring. But this—don't know when. Don't know. Can't think for all the burning." He pants for breath, chest heaving, and I wonder with growing dread if his glassy eyes really can see me.

But I know, now.

"Where's the fresh-turned earth, and where's the trees?" he asks, in a quiet, eerie singsong. "Flowers. Seasons. Fire! The burning, the burning, and I want the rain, but that's later, isn't it? Comes after. I want to know when. When?" he wails quietly, breaking off into a sob.

He lets go of me at last and covers his face with both hands, shaking. My own tears are wet on my cheeks, and I reach instinctively to touch his wrist. His hair is soaked, as if this exertion cost him dearly. His skin feels like he's already burning. I swallow the lump in my throat. "Shh," I whisper, willing my voice not to break. "It's all right. It was only a bad dream."

Lev keeps sobbing, silently, and with a frightened glance at the door, knowing I've taken too long already, I gently tug his hands away from his face. "It's all right," I repeat soothingly, as I reach for my pocket. "I have some medicine to make you feel better."

He doesn't respond, but he doesn't fight me, either, when I tip the vial into his mouth. As his eyes close and his body goes limp, I'm torn between crushing guilt and the knowledge that perhaps this drug is a mercy, after all. At least, lost in the dreams, he won't make himself sick fretting about their meaning.

I've barely re-corked the vial when I hear voices outside the cell door, the key turning, and a jolt of apprehension shoots through me. Hastily, fingers clumsy, I thrust the vial away and wipe Lev's streaked cheeks with my sleeve. The door begins to open behind me with a squeak, and my heart pounds rabbit-fast as I scramble to my feet and try to seem nonchalant, as though tugging Lev's blanket smooth is nothing out of the ordinary. I smile innocently, but my lips freeze when I see the hard-eyed, hateful guard pointing a finger at me, with Lord Tomas on his heels.

"There she is," the guard announces. Rather unnecessarily, I think, seeing as it's a small room.

Lord Tomas's pale gaze flicks from my face to Lev and back, and I try not to flinch. "Healer," he says evenly, "what are you doing here? Did you not come yesterday?"

I swallow and step away from the bed, as if the space will somehow distance me from my guilt. "I wanted to try a second…"

He waves my explanation aside, arching an eyebrow. "Yes, I've heard. But what I don't understand is why Master Thorvald the Physician did not inform me of this new plan. As you are well aware, this prisoner is under my direct supervision. I'm surprised I wasn't told."

"Master Thorvald doesn't know," I reply. "I wanted to see if it worked before bothering him—or you—with such a trifling matter. But I wasn't aware that I required anyone's permission to come here, or to treat him. After all, I've been drugging him with the king's permission…and at the king's request." I fervently hope that invoking Alaric's name will end this quickly so that I can go. The last thing I want is for him to ask me more questions.

Lord Tomas's eyes narrow, and I bite the inside of my cheek, but at last he gives me a slow nod. "You don't require my permission, of course. But for your own safety, I would prefer that you keep your visits to a minimum," he says smoothly.

I nod, somehow managing not to sigh with relief. "I will. Thank you." It takes an effort not to quicken my pace when I walk past him out the door and down the hallway.

Once I'm outside in the fresh air and sunlight, I inhale and do my best to shake off the chill of the tomb-like hallways and Lord Tomas's even colder stare. I don't know why he unsettles me, or why he seems to dislike me so greatly. I know Alaric thinks highly of him, so I try not to think the worst. Maybe I was only imagining that he seemed suspicious of me. Or perhaps he was suspicious, but, I must admit, he had reason to be. I was lying, after all. I try not to think that he dislikes me simply because I'm a Southling. Surely Alaric wouldn't value someone with such prejudices, would he?

My uneasy thoughts swirl as I walk to the main street, scarcely paying attention to my surroundings. The simple fact is, I have too much to think about, all of a sudden, what with Lev, the dreams, Finn's strange behavior, the idea that Lord Tomas doesn't trust me... And now I'm going to the apothecary shop, calling myself a healer, when in truth I feel like a fraud.

I push the heavy wooden door of the shop open with a sigh. Normally I love the way it smells inside, so pungent and spicy, with the dry, sneeze-inducing scents of dried herbs. I love the way the shelves are full of bottles, lined up and precisely labeled, glinting in what dusty sunlight manages to come through the windows. I love the tiny, neatly-rolled pills in little boxes, the scoops and scales for measuring, the thick, scarred wooden counter with the glass cabinet front...all of it. This place reminds me of my father, but today, that just makes me sad.

"'Morning, Red," Josef the Apothecary calls. When Father and I first came to the Northlands, I disliked the hunched, gnarled old man because I thought he was rude to me. I've since learned that he means 'Red' as an endearment, not an insult, and, while he is cantankerous, he knows his trade inside and out and has a heart soft as butter. He smiles behind his long white beard and looks at me over thick spectacles when I approach the counter. "What've you got for me today, hmm?"

"Twenty bottles of wortroot extract," I say. "Five chunks of the lavender soap you liked last time. Some tea to settle upset stomachs, and more of the salve you asked for."

He takes his time examining everything I brought—sniffing the tea and the soap, holding a few bottles of the wortroot extract to the light and peering at them, and testing the salve on the back of his hand. At last, he pushes his spectacles up his crooked nose and fixes me with a glare. "It'll do. But it's not Masters' work. I'll give you five for the lot."

Part of me wishes we didn't have to do this every time, but another part of me enjoys it. "Ten," I snap. "You know as well as I do that the finest ladies in the city adore my soap. And you won't find clearer or stronger wortroot extract anywhere. Besides that, I did something about the salve's stink, like you asked."

"Hmm." He strokes a hand down his beard. "Seven, then. And don't you dare ask for a penny more."

A reluctant smile tugs at the corners of my mouth. "Eight, or I'll find another seller for the soap next time."

Josef purses his lips and narrows his eyes, causing his wrinkles to deepen alarmingly, then nods. "Eight, then. And you'd best take a vial of my rose water, too. It's the good stuff, from Abana, and I'd rather give it to you for your soaps than sell it to some maid who'll douse herself with it."

I laugh, utterly charmed. "Is that any way to barter?"

"Aye, it is, when the seller's a pretty thing, with something besides air between her ears to boot." He winks, then wags a finger. "But don't you dare think of selling the rose soap elsewhere, understand?"

"It's all for you, Josef, I promise." Then I give him a teasing grin. "And I'm sure you'll smell lovely using it."

"Hmph!" He hobbles away to get my payment and the rose water, then presses them into my hands with fingers that tremble a little. I wonder, and not for the first time, if the old apothecary neglects his own health in order to keep his shop open. I certainly hope not. "You stay out of trouble, now, Red," he mutters, sounding cross. "And get me that soap soon!"

I feel much better when I leave the shop than I did going into it. For the first time all day, the sunlight warms me, and I look forward to going back to the castle and having something good to eat. Maybe I'll even start on the soap this afternoon. I'll have plenty of time to worry about Lev later, and as for Finn, well, I'll talk to him later, too. I'm sure whatever he wants to tell me can't be terribly urgent.

Though come to think of it, I realize, maybe he wanted to tell me something about Alaric! It would make sense. Last night, Finn seemed upset when I asked Alaric if he would trust me with his heart. Though I was only half-serious, perhaps Finn could tell that I meant what I asked. And perhaps...after all, he is Alaric's brother. Perhaps he knows that Alaric feels the same way I do. Or maybe Finn knows for certain that Alaric is fond of me, but thinks I was only teasing and wants to ask me not to toy with his brother's feelings. Either way...

My lips curve into a smile, and my fingers tighten on the handle of my basket as I daydream. I'd be in the garden, hair loose and shining in the sunlight. Alaric would stride up behind me, looking truly regal in the blue tunic he has that matches his eyes. He would cast a shadow, and I would turn, startled, to see him holding out a flower. I'd take it, heart pounding, and he would lift one hand to stroke my hair and tell me, again, that he thinks it's lovely. Then he would say that he thinks I am beautiful and that, though he has tried to deny his feelings, he must confess that he is in love with me, can't stop thinking about me, gets tongue-tied and blushing when we're alone, and dreams of kissing me.

And I, of course, will admit that I feel the same way about him. He'll give me a brilliant smile, then will bend and press his lips against mine in a kiss that is far more romantic than the one Lev gave me. Then we'll walk to the castle, hands entwined, where we'll tell everyone that we're in love and plan to marry someday.

I want to dance with him. I want to sit beside him and have tea, with his blue, blue eyes looking deep into mine as he tells me the mundane details of his day, and his hopes for the future. I want to watch as he trims his beard, shaping it neatly. Though the thought makes me blush, I would like to see him without his shirt. I've seen Coll without his, though I didn't particularly want to, but Alaric... I'm sure he must look like one of the great statues, well-muscled and solid. I want to make him laugh. To fix him a cup of spiced wine and have his fingers brush against mine intentionally as he takes it.

I've never been in love before, and I didn't think I wanted to, but Alaric, bright and brilliant as the sun itself, has changed my mind completely.

"Hey!" At the sound of an angry voice, I start as if a bucket of cold water has been doused on me. Jerking my head up, I see that I've walked as far as the crowded marketplace without realizing it, and a red-faced young man holding a big crate stands glaring over the top of it.

I blink at him, confused. "What?"

"You damned near made me spill this all over the place, that's what!" He shakes his head, and I'm mortified to see several people nearby turning to gawk. "Think you're so welcome here now you don't have to watch for us Northlanders walking about? Is that it? Just go wherever you please, and we'll all make way for you?"

I back up a pace. "I'm sorry. You see, I wasn't…"

"Don't listen to her!" a woman calls. "You know how they are. Thinkin' they're better than us, now, don't they?"

"But I don't…"

The man with the box turns his head and spits. "Southlings," he says, as if the word is a curse.

They're all staring at me now, steel-eyed and flat-lipped, and though no one moves, it feels as though the circle is closing in, pressing, trapping me. My heart jumps into my throat, pounding too fast, and I can't seem to stop my eyes from filling with stinging tears no matter how hard I blink.

Without another word, I turn and push through the crowd, shouldering someone who says a word so foul my father once made me chew soap for speaking it. And then, before I know what's happening, someone shoves me from behind, and I go sprawling, landing hard on my hands and knees.

Partly because of the pain, and partly because I'm afraid, I don't move for a moment. Some deep, instinctive part of me hopes that, like prey, if I stay very still, they won't continue their attack. My chest hitches, but I bite down on my lips to keep the sob in check. I won't give them the satisfaction of breaking me.

No one comes to ask if I'm all right. After what feels like a long time, even though it is only a matter of minutes, I push myself, shaking, to my feet. My right palm is scraped and bleeding, wrist aching, and I can feel a trickle of blood sliding down from one of my knees. Holding my arm close to my body, I limp over to my fallen, empty basket and pick it up.

I walk the rest of the way to the castle gingerly, bruised both inside and out. I keep my head down this time for shame, because I can't bear the thought of looking into their eyes, their faces, and seeing such hatred there, still. Shoulders tense, I do glance up every few moments, and look behind me, fearful of walking in someone else's path, afraid of being followed.

I hate this. I hate that they'll still take any excuse to persecute me just because I wasn't born here in the Northlands, because my hair is red instead of blond. I hate the thought of these horrible Northlanders using the medicines that I make, the thought of the wealthy ladies who would just as soon spit on me as use the soap I work so hard to make perfect.

I hate being looked at like that, as if they think I'm so far beneath them. Like I'm some slimy, crawling thing they want to stomp under their boots. It feels like they can look into the deepest, most secret places of my heart and see all of the worst, most horrible things I think about myself in moments of despair…and they agree with me.

I was in the wrong, a moment ago. It's true that I wasn't paying attention to where I was walking, but if he had only treated me like a person—been angry with me, but *listened* to my apology, as he would have if I were a Northlander—I wouldn't have minded. Is it so much to want to be treated the same as everyone else?

CHAPTER SIX

I'M STILL SHAKING when I arrive at the castle, though I'm sure that's more from shock than from the pain of my scrapes. All I want is to wash my wounds and apply some ointment, then fix myself a steaming cup of tea and drown my sorrows in it alone. Maybe then I'll be somewhat composed by dinner.

Intent upon my goal, I head straight for my workroom, walking as quickly as my sore knee will allow. Though I feel guilty about it, I keep my head down and pretend not to see Finn waving at me from the library as I pass. The last thing I want right now is to talk to anyone.

"Ellin!" I can't ignore his mental voice, though. With a sigh, I turn.

"Sorry," I reply with my thoughts, as he approaches with a few long strides. *"I didn't see you."*

"What happened?" he asks at once, taking my hand. *"You're bleeding! Are you all right?"*

Embarrassed, I pull away, under the pretext of needing my hands to talk. In truth, I don't want him looking at me with such concern. I'm afraid I'll start crying again if I let him comfort me. *"It's nothing."* I grit my teeth as the motion hurts my stiffening skin. *"I tripped and fell."*

I hate lying, but the alternative, telling him what really happened, is unthinkable. If Finn and his brothers believe Alaric's peace is perfect, I refuse to be the one to disillusion them by

41

admitting how bad it still is for Southlings like me. I can't bear to give them yet another reason for me to be in their debt, in need of their protection.

Finn winces. *"That looks nasty. Do you want me to help so you won't have to tie a bandage one-handed?"*

I shake my head, and he looks disappointed. Then he takes a deep, slow breath, his gaze even more serious and searching than usual. His hands twitch before he exhales and raises them. *"Could you spare a moment, then?"* he asks. *"And sit in the library, or walk with me to the herb garden?"*

"I'm sorry, Finn," I reply. "I do want to tend to this, and then I—I have work to do," I finish lamely.

He nods, and I would swear, if it made any sense, that I can almost see his shoulders drop with relief. The smile he gives me is small and sad and somehow understanding, though I have no idea how he could possibly know what happened. *"Another time, then."*

I nod, grateful, and reach out with my unhurt hand to squeeze his fingers. "Yes. Soon. I want to find out whatever secret it is you have to tell me," I add, teasing him. "Though I might have guessed what it is."

His eyes widen. *"Did Erik...?"*

"No. I only have a guess. But if I'm right...I'll be very glad."

"You will?" He looks down, cheeks darkening beneath his freckles, but I can tell he's pleased. *"I hope you're right, then."*

"I do, too." And I do, with all my heart. If Alaric does have feelings for me, and tells his people that their king is not afraid to love a Southling, maybe they will see that I'm the same as them. Though even if they don't, if Alaric loves me, I can't imagine I'll care.

———∘∘∘⟡∘∘∘———

After I've tended to my scrapes, my throbbing knee helps me decide not to bother with fetching a mug of tea. Instead, I take a book of poetry I've been studying and go out to sit on the balcony off my room. Squinting at the pages in the bright sunlight, I admit that I don't easily find beauty in the words the way Finn and, surprisingly, Coll do. The formal, courtly language is difficult for me to understand, and the rhythm is entirely different from our poems in the Southland.

In the Southland, there are four forms for poetry. One for love, one for humor, one for sorrow, and one for adventure and battles. The Northlanders have many other types of poems, and I constantly find myself wanting to stress the wrong words when I mouth them to myself. Some of them don't even sound right unless you speak with a Northlands accent, which irritates me.

But, since I live at the castle with the royal family, it's only proper for me to do all I can to be like someone of noble birth. It wouldn't be right for me to seem ignorant of their customs and culture if a visiting lord or distant relative began a conversation with me.

I raise an eyebrow at the book, wondering what the poet could have possibly intended by mentioning a crow's feathers in this particular spot. While Southland poetry is straightforward—albeit with a tendency to exaggerate—the Northlanders use all sorts of metaphors and double meanings that mystify me.

I look up gratefully when a knock sounds at my door. "Come in," I call, closing the book with my finger in it to mark my place. When I turn and see Alaric standing just inside the threshold, I drop the book onto the bench beside me and stand up in a hurry. "Alaric!" I exclaim, barely noticing the pain in my knee as I go to him. Though the younger boys make themselves at home in my room, I don't think Alaric has ever come into my private space before. Somehow it feels more intimate, more improper, for him to be here in the afternoon, with the door open, than it ever has when Garreth or Erik has sat on the edge of my bed to talk.

I'm a little relieved to see that Alaric looks as awkward as I feel, even if he, at least, isn't blushing. "Can we talk for awhile?" he asks.

I struggle to find my voice. "I'd like that. Here? Or perhaps…"

"Let's go to my study," he suggests. "I have something I want to discuss with you."

I follow him out and make some vague reply when he asks me, with typical kind concern, what happened to my hand. When we go into his study, a small, comfortable room with a map-strewn desk and worn chairs, he shuts the door. "Please," he says, gesturing to one of the seats in front of the desk. He pours a small amount of wine for both of us before joining me—not at the chair behind the desk, as I expected, but in the one next to mine. His eyes, I notice, look darker than usual, like deep water. The color I imagine the Northern sea.

Alaric looks at his hands, laced around his cup. His thumb taps the side of it. "Ellin," he says at last, quietly, without meeting my gaze, "there's something I want to tell you."

My breath catches, and my heart seems to, as well. This isn't the garden, and there's no flower, but what else could it be? My fingers are unsteady as I raise my cup and take a sip. Every inch of my skin tingles, practically singing, and I almost think I'm dreaming. "Oh?" I try not to sound as anxious as I feel. "What is it?"

Still, he doesn't look up, and I wonder, with a renewed burst of joy, if he's as shy and hesitant as I have been about admitting to this. Could it be that he feels as pleasantly nervous around me as I do around him?

I wonder suddenly, wildly, if my hair looks nice, and if my skin is still blotched from crying. I hope not. I wet my dry lips and do hope, fervently, that I haven't forgotten how to kiss since Lev. It was only the one time, and I didn't know what to do then, but surely, surely the experience must have taught me something. Though I don't know for certain, I would wager that Alaric has kissed—at least kissed—a number of beautiful women, and I hope that my inexperience won't disappoint him.

He clears his throat, bringing an end to my worrying. "I should have mentioned this sooner, and I apologize," he says. "But I..."

"Alaric." I smile at him warmly, knowing that the contents of my heart must be written on my face. And I don't care. "You don't need to be sorry. I'll gladly hear anything you have to tell me, always."

He takes a drink, then smiles. "Thank you." He stands abruptly and leans over his desk, looking down at it. "You know where Rhodanath is, don't you?"

I'm startled at the sudden change of subject, but nod as I rise to join him. "Of course." I look down at the large, beautifully-detailed map spread out in the center of the desk. "We're here," I say, tapping a fingertip against the parchment. I look at our large island, drawn in bold, dark strokes. Two countries, the Borderlands, facing one another across the river, ringed by the sea. The spot I touch is not far north of the river, in the southern part of the Northlands. Farther north, the land turns mountainous, and I've heard that life is harsh there, the winters longer than they are here and far crueler.

"And then here, to the southwest, across the narrow part of the sea," I continue, tracing the distance, "you reach the continent. First there's Abana, with the roses, and then there's Rhodanath." Turning my head to smile at him, I add, "I've heard what they say here, how Southlings think the world ends at the sea, but it's not true. We may not have much to do with the greater world, but we do acknowledge that it exists. Mostly."

Alaric rubs his mouth with the back of his hand, looking as if he's trying hard not to laugh, then clears his throat. "So, you know of the country. Do you know much about it?"

"Very little. Just bits, from stories."

"Well. It's ruled by a king and queen," he says, "who have a son and three daughters. The eldest daughter will be queen someday, and her younger brother and the second sister are already married. My da was a great friend of King Ilorio," Alaric adds, tracing a fingertip along the western coast of the Northlands. "They each spent a year in the other's country, when they were young, and I remember King Ilorio coming for a visit, once, before the twins were born."

"Oh?" I try to look interested, but I wish we could get back to our previous conversation. "That's nice," I say as I resume my seat, hoping he'll take the hint and rejoin me.

He does, and takes a drink before clasping his hands loosely on his thighs. "They decided then that the third princess and I should marry in order to strengthen the alliance between our kingdoms."

I can't breathe. I'm not certain I heard him correctly. Couldn't have, over the sudden roaring in my ears. My mouth is open, and I can't seem to shut it as he continues.

"Her name is Nathalia, and she is twenty-three," he says, then gives me a smile that's somewhere between tense and sheepish, spreading his palms. "I don't really know anything about her. I sent a letter to her father when Da died."

I press my lips together and swallow hard, hoping he won't see my face wavering as I stare into my cup. I don't trust my voice. Don't know what I would say if even if I did.

"A messenger came today, running ahead," he continues, and I brace myself. "She's in the Northlands and will be here soon, possibly as soon as tomorrow. It's not a long journey with the summer winds, when the weather's good, so her parents will follow when we're prepared for the wedding."

It hurts less with every word, somehow, as if the knife has plunged so deep I can no longer feel it. I take a careful breath through my nose, refusing to allow it to become a sob, and force my lips to curve, though the bottom one still wavers. "That's—that's wonderful, Alaric," I manage, sounding brittle to my own ears but hopefully bright to his. I won't cry. Damn it all, I will *not*. I would die before that. "I'm so glad for you."

He exhales, then reaches over and takes my numb hand in his. His fingers are warm. "Thank you," he says quietly. "What I wanted to tell you is how much I hope that you and Nathalia will become friends. You're a part of our family now, Ellin." He smiles and squeezes my hand. "And you know what it's like to live in a foreign land, far from your life before. I hope you'll be like a sister to her," he says, "the way you are to us."

I only hope that he will think the tears sliding down my cheeks are because I'm overwhelmed, or joyful. Anything but the truth. I have to clear the boulder from my throat before I can speak. "I hope so, too."

——∘◦◦-)◎(-◦◦∘——

I'm pleased to see, when I open the door to go outside, that one of the fast summer storms has come up, and it's raining bucketfuls. I don't think I could bear sunlight. I certainly can't stand to be in the castle another moment, not when Alaric is in his study, no doubt dreaming about his betrothed, glad that his friend—almost a sister—is prepared to welcome her. With a choked, helpless wail like something dying, I stumble out and let the deluge drench me, cold droplets mingling with the hot ones, falling fast and uncontrollable now, on my cheeks.

I put my bandaged fist to my mouth, trying to suppress the worst of it. I force myself to move, all too aware that someone could look out a window any moment and see me. I start walking, blindly, feeling as though I'll never breathe again. It hurts too much.

Thunder growls in the distance, and at last I stop and stand still with my head bowed and shoulders heaving. I don't know what to do. I want to leave, to start running, as far away as I can go. I want to go back and tell him everything, beg him to tell her, to marry me, to love me. I want it to stop hurting.

I don't know how long I stand there, dripping, hearing nothing but the thunder and the rain and my own gasping sobs. I flinch when a thick arm curves around my shoulders and steers me forward. "Come on, now, girl," Coll says, as low and soothing as he speaks to his horses. I think, like them, I respond more to his tone than his words. "Let's go inside."

Blinded by tears and swollen, burning eyelids, I barely register it when he leads me to shelter. It takes me a moment to understand that the rain is only drumming on the roof, not onto my head. Longer still for me to realize that he's brought me not to the castle, but to the stable.

Without a word, he leads me to an unoccupied stall, its floor strewn with fresh, sweet-smelling straw. I stand there, numb, until he pushes on my shoulders gently, and then I sit, automatically smoothing my sodden skirt over my knees. Coll shrugs out of his light coat and drapes it over my shoulders before he sits, too.

He puts his arm around me again, and I still can't stop crying. At this moment, I don't care if he's a prince, and I don't care if it's improper. I lean against him anyway, into his soft, warm side, and am glad when he tightens his hold instead of pushing me away. I wish I were Coll's sister.

He waits patiently, breathing and holding me close, until my sobs taper off into silent tears and sniffling. At last, embarrassed, I straighten and wipe my face on my sleeve. "Thank you," I whisper, surprised how thick and hoarse my voice sounds.

He nods as he withdraws his arm. "You all right, now?"

I shrug and look at my lap, pulling the edges of his coat closer around me. I could fit in it three times with room to spare, but it's drier than my dress, and warmer. I'm suddenly freezing. "Better, I think." I sneak a glance at him. "Do you know...?"

"I can guess."

I wince. "Please—please don't tell him."

"As if I would," he says, with a quiet snort. He reaches up and brushes my damp cheek, lightly, with his knuckles. "Best for him to think you're pleased. And this'll pass, girl. You'll see."

I wish I could believe him, but it's too painful. I feel too empty inside, too raw. Regardless, I nod and wipe my face again, not wanting him to think me more of a bawling child than he doubtless already does.

The straw rustles next to me, and when I look up, I see that he has pushed himself to his feet and has a hand extended to me. I let him pull me up, then stand blankly, feeling as fragile and spindly as a newborn foal. After a moment, it occurs to me that he might want his coat back, but when I make to shrug out of it, Coll shakes his head at me. "Keep it on. You look half-frozen." He nods toward the stable door. "Should get back inside, before you make yourself sick out here."

"I don't..."

"I said should," he says. "Didn't think you'd do it." He gives me a small smile. "Let's take a look at the little one, shall we? I brought him and Snow in just before it started to rain."

I follow him to one of the bigger stalls, where Coll's huge white mare, Snowflower, stands placidly, pulling bits of hay out of her feeder. She whickers in greeting, and I smile. I used to be terrified of horses, especially the muscular Northlands ones, tall and broad, with massive, fur-trimmed hooves, but Snowflower helped to change my mind. As white as new-fallen snow from the tips of her ears to her long, thick tail, she is truly one of the most beautiful creatures I've ever seen. Her deep brown eyes are black-lashed like a lady's, her muzzle pale gray at the end. I still don't know much about how to judge a horse's quality, but even I could see, the first time I set eyes on her, that Snow is a queen among them.

Her foal is, if possible, even more exquisite. He looks up from his dinner to blink at us, milk still on his lips. He's big for his age, all legs and eyes and ears, golden blond with a white star on his forehead and a curly white tail.

As Coll goes to Snowflower, who starts rubbing her forehead against his chest happily, I hold my hand out to the little one. Always shy at first, he ducks his head, then picks his way over to sniff my fingers. After a moment, I set my hand on his neck and begin stroking him, and we're dear friends again. His short coat feels like velvet.

The foal is mine, in a manner of speaking. Since he and Snowflower both would have died if I hadn't helped, the brothers gave him to me as a gift, with their gratitude. Much as I love him, though, I told Coll not long after I came to live at the castle that I couldn't accept him. He is the last foal Snowflower will ever bear, and her finest, the only golden foal she's ever produced. The thought of gelding instead of breeding him made Coll nearly weep, and I'm not—and will likely never be—skilled enough to ride a stallion. Nor would the match be a good one even if he were gelded. I'm a small woman, and he is going to be a truly massive horse, an ideal mount for someone of Coll's or Garreth's stature, but ridiculous for me.

I asked Coll if he would keep the little one for me, let him grow up to be the prized, proud sire of the herd. I said that perhaps I could have for my own one of his children—either a gentle geld-ing or a little filly, depending on how skilled a rider I am by that time. Though Coll protested, the joy on his face was obvious, and I insisted. I did name the foal though, at Coll's request. We call him Sunrise.

When Coll and I brave the rain and walk back to the castle a little later, I feel slightly better for having spent time in the horses' quiet, good-natured company. The pain in my heart is soothed, but not cured. I don't know if it ever will be.

CHAPTER SEVEN

A HANDFUL OF MEASURING spoons falls from my limp fingers, clattering on the stone floor of my workroom. I hear a commotion outside, through the open window. And I know.

I don't know which of these things happens first, or if they happen all at once. I don't know why I'm so certain, but I am. I stare down at the floor blankly, surprised not to see shattered pieces of my heart scattered amidst the spoons. My eyes dart to the doorway, though my feet feel rooted to the floor. Which is just as well, since I never want to leave this room again. Not when she's here.

She's never going to leave, and my chest clenches around my heart to keep it from clawing its way up my throat at the thought. She's never going to leave, she's going to belong here as much as—more than—I do, and they will all adore her, and she will sit beside Alaric at dinner, and she will lie beside him at night someday, and…

I lurch forward and slam the door shut, then stand with my back pressed against it, breathing hard. No doubt she's beautiful. Golden-haired, like Alaric, with wide blue eyes and dainty features and not a single freckle in sight. Her hands are doubtless soft and silken, never having done a day's work in her life.

I wager she sings like a bird and speaks like a princess would, low and melodiously, everything she says phrased in perfect, brilliant metaphors and imagery. Probably, just to make it worse, she knows horses as well as Coll and loves poetry like Finn. She'll sing with Erik, harmonizing like the best of bards, and she'll find "little Garreth" endearing rather than annoying.

Her lips are rose pink naturally, of course, without rouge, and she probably wears dresses that show off her slender, graceful neck and perfect breasts. Alaric will take one look and want to kiss her.

I hate her already, I think, sliding down the door to sit with my knees drawn up, arms wrapped tight around them. I despise her. Princess Nathalia the Perfect.

My head thumps back, and I sigh, looking at the ceiling. Dinner last night was almost more than I could endure, trying to pretend I was fine, happy, even though I nearly burst into tears every time Alaric spoke to me, so normal, as if he hadn't just broken me entirely. I don't think I can live through another hour like that, let alone every moment of every day. And it will be worse, from now on, because she'll be here. The thought of Alaric smiling at her, utterly besotted, makes me want to gag.

A number of possible plans flit through my mind as I continue to stare at the ceiling, though I don't really see it. I could pretend to be sick, and avoid meeting her for awhile. For that matter, I could try to pretend to die, then wait until they've carried my limp body somewhere and run away and never have to see Alaric touching her and kissing her and marrying her. Though it would probably be easier just to run away, without trying to feign my own death first. Were it not for the fact that I have nowhere to go, I might consider it.

I could be awful to her, though that wouldn't endear me to Alaric or any of the others. Besides, I like to think I'm better than that, though the idea of it is very tempting. I'm not usually nasty on purpose, but sometimes I think I might be good at it if I tried.

Or, I think with a sigh, I could do what my father would have wanted me to do. If he were here, he would tell me to make her welcome, not because it is my duty as Alaric's friend, but because it is the right thing to do. For that matter, I was very small when my mother died, but I vividly remember a conversation she and I had once. I came to her, crying, because Kethie Brewer wouldn't let me touch her new doll with the leather shoes and embroidered dress, and yet Kethie still wanted to play at having an inn in the old barn on our property. I said I didn't want to see her ever again, let alone play with her, and yet Mother shooed me out the door with sweets for both of us and some cracked plates for our inn. She said it was important to be kind and good to our friends, no matter what.

I have wondered, now that I know the truth, how my mother could have been so gracious to everyone, so kind, when she knew they hated people with abilities like ours. I have so many questions about her. Could she only talk with her thoughts, like Finn and Erik, or could she compel people like I can? Or, did she have a different power altogether, like the Southling bard Aiddan, who can feel people's emotions, or like Brek, who can make people see illusions? What I want to know the most, though, is how did she find out about her abilities? Was she afraid? Did she have any friends with powers who could share the burden and the joy of her gift?

All I know for certain is that she, like my father, was a better person than I will ever be. I'm ashamed that their daughter is so sour and wretched in comparison. It's just so damned difficult not to be, especially when I want to cry at the mere idea of befriending Alaric's future bride.

After what feels like a long time spent sitting on the floor, long enough for my bottom to get cold from the stones, I know that I'll look like an ill-mannered child if I delay any longer. With a sigh, I climb to my feet and brush off my skirt, then touch a hand to my hair, making sure my braids are still tight and neat. After that, there's nothing left for me to do but take a deep breath, straighten my shoulders, and march out the door with my head high.

-----ooo-)◦(-ooo-----

They have gathered in the great hall. I can hear their voices before I see them, and my feet drag, slower and slower, with every step. My guts knot with dread, and I have to pause and smooth my face out of a scowl before I can go on. I hate to admit, even to myself, that I have only been this afraid of someone a few other times in my life. Another moment, another few steps, and I'll see her, in all of her royal perfection. I'll see with my own eyes how, in such a short time, she has already stolen all those I hold dear, rendering me insignificant. Unwanted.

My feet move, and then my hand is on the doorjamb. I linger, unnoticed, watching them. All of the brothers are gathered around the hearth, no doubt wanting her highness to warm herself since she's fresh from travel and probably chilled from the rain. Coll and Erik are seated on one bench, Garreth and Finn opposite them, with Alaric and a man I don't recognize standing in front of the fire. And, on the middle bench, captivating all of them, is the princess.

I can only see her back, but I can tell she is beautiful, if nothing at all like I expected. Her hair takes my breath away. I've never seen anything like it. It's a deep, rich shade of brown, neither auburn nor dark blond, but true brown, like tree bark or freshly-turned earth. It hangs in glossy ringlets past her shoulders, bobbing as she shakes her head and laughs at something Erik says.

Then Erik catches sight of me, and the princess turns, too. Our eyes meet, and I see again that she is truly not what I imagined. Instead of being willowy, she is tall and sturdy-looking, with a generous chest and rounded cheeks. Instead of pale like fine marble, her skin has a golden cast, as if brushed with honey. Her lips are full, her eyes an odd shade between amber and green, fringed with dark lashes. She is by far the most exotic-looking person I have ever seen.

"To Princess Nathalia Alambil, Daughter of Ilorio and Domitara, may I present Ellin Fisher Healer," Alaric says formally, as I join them. "Ellin, this is Princess Nathalia of Rhodanath."

For a panicked moment, I stand frozen, wondering if I should curtsy, but then the princess rises and extends her hands to me. "Ellin Fisher Healer," she says, smiling. "It's a joy to meet you."

I start when she squeezes my hands warmly. "Princess Nathalia, I am honored." I'm not, but it's the proper thing to say.

"Please, call me Thalia." Her voice is low and smooth, with a singsong accent. She gestures to the strange man, who is as dark-haired as she. "And this is Darius, my cousin."

After we've been introduced, Nathalia starts talking to Erik again. There is space on the bench beside her, but I sit next to Finn instead. He turns and smiles when I put my hand on his arm so that we can converse privately with our thoughts, without shouting and risking Erik, or even Garreth or Coll, overhearing.

"Well?" I ask. "Do you like her?"

He breathes a laugh through his nose. "Are you jealous?"

"No!" Of course, I can't help blushing, and I'm sure he knows I'm lying. "Do you?"

"She's hasn't been facing me much," he replies after a moment, with a shrug, "and Erik's not translating. So, I can't say, yet. She seems friendly."

"That's very helpful."

"Talk to her yourself, then, and find out."

I can't possibly ask the question I most want to know—whether or not Alaric seems taken with her—so I pull my hand away and focus on Nathalia instead. As if sensing my attention, she turns, and I flounder for something to say. "Did you have a smooth journey here, Thalia?"

She nods. "Yes, it was much faster than I thought it would be. I can hardly believe I am in the Northlands at last," she says, looking around the room with wide eyes. "It is so beautiful here! Is it very similar in the Southland, Ellin?"

I shrug. "Not much different in summer, I suppose, but the winters are like day and night."

"I can't wait," she says, smiling. "I've never seen snow before."

Of course, I think, sneering inwardly. She would be looking forward to the bone-chilling cold.

"A Southling bard visited us once, when I was a little girl," she continues. "An extraordinary harpist, and he told us the most wonderful tales of your country. If the Healers there are truly so skilled, you must be very talented."

"The gift comes naturally to a Southling Healer." I shrug off her praise. "Besides, I'm not a true Healer—not yet."

"Even so," she says, "it must be wonderful to have such a gift. I can't begin to imagine. I've always admired those who devote themselves to helping others."

Uncomfortable with her odd gaze upon me, I look away. "You overestimate me," I mutter. "In fact, I'm not even certain I want to be a Healer. But Finn is." I gesture to him. "He's closer to being a physician than I am to being a Master Healer, by far." It's not entirely true, but I don't care if saying it will focus her attention elsewhere.

But she's undeterred. "Yes, I've heard." Her dimple shows again when she smiles at both of us. "It's lucky for me, both of you being here. I trip over my own two feet sometimes!"

She would, I think. They're big enough. "So do I," I say, "but usually only when I'm practicing with a sword. Coll's teaching me," I explain. "And I must admit, I'd exchange my healing ability in a moment for skill like his."

Coll chuckles. "You don't mean that, girl, and you know it."

I do, but before I open my mouth to say so, Thalia turns back to me. "If you would ever like to spar with another woman, please let me know," she says, eyes sparkling. "I'm terribly out of practice, but perhaps we could help one another."

My heart sinks. "You like swordplay?"

"The blade isn't my first weapon." She wrinkles her nose. "My choice is the quarterstaff, with archery second."

Proficient not with one weapon, but with three. Of course. Dismayed, I keep quiet and look at my lap as she and the princes discuss the merits of curved blades versus straight ones. Even Finn joins in, ignoring me.

And I sit practically in the middle of the conversation, feeling more alone than I did up in my workroom. Thalia is nothing at all like I expected. She's far, far worse.

—∘∘∘◦❖◦∘∘∘—

I can still hear her bubbling laughter ringing in my ears, setting my teeth on edge. Though we all left the hall hours ago, I can still see her face before me clearly. So lovely, with her strange eyes and flawless skin and shining, dark hair. Thalia went to her rooms to refresh herself for the feast tonight in her honor, and I cringe to think of how much more beautiful she will be once the grime from travel has been washed off.

Freshly bathed and scrubbed myself, I yank a brush through my damp hair and swear when I hit a snarl. Dressed only in a sleeveless shift, after my bath, I decided to fix myself up in earnest before putting on my good dress for the feast. Ordinarily I would only brush my hair and braid it simply, wouldn't bother with cosmetics, but tonight... I have to admit, I want to look my best.

After I've brushed until my arm is sore, my hair floats, mostly dry, in a wavy, copper-colored mass halfway down my back. I rub at my upper arm and flex my elbow, then take on the task of taming it. It takes forever, but when I crane my neck to see the full effect in the mirror above my dressing table, I know the work was worth it. Two tight braids encircle my head, and at the back, just above the base of my neck, I divided the sections into three. Two of them become loops, and the third wraps around them at the top in a knot. It's the most intricate style I know how to create.

Satisfied, I turn my attention to my face and peer critically at the mirror, tilting this way and that. I've never cared much for my looks. I'm plain and too pale, which makes the few freckles on my nose and cheeks stand out like beacons. I'm grateful I'm not as freckled as Finn, or else I'd look ridiculous.

Painting my face helps, though. Once I've applied rouge to my cheeks and lips, darkened my ginger-colored eyelashes with pencil, I look better. Less like myself, certainly. Just as certainly not beautiful, but more like a lady. Looking this way makes it easier for me to put on my new dress without feeling like I'm playacting.

Soon after I came to live here, Keeper Nan, who used to be the princes' nurse but now manages the affairs of the castle, suggested I buy myself a new wardrobe. Since all of my own clothing had burnt up with my home in the Southlands, the only things I possessed were a dress I'd borrowed from Keth when I traveled with the True Southlings and a Northlands-style dress and nightshift I borrowed from Brigid, one of the castle's maids. So, with money earned from selling my medicines and money borrowed from castle coffers, Nan and I went to the dressmaker's shop. At first, I disliked Nan, and the feeling was mutual, but she began to think better of me when she found out I'd risked my life to try to save King Allard. I began to warm to her when I realized how much she cares about the royal family. I think they're like sons to her, especially since their own mother died when they were young. Garreth doesn't even remember her. It's not just them, either. When Nan helped me choose materials and styles for my clothes, she was as critical and fussy as a mother hen.

It was Nan, in fact, who insisted I buy a fancy dress as well as regular dresses and blouses and skirts for every day. I balked at the cost at first, but gave in when she pointed out, firmly, that I would be an embarrassment to the royal family if I attended a formal event as an honored guest and yet looked like a ragamuffin.

I look into the mirror again after I've put on my dress, and I have to admit that I'm glad Nan made me buy it. Though I'm a Healer's daughter from a tiny village in the Southland, in this, I almost feel like a princess, myself. The fabric is soft as a flower petal, with a surprising weight to it, dyed a deep shade of golden yellow, like the tiny meadow flowers here. The sleeves are short, and with the low, round neckline and tight, reinforced bodice, I almost blush at the idea of anyone seeing me. Which is ridiculous, since the dress is perfectly modest; more so, even, than the dresses I've seen many other women wear. The skirt is my favorite part, full and long enough to brush my ankles, split down the center to reveal the ruffled underskirt that is a pale gold, nearly cream. Though I'm nearly seventeen and ought to be able to resist the temptation to twirl, I can't, and do it anyway.

After I've stepped into the matching slippers, I go out into the hallway. I don't know what I hope to accomplish by making myself look nice for the celebration in her honor. It's not as if I honestly expect Alaric to look at me and send her home. But at the same time, maybe I do want him to look at me tonight and wish, if only for a moment, that things could be different.

I've almost reached the stairs when a door creaks open behind me. I blink in surprise when I see Erik coming out of the bedroom he and Finn share. He looks regal in his finery, a coat and tight breeches, with high, polished boots. When he looks up, the gold circlet on his brow glints in the light. I'm so used to seeing him in tatty shirts with the sleeves rolled up, regular trousers and scuffed, thick boots, it's a shock to see him looking like royalty.

My reaction is nothing compared to his, though. Erik's mouth actually drops open as he stares, and I would blush, I'm sure, if his expression weren't so funny. "Ellin?" he manages at last, sounding strangled. "I can't believe—you look so different..."

I beam and hold out the sides of my skirt. "Do you like it?"

He grins back, looking like the Erik I know again. "'Course I do. Has Finn..." he breaks off and clears his throat. "I mean, have you been downstairs yet?"

"I'm almost afraid to," I admit.

"Well, you shouldn't be." He gives me a bow, and then takes my arm to escort me, surprising me again.

The great hall is brightly lit, the tables laden with food and decorated with flowers. The furniture has been re-arranged to make a clear space for dancing later, and a group of musicians is already playing, adding to the festive atmosphere. Though the feast hasn't begun yet, the room is already crowded with men and women decked out in their finery, conversations overlapping one another everywhere I turn.

Erik leads me to the high table, where Alaric, Coll, Finn, and Garreth are already present, though Nathalia is not, yet. The brothers' reactions to my appearance are almost everything I could wish. Coll eyes my dress and then takes a drink, but not so fast that I miss his amused smile. I think maybe I was supposed to see it, judging from the wink he gives me over the rim of the glass.

Garreth stares for a moment at my chest, then drags his eyes to my face, cheeks fuchsia. As gratifying as that is, I think it's more flattering still that Finn doesn't seem surprised. He just smiles and says simply, *"You look beautiful."*

But the approval I most wanted doesn't come. Alaric glances up from apparent contemplation of the tabletop only long enough to give me a tense, distracted-looking nod. I might as well be wearing a sack, I think with dismay, as I take a seat between Erik and Coll. I try to avoid looking at the empty place at the other side of the table, next to Alaric. I try even harder not to wish that place belonged to me.

A murmur ripples through the room, and I turn, along with everyone else, to see Thalia entering with Darius behind her. As the princes and Alaric and I rise along with every other person in the room, honoring her, I try to swallow past the tightness in my throat. Compared to her, I'm like one of those tiny meadow flowers next to a rose in full bloom. Her dress is pale green, like spring leaves, and beautifully embroidered, though it's not the dress so much as her bearing that makes her stand out. When she nears us, I see how her lips have been darkened to the color of berries, how artfully-applied pencil makes her eyes look even larger and more exotic than before, and I realize how garish my own painted face must look. I look down after murmuring the barest of greetings and try hard not to listen to Alaric's speech welcoming her.

The rest of the meal is excruciating. The food is delicious, with several fresh vegetable dishes and not a piece of cured meat in sight, but that is small comfort. I stare at my plate in silence, chewing like a cow, and listen to the happy chatter around me. Of course she has entertaining stories about her journey and her life at home. Of course she laughs at Erik's jokes, and that, it seems, spurs him to try even harder to charm her. And he's not the only one. Garreth tries to impress her with stories about himself, though the heroic tales' effects are somewhat lessened by the fact that his brothers don't hesitate to snicker and correct him when the exaggerations get out of hand.

Strangely, I notice that Alaric is perfectly polite to her, but he still seems distracted, or uninterested. I sneak glance after glance at him, and each time, he doesn't seem captivated by her. I worry at this puzzle in my mind like a cat with a string. Could it be that he doesn't like her? I wonder, hope flaring. But then I look at her over the rim of my wineglass and swallow with a grimace. How could he not? Not only is she beautiful, cheeks flushed and showing her dimple as she grins at Erik, but she's friendly and obviously intelligent as well. More likely, I admit with a sinking feeling, he's shy around her since they've only met and yet know they must marry. That would make sense, especially considering that, of all of them, Thalia seems coolest toward Alaric. Even if I were as outgoing as she is, I don't know if I would be able to befriend my betrothed immediately after meeting him, especially if I hadn't had any say in the matter. Despite everything, for an instant, I feel sorry for her.

When dinner ends at last, there is nothing I want more than to leave, but I can't without seeming rude. Instead, as the musicians play louder, now with a drum, and the dancing begins, I decide to go sit in a corner somewhere. Not that any of my friends would notice, as long as Thalia is in the room. I've only made it a few paces away from the table when someone touches my shoulder.

"Will you dance?" Coll asks.

"Coll..."

"What?" he replies, helping me find the right position for my hands. "I've said you need to learn to move your feet, haven't I? This way's good as any."

"But..."

"Start with your left," he rumbles, unperturbed, and since he's stronger by far and stubborn as a mule, I know it's pointless to argue.

I look up a moment later and almost smile. Though this dance is unfamiliar to me, he's leading me so well that I think—or at least, fervently hope—that an observer might think I know what I'm doing. The last thing I want is to make a fool of myself in front of Thalia. Coll meets my gaze, and while he doesn't smile back, he's not scowling, either.

Looking at him so closely, I notice that his fine clothes, like Erik's, make him look different, imposing, and surprisingly handsome. I suppose I'm so used to the often dour presence of him that this is the first time I've truly noticed his looks. For the first time, too, I wonder if he has a betrothed overseas, or even a woman here. If any of them do. I know about Erik kissing Katya the pretty barmaid at the urging of his friends—and getting a mug of cider dumped on his head as a result—about all the younger girls who think Garreth is special for some reason, but I've never thought to ask if any of them actually do have sweethearts. Then again, I haven't told them about Lev kissing me, and I can't imagine ever doing so. Maybe there are some things that a sisterly friend—or even a true sister—is not meant to share.

But now that the thought has occurred to me, I'm very curious. When the next song begins and Erik asks me to be his partner, I accept immediately. Almost as quickly, I wish I hadn't. He's less skilled than Coll, and it doesn't help that he keeps craning his neck to stare at Alaric and Thalia dancing together—no doubt trying to see at the last moment how the steps are meant to go.

"Do you have a fiancée, too?" I ask after he's stepped on my foot for the fourth time.

He starts, his grip around my fingers tightening. But at least he looks at me instead of at them. "What?"

"I started wondering," I explain. "Has a marriage been arranged for you, as well?"

"Oh!" he says, sounding, for some reason, relieved. "No, only Alaric. The rest of us are free to marry as we please. Why?" he asks after a moment, giving me a sly grin. "D'you want me to put in a word for you with Garre—ouch!"

Though I stepped on his toes on purpose, and he knows it, I smile innocently. "Was that your foot? I'm sorry!"

He laughs. "That's all right. 'Least you're not a cow the size of a building, with hooves of stone and great, rolling red eyes. Though if you were," he adds, head tilted with contemplation, "perhaps you could go stomp on his foot, so he'd see the difference between you and the perfectly ordinary cow that stepped on him before."

"Don't," I beg, giggling. "You're going to make me forget the patterns and look like an idiot."

"Don't worry, I've forgotten them anyway." Erik gives me a particularly vigorous twirl, and then another. I stumble and clutch at him, but I'm laughing, and I can't be mad.

———ooo-)◯(-ooo———

When the music ends, Erik and I are both red-faced and breathless, and it takes him a moment to compose himself enough to ask Thalia to dance. Garreth and I take a turn together, and after that, Erik asks a lady I don't know, and Thalia goes to sit beside Finn. I'm about to follow her when a light touch brushes my shoulder. "Will you dance, Ellin?" Alaric asks.

My smile falters, but the music is beginning, and Alaric clearly sees nothing amiss, and I have no choice. I nod and take his hands, and spend the next moments dancing on wooden feet, looking at anything but his face. Across the room, Thalia's curls bob as she bends to write something to Finn, and I don't think I've ever loathed anyone more. Were it not for her, this moment would be perfect. As it is, when the dance is over, I murmur something inane and escape as quickly as I can.

Finn holds out my cup as I approach, and I take a deep drink, fighting tears. *"Are you all right?"* he asks.

"I haven't left yet." I try not to watch Alaric and Thalia dancing together. Try not to notice the way she looks at him. *"Are you having a nice time?"*

"I am now," he replies, smiling. *"Now that the prettiest girl in the castle is sitting with me."*

I laugh, but he seems serious as he glances out at the dancers and, after a moment, exhales slowly. *"Well. Would you like to dance?"*

"With you?" I'm startled enough to speak aloud, and he touches my wrist, arching an eyebrow.

"*I do know how.*"

"*Then why haven't you been?*"

He only shrugs, unfolding himself from the bench. "*Will you?*"

"*Of course.*" I take his hand and smile as he leads me onto the floor.

Finn smiles back, but the expression is a little strained, and I hope that my surprise isn't obvious when we begin to dance. "*You're a better dancer than Erik,*" I say with my thoughts, hoping he'll think it's only that and not the truth, that I'm a bit shocked he dances at all.

He gives me a wry look. "*I'm a more careful dancer than Erik,*" he corrects me. "*And I'm counting, so hush.*"

I wince, torn between laughter and sympathy. "*Finn! You shouldn't have offered if...*"

"*If we look foolish, it's going to be your fault...*"

"*As if I care!*" I have a feeling he does, however, so I keep quiet until the song ends. He gives me a quick embrace, then steps back as if to leave, but I catch his hand. "*Would you like to dance another?*"

Finn blinks in surprise. "*Really?*"

"*Only if you want to.*"

"*Always,*" he replies, and takes me in his arms again. This time, I don't mind so much that we can't talk. And when I see Alaric at the table, watching us while Thalia dances with Coll, I smile brightly and move closer to Finn. Just let His Majesty see how nice a time I'm having without pining over him.

Finn holds me close and presses my hand, and I grin. Trust him to play along without even being asked. For a wild moment, I'm tempted to lay my cheek against his chest, as sweethearts dance, but I don't want to embarrass him when I'm only trying to make Alaric jealous.

When this song is finished, Finn inclines his head toward the door. "*It's hot in here,*" he says, and I notice that he does look flushed. "*Would you like to go outside?*"

"All right." I let him lead the way out the side door, to the little paved courtyard lined with flowering bushes. The sky is twilit, deep lavender-blue speckled with only a few stars. I take a deep breath, savoring the cool, damp air. With the door shut, the sounds of the party are distant, muted, only occasional strains of music floating out to accompany the burbling of the small fountain in the center of the courtyard.

"It's beautiful out here," I say with my mind. Though I was shown this tiny garden months ago, the princes rarely come here, and I haven't made a habit of it, either.

Finn nods, his fingers still entwined with mine. *"Did you know it was our mum's garden?"* he asks, then gestures to the bushes. *"She planted these. The fountain was a gift from my da. He laid the stones for the pool himself."*

I'm surprised at the idea of stern King Allard having ever done something so mundane, so tender. But then, I remember the times I saw him talking easily with his sons, the stories I've heard about him letting Coll keep an orphaned fawn in the kitchen, letting them befriend anyone they pleased as children, no matter how common their birth, and perhaps I can believe it. Despite everything, I think my father and I both would have liked him, had things been different. Sometimes, I think my father did anyway.

"What was your mother like?" I ask after a moment, but Finn shakes his head.

"You'd do better to ask Coll, or Alaric," he says. *"I don't remember much about her. I know that she liked to grow things. I think she would have liked you."*

Though I don't think he can really know, it's kind of him to say, and I smile. *"I hope so,"* I reply, then shiver when a breeze makes gooseflesh prickle along my forearms. I'm about to ask him if he would like to go back in when the door opens, spilling light and noise into the courtyard. Finn and I both turn to see Erik crossing the threshold, but he stops abruptly when he spots us.

"Am I interrupting something?" He sounds as if he's had a bit too much to drink, and I laugh.

"Erik, it's me and Finn. Of course not."

"I *know* who it is," he replies, and gives me a loose grin. "Y'think I'm blind or something? A fine pair we'd make then!" He laughs as he throws an arm around Finn's waist. Now that he's closer, I revise my earlier estimation. He's had more than a bit too much.

Finn obviously arrives at the same conclusion. He disentangles himself from Erik's embrace and looks down with amused concern. *"You're drunk,"* Finn says, but Erik shakes his head, making his hair fly out messily.

"I'm not! I'm only relaxed. Feeling much better. You should try it," he adds, craning his neck to wink at his twin. "It'd do you a world of good, y'know. Maybe then you'd have the guts to..." He breaks off with a startled, muffled exclamation as Finn claps a hand over his mouth and drags him to one side of the courtyard. They have a furious, silent conversation, punctuated only by the smacks of Finn's hands against one another as he speaks.

He's angry, I realize, wishing I could see them better, or understand signing this fast at all. But why? After a moment, Erik throws up his arms. "Fine!" he shouts. "I won't, but you're being a damned fool."

Finn sighs and shakes his head, then comes toward me. *"Let's go in."*

I glance at Erik, standing with his shoulders hunched, staring into the fountain, and shake my head. *"I'll stay with him. I don't mind."*

Finn's lips flatten, and he looks as if he wants to protest, but then he nods and goes inside, leaving me and Erik in the growing darkness. I wait a moment, and when he doesn't say anything, I go to him, uncertain. "Are you all right?"

Erik nods, and it seems that his anger left him when Finn did. "Sorry," he mutters at last, more to the water than to me. "I shouldn't've..."

I brush his apology aside, but peer at him curiously. "What were you arguing about, anyway?"

"Don't ask," he says, grimacing. "It's just...d'you ever have something you want to tell someone and can't? Or a problem you can't do anything about?"

"Of course." At the moment, a great many examples spring to mind. I can't tell Alaric that I love him, can't make Thalia go away, can't tell any of them about getting shoved in the marketplace or about Lev and the dreams he's been sending to me...

I hate this, I think dully, looking down at the water, black and cold, like the chill that's been with me these past few days. It seems almost impossible that only last week things were different. The summer seemed warm and full of promise, and we were all easy with one another, without secrets and silence twining between us.

I hug my arms to my chest. "What's wrong, Erik?" I ask quietly, meaning everything, but especially the bitterness I sense coming from him in tense, wine-soaked waves.

"Nothing I can change, that's for certain." He shrugs. "But why're you here moping with me?"

"Besides wanting to make sure you're not going to be sick in the bushes?"

He snorts. "Didn't drink that much. I'm all right," he says, bumping his shoulder against mine, "so you can go back, if you want."

I've only gone a few steps when I turn back impulsively. "Erik? There's something I should tell you." Maybe he will have some insight about Lev, I think. Maybe he's been having the dreams, too, and the headaches are why he drank too much, or they're the problem he can't tell me about.

But when he looks at me, shoulders bowed under the weight of his own burdens, eyes full of a sorrow that's all the more disturbing for being so very uncharacteristic, the words wither on my tongue. No matter what the mood in this courtyard, tonight is supposed to be a celebration. And if Erik insisted on telling Alaric, his evening with Thalia would be ruined. As much as I might wish for that, I can't possibly bring it about. Also, there's every chance that Erik won't remember much in the morning.

"What?" he prods, but I shake my head.

"It's nothing important. It can keep. Truly," I add, when he looks as if he's going to protest.

Erik's lips part, but then he presses them together and gives me a nod. As I go back inside, I wonder how it has come to be that the things we don't say so greatly outnumber the things we do.

CHAPTER EIGHT

A RAINDROP SPLASHES *against a white rock.*
My skin burns.

Then I see a clearing, all sunlight and green leaf-shadows, ringed with beeches and maples and oaks. I look up, and the leaves are green, barely yellow at the edges, not a red one in sight. I blink, surprised, and night falls on the glade.

Firelight and deep black shadows brush the tree trunks. Orange sparks float upward as someone stokes the fire. He straightens, poker in hand. From behind, all I can see of him is the set of his shoulders, his height, and his hair. Grown long, it brushes his shoulders, auburn turned blood-red in the light. I can see the silver strands, paler against the dark. I want to run to him, but my feet are rooted like the trees.

I wake with a gasp that's almost a scream and find that I've already pressed a hand to my chest, where my heart is still pounding like a wild thing. I try to breathe slowly, though I want to pant, and my entire body is trembling. My ears are ringing. My head is going to fall off if I move.

This time the dream Lev sent was different. It was always day in the clearing before, never night, but I only care about one thing. That man was my father!

I've never seen that clearing before. My father never wore his hair so long. But that was Father. I saw him, smelled the smoke and heard the fire crackling. I felt the night air and the soft grass under my shoes. It was real, and he was there.

By the time I've washed up and dressed, I've decided that there's only one thing to do. I have to wake Lev up again and talk to him. Immediately. I try not to let myself hope my father is still alive, but I can't help it. My chest feels like a flock of butterflies has taken up residence, brushing feather-light wings of joy against my heart.

It's not so farfetched, is it? I wonder. I've thought back to what Lev said so many times, trying to puzzle out his meaning. His babbling might have been nonsense, but perhaps it wasn't. He was so concerned with time—wondering 'when' and 'how soon'—I originally dismissed the idea that he could be dreaming of the future, but…well, King Allard did, once, when he was a boy. According to Alaric, his father dreamed that the Southland would attack the Northlands, and that's why all of the hatred against Southlings started in the first place. And if the old king, a Northlander, could do it, why not Lev, who had the strongest mental powers of anyone I've ever met?

I don't go to breakfast, partly because I don't want to sit at the table with Thalia, who hasn't endeared herself to me any more in the days that I've known her, and partly because I doubt I could hide my mental turmoil from my friends. The last thing I want to do is tell them about the dreams or my suspicions or any of it. At least, not yet.

Taking a piece of buttered bread with me, I head into town. The air is cool, the sky gray and heavy with unshed rain. Just as well, I think sourly. I hope it pours, and soon, on all the stupid Northlanders in the marketplace. I'd gladly get soaked for that.

Not for the first time, I wish for skill with a sword, for the guts and meanness to use it. Maybe, with a weapon at my side, I wouldn't keep my eyes on my feet, darting warily upward every few paces. Maybe my shoulders wouldn't be tense, waiting for someone to yell at me. I loathe myself for my weakness, but I wish one of the princes were with me, or even Nan. Then at least I'd feel safe.

But I'm in luck. The people I see on the way to the prison ignore me entirely. By the time I open the door, I'm almost relieved. Would be, except for what I have to do next.

The head guard looks up from some parchments and blinks at me like an owl roused at noon. "What now?"

"I want to see Lev Kinshield again." What else? It's not as if I know anyone else in here. Except Stan the Unlucky, in a manner of speaking, and he doesn't count.

He wipes his pen on his cuff before setting it aside and scowling at me. "Why?"

"I…" I fumble for a lie. "I want to make sure the new potion is working."

He shakes his head before I've even finished speaking. "Unless you've a letter of permission from Lord Tomas or the king himself—or are accompanied by one of them or Thorvald the Physician, I'm not to let you in, 'cept on the appointed days."

"What? Did this come from Ala—I mean, from the king himself?"

"Orders is orders, girl, and them's mine," he says, shrugging. "It's not for me or you to question. Now, get along."

I stare at him, hands twitching uselessly at my sides. I can guess who gave those orders, and the thought sets my teeth on edge. I'm tired of all of it, suddenly—the way Lord Tomas distrusts me, the muttered curses in the street, the way the warden is glaring at me now.

"Get along, now," he snaps, shooing me. "You'll not go in, and that's final."

I force my lips into a smile and walk out, but once the door has shut behind me, I close my eyes and grasp my power before I have a chance to reconsider. Ruthlessly shoving guilt aside, I reach out for his mind and wriggle in, meshing my thoughts with his. I once swore never to compel anyone again, but I don't have a choice.

The warden looks up dully when I enter. "I'd like to see Lev Kinshield."

"Certainly," he says, and gets the keys.

--------‑ooo‑)⊙(‑ooo‑--------

Lev's eyelids flutter open, and he looks around the room, moving his head cautiously on the pillow. When his gaze finds my face, he actually seems to focus on me. "Where am I?" he asks, in a croaking whisper, voice thin as thread.

I choose my words carefully. "You're in a prison."

"Oh." The word is barely a breath past his dry, parted lips, and then they close, and he nods. His dark eyes, once so full of fire, seem even more glazed than before. "Am I a bad person?"

"I..."

"Do you know me?" he presses.

My eyes close, for an instant. "Your name is Levachai Kinshield," I whisper at last. "You're called Lev."

No spark of recognition lights his face at the name, and I know that he truly must not remember. "Lev," he repeats, leaning on the vowel as if the shape of the word is unfamiliar. "Lev. Kinshield."

"Yes."

"Who are you? And why do I feel this way?" he asks, shoulders restless against the mattress. "Am I sick? Am I dying? Is this..."

"Lev," I interrupt, still speaking softly, so carefully, though I'm not sure who I'm trying to keep from breaking: myself, or him. "Please, no more questions. Can we talk, for a bit? I'm not supposed to be here, and you're not supposed to be awake, yet. You're supposed to be sleeping so—so you will get well," I falter, the lie stumbling on my tongue. I bunch my skirt in trembling fingers.

"Oh," he murmurs. The old Lev would have demanded answers. Fought this. At the very least, I think, he would have been frustrated and furious at the idea of being so ill. This new version of him is so different. So very much quieter. I can't say, yet, whether I find this change frightening or encouraging.

I sit on the edge of the bed and start to reach for his hand before I think better of it and smooth my wrinkled skirt instead. "What do you remember?" I ask, watching his face for any sign of deceit.

But his eyes are clear and guileless as he meets my gaze. "I—I don't." His brows draw together, and he shakes his head. "There was a man by a fire. And rocks. And a flower. It was a pretty flower," he adds dreamily, smiling a little. "D'you like flowers?"

I can only nod, choked with pity and disappointment.

Lev sighs. "Flowers are outside in the grass. With the sun. Can I go outside? It's dark in here."

"Oh, Lev. I wish you could."

"If I say I'm sorry, may I?" he presses, touching my hand. "Will you ask them to let me go? Please?"

"I..." I shake my head helplessly, and his face falls.

"I don't like it here," he whispers. "I want to go home."

I feel cruel asking, but I must. "Do you know where your home is?"

His dark eyes are bright with tears, and his lips part soundlessly before he replies. "No...but I have one, don't I? Are you my family? What's your name?"

"It's—it's Ellin."

"Oh." He doesn't seem to recognize my name, either, as he laces his fingers with mine. The gesture is a child's, seeking comfort in the dark. "Ellin, I'm afraid."

I squeeze his hand and know, with certainty, that I'm not afraid, anymore. Not of him. There's no reason to be.

———oooﾒ◯ﾑooo———

When I put him to sleep again and leave, a little later, I wait until I'm outside to loose the hold I have on the anguish threatening to overwhelm me. My face crumples, and I hunch forward, holding my arms tight across my chest. As I watch, sprinkles of rain dot the stones around my boots and coat the leather toes with a fine sheen.

I ruined him. It's as if I took something beautiful and brilliant and tarnished it, scratched it and wrecked it beyond hope of repair. Like a bright flame smothered down to smoke and faded embers.

And yet—there is hope, and I know it despite the guilt I feel. With Lev this way, innocent, remembering nothing, surely no one could see him as a threat anymore. And a new life, child-like as he is, would be better than being drugged to sleep until he dies.

I need to tell someone about him, about what I've been doing. About the dreams. The only question is, who should I tell? Not Alaric, definitely. Not yet. And not Coll, who wouldn't hear me out, I'm sure, if he knew Alaric was in the dark.

I need someone willing to risk Alaric's anger. Someone who will believe me, without question, about the dreams. And, unfortunately, someone who can not only see but hear for himself the change in Lev's voice; the honesty in it. Someone I trust. In the end, halfway to the castle, I decide there's only one person to go to. I think I've known all along.

Erik is repairing a fence south of the stables, calf-deep in tasseled, jewel-green grass. He pauses, hammer in hand, when I shout at him over the dull, pounding blows. "Have you seen Coll?" he asks in greeting.

"Not lately." I shake my head, plucking a piece of grass to twine between my fingers. "Why?"

"He's supposed to be bringing Clare the Weaver's sheep to graze here. Wondered if he was back with 'em yet."

"Sorry. Are you finished?" I add. "Can you leave? I need you to come with me to town."

He glances at the fence. "Almost. I'm supposed to help get them in when they arrive, but Finn won't mind doing it. Let me take these inside and ask him," he finishes, stooping to pick up the box of nails.

I wait for Erik outside, toeing at a crack between the huge gray flagstones. When he comes out again, he gives me a quizzical look before the door has shut. "Where are we going?"

"In a moment," I reply, and wait, feeling his curiosity like a tangible thing, until we're past the yard and on the street that leads into the heart of the city. When I'm positive we're fully out of earshot of anyone near the castle—and far enough that he's not likely to turn back—I glance sideways. "I need to show you something. Someone. At the prison."

He stops abruptly. "Ellin Fisher Healer, tell me it isn't him," he says—spits, rather—in that deeper tone of his that makes him sound so much more like royalty than usual. "Tell me you aren't asking me to go with you and see Kinshield."

And then I stop too, and face him on the path. Turn my palms to him. Feel, suddenly, like I could cry. "Of course it is, and I am. There's so much I haven't told you."

There's only a slight pause before he takes two steps to join me and makes a small gesture suggesting that we keep walking. "Well. I think you'd better."

So I do, as we walk into the city in the late-morning mist. Once I start speaking, I'm unable to stop. I tell him about the guilt I feel for hurting Lev with the drugs, how I tried to Heal him. A little bit about the dreams, though not about seeing my father. I tell him how Lev is now, childlike and harmless. And through it all, Erik, usually talking enough for two, walks beside me, listening. Silent except for booted footsteps that seem heavier than usual.

"You know I'd rather be herding sheep—or swallowing nails—than doing this, don't you?" he asks, when my babbling has finally trailed off.

I bob my head jerkily, like a puppet. "I do. I'm sorry. But I need you to see, so that if you agree with me, we can go together to Alaric, and..."

"And what?" he demands, walking faster. "Pardon him? Set him free? Ellin, he killed the king! He killed my da. What do you expect me to do?"

"I don't know!" I burst out. "At the moment, I'm only asking you to come and see him. Speak with him, and form your own opinion. Is that too much to ask?"

"Asking me not to punch him in his simple head might be," he mutters, but then he heaves a sigh. His mouth quirks when I glare at him. Not quite a smile of forgiveness, but better, I suppose, than nothing. "All right, I won't. I swear it."

"Erik, I am sorry..." I begin, as we approach the prison, but he waves it off and opens the door.

"Just, let's make it quick, shall we?"

To my surprise, the head guard isn't at his desk, and the dim room is empty. I notice Erik's disapproving glance at the empty chair, but I'm too relieved to care. "This way," I say, gesturing, though it occurs to me, after I've already started toward the stairs, that Erik doubtless already knows where Lev's cell is. He follows me without comment, footsteps steady behind me on the narrow stairs.

The last doorway to the last flight of stairs is slightly open, yawning pitch black and a whisper of dank air at us. I shiver, then frown, wondering if perhaps the head guard went down and left it open, but I don't say anything to Erik. Instead, I push it open with a creak and step down. The wall, when I touch it for balance, is rough and cold as ice beneath my fingertips. I can hear Erik's breathing. I tell myself sternly that my skin is only crawling because I hate this place, not because I'm afraid.

But when we open the door at the bottom, I can't deny the eerie feeling any longer. The corridor is entirely empty, without Stan the Unlucky or any other guards anywhere in sight. I nearly jump out of my shoes when Erik puts a hand on my shoulder. *"What is it?"* he asks with his thoughts.

"Something's wrong. Where are the guards?"

"Perhaps they're not as vigilant as they ought to be when they think no one's here to check up on them. It's probably nothing."

I give him a look. *"Then why are we talking like this?"*

"Because I feel it, too," he admits. "But we're here," he adds in a whisper. "So let's keep going."

"It probably is nothing," I whisper back, trying to reassure myself, I think, more than him. Nevertheless, I let him take the lead as we approach the closed door of Lev's cell. The door that should be locked, like all of the other doors should have been and weren't before it, but it opens easily at his experimental try.

Erik steps inside, then stops so abruptly that I stumble to avoid walking into him. "What the...?" He makes a strange, choking sound and swears in a whisper. "Ellin, don't..." he says urgently, but it's too late; I've already elbowed my way past. It's too late for me not to see the empty bed. The blood—a lot of it, dark and drying—on the dirty sheets, blackish splotches on the blanket.

I see Lord Tomas, and the head guard, and Stan the Unlucky, and two other guards across the room, waiting for us. Time seems to race. I gasp and whirl to look at Erik just as Lord Tomas says, "Get her!"

Then my arms are in the iron grip of the hook-nosed guard who hates me, and I'm struggling like a cat, and Erik is shouting and swearing, and all along, the bed is empty and Lev is nowhere in sight, and there's blood, and I'm screaming, too.

"SILENCE!" Lord Tomas roars at last, silken voice fraying for the first time since I've known him. "Your highness," he says, softer, to Erik, "I must beg you not to intervene. I don't know what the girl has told you, but I'm acting on the king's orders. I am to bring her to him at once."

Ignoring him entirely, Erik looks at the guard holding me, and there's something in his eyes that frightens me. "Release her," he says quietly, very calm. "Or your life will be forfeit."

"Are you asking us to disobey our king, Prince Erik?" Lord Tomas asks, just as softly.

Erik's jaw clenches, but before he can speak, I turn to him and try to sound reassuring. "Erik, don't. We'll explain to Alaric. He's not hurting me," I add, even though he is.

"But there's no need," Lord Tomas replies. "His majesty is well aware of where your loyalties lie, Healer." He says my name with twisted lips, like a curse. "And, speaking of your misguided sympathy for the prisoner, there is no need for that any longer, either."

I hate to give him the satisfaction of asking, but I need to know. I swallow hard. "You killed him, then?"

One of his eyebrows lifts. "No, as a matter of fact. You did. They found him after your visit this morning, bleeding from his nose and ears. He died within moments and seemed to be in excruciating pain."

There truly is a great deal of blood on the sheets and blanket. The stains are all I can see. It stinks in this cold room, and I wonder if he died while I was walking through the grass where the raindrops looked like tiny jewels.

I feel like I'm underwater. Distant. Muted. Lord Tomas's face is a collection of mismatched shapes, all of a sudden, dark eyes and a moving mouth I can't hear. His voice laps against my ears like waves.

"Please," I say, loud and harsh. "Please, may Erik be my guard?"

"I'm sorry," Lord Tomas says, a hairsbreadth from sounding sincere. "We have our orders."

Instead, Erik goes in front of me as we walk through the corridor and up the stairs, and then beside me once we're outside. I would hold his hand if I could, like a child, if my arms weren't pinned to my sides like a market chicken by the guard behind me.

It gets worse quickly. Guards, a prince, a Southling prisoner, and Lord Tomas can't walk down the street at noontime without attracting a crowd.

I'm proud that I don't wilt. I walk before my guard with my head high. I can bear them staring at me. I can bear the dozens of people following us, pressing around us on both sides. The whispers, the murmurs, the questions called to the guards and Lord Tomas—I can bear those.

"Ellin Fisher Healer," Lord Tomas replies, in answer. His voice carries like a horn above the din. A clarion call across a battlefield, beautiful and resonant and deadly. "We caught her trying to help Kinshield, the Kingslayer, escape! Don't worry, he's dead now. Treason? Of course it's treason!" And on, and on. I can't look at Erik. I picture Alaric's face instead and hope that he hasn't heard these same words from Tomas's lips. Treason. Betrayal. No doubt loyal to the Southlands all along. Still, I hold my head up. Keep walking, with Erik at my side, silent and obviously furious.

It's only when the crowd begins to cheer and chant for my death, calling me a witch and worse, that, finally, I begin to cry.

CHAPTER NINE

I FREEZE JUST INSIDE the doorway of the throne room, causing my guard to tread on my heel with a muffled curse. I barely feel the scrape, too busy staring. I'm not sure what I expected, but the scene before me is shockingly formal. There's Alaric, sitting rigid in the carved oak throne, his hands clasped on his lap. Beside him on the dais are Coll and Finn, both with mud-caked boots and their sleeves still rolled up from working, and I can smell sheep even from here. Lord Ulric the Wise is seated on Alaric's other side, his walking stick balanced across his knees. To my horror, I see Thalia, too, standing beside Finn. The only one missing is Garreth.

When we enter, the room goes absolutely silent. Of all people, my eyes land on Thalia, who meets my gaze steadily, her expression unreadable.

"Alaric, what in the hell is this?" Erik bursts out, shoving past me and the guard to stride across the room. "Tell me you didn't truly order them to grab Ellin and march her across town like some sort of crimin—"

"Shut up, Erik," Coll snaps. He lumbers off the dais to loom over Erik and jabs a finger into his chest. "Shut it before you make an even bigger fool of yourself. And you," he adds to the guards, "let her go, and leave us."

I hope he'll ask Lords Ulric and Tomas to leave, as well, and Thalia for that matter, so I can give my side of the story in private to my friends. But after the guards have gone, Coll rejoins the others, Erik and Lord Tomas with him, leaving me standing alone before all of them.

At last, Alaric raises his face to me, and I recoil. I don't know what I expected. Anger, perhaps, or frustration. Confusion. But not this expressionless mask with eyes that don't betray the faintest glimmer of friendship. "Is it true, Ellin Fisher Healer, that you did a Healing on Levachai Kinshield, called Kingslayer, and conversed with him repeatedly?"

Despite the knot of apprehension in my gut, I roll my eyes. "Alaric, is this a trial? Are you serious? Can't I explain what really happened?"

"You may answer my question, Healer," he says. "And while I am on this throne, you may address me as 'your majesty.'"

"Oh, for…" I sigh, loudly. "Yes, it's true. Your majesty."

"You therefore aided the man who murdered our father and expressed his intent to seize control of the Northlands. The man whose life you pled for, whose life was granted on the condition that you would do anything and everything in your power to ensure that he remained unconscious and non-threatening?"

"Yes, but…"

"Silence!" Alaric snaps. "Did you or did you not keep your knowledge regarding this most dangerous enemy's condition from me? Did you or did you not abuse my trust—and my name—in order to further your own agenda?"

I shake my head, torn between anger and fear. "And what, exactly, do you think 'my agenda' is, your majesty? Do you think there's even a shred of loyalty to the Southland in me? Have I not proven to you, over and over and over again, that I love the Northlands and am loyal to you? That I love you—all of you?" I draw in a deep, shuddering breath. "Or do you think, truly, that I am the Southling witch, the Southling whore, who has you in her thrall? Who brought Lev here in the first place, brought about your father's death with her own hands, and used her evil powers to coerce you to change the laws?"

My lips twist on the words I've heard whispered so many times, which seem laughable in the light of day but haunt me at night. I shake my head and let my hands drop, limp, to my sides, knuckles brushing against my skirt. "I only wanted information," I finish, and I force myself to meet Alaric's eyes, hoping he'll see the truth in mine. "I've had strange dreams—visions, I think—and I hoped to find answers by speaking with Lev. But I didn't. He doesn't remember anything, so it was all for nothing."

Alaric only nods, elbows on the arms of the throne, fingertips steepled. He looks at his hands thoughtfully, and I look to his brothers. Coll refuses to meet my gaze, watching Alaric instead, but Erik and Finn's white faces and wide eyes tell me clearly that they, at least, believe me.

"You leave me with no choice," Alaric says at last, in a voice that is formal, cold, a stranger's. "Regardless of your reasons, your actions are inexcusable."

"But Alaric, I..."

"Be silent, Ellin!" he roars. I take a step backward, stunned, and my breath catches as he continues. "I will not name you a traitor. Perhaps you are merely confused about where your loyalties lie. But," he adds, lifting a hand, "neither will I allow you to remain here, not when you have abused my trust so grievously. You must go to the Southland at once. Find the answers you seek, and in time, you may return."

"How long?" I whisper, scarcely comprehending any of this.

"Until I say differently." His face hardens, and the long look he gives me is filled with contempt. "Though you may not wish to return, after rejoining your own people."

"My own people?" I think my trembling is due more to anger than fear, now, and I glare at him. "You're as good as condemning me, sending me back, your majesty, and you well know it! The Guardians..."

"Are none of my concern," he finishes flatly. "The Northlands and her people, however, are. As is my family. And you endangered all of those by aiding Kinshield. You brought this on yourself."

"Do I…" But I bite the words off with clenched teeth. I won't demean myself to ask if I mean so little to him, not when the answer is obvious. "Fine," I say instead, though the word comes out wavering, smaller than I'd like. "Fine! I hope I never see you again!" I'm not sure if he hears the last bit, since I say it into my palms, trying to hold in my tears as I run for the door.

CHAPTER TEN

WHEN THE LORDS and Thalia have followed Ellin out, Finn would swear by everything he knows that the room is utterly silent. Of course, it's Erik who rounds on Alaric first, looking as stricken as Finn has ever seen him. "What in the hell are you playing at?" Erik asks. "What do you think you're doing?"

"You're perilously close to treason yourself," Alaric replies. "Don't question me on this."

"Or what?" Erik snaps, stepping closer, hands curling into fists. "You'll exile me next?"

Without any warning except for his face going a shade paler, Alaric lunges for him. "Ask me again and find out, you ass! Don't think you're too old for me to thrash you."

"And don't think I won't knock *both* your heads together," Coll interrupts, moving forward even as Finn does to separate them.

"Say something," Erik says, looking daggers at Alaric as Finn guides him a few steps away. *"He'll listen to you."*

"And what," Finn replies, mouth twisting, *"would you like me to say? 'I'm in love with her and may, actually, consider telling her someday, so please don't make her leave?' Hardly."*

"Well…" Erik breaks off with a start, and Finn follows his gaze to find a red-faced, panting Garreth slamming the door.

"Is it true?" Garreth demands, then stops, taking in the scene, and gapes like a fish. He staggers, turning very white, and Finn takes an involuntary step forward. "I don't even need to ask. You had Ellin executed?"

They all stare. No one moves. And then, Alaric's head falls forward into his hands. His shoulders shake.

"Laughing," Erik clarifies quickly, with his thoughts, and gives Finn a swift, small smile. *"I think."* He turns to Garreth. "Exiled, Youngest. Temporarily. And unfairly, if you ask me."

"Which no one did," Coll points out.

After a pause in which Garreth still looks confused and Coll seems about to say something else but doesn't, Alaric looks up, all traces of mirth gone from his features. He faces Erik. "What would you have me do?" he asks, and for a moment, there is a rawness in his expression that makes Finn wince. "I am king of the Northlands, and like it or not..." He shakes his head. "What would you have me do?"

Alaric looks down at his spread hands, and the mood is broken, replaced by a different, brittle kind of tension. They drift away from their knot of confrontation, with Alaric turning, of course, to Coll, and Erik drawing Garreth aside, no doubt explaining what happened. After a long moment poised between them, indecisive, Finn crosses to his older brothers and touches Alaric's arm before speaking. *"If I asked, would you reconsider?"* He doesn't explain, but then, there's no need.

Alaric regards him, lips pressed together, head tilted, as if gauging his mood. And Finn, meeting his eyes and seeing the answer in them before Alaric speaks, somehow can't be angry. But Erik has already shouted the things that needed to be said—with Garreth likely to repeat it all in a moment—and Finn can't quite bring himself to turn on Alaric along with them. Not when he can see, in the lines on his brother's face and the tension in his posture, what this horrible decision has cost him.

He swallows, throat tight, and nods before Alaric has a chance to say it. And he means to turn away—to look down, at least, long enough to arrange his features into a mask of acceptance—when

Alaric puts a hand onto each of his shoulders. "Finn, I want you to go with her."

He can only stare, certain he must have misunderstood. Almost of its own accord, his hand lifts between them and moves once, jerkily. "*What?*"

Alaric moves aside in order to include the others, who must have overheard. "I want to send Finn to the Southland with Ellin," he repeats. "Not only so you can look out for her," he adds, to Finn, "but so that you, too, can learn about the mental gifts. Perhaps you can discover why the four of you—out of all Northlanders—possess them. Any knowledge you could gain would be a treasure."

The others are crowded around now and all seem as stunned as Finn feels, though in different ways. Coll is staring at Alaric, eyebrows lowered and thoughtful, Garreth seems incredulous, and Erik stands with his mouth slack, cheeks darkening to scarlet. Finn can almost predict to the instant when he will explode.

"Are you mad, Alaric?" Arms flying, throat straining, for the second time in moments it looks as if his twin and Alaric might come to blows. Erik stops short in front of them—intentionally too close, but Alaric doesn't move. Nor does Erik look to Finn, of course. Of course. "Sending Finn alone with her? What would you want him to do if they got separated? And you know Ellin doesn't sign well, and you know it's difficult for him to read speech with accents, and…" He breaks off and stares at the floor. When he looks up again, his expression is calmer, but still panicked. "You'd send him without me?"

Beside him, Alaric shakes his head. "Erik…"

"No!" Erik exclaims, taking a step back. "If you insist on sending Finn, then I'm going, too. Or," he adds, "send me with Ellin in his stead. I'm just as capable of studying and reporting back to you, and without Ellin, won't you want him here? He's a physician, after all, and that's useful, while I'm only…"

"Erik!" Alaric's chest expands in a deep breath before continuing. "No. I forbid it. You're to stay here. As are you," he adds, pointing at Coll, "so don't even suggest it."

Coll scratches his beard, then crosses his arms over his belly, obviously annoyed. "Are we allowed to ask why?"

If Alaric replies, Finn doesn't see it. Besides, where Coll is concerned, he already knows the answer. His solid mountain of a brother is Alaric's anchor. And looking at his twin, the brighter half of his soul, Finn knows that the same need lay, a moment ago, behind Erik's feeble words of protest. For all Erik has always been at his side, ears and voice and self-styled protector, overloud and overcompensating, without Finn, Erik would be just as adrift.

Finn closes his eyes for an instant, thinking of what going with Ellin would mean. So much time shared, multitudes of opportunities for him to finally say the thing he has been longing to tell her for months... Traveling together would bring them closer than a hundred dances ever could. Then he exhales and opens his eyes and sees that they're arguing again. Fiercely, this time, to the point that he has to step into the thick of it and clap his hands to get a word in edgewise.

"*Erik's right,*" he says slowly, resolutely ignoring the deep ache the words cause. He tries to smile at Alaric and thinks he almost succeeds. "*I'm not the swordsman the rest of you are. And you do need me here, and besides, I would be a poor traveling companion. She'll want someone to tell stories while half-asleep, to sing with, not endless silence grating on her.*"

It's not entirely the truth, but the rest of the truth is standing opposite him and gnawing the inside of his cheek, hands shoved in his pockets. Was likely imagining, a moment ago, what it would be like to walk without adjusting his pace to Finn's longer stride. Wondering what it would be like to wake in the morning without seeing features more familiar than his own.

Alaric reaches to cup his chin, gently tilting Finn's face to look at him. "Are you certain?" Alaric asks, and Finn has no doubt that his voice is very soft. "I asked you for a number of reasons, Finnlay, not least because I do trust your ability with a sword. Will you reconsider?"

Finn smiles again, a tiny quirk of his lips, and squeezes Alaric's fingers before stepping back. He looks at the only logical answer to their problem. The one they all love equally—perhaps love most—but who is a support for none of them because they are all his protectors and always have been. *"I think you should send Garreth,"* he says. *"You didn't forbid him, did you?"*

"Me?" Garreth echoes, eyebrows climbing. Then he straightens his shoulders, pulling himself to his full height, and looks at Alaric gravely. It would be an impressive display of maturity, Finn thinks with a trace of amusement, if he left off wetting his lips and wiping his palms on his thighs. "I would consider it an honor to escort Ellin and learn what I can about the powers." He hesitates. "So, am I going?"

Alaric, hands clasped behind his back, studies him for a long, tense moment. Then he smiles and steps forward and ruffles Garreth's hair. "Yes, Youngest," he says, "at my request, and with my blessing. Now, go tell Ellin, and then pack your things. Don't forget extra socks."

CHAPTER ELEVEN

"ABSOLUTELY NOT, Garreth," I snap, for at least the fifth time since he pounded on my door and wouldn't go away. "I don't want companionship, and I won't change my mind. I just want to be alone! Is that so difficult to understand?" I fold a spare nightshift so fiercely I'm surprised the fabric doesn't rip, then stuff it into the depths of my traveling pack.

He throws his hands up in exasperation. "But you need someone to protect you!"

"Protect me?" I throw some stockings in. "What do you think I am, a child? Besides," I sneer, "what kind of guard would you be, anyway? You're barely more than a little princeling yourself."

"I am a guard!" he bursts out, red-faced. "Of the entire city, in case you've forgotten. I think I can manage looking after one girl, even if she is a bitch hellcat more often than not."

"Oh, that's right. You keep the city safe from untaxed cows and runaway pigs. How could I have forgotten how extraordinarily skilled you are?"

"And how could I have forgotten how stubborn you are?" He takes a few steps forward to tower over me like some kind of overgrown stork. "I'm going with you, whether you like it or not." After a moment, a small, hesitant smile tugs at the corner of his mouth. "Don't you want me? It might not be so bad, having a friend with you."

I look at him for a moment, the first Northlander I ever really knew. When we first met, I thought his pale eyes were cold as winter itself, thought his face and voice couldn't possibly be anything but arrogant. Now he's nearly pleading, and I can't find it in me to refuse. Especially since he's right, I have to admit. Not that I need looking after, but that a friend would be welcome. My shoulders loosen. "Fine," I reply at last. "Let's leave as soon as you pack your things. I'd like to be well away from here by dark."

"Why now?"

"Your brother made it abundantly clear that I'm no longer welcome here. I don't want to stay another night in this place."

"'This place' is my home! And has been yours. Don't say it like that, as if…"

"Then stay here." I snap, turning away to thrust some more things into my pack.

He sighs, after a moment, then hands me another dress from the pile on my bed. "Can we wait until morning, at least? It's still raining, and besides, they'll want to see us off."

I hate that he's right again. "Fine," I say finally, reluctantly, "but early, or I'll leave without you."

———◦◦◦ ✦ ◦◦◦———

The sky out the windows is still shot through with pink, the sun still orange, when we gather for breakfast. Garreth has a plate heaped with eggs and bread and meat and fruit and seems happy to plow through it, but my own breakfast is tasteless, and I have to force myself to clean my plate. I look as dreadful as I feel, exhausted and sick at heart.

It's no wonder; I don't think I slept more than a few hours last night, tossing and turning with my mattress like rocks beneath me. On the few occasions that I drifted off, I woke a few moments later in the darkness with a vague feeling of dread…and then remembered what happened all over again. It was all I could do one of those times, very late, not to leave immediately.

Now, sitting between Finn and Coll, with Erik and Garreth across the table, I wish I hadn't waited. It's torture listening to Garreth talking excitedly about our impending trip, peppering Coll with questions about the roads, traveling gear, and any number of other things I couldn't care less about. I have to remind myself that it's different for him. He hasn't been ordered to leave his home. He hasn't been cast aside by someone he loves. Loved, that is.

I sigh and drink my tea, trying to think of anything—anyone— but Alaric. The wounds he's inflicted are too raw yet, too deep, for me to think of him without wanting to kill him, or profess my undying love and beg his forgiveness, or both. I wish I knew.

Somehow, I manage to finish my breakfast. And then, before I know it, the others are standing and moving toward the door. We gather outside in the courtyard, where our packs are already waiting. The sight of my bulging pack penetrates past this fog of disbelief and makes me ache with the realness of it all. My knees threaten to buckle.

"You all right?" Erik asks, slipping an arm around my waist. I lean into him gratefully, near tears, and he sighs and presses his cheek against my hair. "That's a no, then?"

"This isn't fair," I whisper. "I didn't ever mean to…"

"I know." He tightens his hold before pulling away. "But it's not so bad, is it? It's not as if you're going forever."

"And why shouldn't I?" I ask sharply, louder than I intend. "I'm not wanted here. I don't belong here."

For a moment, he looks offended, but then he makes a dismissive face and waves my words aside. "Don't be stupid, Ellin. You know that's not true."

I don't, actually, but I don't want to talk any more about it. Instead, I step forward and give him another, fiercer, embrace. "Try not to do anything too foolish, all right?" I say, trying to smile. "Especially since you won't have Garreth to blame for it."

He laughs. "I won't make any promises, but I might try."

After more words with Erik, too few and far too insignificant, he goes to say his goodbyes to Garreth, and I look to Coll, standing with his thumbs hooked under his belt. He shakes his head. "Not yet, girl," he says. "I'm walking with you to the gates."

Which only leaves Finn because, even though Alaric has joined us, and Thalia with him, I pretend I can't see either of them. It's not the princess' fault, but I don't care. I don't care about a great many things, at the moment, including the king who stands there saying goodbye to his youngest brother as if nothing is wrong. As if the world is the same today as it was yesterday.

Alaric has one hand on Garreth's shoulder and one on Erik's, and his teeth flash in the familiar, warm smile that lights his entire face. I want to hate him. I want to slap him. I want it not to feel like a knife through my heart when he looks at me and his smile fades.

I turn away and go to Finn. If my heart is already bleeding, surely it can't be made to hurt more than it already does. He gives me a sad smile and takes my hands in his, then draws me away from the others. We stand, for a moment, just looking at one another.

"This isn't goodbye," he says, the thought brushing my mind like a caress, not quite a question.

Meeting his steady gaze, I can't argue. *"No,"* I agree. *"Only for a little while. Months. A few years at most."*

Finn nods and tucks a stray piece of hair behind my ear. His knuckles graze my cheek. A lark warbles in a nearby tree, and the breeze smells like damp soil and grass. The sky is nearly blue, by now.

I don't want to go.

He squeezes my hand before releasing me in order to switch to sign. *"Promise you won't forget me?"*

I can't help it. I laugh. *"It would take longer than months or years. Or ever,"* I reply. *"And you know it."*

He grins back and sets his hand on my shoulder, then seems to hesitate. I'm about to ask him what's the matter when he bends and presses his lips to mine.

It's only the barest instant before he pulls away and smiles at me again, blushing crimson. *"To help you remember,"* he says simply, and, despite my heart breaking, I smile.

"As if I need the reminder." I put my arms around him and cling for dear life. *"Thank you,"* I say with my thoughts. *"I'll miss you. I love you."*

Far too soon, he goes to Garreth, and Alaric approaches me. I tense and straighten my shoulders, daring him with my eyes to come closer. My face is a mask, betraying nothing but loathing, and Alaric's steps falter. Before I can change my mind, I shoulder my pack. "Garreth, we should go," I say briskly. "It's only getting later while we wait."

The next moments are a flurry of last, quick hugs and waves and instructions and goodbyes, and through it all, I keep my distance from Alaric. I have nothing to say to him, and I certainly don't need him to tell me, again, to leave. I don't want to give him the chance to tell me not to come back.

At last, we're ready, with Garreth carrying a pack larger than mine and Coll beginning to stride out toward the road. I've barely started to follow him when I hear footsteps on the stones behind me, and someone touches my shoulder.

"I'm sorry we didn't get to know one another better," Thalia says in a rush. Before I can react, she gives me a quick, tight embrace. "When you return, I hope things will be different."

I look at this princess I expected to be cold as ice, who has, in truth, been anything but. And then I smile back and nod. "If I return, I'd like that."

My eyes meet Alaric's over her shoulder, but though he lifts his hand in farewell, I pretend not to see and turn away.

———ooo-)◎(-ooo———

While Garreth and Coll walk together, talking, I hang back a few steps behind them. Strange that the shops and houses and worn stones under my feet should feel so familiar now, when I'm leaving. In the square, many of the shop doors are propped open, with shopkeepers sweeping their floors into the street and polishing their windows, calling to one another as they prepare to start the day. A few shout greetings to the princes, but no one says a word to me. Though I still doubt I need Garreth as a guard, I'm grateful that his presence is enough to protect me from the glares and insults I'm accustomed to.

The wall looms before us, a guard at each gate. To my surprise, instead of going right through, Coll tells us to wait and climbs up, only to return a moment later with another blue-coated guard behind him. "You know Davor, don't you, Ellin?"

"Yes, we've met." Of course I remember Davor, the tall, bearded guard with arms like a blacksmith and a kind smile. I owe him my life, though I didn't learn his name until long after he let me stay in the gatehouse instead of being locked out in the storm. I've seen him at the castle often enough to gather that he is a friend of the family, of Coll in particular, though I don't know him well.

Davor returns my smile, straightening the pack on his shoulder. "'Morning."

"He'll be going with you," Coll explains, and the words are barely out of his mouth when Garreth begins to sputter.

"What, you think we can't manage on our own?" he demands. Coll and Davor exchange a look, and Davor shrugs.

"I'm sure you can, but I'll feel a damned sight better knowing you aren't alone," Coll says slowly. "All right?"

"That's fine," I say, stepping forward. "I don't mind a bit." The thought of having someone besides Garreth to talk to—someone for him to talk with, too, if I want to be left alone—is appealing. And Davor looks like someone I would feel safer having along.

"Fine," Garreth says, sounding put-upon. "You may come."

"Thank you," Davor mutters dryly, giving him an amused glance.

Coll claps a hand on each of their shoulders. "It's agreed, then?"

Garreth sighs. "Agreed."

"Well, then," Coll says, and turns to me. I try to smile, but I know this is the end. The last goodbye before we leave. Before I find myself without a home to call my own. Again. I don't know whether I want to stay or to run so far away that the Northlands will become only a distant memory.

I return Coll's tight embrace and smile at him, genuinely this time, when he gives one of my braids a light tug. "You'll be all right, girl," he says softly.

It's not a question, but I nod anyway and try to swallow the knot in my throat. "I know."

"Wish you weren't taking that, though," he adds, nodding to the short sword I took at the last minute. "You'll only hurt yourself with it, likely as not."

I roll my eyes. "Well, if I do—which I won't, thank you—I'll blame my teacher. But every time I see it," I add, more seriously, "I'll think of him."

His face works ferociously for a minute before he breaks into a reluctant smile. "Well," he mutters at last, "look after yourself, and the Youngest, until we meet again."

The lump is back in my throat, and I nod, silently. Coll looks at me for a moment before he goes to Garreth and the two of them say their goodbyes. Davor and I both make a little space, giving them time to speak privately, until Garreth comes to join us, walking quickly. He stops beside me and looks at the ground, the tip of his nose suspiciously red.

I look away, not wanting to embarrass him, and watch Davor walk over to speak with Coll. The two of them speak too quietly for me to hear, but it's easy to imagine that Davor must be receiving detailed instructions to watch over the two of us, make sure we don't do anything foolish, and things of that sort. No doubt saying farewell to his friend, too, I amend, when I see them clasp forearms and then embrace like brothers.

"All set?" Davor calls, striding toward us. I shift the strap on my pack and nod, and Garreth does the same, straightening his shoulders. With one last wave, Coll begins to head for home, leaving the three of us standing just inside the gates.

Garreth and I look at one another blankly, and I wonder if he feels the same way I do. I think he must, since he doesn't move and doesn't speak and looks a little ill. It's a beautiful morning, warm as I could wish, but it might as well be midwinter again for all I feel it.

"Come on, then," Davor says, his deep, gruff voice as gentle as I've heard it. "We've a long way to go."

"I know," I reply quietly. Garreth sniffles, then clears his throat and doesn't say anything. And then the three of us pass through the gate and fall into step on the road that will take us south.

Chapter Twelve

LATE-AFTERNOON SUNLIGHT bathes the library in gold when Finn pokes his head in the doorway. He's already tried the stables and found Coll, found the kitchen and Alaric's study empty, but it's here, at last, that he spots the brother he's been looking for. Alaric is seated in one of the chairs by the cold hearth, a closed book in his lap, staring at its cover. He looks up when Finn approaches.

"I've already heard enough," Alaric says as Finn sits, "so if you've come to shout, please spare yourself the trouble."

"Erik's been at you?"

Alaric nods. "You know how he is. He won't ever let things *be!"*

"So, you want us all to accept your judgment without question?" Finn asks.

"Ah, you're angry, too." He makes a face. "Wonderful."

"I'm not. Not very," he amends. *"I understand why you wanted her to leave. It would have been bad for her if word about what she did got out. Which you know it will."*

"I know it has." Alaric pushes a hand through his hair. "But if you do understand that I had no choice, why are you angry?"

Finn can only stare, for a moment. *"Because of the way you treated her!"* he bursts out. *"Because you were a complete ass to her. And to Erik, for that matter. Do you even need to ask?"*

"Forgive me," Alaric says, very precisely, face darkening, "if I was angry at Ellin for being sympathetic to the man who

97

murdered our da. And angry at your twin for going with her behind my back."

"Forgive me," Finn retorts, *"for figuring that our mighty king could put aside his feelings and rule objectively."*

"Yes, you're quite the expert on putting aside your feelings where Ellin is concerned, aren't you?" Alaric snaps. But then, perhaps seeing the expression Finn can't hide quickly enough, he gentles at once and touches Finn's knee. "I'm sorry. That was unfair." Finn shrugs, still stung, and Alaric sighs. "I had to, Finn," he says. "When word spreads about what was said in that room—and it will if it hasn't already—how would it seem to our people if I sent her away quietly, without so much as a word of punishment? I can't condone her actions. And I won't."

And yet, if keeping up appearances was all that mattered, Finn thinks, couldn't have Alaric said something to Ellin—given her some signal, even a note—to let her in on the secret? From the expression on his brother's face, however, he knows better than to press the issue. That pinched look around Alaric's mouth and the vertical crease between his eyebrows are clear warnings, and Alaric has been tetchy lately anyway.

"So," Finn says at last, casting about for a new topic, *"what are you reading?"*

With a grimace, Alaric holds up the volume for his inspection. "I wanted to brush up on Rhodanath so I don't look like a fool when I'm talking with Nathalia, or about her. I couldn't remember last night if it was wool from goats or sheep they use for that famous cloth of theirs."

"Goats," Finn says, surprised that he remembers. *"Though I can't imagine she'd mind if you got it wrong."*

Alaric shrugs again. "Well, it's one question of many. I need some topics of conversation, and to know something about subjects she's likely to want to discuss."

Finn's eyebrows climb, and he has to struggle not to smile. *"That's romantic. Is there something besides livestock in there?"*

"It's practical," Alaric corrects him, and lifts a hand. "It never was a match made for love, Finn. You know that."

"You're serious." He studies his brother's face carefully. *"Don't you like her?"*

"Does it matter?" After a moment, Alaric sighs. "She seems very nice. It will be a pleasant marriage, I think. And in time..." He gives Finn a tight smile that doesn't reach his eyes. "You never know."

"That doesn't seem fair to either of you," Finn points out, frowning. *"You certainly don't seem to be trying very hard to get to know..."*

"Oh, shut it, Finn!" Alaric snaps, and hurls the book, which smacks into the far wall. He looks at Finn, red-faced from fury or embarrassment or both, breathing hard. "I'm doing my best, all right? I didn't ask for this. For any of it."

Openmouthed, Finn blinks at him, shocked to stillness. He hasn't seen Alaric's temper flare in years, and hasn't caused it since...he can't remember being the cause of it. *"I know,"* he says at last, for lack of anything better to say, though he isn't at all certain he does.

Alaric is quiet for awhile, staring at nothing again. "Anyway," he says, his anger seemingly passed, "it's not as if she's miserable here. Erik offered to show her around the city earlier, and she seemed pleased to accept. I think it will be all right," he finishes, looking as if he hopes to convince them both.

Of course Erik did, Finn thinks, and tries to push the image of Erik dancing with her out of his mind. Stupid and impulsive as his twin can be, surely, surely he wouldn't be that foolish. He's seen the smile Erik wears while he watches Thalia, though.

"I hope so," he says, and tries to smile.

Alaric nods briskly and pushes himself to his feet. Somehow, in the mere seconds between sitting and standing, the weight settles on his shoulders again, pulling them upright as he accepts the burden. The lines on his face smooth with a visible effort, and Finn's heart twists. Sometimes, he wonders what Alaric would be like if he hadn't spent his life becoming the man he must be. It has only been a few months, but sometimes he wonders if Alaric remembers what it's like not to be king.

But when Finn stoops to pick up the book after Alaric has gone out, he runs a finger along the deep dent in the spine and realizes that he needn't wonder. He stands for a long time holding it, looking at the damaged cover, before he sets it gently on the tabletop and goes out.

———∘∘∘-◦◐◦-∘∘∘———

"Sorry I'm late," Erik says breathlessly, as he drops into his place next to Coll at the dinner table.

Finn eyes his brother's damp, slicked-down hair and shining face. *"At least you're clean and late,"* he says, smirking a little. *"Nice of you to make the effort."*

"Oh, shut it," Erik retorts, pink-cheeked, before nudging Coll. "Pass the bread?"

Finn glances at Alaric, who sits staring at his plate, eating methodically. Though the main dish is a favorite of Alaric's, duck in herb-seasoned cream sauce, he doesn't seem to be enjoying it. Doesn't seem to be enjoying Thalia's conversation, either, despite preparing for it. Not that she seems to notice, fortunately, but to one who knows Alaric well, it's easy to see when he's simply nodding along.

Unlike Erik, Finn notes with a grimace. His twin's eyes are shining as much as his freshly-scrubbed cheeks, and he has that look about him. As if he's more alive than usual, talking faster, gesturing more, at his most charming. If they were a few years younger, Finn would be tempted to kick his shin under the table. Would do it, even now, if he weren't afraid that Erik would yell, or that he'd accidentally kick Coll instead.

The worst part of it, he thinks, stabbing some greens, is that Erik might not even realize he's doing it. Probably doesn't, at that.

Or, no, he amends, watching Erik duck his head, grinning at something she said. All white teeth and his heart on his face. The worst part is that Erik is going to be hurt by this, and badly.

With a sigh, he looks to Coll, who seems to pay no mind to any of his brothers' moods as he spreads butter on another piece of bread. As Finn watches, Coll nudges Alaric, who straightens with a start.

"I sent Davor along with the youngsters," Coll says, gesturing with his bread. "Thought you ought to know."

Alaric sets down his knife. "What did you say?"

"Davor. I asked him to go along with Garreth and Ellin." Coll shrugs. "Told Garreth it was mostly to set myself at ease, and that's the truth."

"You dismissed a guard without my permission? Without even mentioning it?"

"Hells, Alaric, I'm telling you now, aren't I? Would you have said no?"

"Does it matter?" Alaric cries, throwing his hands up. "He's gone by now, whether or not I would have minded. Damn it, Coll! You had no right."

And Finn, already startled, is even more shocked to see heads turning in their direction. For Alaric to disagree with Coll is one thing, but loudly and in public? He glances at Erik and finds his twin looking equally flabbergasted.

Coll's face is hard as stone, and he sets his half-eaten piece of bread down before pointing a finger at Alaric. "And you know damned well that I…" He breaks off abruptly and shakes his head, red-cheeked, then climbs to his feet. "I'm through here. Find me when you've found your wits." He stalks away, heedless of the stares that follow him.

Stares that land on Alaric, who takes a long swig of his wine before giving Finn and Erik and Thalia a shrug. "He overstepped his bounds, and he knows it," Alaric says shortly. But before any of them has a chance to respond, Lord Tomas appears at Alaric's side and, at Alaric's gesture, lowers himself into the seat Coll recently vacated. After accepting a glass of wine, he leans close to speak near Alaric's ear. Finn tries not to eavesdrop, but he still sees the words "Southlings" and "fighting" and "dealt with accordingly."

Despite it being summer, his hands are suddenly cold.

CHAPTER THIRTEEN

THE FIRST OF THE EVENING stars are beginning to come out when Garreth and Davor and I clump wearily into Wayton. It's the first town we've seen since ferrying across the river two days ago, and I smile as I push a few limp strands of my hair off my forehead. "I'll be glad to see an inn," I say, then wince when I shift my pack. The strap has rubbed raw places on both shoulders, which match the blisters on my feet nicely. We haven't set a particularly brisk pace, but we've been walking for days, stopping only to eat and to sleep.

A little ahead of me, Davor nods. "I'll be glad to see a mug of ale."

"And gladder still to pour it down your throat, aye?" Garreth asks. "So will I."

I roll my eyes. "Isn't it just like men to come into town, filthy and stinking and hungry and tired, and give their first thought to having a drink."

Davor gives me his slow, crooked grin. "Well, now. Isn't it just like a woman to nag 'em about it?"

"If you think that was nagging…" I shake my head. I've come to like Davor a great deal in the few days I've known him, and it's easy to see why the princes think so highly of him. Though Garreth hasn't complained about traveling as much as I expected and has, in fact, been strangely quiet, it's Davor who has built our fires and chosen good spots to make camp and smelled rain on the air and a dozen other useful things.

Wayton isn't a large town. It's bigger than Harnon, the village where I grew up, but it's certainly no city with a paved town square and statues and fountains and great tall buildings. Instead, the dirt road widens on the main street, and that's the center of town.

"So," Garreth says, looking around with amused interest, "this is a Southling city."

"Town," I correct him, nettled, "not a city, and you needn't sound so haughty about it. It's no different than small towns in the Northlands."

"No different?" He snorts. "Is that a joke? Since we crossed the river, everything has been different. This is nothing like the Northlands."

I walk past him, leading the way to the inn. Strangely, I don't feel it, though I do know what he means. The first time I crossed into the Northlands, it seemed utterly strange to me, and even the air smelled different. Then, when Father and I went home to the Southland, it was as if my very bones breathed a sigh of relief and felt soaked in the familiar. But this time, if I'd been blindfolded or asleep when we crossed the river, I don't think I would have known when we entered the Southland. If I didn't know better, right now, I could easily mistake this place for a town in the Northlands.

The inn is the only building two stories tall on this street, with many of its windows glowing against the growing dark. The white sign above the door is neatly painted with the name, The Golden Stag, as well as a picture. Warmth envelops us when we enter, sniffing the heady smells of food and drink and pipe smoke. It's like any other inn, and yet, in this one, the cheerful babble seems to pause, just for an instant, when we enter. My skin crawls, but before I'm even certain the odd moment really happened, it's over.

"Nice place," Garreth mutters, after we've sat.

"What do you mean?" I ask, but his shoulders only hunch toward his ears in reply. Before I can press him about it, a pretty barmaid approaches our table, and pushes her thick braid, as flaming red as my own, behind her shoulder. I smile at her, unreasonably pleased to see someone who looks like me, but she doesn't smile back.

"What'll you have, then?" she asks.

After we've ordered, Garreth gives me a look across the table. "What did I mean?" he repeats, mouth twisting as if he tastes something unpleasant. "Look around."

"What?" But when I look, truly look, around the room, I think I see what he means. There are a few other Northlanders in the crowded dining room, blond heads shining like pale beacons amidst the many shades of Southling red, but every Northlander in the place is alone or at a table with other Northlanders...and only other Northlanders. Ours is the only mixed table in the place, and, judging from some of the narrow-eyed glares we're getting from the other patrons, they don't approve. "Oh."

I bite the inside of my cheek, glancing around the room again. Maybe I'm wrong. Maybe I've got nothing to do with it, and Garreth and Davor are the ones drawing the dark looks. That would make more sense. Unlike the two of them, I clearly belong here. And it's only fair, I think, turning my gaze to the worn, scarred wooden tabletop. I've been made to feel as if I'm an outsider plenty of times in the Northlands. I've faced dirty looks and worse, and it is only fair for Garreth and Davor to get this small taste of the same medicine. So why do I feel so guilty about it? Why do I feel as if I'm just as unwelcome here as they are?

I'm grateful when the barmaid returns with our drinks. "To our arrival in the Southland," Davor says, raising his cup.

"And a continued safe journey," Garreth adds, and does the same. I lift my mug of tea along with them, blow on it and sip, and try to smile. The room is noisy again, and no one seems to be staring at us anymore, and maybe Garreth and I were both wrong.

"So," Davor says, with a small gesture. With his sleeves rolled up, the fine blond hairs on his thick wrist glint in the light. "Due south again in the morning, or do we start heading east?"

"Well, that depends," I reply, looking from him to Garreth. "If we were planning the shortest route, we'd continue south on this highway. But, it passes closer to Harnon than I like. So, I say we go east, then turn south near the coast."

Garreth takes a drink. "And that'll take us to the college?"

"To the one in Whiteriver." I nod. "It's the oldest and best of the three colleges. It's where the Healers train, with the most extensive library. If we're going to find answers about…everything," I say significantly, lowering my voice, "it will be there."

"Not to mention, if it's the Healers' college, it's where you'll want to finish your training," Garreth says. "Did your da study there?"

I nod, looking into my cup. Strange how the mere mention of training as a healer can set my teeth on edge. Beneath the table, I wipe my palms on my skirt.

When our dinners are brought out, we eat quickly. Davor and Garreth talk a bit, but I just chew and swallow. I wish Garreth hadn't mentioned my father. We had dinner at an inn the night he died, soon after we returned home from the Northlands, and now…

Now I have only to close my eyes, and my father will be across from me in the smoke and noise instead of Garreth. The big man beside me will be Donnal Marthen instead of Davor, this town will be Harnon instead of Wayton…

"And a glass of cider for me, I think," Father said. "A small one for Ellin, too. She worked hard today." And then he smiled at me, brown eyes crinkling at the corners. Somehow, some trace of bitter-sweetness in the set of his lips, the seriousness in his tone, told me that this was more than a drink for a girl not quite old enough to have it. It was a gesture of acknowledgement that I was growing up. That he was proud of me. That he trusted me. It was a moment, a smile, that said we were going to work together, that this was how it was going to be. Rowan and Ellin Fisher, Master Healer and apprentice.

It was a smile, a moment, that let me see the future he had planned for us.

I remember so few of the words we exchanged that night. If only I'd known, I would have listened better, remembered better… I would have told him so many things. Would have asked him so many more. Everything I could think of that I might someday wish to know.

But even if I had known, there wouldn't have been enough time. There never is. Those words, though, that smile, I remember. I remember a few other bits of our conversation exactly. For the rest, I recall what we talked about, but I'm not sure if the words I remember are truly his or ones I've made up that sound like things he would have said.

I remember, precisely, what the cold mud felt like under my feet when I heard he was dead. The way the night air smelled. Raindrops like pinpricks on my skin. Sometimes, that night seems a lifetime ago. Sometimes, only yesterday.

My head jerks up when something raps my ankle under the table. "What was that for?" I demand, giving Garreth a sharp look. "That hurt!"

He raises a finger to shush me and leans forward, darting a sideways look out at the room. *"Aren't you listening to this?"* he asks, moving his hands surreptitiously.

"What?"

Garreth rolls his eyes. *"The song, Ellin. The song."*

I hadn't even noticed the music until now. The singing and fiddling blended into the background noises of the inn, along with talking and shouting. I don't turn to see the musician, since Garreth obviously doesn't want us to attract notice, but I do sit up and pay attention.

After the next verse of the song, received by laughter and hoots of approval, my mouth hangs open like a fish's. My hands are suddenly freezing. *"Garreth, did he just call Alaric a..."*

He nods grimly. I can't stop listening now that I've started. Can't avoid hearing about how the king is telling Southlings they're welcome to come and live in the Northlands, and then knifing them in the back. Taking the Southling women and—I blanch.

The song is a clever Southling's tale, telling the Northlander king just what he thinks of him. Saying he knows the king's a liar and a fool and so are any Southlings who think the new laws and promised peace are true. It's supposed to be funny, mocking Alaric, but it makes me sick. I might be furious at him myself, but to hear other people say such things is another matter entirely. They don't even know him.

"I'm going to kill him," Garreth mutters, but I grab his forearm, which flexes under my touch.

"Garreth, don't," I hiss. "Are you mad? Do you know what they'd do if they knew who you are?"

He jerks away. "I don't care!"

"Well, I do," Davor rumbles, gripping Garreth's wrist. Unlike me, he's strong enough to hold him if Garreth decides to be stupid. "Now's not the time or the place, an' you know it."

Garreth exhales shakily. "I..."

"What's the trouble, then?" A tall Southling, with a brighter-haired one at his side, slaps a hand on each of Garreth's shoulders. I try not to flinch as the man, obviously drunk, leers at me before turning his red-rimmed gaze to Garreth. "Don't you like the music?"

"It's fine," Garreth says, through clenched teeth. His shoulders hunch, trying to shove the offending hands off, but the Southling holds tighter. Out of the corner of my eye, I see Davor tense. His fingers twitch, but he doesn't reach for a weapon. Yet. I know the second man's gaze is likely fixed on him in case he does.

"Oho, but you don't seem to be enjoyin' it much to me," the Southling says, leaning closer. He flicks a glance at me. "'S it 'cause we didn't describe our women to your liking? Wanted more detail, did you? Or did we get it wrong, the way she likes it when you..."

I want to do something, anything. To throw my mug at his grinning face. Break his nose and watch it bleed, damn him. But I can't move, and I'm too afraid of what would happen to Garreth even if I did. So I sit, and do nothing.

Don't, I beg Garreth with my eyes. Don't do something stupid. They're not worth it. But he bucks under the man's hands again; cranes his neck to glare daggers. I've never seen his face so flushed. "Stop," he breathes, very low, and the sinews on his neck stand out. "Stop now, or I swear..."

"What the lad means to say," Davor says loudly, turning his hand palm-upward, "is, we mean you no harm, an' we're just passing through. No great fans of his fool of a majesty ourselves." He turns and spits on the floor. "The girl's da died in the Northlands, and as a favor to a dyin' man who was a friend to us, we're escortin' her home to her mother on the coast. That's all. It was the girl's honor the lad was gettin' riled up about."

"That so?"

If Garreth doesn't agree, I'll kill him myself and spare them the trouble.

"It's true," he mutters at last. His throat bobs. "I—I apologize."

No one moves, and the two Southlings exchange a glance. The one holding Garreth tightens his grip visibly and leans down, and I flinch.

His laugh breaks the silence at our table like glass, sharp, with an edge. "Should've known you bloodless lot would be so easily cowed," he says, slapping Garreth on the back before releasing him. "Northlanders." The word is a curse or a joke, or both, and his companion laughs along with him as they lurch away.

Davor takes a deep drink. "Finish your food," he says to Garreth. His broad accent of a moment ago is almost entirely gone, replaced by a quiet note of command. "We'll not leave just yet."

"But…"

"Do as I say, lad." Davor's voice is rough, hard as stone. "I'm speaking for your brother on this. We'll not run as if we have something to hide." For all his brave words and untroubled face, I notice that his knuckles are white where he clutches his glass, and his other hand stays beneath the table, no doubt gripping the hilt of his knife.

When Garreth picks up his fork, Davor turns to me. "Are you all right?" he asks softly.

I nod. I'm not, of course; I'm still tied in knots, but I don't want to talk about it. I don't think any man would understand. I want nothing more than to forget the things he said.

It's not easy to forget, though. As Garreth chokes down his food, I try to finish my tea, all too conscious of the sidelong glances we're getting from those at nearby tables. I'm sure they heard what the drunk man said, and my cheeks burn with a dull heat that my lukewarm tea does nothing to cool.

At last, Davor pays for our meal and says we can leave. Garreth and I shoulder our packs quickly and follow him to the door with our eyes downcast. I sigh with relief when we step out onto deserted street. "What are we...?" I begin, but Davor shushes me.

"Not yet, Red. C'mon." Gesturing for us to follow, he turns up the street the way we came. Garreth and I fall into step behind him, side-by-side. Our boots crunch on the dirt and gravel, and once we reach the edge of town, I can hear crickets chirping. A pond must be nearby, too, since a frog joins in sometimes with a low, booming bellow.

Davor goes perhaps half a mile out of town, past trees and meadows and the occasional farmhouse set back from the road, with candlelit windows. When we come to the top of a low hill, he veers off the road and leads us through grass that looks blue in the darkness and swishes against my ankles. In the black trees up ahead, a nightbird screams, and I shiver.

"This'll do," Davor says, unslinging his pack.

"And to think, I was looking forward to a bath and a real bed tonight." I sigh, easing the straps of my pack off my aching shoulders, and let it thump to the ground. "Isn't it just our luck."

"Luck has nothing to do with it," Garreth snaps. A spark illuminates his face as he lights his lantern. "I'm going to get some wood." With that, he stalks off, leaving me and Davor in the darkness.

Before I can decide whether or not to follow him, Davor puts a hand on my arm. "Leave him," he says, once Garreth is out of earshot. And, after a moment of watching the lantern's light bob away, growing smaller, I nod and set about making camp.

———ooo-◦◖◗◦-ooo———

By the time we have a fire blazing and our blankets rolled out, the edge of Garreth's anger seems to have dulled. He still looks sour, though, especially with the firelight casting harsh shadows

on his face. I boil tea in a tin pan and pour some for each of us, and
Garreth gives me a small smile when he accepts his cup.

We sit for awhile, not speaking, and I watch sparks fly up into
the sky. Davor looks to the road, tight-lipped, and Garreth seems
fascinated by his hands around his cup. At long last, he heaves a
sigh. "Davor, I wouldn't ask this if I weren't Alaric's eyes here, if I
didn't put love and loyalty above all else," he begins. Davor looks
a question at him, and Garreth inhales. "I'd like you to turn for
home—now, tonight—and tell Alaric what has happened. What
they're saying here. Without us, you could be almost halfway to
the river by morning, and if you buy a horse tomorrow, you'll be
home in no time at all."

Davor snorts. "Garreth…"

"No!" Garreth holds up a hand. "Surely you agree that he needs
to know, and it's our responsibility to tell him."

"'Course I do, lad, but so is it my responsibility to look after
the two of you. I gave my word to Coll…"

"Leave Coll to me, if it comes to that," Garreth says. His eyes
close for an instant, and when he speaks, his voice is strained, very
low. "Davor, I'm not asking."

I gape at him. "Garreth, of all the arrogant, pigheaded things
to…"

"No, Red," Davor says. "It's his right. An' he's right," he adds,
sounding, to my ears, strangely relieved. He drains his tea, then
pushes himself up. "I'll gather my things an' be off, then."

Shooting a poisonous look at Garreth, I jump to my feet, too.
"Davor, you can't be serious," I protest, standing beside him as he
kneels to roll up his blanket. "It's late, and it's dark, and his highness over there is being an idiot. Can't you wait until morning?"

He chuckles in answer and squeezes my hand. "Oh, girl, y'worry
too much. I'm a soldier to my bones, don't forget. Travel in the dark
is nothing. He's right, by the way," he adds. "I shouldn't waste time."

My arms fold themselves across my chest. "I still don't like it."

He laughs again, tightening a strap. "Take care, Ellin," he says
when he's stood and shouldered his pack. I clasp his proffered

hand in farewell, and though I want to beg him not to go, to stay and help us and protect me, because I've seen what the Southland is like now and it frightens me, I don't say any of that.

"Safe journey," is what I say instead. "Thank you, for coming with us this far." I busy myself with smoothing out my blanket, arranging my things, while Davor and Garreth say their goodbyes. I don't want to have to listen to Garreth being such a haughty bastard again, and I don't want either of them to see my face. It's bad enough being afraid without anyone else knowing it.

When he leaves, I wave and watch his lantern bob off into the night. Behind me, Garreth sighs, and I poke the fire with a stick, causing the edge of a log to crumble in a shower of sparks.

"Ellin..."

"I don't want to talk to you right now." I jab the log again, harder, then ignore him as I pour more tea for myself. I don't even look in his direction. The cup burns my hands, but I'm angry enough not to care. Serve him right if I dumped the contents on his foolish head.

"Fine," Garreth mutters, sounding cross, and there's a rustling sound from his direction that I assume is him sitting, too. I still don't look. I don't care what he's doing.

It's easy to forget, living in the castle, how loud nighttime in the country is. I always think of moonlit meadows as being serene, but in reality this place is anything but. The frogs are still booming and creaking, the bugs chirruping, owls hooting, small furred things or the wind in the grass rustling... The fire crackles and pops, and Garreth keeps sighing heavily.

Strange how, with all those noises, I can feel the weight of the silence between us. With a sigh of my own, I set aside my cup and draw my knees to my chest, tenting my skirt, and wrap my arms around them. My bare toes dig into the cool grass and powdery dirt.

"Ellin," Garreth says again.

"I'm still not speaking with you." But I do glance at him, this time, and see that his position mirrors mine, only more awkward-looking, with his long legs and jutting elbows. While I'm angry and afraid, he looks simply miserable. "Oh, what?" I snap, even more irritated with him for making me want to be kind.

"I'm sorry," he mutters at last. "Did I truly sound like an ass?"

There's an easy answer, but I can't bring myself to give it. Instead, I look at the stars, bright against the blackness that seems more immense than usual, and shrug. "You sounded…like a prince," I admit, "who puts his kingdom, and his king, ahead of himself and his friends. All right?"

"If it's worth anything, I didn't want him to go, either," he says, after a moment, hugging his knees tighter.

Tempting as it is to snap something rude, there's an eloquence in his face when he meets my eyes that makes me swallow and nod, slowly. "Are you afraid, too?"

"I…" His head jerks up, bright and quick as a comet, and he stiffens, and I go still.

"Garreth?"

He darts a glance at me, wide-eyed, and shakes his head. "Shh!" he hisses, peering into the night. "Thought I heard…"

"Us?" a deep voice interrupts, right behind my ear.

I shriek as my heart seems to explode in my chest. Before I can scramble to my feet, hands are on my arms, yanking me backward. There are more of them, nightmare shadows in the flickering light, footsteps pounding.

I twist, trying desperately to free myself, and can only watch as Garreth throws himself headlong at the two going after him. Fists are smacking dull on skin and clothing, men shouting, grunting, and I try, kicking my useless bare feet, aiming for his boots, his shins, wrenching my shoulders to free my arms. I throw my head back, teeth bared.

"Let go!" I scream. "GARRETH!"

Behind me, holding me with a terrifying strength, the man laughs. "Whoa, easy, wench! We're only after a bit o'fun, aren't we?"

The world drops out from under me when he twists, a wrestling maneuver, and we land hard. Before I can squirm away, he's flipped us, is on top of me, straddling me with strong knees squeezing my hips and my arms pinned, and I am going to die.

My eyes have filled with tears, whether from the terror or the pain of banging my head against the ground, I don't know. He's heavy as a boulder, and disgusting, reeking of drink and sweat when he leans down and breathes on me, but not close enough that I could fling my head up and break his nose...

I turn away, squeezing my eyes shut tight. To one side, another hit, a grunt of effort, and Garreth cries out, then moans. I have the sudden, horrible picture of him sprawled on the dirt, bloodied, but I can't bear to look.

Rock digging into my shoulderblade. I'm gagging. Can't get my knee up...

"C'mon, sweet'eart," the man slurs. "Don't y'like us Southling men anymore? Haven't been spoilt for us by them frigid Northlanders, have ya?"

Suddenly, I know him. Remember his leering face from the inn, and I should have known they wouldn't let us leave without a fight.

He shifts, and I bite back another scream. He's going to snap my wrists like twigs, thick fingers bruising my skin, fingernails digging. My breath is coming in wracking sobs that can't seem to claw their way out of my throat; feels like a stone is on my chest, though he's not touching me there, not yet; can't breathe...

"The hell d'you think you're doing, Jak?" another, different voice demands, and then he's being dragged away, kicking my hip in the process, but I don't care, and I can't move, and he's gone. Spurts of air through my nose, sharp and cold; stars behind my eyelids. "Can y'not see her hair, you damned fool? She's one of ours!"

The man—Jak?—spits. "She's with him, isn't she?"

"Not on my watch, Jak," the other man says. "What d'you think we are? Animals?"

"Wasn't going to do anything," Jak mutters, sounding sullen. "Just scarin' the trollop, havin' a bit of fun."

"An' now you've had it, so let's get what we came for and be done with it."

Still shaking like a leaf, I dare to crack one eye open, hoping to see what they're going to do to us. There are four of them, the one called Jak and a smaller, older man he's talking to, with two brutish, ugly ones across the fire, standing guard over Garreth.

At a word from the older man, one of them drags Garreth upright, and I gasp, soundlessly, at the sight of him. He looks barely conscious, with the man's grip under his arms, head lolling, nose dripping blood. The man deposits him next to me unceremoniously, and I'm relieved to hear a faint groan from the limp heap beside me.

"Don't move," the old man says, looming over us. Though I close my eyes, he nudges me in the side with the toe of his boot. "Don't pretend to faint, now. We'll not harm *you*—it's your coin we're after. Where is it?"

I turn my head to look at him. Tears are streaming down my cheeks, but I can't help it. Don't want to cry, but I can't stop. I force my mouth to open, but there are no words. Only air over my tongue, drying my lips, and a sour taste at the back of my throat.

"Your coin, girl!"

The answer comes from beside me, weakly. "The leather purse in my pack," Garreth whispers. "The bigger one. There's a bit in hers as well, but it's mine you want."

At a gesture from the old man, Jak and the others start rooting through our packs, tossing our belongings left and right. I wince at the sight of Garreth's bloody face.

"Are you all right?" he whispers.

I close my eyes and nod. I'm not, not at all, but it could have been much worse. "Are you?"

Garreth nods, too, then looks to where the old man is watching the others instead of watching us. And no surprise, I think. What threat are we, an unarmed, skinny boy and a small girl, who didn't hear them coming until they were upon us?

A light touch on my hand makes me look at Garreth again. He wets his swollen lips, then winces, obviously touching a sore spot. After glancing at the old man again, he nods significantly down at his hands. *"Stop them,"* he says, signing almost too quickly for me to understand, especially in the dim light. *"Use your powers!"*

The mere mention of my abilities is enough for me to feel the urgent itch under my skin, the tightness at my temples. Were I to compel the leader, I could make them stop this instant. I might be able to kill Jak, or hurt him. At the very least, I could force them to go away and forget about us.

I want so badly to do something, anything, that I find myself reaching for my powers before I've had time to think it through. My breathing is slower, now, and my limbs feel heavier, more real, less in danger of trembling to bits or shattering. So very close… And then, suddenly, I shy away as if the barest touch burns.

"Garreth, I can't!" I whisper, stunned at my own foolishness. "The Guardians!"

His sharp breath tells me that he forgot, too. His eyes close, and he nods. I don't need to hear his thoughts to know what he's thinking—that there's nothing for us to do except wait. Wait, and hope they don't kill us.

It feels like a long time, but I think it's really only a matter of moments before the men stand, and Jak lifts Garreth's purse, jangling it triumphantly. "Got it!"

"And the girl's?"

"It, too," the other man says, tossing it over. The old man opens the drawstring with two fingers and peers inside, then snorts. "Hope the other one's more worth our while than this." Then, louder, over his shoulder, "We're finished here, boys."

He looks down at Garreth and me, a dark shadow with the light behind him, and holds up a warning finger. "Come after us, and we kill you." I fight a bone-deep shiver, absolutely certain he means it. "Understand?"

We nod, and he snorts again. "I'd find a better traveling companion if I were you, girl. You're in for naught but trouble with this one."

With that, they fade into the darkness. After a moment, a piercing whistle splits the night, followed by a horse's whicker and the jangle of tack. Garreth and I don't move, listening to the hoofbeats becoming fainter and fainter in the distance.

When I'm certain they've gone for good, I pick my way over to our ransacked belongings. I move gingerly, afraid I might break. I've barely knelt down and started re-packing our satchels, fingers shaking, when I groan. "Oh, Garreth, they ruined our food, too." Rocking back on my haunches, I grip my forehead in frustration. "What are we going to do?" I wail. "No food, no money, and you heard what the man said. And what happened earlier. What are we going to..."

His footsteps crossing the distance between us are quiet, and the hand he sets on my shoulder is cold. Nevertheless, the reassuring gesture is welcome, and I try to smile when he kneels with a soft hiss of pain. "It's not so hopeless," he says, picking up one of his shirts and stuffing it into his pack. "Wouldn't want to eat anything they'd touched anyway, would you?" The skin around his left eye is darkening, his nose ringed with dried blood. Just looking at him is painful, but feeling sorry for him is better than feeling sorry for myself.

"Besides," Garreth adds in a whisper, "they didn't take all our money. I've got a smaller pouch on the inside of my boot, and another around my neck. Lucky they didn't find that one, actually." He sounds so matter-of-fact that I can only stare, wide-eyed. After a moment, the corner of his mouth quirks upwards. "What?"

"I can't believe—you..." I trail off with a useless gesture and reach for another shirt, and his smile starts to widen before he flinches. Funny how, even with a swollen lip and blackening eye, he looks...better, somehow. After touching a finger to his mouth and wincing again, he hesitates, then reaches for my shoulder.

"Ellin, stop," he says, with that same tone of command he used with Davor. Sounding very like Alaric, come to think of it. "I'll finish up. Why don't you get some sleep?"

"I'm not tired," I mutter, looking aside. I must sound like a child, but I don't care. I can't tell him that I'm afraid I'll fall apart—rather spectacularly—if I try to rest. If I stop moving. Stop thinking. If I...

"Ellin," he says again, very softly, and he rises to one knee, taking both of my restless hands in his. His eyes are strangely bright. "If that one comes back, I will kill him. I swear it."

I squeeze his hand. "If they come back," I manage, hoarsely, "I'll use my powers. Guardians be damned."

He smiles a little and nods. "Agreed."

CHAPTER FOURTEEN

"YOU'RE NOT SERIOUS," Garreth says flatly, as he scatters dirt on the dead remains of our fire. He looks awful in the light of morning, all bruised and dirty, with bright red rimming his eyes. I'm sure I look hardly better. What sleep I had was plagued with nightmares, and I woke up stiff and aching. Irritable, too, which is why I give him a truly withering look as I tighten the fastenings of my pack.

"Give me a better plan, then," I snap. "Or, better yet, tell me it isn't true. Tell me I'm safer dressed like this. Looking like myself. Tell me it's fair, Garreth!"

"Fine!" He throws up his hands, face closing in on itself. "Do what you like. I certainly don't care if you make a fool of yourself."

"Well, good." Shouldering my pack, I stomp off toward the road without a backward glance. After a moment, there's a muffled curse behind me, and his footsteps pound in a few running strides to catch up. "I think we'll be safe to go back through town," I say when he's in step with me, "as long as we're quick about it."

I sense his nod. "I'll see about buying us some food."

"And I'll meet you at the far edge of town," I finish. "Fine."

The main street bustles now that shops are open, and Garreth gives me a quick, searching look. It seems as if he's about to say something, but then he shrugs and goes off his own way.

I stand still for a moment, watching people come and go. Without Garreth, no one looks twice at me, another red-haired girl in a Southling town. It's refreshing, but unsettling at the same time, since I'm not sure I want to fit in here. I certainly don't like the knowing that if they knew the truth about me, things would be very different.

With a sigh, I square my shoulders and search the shop signs for the one that I want. Luckily, I don't have to look long before I see the local tailor's. A mixture of anticipation and dread flutters in my chest as I go in.

A small woman with graying strawberry hair doesn't look up at the sound of the door, busy in the center of the shop with a half-made dress and a mouthful of pins. "With you in a moment," she murmurs, sliding another pin into place. I browse around the shop, admiring the ready-made dresses and skirts, until the seamstress takes the last few pins out of her mouth. "There," she says briskly, standing. "Found anything to your liking?"

"No, Madam," I reply, before realizing that's rude. I hurry to add, "I mean, they're lovely, but I only came to ask if I might borrow your shears for a moment, please."

Her eyes narrow. "What for?"

"For—for my brother," I stammer, wishing, as always, that I could lie more easily. "He's a Healer, and he needs to cut some string to bind the bundles of herbs he wants to sell at the market. His knife's too dull," I add, suddenly inspired.

If the seamstress doesn't believe me, she doesn't show it. She squints at me for another moment, then nods. "All right. But only for an hour. I'll need them back."

"And you'll have them back, much sooner than that," I promise. "Thank you!"

I clutch the shears tightly as I leave the shop, as if they're precious, and hurry down the street. My heart is still pounding with dizzying fear and excitement, and though the next part of my plan should be difficult, it isn't. I turn down a side-street and find people's homes instead of shops, and on this sunny morning, many women have their washing hanging out to dry. All it takes is a bit of quickness and a lot of bravery to dart to a few of the lines and snatch what I need. I feel guilty, but I've done worse.

The difficult part is finding a place to do what I've decided to do. I consider the inn, but I don't have coin for a room and wouldn't spend it for only a few moments if I did. I could shut myself in a privy somewhere, but that idea is worse than getting a room. I wander around town aimlessly, my stolen bundle under my arm, and at last, I find it: an old, ramshackle barn on the fringes of town. I'm half-afraid the roof will cave in on top of me, but I hurry over and slide the door open.

It's dim and smells like moldy hay, but at least it's private. I'm in no position to be choosy, either, so I go without hesitating to the most shadowed corner and reach for the ties in my hair.

Once it's unbraided, tumbling down my back, I pause for a moment, holding a soft handful with my eyes shut tight. I wish for a mirror, so I could see it one last time, and so I could see what I'm about to do. But if I had one, I'm not sure I could force myself to go through with it.

My heart is in my throat as I lift the shears. I open them, take a shuddering breath, pull the hank of hair out straight, and aim.

With a tiny, inarticulate noise, I lower the shears again. I can't do this. I can't. Not my hair...

All it takes is another steadying breath, the memory of Jak calling me a trollop, remembering what he did. An uncaring fire burns through me, and this time, when I lift the shears, I don't hesitate before I snap them shut.

The *shhkk* seems deafening, just below my left ear. When the hair comes free in my hand, somehow brighter and lovelier than it ever was on my head—but gone, now—I stare for an instant in disbelief before dropping the strands in a pile on the floor. Then I snip again, quickly, before I lose my nerve. Another cut bares part of my neck and makes me shiver. Then another.

Soon, the pile by my feet has become a pile in truth, so much that I can scarcely believe I've any hair left. But I do, I find, when I examine my handiwork as best I can by touch. I have a cap of hair left, somewhere between my jaw and my chin, cut evenly enough, I hope, though the ends feel strange, too thick, and unruly. I feel oddly light.

The next moments are even stranger. As if I didn't feel exposed enough with my neck bare, stripping off my clothes in a barn is even worse. Gooseflesh shivers up and down my back, and I hurry into the boys' clothes that I stole.

The trousers are a good fit. The cream-colored shirt is a bit loose, but that's for the best, I suppose, casting a dubious look down at my chest as I do up the buttons. The vest I took helps, too.

Once I've got my boots on, I look down critically. As best I can tell, I look boyish enough. Just in case, I rub a bit of dirt on my cheeks and nose and vow to keep my head down.

On the way back to the tailor's shop, I try to improve my disguise, walking with a longer, wider stride and swinging my arms. I could be a twelve-year-old boy, I think, enjoying this fine morning, with badly-cut hair and a dirty face. I'd like to be the type who's full of impish mischief, complaining about chores and making smart comments. I smile to myself, realizing that, without meaning to, I've patterned my new identity after Brek, the True Southling boy I used to know. Though I'm no playactor, I decide to encourage this line of thought as I shove open the door of the tailor's shop and amble in.

Though I feel horrifically nervous, I force a grin and hope it's cheeky. "Mornin' Madam!" I say brightly, striving for a tone different than my own. "Them's your shears my sister borrowed, right?"

When the lady looks at me, eyebrows rising, I nearly drop the act on the spot. Then I remember my lie and remember that I'm being a *young* boy. "Our older brother, the Healer, says thanks kindly for letting us borrow 'em," I hasten to add. When she takes the shears, still looking a bit perplexed, I wipe my nose roughly with the back of my hand, then shove both hands into my pockets.

"You're welcome," she says, as if she doesn't see anything amiss.

I grin, not forcing it at all this time, and duck my head. "Thanks again, an' good day to you!"

Once I'm out on the street, simply because I can, I run a few steps, and leap, and give a little whoop of triumph. No one looks at me twice, because they only see a Southling boy in high spirits, not a young woman who's old enough to know better. The freedom almost makes the loss of my hair worth it.

I approach our meeting spot and see Garreth there ahead of me, and I can't resist the temptation to walk past him with my new, boyish stride and see if he calls out. When he doesn't, and when I'm a few steps past, I turn around. He's so intently looking for me in the opposite direction that, again, I can't resist, and I jab him in the ribs. "Oi!" I say broadly. "You! Lookin' for someone?"

He starts. Then swears under his breath and stares at me.

My grin widens as I stick out a hand. "Eland Fletcher, at your service, sir."

Garreth snorts, but shakes it anyway. "Eland Fletcher?"

"It sounds close enough, doesn't it?" I shrug. "If one of us says 'Ellin,' by accident…"

"Right, it's clever." He studies me, half-squinting. "You look better than I thought you would. With your hair short, I hardly recognize you."

"But can I pass for a boy?" I press, as we begin to walk down the road. "I fooled the tailor, but I think she was nearsighted."

He spreads his hands. "Don't ask me! I know you're not. But…" he frowns at me again. "Aye, I suppose you could, as long as you act the part. You're a bit pretty for a lad, but then, some are." He laughs after a moment, shaking his head. "I can't get used to the sight of you in those clothes. Good thing you're not like Thalia."

"What, not beautiful? Thanks kindly, Garreth."

Garreth rolls his eyes. "Say things like that, and anyone'll know you're a girl. I meant built like a prize heifer, with tits to match."

"Garreth!" I gasp, and he shoots me a wicked grin, though his cheeks are flaming.

"What? Are you a lad or not, Eland?"

"Yes, but..."

"You'll hear a lot worse, if you're going to do this," he says. "I'm trying to help get you used to it. And quit bouncing so much."

Unable to argue with any of that, I stop and watch him walk a few paces and then follow, trying to copy him. It feels strange, as if each step is twice as long as it needs to be. "This isn't going to be easy, is it?"

"You thought changing who you are would be as easy as changing your name?" He gives me a shrug. "But you'll manage."

By the time we reach Greenhaven, two days later, managing has become easier. It still doesn't feel natural, but every time we've passed other travelers, I've been glad of my decision. Two boys traveling together, even if one of them is a Northlander, attract less attention. And I'm relieved.

The houses on either side of the road get closer together as we enter the town, and scrubby weeds give way to occasional neat, tended beds of flowers. Garreth turns to me, face shadowed with evening and travel grime. "Want to chance the inn?" he asks, stretching his arms. "Can't be worse than last time."

I worry the inside of my lip with my teeth, but it doesn't take long before the thought of a hot meal wins out, and I nod. "Do we have enough coin for it, though?"

"For a rundown inn in the Southla—" he begins derisively, then stops at my glare. "Er, I think so."

The common room of the inn is crowded and warm, cleaner than most, with windows open to let in fresh air and take out the smoke. I don't know whether it's because of my disguise or if people here are simply more pleasant, but Garreth and I don't draw anything harsher than a few interested glances. One or two people even give us curt nods.

Our dinner is delicious, especially after nothing but cold food seasoned with the taste of road dust. Halfway through stuffing ourselves, Garreth meets my gaze across the table and smiles.

"What?" I ask when I've swallowed. I wipe at my mouth with a knuckle. "Do I have something on my face?"

"It's nothing. I was just thinking..."

"Shh!" I hiss suddenly, skin crawling at a word half-heard behind me. "Wait a moment."

His brows draw together, and he leans forward, no doubt pricking his ears up, as I am, in order to listen to the conversation at the table next to us.

"...and burnt it to the ground anyway, of course," the woman behind me says, sounding satisfied. "What do you expect?"

"I thought they might have spared the family that," another woman says, higher-voiced and indignant. "You know what they're like on the coast."

"Not anymore," the first one replies, smugly. "Have you been living underground, Valeria? The Guardians down there are run practically off their feet! So many of *them* thought as you do about the coast and ran to Glennig and Aurora at the first sign of trouble." She clucks her tongue. "My sister lives right in Glennig, you know, and she told me on market days they'd be performing with those black arts of theirs. Performing! Right in *public.*"

"Tch," the other one replies, and out of the corner of my eye, I watch her shake her head. "Well," the woman says at last, "didn't they just fall apart, and all, after that one got killed? He was the worst of 'em."

"Kinshield, you mean? The one on all the notices?" The smug one sighs again. "Valeria, sometimes I wonder about you. Haven't you seen the newest? There's another one they're looking for now. Quite a handsome reward, too, I might add."

"Really? Who is it, then? Who's his family?"

"No one knows, dear! The description only says tall, about forty, long dark hair, and a rich voice. Sometimes wearing a mask over his eyes. Which could be practically anyone, of course. But the rumors originated near Harnon, you know, and I told Fern, I think..."

She breaks off at the sound of shattering glass. I start at the sound, too, and only realize when the tea seeps through my trousers that I was the one who dropped it. I look down blankly and watch my hands fall to my thighs, limp and unfeeling. My father...

"Oh, hells, Eland!" Garreth says loudly. I raise my eyes, uncomprehending until I notice that everyone around us is staring. There's a fog around my mind, and I can't..."Do you have to be so clumsy?" he asks as he kneels gingerly beside the mess to pick up the pieces. "Go get a mop!"

But the bar madam is already bearing down upon us, rag in hand. "What's this, then?"

Garreth looks at her sheepishly. "Just an accident, ma'am. I'm sorry. The lad had some cider earlier, and he's not used to it. Been staring like a frog, an' clumsy, too."

When she shifts her sharp eyes to me, I'm sure my red cheeks do much to help me look drunk.

"We'll pay you for the mug," Garreth adds helpfully, his hands full of broken glass.

At last, she nods and holds out the rag for the shards. "Well, that's right of you." Then she smiles, dimples showing in her ample cheeks. "Maybe next time, don't let your young friend drink so much, hmm?"

Garreth laughs. "Maybe not at all," he replies easily. "Thank you."

When we've gone upstairs, Garreth barely waits for me to shut the door before rounding on me. "What in the hell were you thinking?" he bursts out, in a stifled shout. "Did you want them to see you turn white at the mention of the Guardians? That was stupid."

"Oh, shut it." I push past him in the cramped space to perch on the edge of one of the two narrow beds. My head falls into my hands, and for a moment, I feel like I did have too much to drink. My skull is too tight. I can't think.

"Ellin?" he asks softly. "What's wrong?"

The heels of my palms are cool against my eyelids. I sigh, shoulders aching with tension. "I think—Garreth, I think it's my father."

The bedframe creaks as he drops beside me heavily, and his sharp breath is audible even above the distant drone of conversation downstairs, murmurs down the hall. "Oh." He clears his throat. "Er, why?"

My hands drop to my lap, and I turn just enough to look at him. "A tall man with long, dark hair leading the True Southlings? About forty? Near Harnon? Garreth…"

"Ellin." His face twists, and the look in his eyes is so pitying, even in the dim light of the dirty lamp, that I look away again. "Imagine I told you to look for a tall blond lad, about twenty, back home. Would you go to me? Sven the stable boy? Finn? Any of a hundred others?"

"You don't understand. It's not like that. I've seen him."

"How?"

I look at him bleakly; raise a hand that looks pale and wavering, insubstantial. "In—Garreth, you have to believe me. It was in a dream."

His throat bobs as he swallows. "I believe you. It's your powers, isn't it?"

"I think so." Or Lev's, but I don't want to tell him that yet. If ever. "I—I can't explain it. But I saw him. Not his face, but even so, I would swear it was my father." My lips shake on the last word.

His boots scrape softly on the floor as he pushes himself to his feet, then quick, measured, as he paces. Over to the door and back. Turn. "You know we can't go after him. We can't," he adds, when I jerk my head up. "To your town? In search of someone the Guardians themselves are hunting for?" He shakes his head, pale hair fanning out to catch the light. "It would be past foolish, from what you've told me about them. What we've heard. If things are worse now than when you left…"

"What choice do you think I have?" I exclaim, jumping to my feet. "What would you have me do—go on to Whiteriver as planned? Ignore this?" I want to shout, but I settle for snapping venom.

"For now, yes!" he retorts. "You don't know where he is, what he's doing, or even if it's really him."

"I don't care."

"Well, I do!" He glares. "How am I supposed to protect you against them? Against this?"

My cheeks are hot, and he must know I'm near to losing my temper because he holds up his hands. "Look here," he says. "I simply don't want to risk both our lives before we know anything, all right? I don't want to jump into this when we can't see the bottom. And..." he hesitates, just for an instant. "And you know I'm on a mission from Alaric. I gave my word to come here and find out what I could about these powers."

"And you think a library would be a better place than among the True Southlings themselves? You sound like Finn."

He makes a face at me. "Besides, haven't you considered that your father—if it is him—is leading the True Southlings? Ellin, they hate you!"

"Eland, damn it," I correct him, and he sighs.

"Eland. They tried to kill you. They tried to kill me, and Alaric, and Coll, and..."

"I know!"

"They did kill my da," he finishes, harshly, breathing heavily. He looks at me beneath lowered brows, his face sharply shadowed. "And I have to ask myself, if your da is alive, somehow—why's he with them, and not looking for you?"

The room is too hot, too close. I can't breathe. I stumble to the window and push it open, then stand there, gulping, the night air like cool water on my flushed skin. Of all the things he could have said, why did he have to say those things? The ones I've been trying my hardest not to wonder. I look down at the street blankly. Lit windows and a pair of shaggy dappled ponies hitched below. Somewhere, either downstairs or down the street, someone is singing.

I turn to Garreth at last, leaning with my hands splayed on the sill. For a moment, I watch him quietly, sitting on his bed and bending to take off his boots. Not looking at me.

"Garreth, I don't know." I'm surprised how thin my voice sounds. "I don't have any answers. But how can I go to Whiteriver as if nothing has happened? If it is my father..."

"If it is, don't you think he'd want you to learn to be a better Healer and not risk your neck?"

"You know, I'm tired of wondering what he'd want me to do. I'd like the chance to speak with my father again and ask him."

"We all would," he says, under his breath. He swings his legs up onto his bed, hands crossed beneath his head on the thin pillow. He looks at the ceiling instead of at me. "Well, if we can't agree, why not delay this decision? Maybe we'll hear more in the next town."

I shake my head as I go to sit on the edge of my bed. After I've removed my own boots, my hands reach up to loosen my braids before I remember and run my fingers through the short, tangled mess of curls instead. "I wish we could, but we have to decide," I say, picking a bit of leaf out of my hair. "There's a crossroads on the other side of town. Harnon is west, and to get to Whiteriver, you take the coast road south. Then east, later on."

"Even so, we don't have to decide right now. Let's sleep, and choose in the morning."

"I'm not going to change my mind overnight." But I lie back anyway, pulling the blanket up without undressing, and don't make any protest when he douses the light.

I might have expected both of us to take a long time falling asleep, but I can hear him snoring after a matter of moments. Strange as it is, the sound is comforting, and I smile to myself in the darkness.

CHAPTER FIFTEEN

GARRETH RISES WITH the sun, and I wake to the sight of him, bright-eyed, with his hair already wetly smoothed down, doing stretches in the corner. He's told me he wants to stay in fighting form away from the guard company drills, but I think he looks ridiculous. "Good morning," I say, and he nearly falls over.

"'Morning."

"Would you mind going down without me?" I ask as I climb out of bed and look with dismay at my rumpled appearance. Boyish is one thing, but I'm beginning to look—and smell—like a vagabond. "I'd like a wash."

He gives me a sly grin. "I hate to tell you, lad, that boys wouldn't ask one another to…"

"Oh, get out!" I retort, laughing. I'm not at all surprised when he does, since I know that, for all his teasing, I'm as much a sister to him as he is a brother to me. The last thing I'd want is to see Garreth without his clothes! The thought makes me wince, then laugh again, as I bathe with cold water from the basin and a cloth.

When I go downstairs, I find that Garreth has already ordered the breakfast special for both of us, and I inhale appreciatively as I sit. The oat-flour breakfast cakes, sprinkled with starberries and drizzled with honey, are a purely Southling food—and one I've missed.

Across the table, Garreth plows his way through half his plate before he comes up for air. "So," he says at last, setting down his cup of water, "have you reconsidered?"

"Garreth…"

"Have you thought about this, then?" he asks, lowering his voice. "If you go to Harnon, disguised or not, you will be recognized. People knew you, there."

"Maybe not," I say, but a note of doubt creeps into my voice. "Besides, I do have friends there…"

"You did," he retorts, "before they knew about you. Which, at this point, everyone must, and you know it."

I glare, stabbing a piece of cake harder than necessary. I hate that part of me agrees with him.

He takes another drink and sets his cup down heavily. "Don't know why you're so eager to go running after them anyway," he mutters. "Seeing as they killed my da. Thought your loyalty was to the king."

I look up, startled. "Garreth! Not you, too!"

"What?"

"First Alaric doubted me, and now you? Do you all think I'm as fickle as that?" Breath huffs through my nose, and I'm certain I've gone pale. "I want to see my father. That's all. Don't you dare tell me you wouldn't do the same."

He nods once, jerkily. Swallows. "But I'll tell you I won't now," he says, sounding strangled. "I promised I would go to Whiteriver, to the College. And that's what I have to do. With you, or without you." He hesitates for a moment before adding, "And if you want to walk into trouble, I can't stop you. But I can ask you not to. And I am. Asking, I mean."

I don't know what I want to do, anymore, and I look at him bleakly. When my eyes meet his, the understanding I find there almost undoes me. But he doesn't say anything more, waiting for me to decide.

I close my eyes, feeling them sting. Not quite in tears, but closer to it than not. Behind my eyelids, I see the image from my dream again. My father, poking at the fire, and then half-turning toward me... I swallow and shove the memory away, hard.

"Fine," I say, voice hitching on the word. "We'll go to the College. Fine!"

I've lost my appetite, so it's only a matter of moments before he has finished both our breakfasts and we've gathered our things. When we step, blinking, onto the sunlit street, I try to resign myself to going the wrong way. Maybe it won't be so bad. Maybe Garreth is right. Even so, I shove my hands into my pockets and lower my head on the way out of town. Even if the decision was mine, I still don't want to speak to him.

Not that he notices, of course. He seems relieved. Cheerful. Probably, I think spitefully, he's just glad to have gotten his way. I belatedly realize that he's asked me a question, and look up, mouth twisting with annoyance. "What?" I snap.

"I said, what's the Whiteriver College like? Is it anything like the one at home?"

"Oh." I shake my head. "Not much alike, no. I haven't been there more than twice, but I think it's less...formal, perhaps? The scholars don't wear robes, for one thing, and you needn't pledge yourself to the College for years the way they do in the Northlands."

"Then how d'you guarantee that the scholars will stay on?"

"Well, you don't," I reply slowly, "but I think—I think the entrance requirements are stricter to begin with. You can't even begin to study Healing if you don't have a bit of the power. So..."

"So they want to stay, because it's in them already? They just don't know how to use it?"

"Something like that, yes."

Garreth nods, and kicks at a roundish stone with the toe of his boot. It skitters ahead before rolling into a clump of weeds. "Well," he says, "what about you?"

"What *about* me?"

"The power's already in you, isn't it? Don't you want to learn?"

I groan. "Garreth, does it matter? We're going to the College, whether I like it or not. There's no need to..." I break off with a gasp as a bolt of pain stabs inside my left ear. Clapping my hand to it, I stumble.

"Ellin!" Garreth grabs my elbow. "What...?"

"Shh!" I snap. The pain is all over now, knifing through my head, but in it, somewhere, there are words.

"Help me!" Someone is saying, panic mounting with each word. *"Oh, please, please help me!"*

Gritting my teeth, I build up my mental shields, shutting out the *noise* for a moment. I can't silence it entirely, but this lets me have enough space in my head to think. I straighten and look at Garreth, who has led me to the side of the road. "Are you going to puke?" he asks warily. "It wasn't breakfast, was it?"

"Someone's calling to me," I explain, voice low. "They want help."

"Someone's...? Ohh! Where?"

"I don't know! It's just noise. A voice begging for help."

His hand tightens on my elbow. "Well, can you ask them?"

"Oh, wait a moment," I say crossly, and close my eyes. Bracing myself, I lower my mental shields. The pain nearly overwhelms me, but since I'm prepared for it this time, it doesn't seem quite as bad. The voice is still begging for help, more panicked than before. I cast out with my thoughts, like a fisherman with a line, thin and taut. I reach, stretching, seeking out the source of the voice. At first, it's nearly impossible; its presence seems to be everywhere and nowhere, all at once, all around me. But the more I focus, tightening my hold on my powers as my thoughts fly farther, everything seems to clear, like a form seen through dispersing smoke, or mist. At last, I'm able to grasp the other mind, and though it recoils at my mental touch, I cling tight.

"Stop it!" I say, irritated at all the squirming. Like I've caught a fish, indeed. *"I heard you, and I want to help."*

A long pause, and then, *"What?"*

"Where are you?" I ask. *"My friend and I will come if we know where you are. We're in Greenhaven."*

The voice gives me directions, tripping over the words, constantly interrupted with other thoughts. I'd wager everything I own that this is their first time using their gift, and I feel sorry for them. *"Please, please hurry!"* they finish, and I withdraw.

"They're locked in a shed outside a whitewashed house on the orchard road, south of town. That's this one, I think," I say, in answer to Garreth's head-tilted, curious look. I set off before he has his pack shouldered again. "They want us to hurry."

"Locked in a shed?" he repeats, catching up with a few long strides. "That sounds like..."

"Trouble, I know." I shake my head, irritated. "And to think, you were worried about the Guardians if we went after my father," I add, under my breath. "I think we're going to find them a lot sooner than that."

"They might not have heard you," he says, sounding like he's trying to convince himself. "You weren't using the power for long."

"No, but the person we're going to rescue was loud," I reply, "and obviously untrained. Any True Southling within ten miles must have heard." And the Guardians seem to hear even better than that, but I don't voice this aloud.

I scan the sides of the road for the house, walking quickly. We're not far out of town when we pass a fenced orchard, trees laden with fruit. Some chickens make way for us, clucking indignantly.

"Is that it?" Garreth asks, pointing. I follow his gaze.

"Has to be," I say, breaking into a run. "There's the shed. Come on!"

"El—Eland, wait," he calls, and hurries to catch up. "What if it's a trap?"

I stare at him, stricken. "It couldn't be," I say slowly. "I mean, it could, but..."

A wail interrupts me, muffled, from the direction of the shed. Garreth's eyes meet mine, and he nods, then leads the way at a run, drawing his sword.

My hand fumbles for the hilt of my own weapon before I realize that, if it is a trap, the Guardians already know I'm here, and I'd be more useful fighting with my mind instead of sharp steel. I let my hand drop and follow Garreth, listening to the sobbing ahead of us.

"Is someone there?" the voice asks, aloud this time, when we approach the door.

Garreth shrugs. If it's a trap, well, we're already in it. His hand tightens on the hilt. "We're here to help," I call softly.

At a gesture from Garreth, I lift the bar, then slowly pull the door open while he crouches in wait on the other side. He tenses, and I do, too, teeth on edge and every muscle clenched. The hinges creak, and I hold my breath, waiting for an explosion of angry Guardians.

But no one comes. And then Garreth, taking a wary step forward, huffs out his breath in a sigh. "Eland," he says, sounding strangled. When I step out from behind the door, I see why.

Spare boards and tools and rubbish crowd the inside of the small shed, and it takes me a moment, eyes adjusting to the dimness, to see the small, wretched form cowering in the corner. I try to look reassuring as I hold out a hand. "It's me," I say. "We talked a moment ago."

A sniffle is my only answer. Then, in a whisper scratched from sobbing, "How do I know it's really you?"

Sighing, I reach out with my mind, even though doing so makes my skin crawl at the thought of the Guardians. *"Because of this,"* I say quickly. "Do you believe me now?"

"I—I think so."

"Well, then." I extend my hand again, reminded of trying to pat Sunrise when he's feeling skittish. Conscious, every second, of the danger we're in. "Come on," I say. "We have to hurry."

She finally comes toward me, picking her way through the mess. I try to be patient, but the open doorway at my back, even with Garreth just beyond it, gives me chills. At last, small fingers grasp mine, a tentative touch that quickly turns into a death-grip, and she lets me lead her out into the sunlight.

Garreth's breath catches when we emerge and, when I get my first good look at her, mine does, too. Without thinking, I reach toward her cheek, but check the movement when she ducks her head. "What happened?" I ask instead. Though it's obvious enough what happened, I think angrily. Someone slapped her, hard enough to bruise.

"My uncle," she mumbles at last. "I woke up this morning and could—could hear him and my auntie. Inside my head. But they got really angry when I told them." Her swollen bottom lip begins to quiver as she struggles not to sob again. "He told me not to tell lies, but then—I thought I could prove it? But when I did, Uncle hit me."

I squeeze her hand and am reassured when she looks up at last, seeming less afraid—of us, at least—than a moment ago. "Did your uncle say anything about the Guardians?" I ask.

"How'd you know?" she replies, wide-eyed. "That's where he and Auntie went. To get the Guardians to take me." She pauses to wipe her nose. "Who are the Guardians, anyway?"

I cast a desperate glance at Garreth, who shrugs, helpful as always. "They're...very bad people," I say at last. "They want to hurt you and me, and others like us. So, we have to go before they can find us."

"Are you running away from them, too?"

"Right now, yes. Will you come with us?" I press, wanting to be sure. "I promise, we'll do our best to keep you safe. If you stay here, they will kill you. But if you come with us, you can't ever come back. Do you understand?"

"I'm twelve, not stupid," she retorts, crossing her arms, and I'm startled enough to laugh.

"Is that yes?"

She looks longingly at the house, but then nods. For a moment, her eyes look far older than twelve. "Yes."

"Good," Garreth says, surprising me. "I'm Garreth, by the way, and this is Eland."

"I'm Rose." And then, looking past us to the road, she screams.

CHAPTER SIXTEEN

I WHIRL, HAIR WHIPPING into my eyes, and Garreth swears. Three men and two women are approaching up the road, too quickly, exclaiming.

"There she is!"

"Hurry!"

"Who's that with her?"

"Hey! You there!"

I bounce on the balls of my feet, every muscle taut, heart pounding. My hand fumbles for my sword again, unsure whether to fight or run. Before I can decide, a tall man and curly-haired woman break away from the others, half-running toward us, closing the distance step by menacing step. With another shriek, Rose dashes across the yard at an angle.

"Oh, hells," Garreth breathes, his hand shooting out to clutch my wrist. "Come on! Run!"

Nearly yanked off my feet, I struggle not to fall as he drags me along, running across the grass as the Guardians yell and give chase. Garreth's legs are so much longer that it's all I can do not to go sprawling.

"Run, Rose!" Garreth shouts, and we follow her, vaulting over the stone garden wall, squashing vegetables and leaves under our trampling feet.

I don't look back. Couldn't if I wanted to, when the whole world consists of Garreth's iron grip around my wrist and my legs moving and the pounding of my feet against the earth. I'm not used to running in thick boots. We're gaining on Rose, but I don't know—or want to—if the Guardians and Auntie and Uncle are gaining on us. They're still shouting.

Garreth releases me when we arrive at a wooden fence, and he climbs over, but I go through the middle slats, and then we run side-by-side, flat out, through a muddy field with yellow grain up to my waist, shoots slapping against my hands and tangling around my feet. A little in front of us, Rose lets out another scream and disappears.

Garreth and I push ourselves even faster. My lungs are going to burst. Sides aching. And then, half-blinded, my feet hit something soft that grunts, and I go flying.

Immediately, Garreth crouches down, too. He looks at me and Rose as we pick ourselves up where we tripped, panting and filthy. "Follow me!" he hisses. "I've got an idea."

He lowers himself to all fours and begins to crawl off to the side, a quarter turn from the direction we were going a moment ago. Seeing what he means, I nod. "Go," I whisper to Rose. "I'll follow behind."

"Shh," Garreth says, already lost in the grain ahead. "Stay low!"

It takes Rose a moment to get her skirt hiked up, but once she has the knack of it, she moves swift as a snake, without a noise of complaint about the mud.

I follow her, having an easier time of it in trousers, though they're soaked immediately. Mud coats my hands, and I slip in it, and the pack on my back feels awkward, trying to move like this. Wet stalks slap my face as I maneuver between them, keeping my eyes on Rose's feet.

The only sounds are the rustling of grain and our heavy breathing. Then I hear voices behind us and drop flat, not wanting them to see where we are by the grain moving. I grab Rose's ankle, urging her to be still, and hope she'll understand and tell Garreth. We don't dare move, not with them so near. Not unless we have to.

The moments stretch out, and I'm aware—too aware—of everything. Sweat running down the back of my neck. Cold, heavy spots on my trousers where my knees, now sore, have dug into the ground. A rock pressing into my arm. Hair stuck to my forehead. I don't know how long we lie as silent as possible, waiting to be trampled on and found. My skin crawls as I wonder—did they see us, and now they're quietly sneaking up to catch us unawares? Are they waiting for us to stand up again? Or have they gone?

A gust of wind rustles the stalks overhead, and somewhere behind us, a crow caws. My nose itches, and I wrinkle it, not daring to move and not wanting to scratch it, in any case, with my dirty hands.

I've begun to feel chilled and clammy instead of hot and sweaty by the time Garreth slithers around Rose to talk with me. "They must be gone by now," he whispers. "Don't you think?"

I gnaw the inside of my cheek. "I hope so," I reply. "But what are we going to do?"

He gives an odd little shrug, hampered by his pack. "Hide until nightfall, or keep moving, I suppose."

"We can't hide all day." I shake my head. "Not here. If they've gone, I wager it's to fetch others to help with the search. They're not going to give up so easily."

Garreth wipes his forehead with his arm, leaving a smear of dirt. "Then, I say we get far away, as fast as possible. We'll have to stay off the road."

We crawl the rest of the way through the field, until at last we part the grain and find shorter grass and a fence. After scrambling under the fence into a farmyard, standing up again—even with creaking knees and filthy clothes—feels wonderful. I take a breath and tilt my head back, relishing the sensation of my pack being where it belongs, for a change. I don't have long to relax before Garreth takes off at a run again, leaving me and Rose to follow.

I'm not sure how many fields and pastures we cut through, weaving and jogging our way through tall crops and taller grass, the monotony broken only by the occasional orchard or bit of woods. With Rose to guide us, we skirt town by going south, avoiding the crossroads.

Before long, the sun shines down full overhead, drying our clothes and baking our hair. The fences and farms give way to open grass and gentle hills and, at last, I see the dark smudge of trees in the distance. I hurry a few steps to catch up with Rose. My voice comes out a dusty croak when I first try to speak, and I clear my throat. "That's the Greatwood, isn't it?"

She nods. "The northern reach."

I call Garreth, and when he's dropped back, point to the woods. "That's the Greatwood. The road runs through it, and Harnon's on the edge of it. And," I add, glancing at Rose, "if we're going to find...anyone...it'll be in there."

His lips thin, but instead of arguing, he points ahead, too. "Look, there's a stream by those trees. See how the grass is greener? Let's make a run for it, and stop there for a rest. We can talk then."

We set off wearily. My boots are stone, my legs made out of jam. *Sore* jam. It only takes moments to reach the stream, and when we do, I kneel on the bank and give my dirty hands only a cursory rinse before I start scooping water up to my mouth greedily. The first icy mouthful tastes better than anything I've ever had to drink before. Beside me, Rose and Garreth do the same.

After I've splashed my face and the back of my neck, I feel almost like myself again. With a groan, I lean back on my hands with my legs stretched out. After a moment, Rose sits beside me, legs crossed beneath her skirt. Glancing from me to Garreth, sideways, obviously studying us.

Even with the darkening bruise on her cheek, she's a pretty girl, now that her face isn't swollen from crying. Her hair, worn long and loose, is straight, and darker than mine. A true blood-auburn, like my father's was before it started to fade to gray. Her eyes are dark, too, brown as rich earth, and she has a smattering of freckles scattered across her long, sharp nose.

She seems shy, and half-stunned, and my heart aches for her. She reminds me all too much of myself.

"I'm sorry this happened, Rose," I say gently, sitting upright in order to draw one knee up and hook my hands over it. I hesitate for the barest instant. "The Guardians came after me, too."

"But why? I don't understand..."

"It's the power," I explain. I don't know quite how much to tell her. "Talking with your mind. It's—it's special," I add, thinking of the True Southlings, trying to remember what they told me. "It's a gift. But the Guardians—and a lot of people—don't want us using it. So, if they sense you talking with your mind, or listening to people's thoughts, or anything, they will come for you. That's why you mustn't do it. You see?"

She makes a scrunched-up face, wrinkling her freckles, and plucks a blade of grass. "Not really. Why don't they want us using it? Why do I have it? What will they do if they catch us?"

"We don't know why some people have it," Garreth replies. His posture mirrors mine, and I almost smile, wondering how much I've based "Eland's" mannerisms on his without realizing it. "And if they find us, they won't hesitate to kill us. I'm sure of it."

For a moment, I think Rose might cry. Her lips quiver, but then she nods, slowly. "Why?"

"Because they're afraid," Garreth says, and I know he must be thinking of his father. As I'm thinking of mine.

Rose nods again, twisting the stem in her fingers, studying Garreth frankly. "You're a Northlander, aren't you?" Her gaze shifts to me, and I wonder, for an instant, if another girl, close to my own age, might see through my disguise. But I make a better boy than I thought, or she can't see past the dirt, because she asks, "You're not brothers, surely. Are you friends, then? Do you go to a college together?"

Garreth grins. "You ask a lot of questions. Aye, I'm a Northlander." I'm certain he exaggerates his accent to make her smile, and it works. "And Eland and I are friends, true, but we're not at college. We're on a mission."

"What for?"

"Well," Garreth begins, but he stops when I clear my throat loudly.

"Actually, Rose, we're not certain we *are* on that mission any-more," I interrupt, giving Garreth a significant look. "It might be too dangerous now." While I speak, I also move my hands near my lap, adding, *"We can't take her with us."* As I'd hoped, she doesn't notice.

Garreth does, of course, and grimaces. "It might indeed," he says aloud. *"But do you trust the True Southlings?"*

"I don't think we have a choice," I reply, in answer to both. When he gives me a resigned nod, hands spread, I look to Rose again. "What we're going to do instead is find others like us. We've heard there's a group of them living in the Greatwood, near Harnon."

CHAPTER SEVENTEEN

WITH HEAVY CLOUDS obscuring the moon, making the bedroom he shares with Erik pitch dark, it's easy for Finn, lying awake, to see the glow of a candle in the hallway, under the crack of the door. He rolls over and looks toward the ceiling; inhales as cool wind through the window brings the scent of rain. After a moment, he faces the door again, now indistinguishable from the wall around it. Hesitates for only a moment before pushing the blanket aside, swinging his legs off the edge of the bed. His trousers are where he left them, folded, and he steps into them quickly but forgoes shirt and shoes. The flags are almost cold beneath his feet, and he takes care to shut the door softly when he goes out.

A short walk in the dark later, and the soft, flickering light from Alaric's study beckons, confirming his suspicions about who else might be awake so late. He knocks lightly on the open door, and Alaric, seated in one of the chairs with a cup of liquor in hand, sets it aside, next to the candle.

"What are you doing up?" Alaric asks.

Finn shrugs as he takes the other chair. *"I was asleep, but I think the wind woke me. And then I saw your light."* He notes the faint, bruised-looking shadows beneath his brother's eyes. *"And you?"*

"I was thinking, and wanted a drink."

"To help you sleep?" Finn can't help his brows drawing together, torn between disapproval and concern.

Alaric shakes his head but doesn't elaborate. After a moment, he gestures to the decanter. "Shall I pour for you?"

"*That depends,*" he replies, trying to gauge his brother's mood and failing. The candle's flame dances as a breeze finds its way to this windowless room, and he shivers, wishing he'd brought a shirt. "*Do you want me to stay?*"

In answer, Alaric rises and retrieves another cup. He pours a measure of the amber liquid neatly and replaces the stopper before handing the cup to Finn. When he resumes his seat, he takes a deep drink, and even in the poor light, Finn can see his brother's dark, searching gaze. But Alaric doesn't speak, and with a small sigh, Finn sets down his untouched drink.

"*What's troubling you?*" he asks. "*If you can't sleep, tell me. I can give you something…*"

"It's not that," Alaric interrupts, with a dismissive, sideways gesture. "It's nothing I want to burden you with, Finn."

Finn gives him a sharp look over the rim of his cup. "*Oh? And nothing you'd tell Coll, either. You've barely spoken to him since Davor got back. Shall I wake Erik?*"

"Stop," Alaric snaps, gripping the arm of his chair, hard. "Can't I have my own, private thoughts?"

"*If something was bothering one of us, you'd try to help,*" Finn points out. Sensing Alaric waver, he leans forward slightly. "*Whatever it is, you can tell me.*"

Alaric closes his eyes as he swallows. When he opens them again, and sets aside his cup, he gives Finn a small smile, surprising him. "Do you remember that summer—it must be ten years ago, at least—when we were all supposed to go with Da to see the ships at Tarmorrin?"

Finn smiles, too. "*Not all, remember? Garreth was too young.*"

"That's right. And then Coll and Erik got caught fighting and had to stay home with Nan, too."

And so it had been the two of them, Finn and Alaric, only boys on the trip, since junior members of the Guard didn't travel. They'd been allowed to ride ahead, or lag behind, so long as they arrived at camp by sunset. They'd made the most of their freedom, stopping to swim, exploring woods and towns, buying and eating enough pastries for an army.

"That was the first time I saw the sea," Finn says, remembering the sense of wonder he'd felt at the sight of the glittering waves, the tall ships with their carved prows and colored sails.

"Do you remember the ships?" Alaric asks, as if echoing his thought. At Finn's nod, he smiles, a strange mixture of remembered boyish delight and a sadness Finn can't fathom. "You know, I've never been back to Tarmorrin. I asked Da on that trip if I might join a crew the next year, if only for the summer, but he said I couldn't. I still think of it sometimes," he adds, shaking his head.

And Finn, eyeing the maps and lists and sheaves of requests piled on the desk sees, again, the weight on Alaric's shoulders. *"You could visit Thalia's family someday,"* he suggests, knowing it's not the same.

Alaric nods thoughtfully. "Perhaps," he says, and finishes his drink.

Back in bed, a little later, Finn goes to sleep smelling damp air and dreams of ships in sunlight, bright sails billowing in the wind.

———ooo-)(oo-———

At breakfast, Alaric announces that the wedding will be delayed indefinitely. Thalia says nothing and smiles graciously, as if this decision was hers as well, but Finn notices the faint line between her eyebrows that wasn't there yesterday. The way she doesn't meet any of their eyes.

Nor will Alaric, for that matter. He grabs a bun from the basket and excuses himself from the table, leaving confusion and an intensely uncomfortable-looking fiancée behind. Finn smiles at her across the table when she looks up at last, but he is no closer to the princess now than before. Besides, Erik is quick to offer her a plate of fruit and a witty remark, earning a more genuine smile than the one she gave Finn. The two of them have become fast friends, and Finn would be glad, were it not for the longing glances his brother thinks no one notices.

Pushing aside the rest of his porridge in disgust, Finn goes out with the vague thought of looking for Alaric. After only a few steps in the corridor, though, he stops and shakes his head, suddenly exasperated with all of them, and heads for Ellin's workroom instead. Grinding herbs would be better than arguing with Alaric or Erik, surely. This morning, even Coll is fraying his nerves, with his taciturn lack of interest. Even if things aren't well between him and Alaric, surely he could have offered more than a raised eyebrow at the news about the wedding.

Grinding wild mustard seeds to powder does help. At first, his strokes are angry, but when he settles into the rhythm of it, the monotony is relaxing. Being here makes him think of Ellin, too, which helps to ease his sour mood. Just the memory of her face is enough to bring a smile to his lips. They've shared hours together here, at this counter, talking of everything, so much that Finn knows the touch of her mind as well as Erik's.

Sometimes, when she's frowning with concentration, with stained, dirty hands and her hair coming unraveled, it takes an effort not to put his arms around her. She would fit well in his arms, and he could rest his chin on the top of her head, and kiss her when she turned. Sometimes, he imagines unbinding her hair, gently, and combing his fingers through the bright strands. Imagines more than that, and Erik's teasing isn't far from the mark, though he doubts his brother has loved—or even known the names of—most of the women he's been with, which makes a difference.

Finn is measuring the mustard into small paper packets when the workroom door is thrown open, scattering paper and powder across the counter. He turns, irritated, but his anger turns to ice down his back at Coll's stricken expression.

"Come quick," Coll commands, one hand still on the doorknob. He leads the way down the hall, and Finn, annoyed and afraid, runs a few strides to catch his arm.

"What is it?" he asks, searching Coll's face. *"What's wrong?"*

Coll's shoulders tighten, and his cheeks are darkening, now, with anger. *"There's a riot in the marketplace,"* he says tersely, lips clamped, not bothering to speak aloud. *"I don't know whether our own started it or the Southlings did, but all hells broke loose."* He pauses, walking faster. His jaw works for a moment, and he doesn't look at Finn. *"Erik's out there."*

Finn stops halfway down the stairs. The words don't make sense. Erik was at breakfast, talking with Thalia. He wasn't in town. Isn't...

He's not aware that he's closed his eyes until Coll grips his arm, hard. "Come on," Coll says, tugging. "We don't know anything yet."

Finn nods jerkily. His hands won't move, except to grip Coll's tightly, like a child. *"And Alaric?"* he thinks, as strongly as he can, knowing there's only a chance Coll will hear.

But, thankfully, he does, and gives Finn a swift, surprised look. "He's fine," Coll says aloud. "Furious, but he was here when they brought word."

In the throne room, Alaric stands with his back to them, a knot of the lords and captains of the Guard gathered around. Finn doesn't miss the sword at Alaric's hip, the helm under his elbow. He drops Coll's hand, shocked. Surely Alaric wouldn't...

But then Lord Ivan moves a step to the left, giving Finn a glimpse of another figure in their circle, and all thoughts of Alaric are driven aside. He closes the distance with only a few strides, heedless of the conversation going on around him.

"What happened?" he demands, hands shaking as he takes in Erik's swollen, bloody face and the arm cradled awkwardly in front of him, shirtsleeve dark with blood. *"I thought you were dead, you ass! What were you doing?"*

Erik squints at him out of the eye that isn't blackened; gestures to his lopsided lip, then to his injured arm. *"Later,"* Erik thinks, his mental voice pained. *"Kind of a giveaway if we did this in front of everyone, aye?"*

At a touch on his shoulder, Finn turns to see Alaric glaring at him. "We don't have time for this," he says flatly. "Before you interrupted, Erik was telling us what he saw."

"He needs his wounds treated," Finn protests, but Alaric shakes his head.

"Not yet! This is important, Finn. See if Coll will sign for you, if you must." He turns to Erik, as do the others, clearly a dismissal. And Finn, cheeks burning, turns furiously to Coll.

"If you don't mind," he snaps, but Coll shushes him.

"He didn't mean it that way."

But his brother's face is closed, doubtful, and Finn snorts his derision. *"Just tell me."*

After a moment spent listening, Coll does.

Erik doesn't know where the fighting began, or who started it. He arrived in town after it had already begun, turned a corner, curious about the commotion he heard, and saw chaos. Men and women brawling in the street, food and broken wares spilled everywhere, children crying, or fighting amongst themselves, or both.

It was pandemonium, but he'd dashed forward, heedless of the fact that he was unarmed. Hoping to break it up with his presence, or in Alaric's name, but he never got the chance.

"It's good you didn't try," Alaric interrupts. Erik gives him the barest of nods before continuing.

He didn't intend to join the fight—wasn't sure which side to join, anyway, and it *was* apparent, up close, that there were sides. Southlings against Northlanders, that much was clear. As he approached, someone grabbed him, and someone else punched him, and a shoe hit him in the face, and soon he was in the thick of it, struggling to break free, hitting anyone who grabbed him.

He was on the edge of the crowd again, bent double and panting, when glass shattered behind him, and he whirled to see. A group of Northlander youths with rocks were heaving them at the apothecary shop. The windows were already broken when they started on the door. One of them threw an iron pot, and the door splintered.

They were shouting—calling the old man out, accusing him of dealing with 'the witch,' selling 'witch wares and potions.' And worse.

"And then," Erik chokes, shaking his head angrily as a tear spills down his cheek, "then the apothecary came out. Old Josef, you know him? Opened the broken door as calm as you please and stood there with his hands spread, wanting to reason with 'em. They didn't even listen before they grabbed him.

"I ran toward them—they took him into the shop, and two of them started throwing everything, breaking things for the fun of it—and the other two were shouting at him. One was holding Josef, but I don't think he would have..." He wipes at his nose with his sleeve and winces. "Anyway, I jumped the one holding him, but the bastard had a knife, and then Josef tried to do something—hit the other one with a book, I think—but the man threw him off, and—Josef flew back, he was old, and hit—hit his head on the counter..."

Erik still looks dazed, and Coll looks hardly better. As for himself, Finn can't quite believe it. He knew Josef, and liked him, and to think of such an end...

"When they realized he was dead," Erik says after a moment, "they ran away. I wanted to take his body, but I couldn't carry him with my arm, and—and so I came home." He hangs his head.

"You did well," Alaric says, placing a hand on Erik's hair. Erik doesn't look up, but Coll does.

"And you, Alaric?" he asks. "What do you plan to do?"

"Ride out, of course," Alaric replies, taking his helm between his hands. "What did you think?"

"And do what, against a mob?" Coll presses. "Reason with them? Raise your sword against your subjects?"

"He's right, my lord," Lord Ivan says, turning one paper-skinned hand palm-upward. "Seeing you may only anger them further."

"And they'll think I'm a coward if I stay here," Alaric retorts, but he drops his hands to his side in defeat, helmet dangling. Narrow-eyed, he turns to Lord Tomas and Captain Fenrith. "Arrest all you can, until tomorrow at least, and fine everyone involved. Compensate those whose wares were damaged, provided they didn't take part. And I want to know who started it. Have the instigators brought to me as soon as possible. If you can find the ones who killed Master Josef, bring them to me as well."

When they have bowed and gone out, he touches Erik's shoulder, gentle despite the lines still etched deep on his face. "Go," he says. "Let Finn patch you up."

---ooo-)◉(-ooo---

"I'm sorry," Erik says, seated at the small table in the workroom. From the short walk down the hallway and up the stairs, his face is ashen beneath the blood, covered with a sheen of sweat. He winces as he speaks, and Finn knows without being told that his brother has a bad headache on top of everything else.

"What are you sorry for?" he asks with his thoughts, glancing over his shoulder as he assembles the things he needs from cupboards and drawers.

"Worrying you. All of it. Managing to get my mouth and my arm hurt, so I can't..."

At that, Finn smiles despite himself. *"Just as well. You shut it, and I'll talk, for a change."* Sobering, he takes in the extent of the damage. *"I'm glad you're all right. Can you manage your shirt?"*

Erik reaches awkwardly for the buttons, one-handed, then wriggles his injured right arm out of the sleeve, grimacing as the fabric sticks to the wound. It starts to bleed again, and it takes several moments, dabbing gently with a cloth and cold water, to see the cut beneath the mess. At the sight of it, Finn winces, too; the deep gash is as long as his hand, slicing across Erik's shoulder and upper arm.

"I'm going to have to stitch it," he says reluctantly. *"I'll get you something to numb it."*

Erik swallows the vial of blackish liquid Finn gives him readily enough, and only clenches his jaw when Finn pours from another bottle into the wound, though he knows it stings like bees and fire mixed.

Finn threads the needle while he waits, trying to remember everything Master Thorvald taught him. At last, he gives the skin near the wound a light jab. *"Did you feel that?"*

"Only a little." Erik closes his eyes, face tight. *"Go ahead."*

It doesn't take as long as Finn expected, but by the time he ties the last knot, he's sweating almost as much as Erik. After that, covering the cut with ointment and applying a bandage seems ridiculously simple.

"*Finished,*" he says at last, giving Erik's uninjured hand a squeeze. "*Did it hurt?*"

"*I'll sew you up sometime, and you can find out,*" Erik replies. But then he turns his hand beneath Finn's and holds his fingers tightly. "*Thanks.*"

"*Why were you in town, anyway?*" Finn asks a moment later, cleaning the cut on Erik's cheek.

Strangely, the skin beneath his fingers turns bright pink, and Erik looks away. "*I wanted to get something for Thalia,*" he admits. "*We were at the market yesterday, and she saw some carved combs she liked. I thought, with the wedding being delayed, they might cheer her up.*"

Very precisely, Finn sets down the cloth and looks at him, and Erik's color deepens. "*I only…*" he begins, but Finn shakes his head.

"*I was serious about wanting you to shut it and listen, for a change,*" he says sharply. "*Erik, what are you thinking?*"

"*Thinking has nothing to do with it!*" Erik looks so miserable that Finn almost feels sorry for him. He touches Erik's hand again, and sighs.

"*From the moment you saw her, wasn't it?*"

"*It was like I'd been kicked in the gut,*" he says, his gaze pleading for understanding. "*And then I talked with her, and—Finn, we're alike! She enjoys the same things I do, makes me laugh—we're easy with one another.*"

"*You should be,*" Finn replies. Slowly, because these words are so difficult. "*Seeing as she's going to be your sister.*"

Erik flinches, then glares, one-eyed. "*It's not as if I don't know that. I'm not going to do anything stupid.*"

"*Except, perhaps, get **her** to fall in love with **you**,*" Finn says flatly. "*If you haven't already.*"

"*Well, it's Alaric's fault! If he weren't being such an ass lately…*"

"*But he is,*" Finn says, "*and how they are together is none of your business or mine.*"

Erik quirks an eyebrow at him. "*And how much of this is you being jealous? You didn't have the nerve to tell Ellin, and now you're miserable...*"

"*Stop.*" Finn shakes his head, more sympathetic than angry. "*How I feel about Ellin is beside the point. I just don't want to see this hurt you—or Thalia, for that matter, or Alaric.*"

Slowly, carefully, Erik leans forward and rests his forehead in his palm, elbow on the table. His shoulders heave once, and then are still. "*I'll stop being around her so much, but I don't think I can stop loving her,*" he says at last.

And Finn, heart twisting for him—for all of them—can't think of anything at all to say to that.

CHAPTER EIGHTEEN

AFTER WE SPENT MOST of the night walking, chancing the road in the dark, we arrive in Harpersfall when the sky is pink-streaked. This is the first town we've been through that I know well, here in the Southland, and it's strange to walk down the street now, seeing the familiar shops with Garreth and Rose beside me.

While Garreth looks around—searching for danger or with interest, I can't tell—Rose, who's been clinging to my hand for the last mile at least, yawns behind the tangled curtain of her hair. "Are we going to stop here, Eland?" she asks. "My feet hurt. And aren't you hungry?" Smoke is billowing out of the baker's chimney up ahead, and the day's warm loaves perfume the air. My stomach growls.

"We may as well stop," Garreth says, dropping back a few steps to walk with us. "We've enough coin to stay at the inn, if they'll let us have a room during the day."

"I think they would." I remember the kind, short innkeeper and his wife. "And then what?" I ask, lowering my voice, though there's no one around to hear. This early, only farmers and milkers and the baker are up and about. "Leave at dusk and walk in the dark again?"

"Ooh!" Rose sounds excited rather than exhausted, suddenly. And more than a little afraid. "At night? In the Greatwood?"

Well, yes, since we're looking for the people everyone is afraid of, I think, but I don't say it. Instead, I squeeze her hand. "It's the safest way, Rose. We'll have nothing to fear."

Her eyes shine as she gazes up at me. "I won't, with you there, Eland," she says, a bit breathlessly. Garreth makes a strange, choking sound, but when I look at him, he's all bland innocence.

I've never wanted to kick him quite so much, but I settle for giving him a warning look. "You'll be safe with both of us," I reply, trying not to sound too pointed.

All other thoughts are driven from my mind when we arrive at the inn. My breath catches, and Garreth swears, very quietly.

"What is it?" Rose asks, peering over my shoulder on tiptoe. "What's the matter, Eland?"

I can't answer. Tears well up in my eyes and threaten to spill over as I read the notice tacked to the door over and over again.

The Following Persons Are Not Welcome in This Establishment for Reason of Being Tainted or Near Kin to Those Such Declared, it says. And then, in smaller letters, *List of Undesirables.*

I don't realize that I've started to run a shaking finger down the list until Garreth grips my wrist. "Don't," he hisses, and I look at him blankly, still seeing the names in front of me.

Amos Brewer. Lorlee Brewer. Jennet Brewer. Kethrinn Brewer. Keth, and her parents. Her little sister Jennie, whom Keth and I used to look after. So many other names I know, like Padrus Miller and his son Jonah. Mathias Oakenfold and two others who must be his parents. Cedran Hill. Levachai Kinshield, of course.

And, near the top of the list, Ellin Fisher and Rowan Fisher.

I think I might fall apart on the front step of the inn. I close my eyes and hope I won't faint.

And then Garreth's hand is on my arm again, shaking me. "Eland Fletcher, what's the matter with you?" he asks brightly. "Not going to fall asleep standing here when there's a bed waiting inside, are you?"

I shake my head dully, trying to clear it, and stumble inside when Garreth opens the door. "Ah, little Rose," he says, still in that too-loud, cheerful tone, "you must be half-asleep, too! Pale as salt, but a rest and a meal will do you good."

Leading her by the hand, he heads across the empty dining room, nodding for me to follow. Before we're halfway to the kitchen door, the innkeeper strides out. If I weren't already numb with shock, I would gasp at the sight of him. I remember him as a gentle man, with a ready smile and eyes that wrinkled at the corners. Now, his face is set in a scowl, and the sharp, suspicious look he gives us isn't the least bit friendly.

"Bit early for breakfast," he says. "And y'look awfully tired for the hour. Been traveling at night?" Something about the way he says it makes me feel guilty, but Garreth seems unruffled.

"We have at that, kind master," he says, his accent broadening again. I realize belatedly that he must be trying to sound common-born. "We're on our way to Whiteriver an' got accosted by brigands as we made to camp last night. These two were frightened," he says, with a dismissive gesture, "an' so I thought we'd walk through the night and stop at the first good inn we saw."

The innkeeper thaws a bit at the compliment, but still seems wary as he points a finger at Garreth. "And what business have you with a Southling lad and lass?"

"It's a tale, master. I'm bound for the coast. Formerly of the Guard in the Northlands, an' their mother heard me mention I was in need of coin and hired me to see Eland and his sister Rose, here, to their grandfather's for a visit." He shrugs. "We'd like a room until tomorrow morning, if you have one to spare."

"I do, at that," the innkeeper says, apparently deciding we're no threat. He names the price of a double room and adds that meals are extra and we're required to pay up front.

But Garreth only nods agreeably, reaching for his purse, and we follow the innkeeper upstairs to a room near the landing. "Send down for more towels if you like, but they're extra," he says, as Garreth unlocks the door. "My girl Sarette will do your washing, but it's extra. We'll send a pot of tea up, but…"

"Thank you, master," Garreth interrupts, smiling. "This will do us nicely."

The innkeeper harrumphs at that, but bids us a pleasant stay. Garreth shuts and locks the door behind him, then leans against it, one hand and his forehead pressed against the wood. His shoulders hunch beneath his pack.

I swallow with difficulty, finally coming to my senses a bit, and turn to Rose. This room is on the east side of the inn, with sunlight streaming in brightly, pale yellow, turning her hair scarlet. But her face is pale and drawn, with her bruises and the dark smudges beneath her eyes standing out in sharp contrast. I touch her shoulder, and she starts, blinking.

"Come, Rose," I say, leading her toward one of the beds. "Take your shoes off and lie down before you fall over."

When she does, unable to care that I'm supposed to be a boy right now, I tug the quilt snug, as my father used to do for me, and smooth her hair. "Sleep well." By the time I've shrugged out of my pack and unlaced my boots, she's breathing deeply and evenly, fast asleep.

"You'll take the other bed, of course," Garreth whispers, sitting in the other spindly chair to begin on his own laces. "I'll spread my blanket on the floor."

I make a face. "Garreth..."

"Don't."

Honestly, I'm too exhausted to argue, and I shrug and pad across the floor silently in my sock-feet to climb into the empty bed, fully clothed. A moment later, Garreth kneels between the beds and sets about arranging a place for him to sleep.

I roll over to face the wall, arms clutched across my chest. Despite the warm day and the soft, musty-smelling quilt, I'm chilled to my bones. I can't stop seeing my name written for all to see. My father's name. Can't stop thinking of the innkeeper's hard face and harder voice.

What has happened to the Southland? This was my home, and now I barely recognize it. Everything seems different, and so very wrong. At the center of it all, my name is on a list tacked to a door. And I feel ashamed, as if I, too, am stained with ink. Tainted.

Even though I squeeze my eyes shut and cover my mouth with my hand, tears still trickle sideways down my cheeks, and my breath still comes in hitching gasps. I press my hand against my lips harder, but it's no use. Down on the floor, Garreth stirs.

I tense, waiting for him to ask what's the matter, or tell me to shut it and go to sleep, but he doesn't say a word. The mattress dips as his weight settles on it, and he lies down next to me, on top of the quilt. Hesitantly, he puts his arm over me, as if he thinks I'm made of glass, or might slap him.

I fumble for his hand and clutch his warm fingers tightly, since my own feel like ice. Behind me, I feel him relax, and he shifts, holding me closer. "It'll be all right," he whispers, the words brushing my hair. "We'll be all right. That list doesn't matter."

I don't think he means it, and I don't believe him, but I nod anyway.

———∞∘-)⊚(-∘∞———

Banners snap and dance in the wind, their colors bright against the blue, blue sky. I turn my eyes from them, dazzled, and see that the grass at my feet is soaked with blood.

The scrubby grass becomes gray stones, white stones, round ones, piled into a cairn. Flowers seem to spring from the rocks themselves. I watch one spin, falling. Deep, crimson red.

Raindrops splash down, dark spots on pale stones. The wind is keening, a flash of the banners again, a stain on the cloth…

I see a clearing, all golden sunlight and green leaf-shadows, ringed with beeches and maples and oaks. A sword and a pair of shears lie at my feet, bright on the grass, and I know I must choose.

"ELLIN!"

That voice…

Firelight and deep black shadows brush the tree trunks. Orange sparks float upward as someone stokes the fire. He straightens, poker in hand. His hair brushes his shoulders, blood-red in the light. I want to run to him, but my feet are rooted like the trees.

A whisper, this time. "Ellin..."
"FATHER!"

I've leapt to my feet before I'm fully awake, clutching the wall with one hand and my heaving chest with the other. I'm shaking violently, liquid fire in my veins, skin prickling and sweaty, hair on end.

"What is it?" Garreth hisses, scrambling to his feet. "Ellin?"

I can't answer because I'm running for the basin. I haven't eaten since yesterday afternoon, which only makes it worse as I'm violently sick.

"Oh, hells," Garreth moans, sounding disgusted as he touches my shoulder. "Ugh. I'll get you some water."

I nod with my mouth clamped shut and close my eyes. I only barely pay attention to Rose asking Garreth what's the matter with me.

By the time Garreth has fetched a cup of water, I feel well enough to thank him. He leads me to one of the chairs and watches me. "Are you all right? You're still green."

After a few more cautious sips, I nod. "I'm fine." I try to sound like it, too, since Rose is sitting up in bed and watching me with worried eyes over her drawn-up knees. I glance at the window, trying to get my bearings. "What time is it?"

"Late," Garreth replies, folding himself into the other chair. "Dinnertime, if we haven't missed it already."

I feel strangely distant from him and Rose, distracted. I can still smell smoke from my father's fire; can still hear his voice in my ears. I try to banish the prickling sense of unease. "If it's that late, why don't the two of you go down and have something to eat?" I suggest, mostly because I want to be alone.

"We ought to," Garreth agrees. "Rose?" he says, when she pauses in putting on her shoes.

"Well—are you certain you'll be all right, Eland?" she asks. "I can take care of you."

I resolutely do not look at Garreth. In truth, I'm touched by her concern, and strangely flattered. "I'm fine," I assure her.

She purses her lips at me when she stands. "At least let us bring you something up. Would you like some soup?"

"Soup would be good, if they have it. And tea, please."

When they've gone, I put on my boots and go to the open window, wanting some fresh air. Though the street down below is quiet—strangely quiet, with people walking in small groups without speaking, darting glances over their shoulders—my thoughts are anything but. They race through my mind so fast I don't have a chance to grasp any of them and truly think.

The cup rattles against mouth as I take another drink, shivering. How could I have had the strange dream again? Lev died in the Northlands weeks ago! I haven't had a true dream since before he died, and I thought...

I was so certain the dream was his, and I was somehow sharing it. But he's dead, and if he wasn't sending it, then who was? Or, what if...

My lips part as gooseflesh ripples over my arms, up the back of my neck. What if I had it backward all along? What if I wasn't sharing Lev's dream? What if he was sharing mine?

It makes sense, I think, fingers clenching the cup almost hard enough to dent it. If Lev, in his sleep, was instinctively seeking out another gifted Southling, wanting contact, he would have found me at night, when I was sending out the dreams. And perhaps he shared my dreams, instead of Erik or Finn, because his mind was so damaged. Perhaps he had no way to keep the dreams out.

But one thing is certain. This power is mine, not an echo of someone else's. There's no other explanation for it.

And I don't want it.

Finding out I could speak with my mind was one thing. For that matter, having the Healing talent was, too. Both of those were good things. Neither of those terrified me. But the other powers I've discovered, like the ability to compel people, and what I did to Lev, and this new ability to dream the future... These make me afraid of myself. Make me feel I don't know myself anymore. They make me wonder if I am tainted, after all.

I gasp at the thought. The cup, hitting the wood floor, makes a dull sound and rolls, leaving a puddle of water behind. I lunge for the door, then hurry down the stairs, two at a time. I hope I'm not too late, but there's little chance of that, and my racing heart knows it. I curse myself for my utter stupidity. I am worse than a fool.

I am Tainted. And, by dreaming like that, dreaming what will be, I just used my powers in the Southland.

———ooo-)◯(-ooo———

I search the crowded common room frantically, my gaze darting from table to table in search of Garreth's hair. And then I see him and Rose across the room, both of them smiling, unaware of what I've done.

The common room, like the town itself, is unsettlingly quiet. People hunch over their food and talk to their companions in hushed voices, glancing sideways at their neighbors. The air is heavy with tension, and I feel like I can't breathe.

And of course half the patrons stare when I burst into the room with my hair looking like a bird's nest and rumpled clothes. I slow my pace and lower my head, winding my way past full tables where suspicious eyes follow me.

Garreth looks up, obviously surprised. "Did you change your mi—" He breaks off, face closing in on itself at the look on mine. "What's wrong?"

I lean down. "Garreth, we have to…"

The door crashes open, and the first two Guardians burst in. Gasps and screams ripple throughout the room, before the taller Guardian raises his short sword. "Everyone, stay still!"

Silence. Immediately. For an instant, I don't think anyone even breathes. I stand frozen, leaning over the table, as three other Guardians file in, blocking the door. I think one of them was in the pair who came for Rose, back in Greenhaven.

I shudder and watch the sinews jump out on Garreth's hand, fingers digging into the tabletop. My gaze travels to his white face, and he meets my eyes with a look that tells me, clearly, that he knows exactly what they are, and who they've come for. On my other side, Rose's breathing is shallow, her eyes terrified. I want to reassure her, but I don't dare call attention to us, and anyway, there's no reason to.

"Where?" the tall Guardian asks a shorter one whose head is bald at the top. His voice isn't loud, but right now, a mouse skittering across the floor would sound like pounding hoofbeats.

The shorter one looks around, slowly, squinting. He's dressed differently than the others, wearing a black vest instead of a black coat. Maybe he's their leader, though he doesn't look it, all pinched and pointy-faced, with a red-tipped nose overrun by golden freckles.

After what feels like hours, he looks at us. Meets my eyes across the room, and I fight the urge to scream. He begins to raise his hand, but another Guardian—the curly-haired woman from Greenhaven—gasps and points, too. "Those are the ones from yesterday!" she exclaims, voice cutting like a knife. "That's the Thornwood girl!"

Suddenly, between one heartbeat and the next, the stillness of the room shatters into a flurry of chaos and motion. Rose makes a small, strangled sound—somewhere between a whimper and a swallowed scream—and Garreth jumps to his feet, grabbing my arm with one hand and reaching for his sword with the other. His chair falls, clattering against the floor, and he pulls me close and speaks into my ear since the room is deafeningly loud. "Pretend to run, but use your powers! Do whatever you have to!"

"Garreth…"

But his face is set, and he shoves me roughly at Rose. "Do it!"

Before I've made the decision to move, my fingers have clamped around Rose's wrist, yanking her to her feet, and I'm scanning the room for a way to safety, an oasis of calm where I might reach inward, just for a moment. But the Guardians are coming at us from all directions, the others here in the inn look likely to help them, and…

And next to me, Garreth is throwing things at the approaching Guardians. Plates, mugs, everything off the table, trying to distract them, make them angry with him, trying to give me *time…*

Clinging to Rose, I begin to run, darting past tables, elbowing and slapping and jerking away from the hands that reach for us. I think about reaching for my sword, but I know I don't have time; can't maneuver well enough in here to draw it.

At last, near the doorway to the kitchen, we have an instant, since the ones chasing us have to skirt a table full of fat men with their chairs pushed out. Holding Rose's hand hard enough to crush it, I close my eyes and reach for my power, which burns beneath my skin. A coiled beast, ready to strike at a touch. I lash out, directing the force of my fury and desperation at the woman, since she's closest...

And I reel back at the impact. It feels like the first time I hit a wooden dummy with my sword—the shock of pain made me gasp and drop the blade. This is like that, but a hundred times worse. Behind my eyelids, I see black whorls and colored sparks. I fall back another step, Rose stumbling after me, when my other arm is gripped like a vise.

I gasp, but it's only Garreth. Red-faced and panting, he drags us through the kitchen, past the hearth and bubbling pots and cowering maids. In a moment of brilliance, Rose squirms out of my sweaty grasp and knocks a basket of potatoes to the floor, followed by the pile of peelings.

Behind us, as we dash out the back door, someone slips with a thud, swearing, and I squeeze Rose's hand in triumph.

Garreth slams the door, and he and I throw our backs against it, breathing hard. We don't have more than a moment to spare; I can hear them out in front of the inn, angry voices in the kitchen behind us.

"Run," Garreth pants. "Take Rose and run. Not to the woods—they'll expect that. To that farmhouse we passed—the one with the yellow shutters, all right?"

"Garreth, no!"

"*Go!* I'll find you."

Rose's hand is still clutched in mine, and the door is shuddering beneath our shoulders with their pounding, and I know he's right. I step away from the door, Rose at my side, look over my shoulder at Garreth...

"Ellin, watch out!" he shouts, sounding terrified.

I push Rose ahead and whirl around, jerking my sword out of its hilt. Fumbling, wrenching my shoulder. Barely have time to lift it before the short, bald Guardian is upon me, his own blade raised, shining in the window's light as it slices down. I'm not ready...

I bring my blade up, instinct rather than thought, half a second too late; feel his strength as I barely deflect the sweeping cut; know I'm overmatched...

This isn't like the forms Coll taught me; isn't like playing. This is real, and he wants to kill me; Rose is screaming...

Light floods the darkness as the door swings open, and Garreth is at my side, the Guardian's sword not for me, anymore, but for him. I barely have time to jump out of the way. They circle one another, swords flying, clanging and flashing in the light from the kitchen. Others are coming from both the back door and around the corner, now, shouting, but I barely notice the babble, so intent on watching Garreth. I see the fury on his face, the sharp shadows, the way he seems to dance with the blade, moving it faster than I've ever seen anyone, even Coll...

All of this has happened in the space of a few heartbeats, and now there is a different ringing sound as the Guardian's sword goes flying. But Garreth's momentum carries him forward, and suddenly his blade thrusts through the man's back, and I look at the dark, dark point of it blankly.

Garreth stares at me, white-faced, then, with a strangled cry, drags his sword free. "Damn it, Ellin, GO!" he shouts, and rushes headlong toward the others.

My feet pound on the hard-packed road in time with my heart, and I scream, raw-throated, for Rose, and everything happens very fast and too slowly, all at once. She finds my hand again, and we dash off into the night, our frantic breathing rasping in my ears.

Chapter Nineteen

DARKNESS. L<small>IT WINDOWS</small> flashing by. My side cramping, heart hammering in my throat, in my ears, pounding shuffle of feet against the gravel. Bouncing, a sense of pushing myself so fast I'm going to trip and fall at any moment, Rose's weight dragging at my shoulder, sword banging against my thigh. Hot, dry air dragging through my nose and mouth, never enough, and the sound of her panting next to me. I don't look to the side. Just run, head lowered, moving legs and can't think of anything but my feet and flying forward. And the terror, can hear them behind us; we haven't lost them yet, aren't fast enough, have to run…

It feels like we race in the darkness forever, but it must be only a matter of moments before we reach the house Garreth mentioned, with the yellow shutters, a ways outside of town. I almost miss it, but Rose makes a rasping sound and tugs at my hand, and I follow her, cutting across a yard and then another. We scramble between the slats of a fence and collapse, at last, just inside the open door of a barn behind the house.

Lying on the cool, packed-dirt floor, I press my hand to my heart and feel it banging against my ribs with the force of a smith's hammer. Beside me, Rose is breathing too fast, and, still dizzy, I shove myself to kneel at her side. "Shh," I whisper, more an exhausted exhalation than a word. "We're all right. We made it."

Her breath hitches. "But Garreth…"

My heart skips a beat. There were so many. I should have stayed, even if my powers were useless against them. I should have...

But Rose needs reassurance, not more worry, so I swallow my own bitter fear as I place an arm around her shoulders. "I know," I murmur, unable to keep my voice steady. "But he'll be all right, too." I hope. Oh, I hope.

She puts her arm around my waist and clings, hard, as silent and tense as I am as we watch the door. And wait.

The minutes stretch taut and thin as threads. Rose and I sit motionless, jumping at every sound, no matter how small. My bare neck has never felt so exposed; every hair on it is standing upright. My skin crawls, and every time I shiver, Rose starts and shivers, too.

With each passing moment, the cold feeling in my chest threatens to turn to ice and drop into my stomach. I know this feeling well. It's hard to remember that this is now, this is different; I'm not drenched with rain and slick with mud, crouched in a patch of thorny bushes, waiting for my father to come. This is different. Because Garreth will come, any moment, and...

At the sound of heavy footsteps, Rose and I clutch one another's hands hard enough to hurt. My eyes have adjusted to the darkness, and when I turn, I find her looking, wide-eyed, back at me. We don't say a word, don't make a sound, and my teeth are on edge again. What if it's not Garreth at all? It could be a Guardian, or the farmer who owns this barn, or...

"Ellin?" The voice outside is strained, so quiet that I barely recognize it *is* Garreth. I let out a breath I didn't realize I was holding as I let go of Rose and lunge for the door.

"Garreth!"

"Shh!" he hisses, and the sight of his shadowed form in the light of the sliver-thin moon is enough to stop me cold. I swear, horribly, running to him as he topples forward. I stagger backward under his weight, and he moans.

With Rose's help, I manage to drag him into the barn, and then she shuts the door, stealing what little light we had. It's safer this way, I know, though I curse our situation as I lower Garreth onto the floor.

"What happened?" I demand, voice shrill and thin. "Where are you hurt?"

His shirt is stiff and damp in some places, soaked in others, and my hands—my hands are wet. And shaking violently, all of a sudden. I can't...

I can't see...

He doesn't answer, and my heart stops. "Garreth!"

"Stray cut to my ribs," he whispers, sounding dazed. "Not too bad, I think. Just grazed me. And my leg. And I—Ellin—I've never killed a man before..."

"Oh, *Garreth*." My hands bunch his shirt. "It's all right. You're going to be all right." I try to keep the fear from my voice as I continue. "Now, lie still, and I'll see what I can do to Heal the worst of it, all right?"

At his vague noise of assent, I close my eyes and take a shuddering breath, trying to calm myself. It doesn't work, but I don't have a choice, and I reach for my Healing power, as I have done countless times before. Usually, it comes to my touch like a flower unfolding, like warm liquid pouring through me, pooling beneath my hands to flow outward. Gentle and beautiful and right. Now, reaching for it is like reaching through mud, sluggish and slimy. I would swear I smell something rotten, and when I finally grasp the power, it burns. I've only felt it this way once before, and now it's itching, stinging like nettles, insisting to be released...

I jerk away, sitting bolt upright. The thin slices of moonlight coming through the cracks in the walls seem bright as beacons, and I focus on them gratefully, still feeling it roiling within me, too big to be contained... I shudder, horrified. "I can't do it." The words are shoved past my unmoving lips. "Garreth, I..."

"It's all right." But it isn't, it very obviously isn't. Not with his voice so weak. I nearly jump out of my skin when something rustles next to me and Rose's fingers wrap around mine.

"El—Ellin?" she says, and she must know, or at least guess, that I'm not a boy. But that's so unimportant now. "What are we going to do?"

There's only one thing for us to do. I swallow. "I'm going to call for help."

———∘∘∘-◦◖◗◦-∘∘∘———

"We're on our way." The words brush my mind skillfully, and I fight the urge to cling to the voice like I'm clinging to Rose's hand and Garreth's limp fingers. Even with the two of them beside me, I feel alone and utterly helpless.

The words remind me of another night, a long time ago. Lying in my prison cell, holding on to a voice heard in my thoughts. And then I lost Lev.

If I think too much about the blood in Lev's cell, when they told me he was dead, I'm going to cry. My palms are sticky, and Garreth's clothes...

I exhale and fumble my hand down Rose's leg. "Let me tear a strip from your skirt," I say, when she starts. "It'll rip more easily than my shirt, and I want to stop the bleeding."

"I'll do it." A soft rasping rends the silence, and by the time she presses the soft bundle into my hand, I've found the tear in Garreth's trousers on his thigh. The fabric there is even more soaked than his shirt. He moans when I tie the bandage above the wound, as tightly as I can.

Before I know it, a presence touches my mind again. *"We're here,"* the voice says, as the door creaks open, revealing several shadows.

"Oh, thank you!" I scramble to my feet. "My friend was hurt by the Guardians, trying to protect us. And I can't Heal him, and..."

"Shh," a man says aloud. "We'll get him looked after."

There are three of them, and the other two lift Garreth between them. He makes a weak protest, somewhere between a cry and a moan, and I flinch, wanting to run after them. But I can't, because the man is still speaking to me. "How many are you?"

"Three," I reply, as Rose joins us. "I'm Eland Fletcher, and this is Rose. Our friend is Garreth, of the Northlands."

"I'm Brendin," he says, voice low. "We should go now, quickly, before we talk any more. It's not safe here."

"All right," I reply, and we follow him out into the night.

———∘∘∘–❃–∘∘∘———

The Greatwood is very dark, with the thick canopy of leaves letting through only the tiniest slivers of moonlight. What little light comes through casts long, weird shadows. When the wind blows, the leaves rustle like dry voices whispering, answered by creaking branches and unseen things shuffling through the underbrush. Owls hoot and scream, and crickets chirp, and sometimes, if the path winds close to the stream, one can hear it chuckling to itself. In daylight, the sound is merry, but at night it just sounds sinister.

If I were alone at night in the Greatwood, in summer when it's most alive, I would be terrified.

Tonight, I don't have time to fear the wood itself, or the nameless things lurking in it. The path underfoot is clear, and our guides know the way well. I don't even think Rose is very afraid, though she holds my hand again.

The path winds to the right, and I hear voices up ahead, and a fire glows in the distance.

"Take him to Mistress Freya," Brendin instructs the ones carrying Garreth, when we approach the clearing. Tents are nestled amid the trees, in the night-shadowed forest, and smaller circles of lantern-light dot the darkness for a ways back. A few tents are lit from within, with vague shadows moving inside.

"Welcome," Brendin says, and now it's light enough for me to get a good look at him. He's younger than I expected, with a shock of messy orange hair and a short beard, and broad, muscled shoulders. "You're safe now," he continues, "and your friend will be Healed if it's possible. Are you more hungry, or tired?" he asks, turning to Rose with a crooked smile. "Everyone's one or the other when they come to us."

"Hungry," she says at once.

"Come, then. Dinner's finished, but we'll find something for you."

"I want to go with Garreth," I say, but he shakes his head.

"Let the Healer do her work, lad," he says. "Eland, isn't it? Have a bite to eat, and give them a bit of time, and you can see your friend after, or in the morning."

I open my mouth to protest that I'm a Healer myself, but swallow the words when I realize that a boy as short—and young—as I look couldn't possibly be. With a reluctant glance in the direction they took Garreth, I sigh. "All right."

Brendin leads us to a tent on the other side of the clearing. There's a lantern lit in this one, and a table, really just planks on sawhorses, and many crates and casks, some filled with food, others with kettles and dishes. There are larger barrels pulled up to the table like stools, and a man and a woman are already perched on two of them, eating.

The woman looks up when we enter. "These the ones you went after, Bren?" she asks, and sets down a half-eaten piece of cheese.

"Two of them. Rose and Eland. Their friend's with Freya."

The woman makes a sympathetic noise. "I'm Marilee," she says, pushing her long braid behind her shoulder. "And this is Jaysen. Would you like some?" she adds, and gestures to the food on the table. "We missed dinner, so we're just eating cold stuff."

"Go on," I say, when Rose looks at me. With that encouragement, she clambers onto a barrel and eagerly accepts a thick piece of bread and a slice of cheese Marilee cuts for her. My stomach growls, too, reminding me that I haven't eaten all day.

Brendin chuckles as he chooses a piece of fruit. "Help yourself, Eland."

But I can't, yet. I remember being here before. Not here, precisely, but another camp like it. I remember eating hungrily, as Rose is now, and feeling safe, and realizing with a sense of wonder that these people were like me. I remember Lev.

They're all regarding me with bemusement, even long-faced Jaysen, and I take a step back, away from the table. "I—I need a moment, before I can eat," I stammer, and, inspired, hold up my stained hands, only now remembering them. "I want to wash, and I saw the stream nearby..."

Brendin makes to stand. "Would you like me to go with you?"

"No, I know the way. Thank you. I'll be back." I try to give Rose a reassuring smile before hurrying out of the tent.

Outside, I decide I might as well go to the stream, in truth, and wash my hands. It's only a short walk, and when I kneel beside the water and feel its cold, clean touch, I feel a little clearer-headed. It's too much, I acknowledge, drying my hands on my trousers as I walk. Remembering Lev, and being in a True Southling camp again, like I was right after my father died.

My father.

I stop on the edge of the clearing, transfixed. I would move, were it not for the knife in my heart and the fact that my feet have turned to stone. Rooted like the trees. Would breathe if I could.

I've been here before. Have seen this before, and I know it with a certainty that makes my skin prickle. I've seen this clearing. This night. That man. Orange sparks float upward, shimmering, as he stokes the fire. He straightens, poker in hand. From behind, all I can see of him is the set of his shoulders, his height, and his hair. Grown long, it brushes his shoulders, auburn turned blood-red in the light. I can see the silver strands, paler against the dark.

And then he blurs, and the light becomes too bright as tears fill my eyes. I would call his name, but my throat is tight, closed... Finally I stumble toward him, and I think my heart might burst...

He turns at the noise, and I freeze. I know him. Know his face. But he is not my father, and the wordless cry that wants to leave my throat only emerges as a half-caught sigh. It hurts.

"Good evening," he says, in his rich, gentle voice. His voice is beautiful, of course it's beautiful, because Aiddan Innys was once one of the most renowned bards in the world. But he's not my father. "Are you Eland?"

I don't know how, but I manage to nod. Swallow the lump in my throat, which sticks like something sharp going down. "Y—yes, sir."

He smiles and beckons me closer with a small motion of his head. "I'm Aiddan," he says, and tosses the stick he was using as a poker on the blaze. Then he looks at me sideways, considering. "I'm the one you spoke with, earlier," he says neutrally. "You knew of us when you called out for help, didn't you." It's not a question. "Knew we were nearby."

I feel trapped, all of a sudden, and nervous. I don't want to betray too much. "Well," I reply slowly, "of course I've heard of people in the Greatwood. Tainted people, I mean, and…"

But Aiddan is shaking his head at me, and I curse myself as my stomach drops down to my toes. How could I have forgotten that his particular gift, beyond thought-speech, is to feel people's emotions? But I don't know how to stop myself from feeling, no more than I could stop my heart beating if I wanted to. It seems to be doing that, all on its own, as I stare at him.

He gazes back at me with his eyes narrowed. Not angrily—I don't think—but very thoughtful. "Step closer to the light," he says at last.

I can't refuse. Not now. I take a step forward, feeling even worse than before. There's no point in hanging my head and avoiding his gaze, so I look up defiantly, jaw tense.

To my surprise, he laughs, the fine lines on his face crinkling. He sets his hand—his only one—on my shoulder and gives me a warm smile. "Well met, Ellin Fisher," he says. "I thought it was you, when you called out to us."

For a moment, I can only stare, dumbfounded. "But you helped anyway!" I blurt out at last.

Aiddan's brow creases as he withdraws his hand. "Of course we did. What did you expect?"

"I—you…" I frown and start over. "Don't you hate me?"

He exhales, slowly, and gestures to several logs placed near the fire, as benches. "Come," he says quietly. "We should talk."

When we've seated ourselves, he turns to me, his good hand clasped loosely over his other wrist on his lap. "You've been in the Northlands all this time, have you?" I nod in reply. "Well. Things are very different here, now. We are different."

"The True Southlings?"

"Yes." His mouth tightens. "You know the mission to the Northlands was borne out of desperation," he says, and that also isn't a question. "Lev...had a very good idea of how bad things would become here. He hoped to prevent it."

"At the cost of innocent lives!" I'm startled at the bitterness in my tone, after all this time. "What he wanted to do to the king, and the princes..."

"...Was wrong," Aiddan interrupts. "I'll admit it, and I think Lev knew it, too. Or would have, if he'd let himself dwell on it. But, what's done is done. I'm not a bad man, Ellin, nor an unreasonable one."

"I never thought you were."

"And yet you were surprised that I'm not your enemy."

"I fought against you," I say, but he shrugs.

"As I said, what's done is done. Now I welcome you among us," he replies. "We could use someone with your gifts."

"For a little while, at least. Thank you." I give him a tentative smile. "What about Rose? Garreth and I saved her from the Guardians, but we can't take her with us. And, for that matter, what about Garreth? He's a Northlander, and my friend. Is he welcome, too?"

His eyebrows rise. "Prince Garreth the Youngest, you mean? Is that who you've brought?"

I wince. "It's complicated."

I'm not surprised that he doesn't press. I didn't know him well before, but Aiddan always struck me as the sort not to stick his nose into others' business. "They're both under our protection, now," he says. "And we'll have a place for the girl, of course, if she wishes to stay. How old is she?"

"Twelve."

He makes a face. "That's young to be showing abilities already. But old enough, I suppose."

"I should get back," I say, making to stand. "They were waiting for me..." But he holds up his hand.

"I've told Brendin you're with me," he says, and smiles. "It's been some time since you've used your powers freely, hasn't it?"

"With the Guardians about? Of course."

"They won't attack us here. We know the wood too well, and there simply aren't enough of them. Yet," he adds, under his breath.

"How bad *is* it, Aiddan?" I ask, folding my hands on my lap. "I saw the sign on the door of the inn..."

By the time he directs me to the tent I'm to share with Rose and Marilee, later, the fire has burned low, and the bread and cheese Brendin brought me sits like stone in my stomach.

I always believed that the Southland would stay the same, even though I left it for the Northlands. But now everything is so different. According to Aiddan, the Guardians have increased their numbers, and the attacks on "tainted" people are becoming more frequent, the punishments more public, and more painful. People are encouraged to report their friends and neighbors if they suspect them, and are rewarded if the charges are true.

At home in Harnon, Alder's Inn closed down because the Alders refused to put a sign on their door. Now it's a meeting place for the Guardians who seized the building, a sort of barracks for them.

The Southland is at war with itself, and the thought makes me shudder. Though I've come to love the Northlands, this is my home. Or was, I suppose.

Such a short time ago, I thought the True Southlings were my enemies. All I remembered was the way they coerced Alaric and King Allard, the way they fought in the castle in the Northlands. How they looked at me, after, with hatred. As if I was the one who had done something evil, by betraying them.

But everything Aiddan said, as we sat and talked beneath the rustling leaves, made sense to me. The True Southlings don't want to invade the Northlands anymore. Now, they keep busy rescuing gifted Southlings from the Guardians and helping the families of the Guardians' victims. They help gifted Southlings travel to the Northlands, where they'll be safe, or let them join the camps and teach them how to use their powers. Truly, they have changed as much as the Southland itself.

CHAPTER TWENTY

I WAKE TO THE FEELING OF being shaken. Groaning, I flail my arm out to the side blindly. "Mmmph. Go away."

"El-*and*," Rose hisses, somewhere between urgent and a singsong, and I crack an eye open. The grayish dimness in the tent tells me it isn't fully sunrise yet, and I've only been asleep a few hours.

"Rose," I whisper, trying to keep my cracking voice even, "it's very early. What is it?"

"I need to talk to you."

My head feels like it's stuffed with wool. "Now?"

"It's important!"

"It had better be," I grumble, pushing off the soft blanket irritably. The morning air is unpleasantly cold as it rushes in, stealing the last of my warm, drowsy haze, along with any hope that I might go back to sleep any time soon. I scrub my hands over my face, then peer at Rose where she kneels next to my cot, looking all too bright-eyed for the hour. Behind me, Marilee snorts softly in her sleep. "Let's not talk here," I whisper.

This early, no one is about. The camp is still and peaceful, the fire nearly dead. The cold, wet grass under my bare feet makes me shiver.

"What is it?" I ask once we've walked over to the remains of the fire, out of earshot of the tents.

Rose looks at me, head tilted slightly. She hooks a strand of hair behind her ear, and her eyebrows draw together. "Last night, Garreth called you Ellin," she says at last, very quickly, sounding shy. "Is—is it true?"

"Is that all?" I exclaim, and then recall myself and lower my voice. "Yes. I'm a girl."

"Then why…?"

I hesitate, not knowing how much she knows about what drunk, horrible brigands are capable of, and decide to give her the simplest answer I can. "Because I thought it would be safer," I reply. "Traveling with Garreth, especially since he's a Northlander, I thought it would be…better. Do you understand?"

"I think so." She shrugs. "So, you're really Ellin Fletcher?"

"Ellin Fisher," I admit, wondering at how strange it feels to speak my own name. "My name was on the notice in Harpersfall. That's why I was so upset."

"Well, mine was, too," she says, obviously unimpressed. I must look as startled as I feel, because she shrugs again. "Auntie and Uncle's name is Thornwood, but my real name—my parents', though Auntie and Uncle call me the same as them—is Kinshield. Same as the one on the sign."

My knees threaten to buckle. One of my hands, of its own accord, finds its way to cover my mouth, and I stare. Now that I know, how could I not have seen the resemblance before? Her slightly upturned eyes and high cheekbones are the spitting image of his. Her hair is the same flyaway, nearly black auburn. Even her crooked, mischievous smile is the same. Rose looks… like Lev's little sister.

"Rose," I say, when I can speak, "what do you know of your family?"

"Nothing, really." I can hear the ache in her words that I feel whenever I think of my mother. "My parents and brother died when I was a baby, in an accident. Auntie and Uncle don't ever talk about them."

"Your brother?" I echo. "Do you know how old he was?"

She shakes her head. "Sometimes I used to dream about him, though," she says, barely above a whisper. "I'd dream that he'd talk to me, right as I fell asleep. He used to tell me stories about our parents, about us when we were together..."

I put my arms around her, but I think the tears stinging my eyes aren't for her, but for him. I don't know what happened, but I know how this story ended. And I can guess that, all of those years spent traveling with the True Southlings, he must have remembered her, and wanted her to remember him. I'd wager he planned to rescue her someday, if her powers ever manifested.

I catch sight of movement at the edge of the clearing and release her, wiping the back of my hand roughly across my eyes. When I see who the tall figure striding toward us is, I wince, tempted to tell Rose to hurry back to the tent. I don't, however, because I think this is one person who really ought to meet her.

"Hello, Mat," I call quietly, with a hesitant wave. And then I tense, wondering just how much of Aiddan's forgiveness is shared by the others.

He stands stiffly, his freckled, homely face unreadable. "Ellin Fisher?" He gives a small, strange-sounding laugh. "I never would've recognized you if Aiddan hadn't told me."

"I'm sorry," I say, putting it bluntly with my hands spread. I liked him once, and he was Lev's dearest friend. The thought, with Rose so near, almost makes me want to weep again. "Mat, I never meant—I tried to Heal him, later. And got exiled for my trouble, but..."

His hands curl and uncurl at his sides, but no sound escapes his open mouth. Then he looks at Rose beside me, and his startled gaze finds my face, and I know that he knows. Indeed, I think he knows far more than I do. Of course Lev would have told him.

"This is Rose," I say quietly. "Rose Kinshield, meet Mathias Oakenfold." My smile wobbles at the corners. "I think the three of us have a lot to talk about."

And I know from the way Mat nods, slowly, that for now, at least, I am forgiven.

———∘∘∘-)◯(-∘∘∘———

When I leave Rose with Mathias, listening raptly to stories about her brother, it's late morning, all gold and brilliant green in the clearing. The camp is bustling now, and I'm surprised that people I used to know wave at me and call greetings. No one comments on my appearance, but I realize that Aiddan must have said something. Of all people, the True Southlings understand the need for disguise. Even so, for the first time in weeks, I feel uncomfortable in my shirt and trousers, out of place. I resolve to ask Marilee, later, if she has a spare dress I might borrow.

Before breakfast, I hurry to the Healer's tent, determined to see Garreth since Aiddan said I couldn't last night. I find the Healer herself outside the tent, working in the sunlight. At first, I think she must be an old crone, bent over with her white hair gleaming. But when she looks up at my approach, I'm startled to see that her face is not creased as I expected. I would guess her at a few years older than Aiddan, certainly, but her cheeks are still pink, and her eyes sparkle at me, blue-green. She beckons me closer. "Well, now. You must be Rowan's girl."

"You knew my father?" I exclaim, then stop and give her a nod, remembering my manners. "Ellin Fisher, Mistress."

She smiles as she stands, setting a pile of bandages on the camp stool behind her. "Call me Freya. There are no formalities here." She clasps my hand with a startlingly firm grip. "And yes, child, I counted your father a friend, a long time ago."

Of course I want to ask her when, but I gesture instead at the tent. "How's Garreth? Is he all right? I tried to Heal him last night, but..."

"He's fine," she says. "He lost a great deal of blood, and the wound on his thigh was deep, but I Healed that one completely and bandaged the other. He'll be walking about tomorrow."

I didn't see his leg last night, but..."You Healed that?" I gasp. Of course, I've seen bruises fade beneath my father's touch, or

Donnal's, have seen cuts and scrapes go from gushing to partly-healed, but a complete Healing? On a cut so deep? I look at her with new respect. "Thank you," I say, and duck my head. "I wasn't sure you would, because of me. And because he's a Northlander."

An odd look passes over her features, but then she smiles at me, and I think I must have imagined her strange hesitation. "You should know Healers better than that," she says lightly. "Come, let's see to your friend."

The tent is large, with a front area for treating people and a back room, separated by a partition, that must be where Freya sleeps. Though there are several cots in the front part, only one of them is occupied. "Garreth!" I exclaim, and then wince when I see he's asleep.

Or was. He shifts, mumbling a little, and blinks. "Ellin?" he asks thickly. "What—weren't we...?"

"You were hurt fighting the Guardians," I explain. "Do you remember? The True Southlings came and helped us. Freya healed you," I add, nodding at her. "She says you'll be fine tomorrow, but today you're supposed to sleep."

He gives me a small, half-awake smile. "Don't think that'll be very difficult."

"It's the Healing." I squeeze his hand. "It makes you tired, especially with such a serious wound. Garreth, we would've—I don't know how to thank you, for what you did."

He makes a dismissive face, but it turns into a jaw-cracking yawn halfway through. "You'd do the same."

"Well, of course, but..." I stop when his head falls to the side, asleep again already. I tug the blanket up over him.

"Thank you," I say to Freya, again, on my way out. "If you hadn't been here, I..."

She touches my shoulder. "I know who he is," she says quietly. "There's no need for thanks. It would have been my duty to heal him, even if I hadn't known." She arches an eyebrow at me, with a hint of rebuke. "Our gifts don't differentiate between Northlanders and Southlings—or anyone else, for that matter. So, what right have we?"

───∞o-◦❦◦-∞o───

Deep in thought, I eat my breakfast, a leftover buttered biscuit and a cup of strong tea. With my fingers curled around the warm cup, I feel truly safe. But how is it, I wonder, that I felt like this in the Northlands, too? I may be content now, but I remember being surrounded by my friends at the palace, friends who were like family, and I'm confused. Torn in two. Am I a Southling, born to be a Healer? Or am I the girl who left the Northlands with a sword she wanted to use?

I take a deep swig of my tea, trying to swallow my troubled thoughts along with it. I nearly spill the rest of the cup when strong, skinny arms are thrown around me from behind. "Ellin! Is it really you?"

"Brek?" I gasp at the sight of him. "I can't believe how you've grown!" I scramble to my feet and give him a quick, tight squeeze. "What are you doing here? Is Donnal here, too?"

He laughs at me, his masses of freckles crinkling, green eyes bright as glass. I can't believe the little boy who left the Northlands last winter has grown at least a handspan, maybe two, and is gawkier than ever. Not to mention different. His clothes are no longer patched and threadbare, and his hair is neatly cut.

"I'm here with Aiddan," he says. "Didn't he tell you?"

"Tell me what? Is Donnal all right?"

"Oh, Father's fine," he replies airily, and from the way he glances at me, I know he means me to notice the word he used. I smile so hard my cheeks hurt.

"Father, hmm?"

A look of mingled pride and pleasure passes over his features. "Well, I didn't have any parents. An' Donnal said, if I wanted, I could be his son, and I said all right."

He says it all so simply that I'm tempted to giggle. "That's wonderful. But where does Aiddan come in?"

"Oh. Well," he says, looking even cockier than before, "*he* said that, with my voice, if I could learn to play the harp, I could be a bard as good as him, and did I want to be his apprentice? So, Father said I could if I wanted. An' I did."

"Lucky for me," Aiddan says from behind me, sounding amused. When he puts his hand on Brek's shoulder, I notice the change in Aiddan, too. Before, he seemed sad and withdrawn, prickly, but now the lines on his face seem softer. He looks like someone from whom a weight has been lifted, and I suddenly understand.

"You're singing again, too, aren't you?" I ask, hoping very much that I'm right. I've never heard him sing or play, but I know that Aiddan Innys, Master Bard, once played for kings, and they considered it an honor.

"I am," he agrees, and holds up the stump of his missing hand. "With this, I thought I was finished. Then it occurred to me that, should I find someone willing to play for me, there was no reason to retire altogether. Especially not when it's so useful to be a bard, is it not, Brek?"

Brek laughs, and I shake my head, confused. "What?"

"You should remember better than that, Ellin." Aiddan grins. "Who better to hear gossip and rumors than musicians who are welcome anywhere? Who better to steal one of our own away before the Guardians get to her than a traveling bard and his apprentice, passing through town?"

"You don't get caught?"

"An' now you're forgetting what we can do." Brek sighs. "They don't suspect a thing, with him to make 'em feel calm and me to make us look different."

"I'm only Aiddan Innys sometimes," Aiddan adds. "Only when we're far from here and above reproach."

"So Master Innys won't be connected with the True Southlings," I say, understanding. "Since they have a description of you as their leader. That's clever." They both look amused again, and I sigh. "What else don't I know?"

"I'm not, in fact, the leader of the True Southlings," Aiddan replies. "We merely want people to think that I am. Our commander is out doing far more than the rest of us, and in far greater danger."

"Who?" I ask, but he shakes his head.

"That's not for me to tell."

CHAPTER TWENTY-ONE

"*You know,*" Erik says with his thoughts, out of nowhere, "*Coll told me he's thinking of wintering Weaver's sheep here.*"

Finn doesn't glance up from where he sits by the small hearth in their bedroom, oiling his boots. Instead, he makes a noise of vague interest, frowning at a small crack on the toe of his left one. He knows without looking that Erik is similarly absorbed with sharpening his hunting knife, bent over it in the other chair.

"*Well, I said to him, where's he going to put 'em?*" Erik continues. "*Not to mention the extra feed.*"

"*The south barn would be fine for sheep, and you know it,*" Finn points out, amused, as he rubs small circles in the leather. "*And they can eat what they like, given how they've improved the land by eating what the mares won't. You're just being lazy.*"

"*Well, so would you if...*" Erik's thought breaks off abruptly. "Yes?" he calls aloud, toward the door, when Finn looks up in surprise.

Nan, in the open doorway, tucks a strand of faded hair into submission. "Your brothers asked me to fetch you," she says, and tugs the quilt on Erik's bed straight at the corner. "They're in the study. And what are you thinking, setting that so near the fire?" she scolds, pointing at Finn's other boot.

"*It's only been a minute,*" he protests, but he nudges it away with his toe, anyway. "*Do you know what they want?*"

Nan shakes her head. "I asked if they wanted a bite—they've been closed up with Tomas for hours—and they sent me to get the two of you. I don't think it's good, though, love."

"If it's Tomas, it can't be," Erik grouses. "More Southling trouble here, or there, and shouldn't we just send 'em all home and get rid of them once and for all?"

"Be nice." Nan gives him a stern look and a good-natured cuff on the head. "You know he's a good man."

"I'll believe it when I see it," Erik says, and Finn, standing in his sock-feet, agrees.

In the hallway, they pass Lord Tomas, striding with a fierce scowl that doesn't soften when he bids them good evening. Of course, after that, Erik sticks out his chest and stamps along with a baleful eye, stroking a nonexistent moustache, and they're both chuckling like idiots when they stumble into the study. After one look at their brothers' faces, they sober immediately.

"Sit," Coll says, before either of them has a chance to ask what's the matter. Erik perches on the edge of Alaric's desk, hands dangling between his thighs, leaving the chair beside Coll for Finn. Alaric, of course, is seated behind the desk, leaning his elbows on it.

"Well?" Erik demands.

Coll lifts one hand and drops it to his lap again. Alaric looks from Erik to Finn. "Tomas was just in," he says at last. "Diedrick the Valiant is gathering support, up in the Northwatch."

"Cousin Diedrick?" Erik echoes. "Gathering support? Not for..."

But Finn, seeing the shadow in Alaric's eyes, swallows hard. *"Are you certain?"* he interrupts. *"And does Tomas know how many?"*

It's Coll who touches his sleeve and answers. "Absolutely certain. He'll have most of the north behind him, and everyone here who resents the Southlings. That's his rallying point—as king, he would reinstate the old laws and send them packing."

"So, was Tomas defecting?" Erik asks sourly, earning a stern look from Alaric.

"He may not agree with me—or, more accurately, he knows what I've done does not endear me to our people—but he would die before betraying our family."

"All of this is beside the point, anyway," Finn points out, sharper than he intends. *"What are we going to do?"*

"Nothing, yet." Alaric shakes his head. "If I know Diedrick, he's not going to make any overt move on the throne until he's sure he has a chance. And he doesn't. Yet."

Erik frowns. "But you can't..."

"But nothing!" Alaric shouts, jumping to his feet so violently that his chair falls over backward. He looms over the desk, arms braced. "I don't know, all right? I don't know what to do! "

"Alaric." Coll pushes himself to his feet, but Alaric raises a warning finger.

"Don't," he snaps. "Don't you tell me what's best, or what the Guard would do. You're *not* king, Coll. And don't *you* try to placate me," he continues viciously, turning to point his shaking finger at Finn. "If I want womanish kindness, I'll speak with my betrothed."

Before Finn can recover from the insult, which stings like a physical blow, Alaric has rounded on Erik. "And you," he snarls. "When are you going to grow up, Erik? Do it soon, or you'll end up a drunken tavern lout before you know it. I want *men* as my brothers, my advisors, not sniggering boys at school."

"Up yours!" Erik springs to his feet. "Think you're such a prize, just because you're the frigging king?" His hands curl into fists, but Coll grabs him by the arm and drags him back.

"Leave him, boyo," Coll says, looking at Alaric with disgust. "Let his majesty stew in it. You, too," he adds, nodding to Finn. "I think we've heard enough."

"Oh, piss on the lot of you!" Alaric retorts, knocking a stack of maps to the floor with a furious swipe of his arm. "All of you can deal with the mess, then. Go on! Figure out a plan, and when you do, let me know. All I know is that there's not enough damned time, and I can't..." Face crimson, he clamps his mouth shut, then shoves past them and out the door.

"And what in all hells was that about?" Erik asks, in the stunned pause that follows.

Coll scowls as he kneels to pick up the papers. "The news about Diedrick hit him hard," he says after a moment. "This could well mean war. But that's no excuse for flying off at us."

"No," Finn agrees, and hands Coll a fallen map. *"It isn't."*

The three of them work without speaking, smoothing pages, straying glances at the door.

— ∘∘)◦◎◦(∘∘∘ —

At breakfast, Alaric's chair is empty again. Coll is absent as well today, Erik deep in conversation with Thalia, and Finn eats quickly, alone with his troubled thoughts. Alaric isn't present at lunch, either, though Erik says Alaric snapped at him again, in passing, for something inconsequential.

They barely speak at dinner. Thalia tries repeatedly to draw Alaric into conversation, but she gives up after several failed attempts and stares glumly at her plate, then leaves, with an irritated look at Alaric, immediately after.

The next day is no better, and the one after is worse. Even the maids notice; Finn sees them exchanging glances behind Alaric's back, rushing out of the room when he approaches.

Word is out about Diedrick, speculation on everyone's lips.

It rains for days, steady, chilly drizzle, a herald of autumn that does little to improve anyone's mood. When Finn chances to pass Alaric in the hall one evening, he's startled at the change in him. With his disheveled hair and red-rimmed, sunken eyes, Alaric looks as if he hasn't slept in a week.

A few days later, Finn is in the workroom, the window open to let the warmth and sunlight in. The air has changed, is almost imperceptibly sharper since the rain. His hand pauses on the pestle as he gazes out, thinking of Ellin. It won't be long before the leaves are the color of her hair. He'd hoped they'd be back by winter, but he knows better, now.

He wonders often how different things might be if Garreth were here. Ellin too, but it's not her absence that sets them all off-balance. Sighing, he scrapes the pestle through the ground hornroot, then stops again at once, feeling a vague sense of unease even before the door is shoved open.

He's on his feet immediately. *"What happened?"* he demands, taking in the sight of Erik and Sven the stable boy supporting a limping Coll between them. He pulls out a chair before any of them can answer. *"Well?"* he asks, when Coll is settled and the others have gone.

"It's nothing." But Coll's fierce grimace belies the words. *"I was working Bramble, and a rabbit spooked her, and she threw me."* He swallows, throat bobbing beneath his beard. *"Landed badly on my knee."*

"Apparently." Even through Coll's muddy trousers, he can see the swelling. *"Do you want me to have a look, or fetch Master Thorvald?"*

Coll gives him the ghost of a smile. *"You, if you know what you're doing."*

It looks bad, he sees a few moments later, huge and already bruising. But though Coll's hands clench in pain as Finn examines it, he's relieved to find nothing seriously wrong.

"It looks worse than it is," he says at last, standing. *"I'm going to wrap it and find you a crutch. You should keep it propped up as much as possible for a week."*

"A week?" Coll repeats, looking sour, when Finn sets the bandages and ointment on the table.

"You need to keep your weight off it. Your knees are bad enough." Coll shrugs in reply, then sits quietly as Finn coats his knee with ointment and wraps it. *"That's not too tight, is it?"*

"It feels better already."

"It's going to be stiff later. But resting it—and ice, I'll fetch some—will help."

When Coll is dressed again, Finn washes the ointment from his hands in the basin, then rummages in the tall cupboard for a crutch. *"Here it is,"* he says, after he has handed it to his brother. *"It's from a few years ago, when Garreth broke his leg. It might be a bit short,"* he adds, squinting, *"but that's just as well, since you're not to use it much."*

Before Coll can reply, Alaric storms in. "What were you thinking?" he demands, by way of greeting. "Erik said you were riding Bramble?"

Coll's hand holding the crutch tightens. "I was thinking to train her," he says. "Thought that was my prerogative. And I'm fine, by the way, thank you." His mouth twists, but his sarcasm seems to have no effect.

"She's had a saddle on her thrice, if that?" Alaric shakes his head. "Should've left it to Sven, or anyone else who's not a fat lump who'd land like a sack of rocks!"

"It was a rabbit!" Coll snaps, red-cheeked with embarrassment and fury. "The horses are my responsibility, Alaric, and so help me, if you think for one moment..."

"Stop it!" Finn interjects, moving between them. He shoves Alaric hard, breathing heavily. *"Get out, if you don't have a kind word to say. Mind your own affairs and domains, damn you, and leave us to ours."*

Alaric stumbles back, obviously shocked. Stares at Finn for a moment, then at Coll, and then his shoulders sag. He closes his eyes briefly. Stepping around Finn, he goes to Coll. He says something Finn doesn't catch and then bends, slowly, until his forehead rests against Coll's hair and his arm is around his shoulders. After a long moment, Alaric turns to Finn, hands spread. *"I'm sorry, Finn. I shouldn't have said that. Any of it,"* he adds, and Finn has a feeling he doesn't only mean the insults he gave to Coll, just now.

"Alaric," he begins, and shifts his glance to Coll. *"If something's wrong..."*

But Alaric shakes his head, smiling ruefully. *"I was crazed with worry. I don't want to lose any of you."*

At that, Finn wonders how much of all of this *does* have to do with Garreth. But he says nothing, and instead puts his hand on Alaric's shoulder in forgiveness. Alaric nods at Coll. *"Come,"* he says, *"I'll help you get him settled.* The four of us can eat dinner in your room," he adds, to Coll. "Together. I'll tell Erik."

Chapter Twenty-Two

SINCE WE ARRIVED in the town square, every-thing has been a blur of noise and color and whirling movement. I gasp, ducking, as the short, fat Guardian's staff nearly takes my head off. Then I lunge, tightening my grip on the hilt of my sword, and meet his next blow. He's not very good with the staff, which tells me that he must be a new Guardian, since I know they're trained to fight. Even so, it takes all of my meager skill to defend myself. We're both sweating; I can feel it trickling down my forehead, can hear blood rushing in my ears. I know Marilee, Mathias, and Jaysen were supposed to release the prisoners from their cell, leaving me, a woman named Alma, Garreth, and Brendin to deal with the Guardians, but I don't know how the others are faring.

Finally, I can sense him tiring. My arms and legs feel sluggish, out of practice as I am, but I try to move faster, like Coll taught me. My size is my one advantage. With each burning breath, eyes stinging, I dance faster, widening the distance between us. Making him come after me, making him block lighter, swifter strokes.

He stumbles, off-balance, when I switch direction. Without thought, I finish the motion, bringing my blade back up...

A scream.

I don't understand. Everything seems to happen too slowly, too quickly, and I don't...

He falls, clutching his wrist. Two things fall onto the dirt beside him. His staff.

The other thing beside him is his hand.

I can't stop staring at it. At him. There's a smear on my blade. My breath hitches.

"Come on!" Garreth shouts, grabbing me by the arm. His hair is dark with sweat, and I can't make sense of his features. He looks like a stranger. My feet feel like someone else's as I allow myself to be dragged away.

I don't look back, but I can still see him. "Garreth, I didn't mean…"

"Come on," he says again, roughly, and I don't say anything else as I sheathe my blade and run.

———oOo-◦◦◦◦-oOo———

Mathias grabs my shoulder as soon as Garreth and I arrive, panting, at the clearing. "Freya wants you," he says, freckles standing out on his pale face. "Now. There's twelve of 'em, and some of them are in bad shape. Said she needs another Healer."

"Twelve?" Garreth repeats incredulously, but I can see that it's true. Everyone is shouting, bustling from one tent to the next, looking tense.

"Where's Rose?" I'm pulled out of my shocked stupor enough to be worried.

"Doing something for Aiddan, I think. Dishes? It doesn't matter. She's fine." Mathias waves an impatient hand. "We'll need more tents, Northlander, if you want to help."

I leave them to it and rush to Freya's tent. Some of the prisoners are gathered outside, standing with dazed expressions or sitting on the ground. Aiddan and Rose are tending to them, offering tea and food. As I watch, Brek comes from the kitchen tent with another tray.

I don't have time to give Rose more than a quick nod of encouragement as I hurry into the tent. I don't know what I expected, but compared to the commotion outside, the Healer's tent is a cocoon of quiet. I would be at my wits' end if I had twelve people to tend, but Freya doesn't look the least bit frazzled, not even working quickly with her sleeves pushed up and a line outside her door. "There you are, Ellin." She looks up from the man she's tending to give me a small smile. "Another set of hands will be welcome. Why don't you wash up and see what you can do for Jodith?" she asks, indicating the young woman curled up on the far cot. "I'm preparing to do a Healing on her brother Simon, here, for his broken ribs."

When I approach Jodith, I stifle a gasp. She doesn't open her eyes, and I'm glad, because I'm not sure I could stop staring if I wanted to. She's so thin that her skin seems stretched over her bones, birdlike hands crossed in front of her chest, clutching the bodice of her dress. Her red-gold hair is chopped shorter even than mine, and roughly—I can see her scalp through it, in places. On her angular face, I can't tell where the shadows end and bruises begin. There are cuts at the corners of her mouth, caked with dirt and dried blood.

Swallowing hard, I touch a hesitant finger to the back of her hand. I don't think I've ever been so afraid of hurting someone. "Jodith?" I say softly. "My name is Ellin, and I'm a Healer. Are you awake?"

She blinks, and the beauty of her eyes, huge and green, fringed with dark lashes, makes the devastation of her face seem worse. Her dry lips part, and she frowns, and presses them together, and tries again. "My back," she whispers. "That's the worst of it, Healer."

As soon as she speaks, I look at the dark spots on the gray fabric of her dress, soaked through and dried, sticking cloth to raw skin. The stains are long, and thin, crisscrossing one another. It's all too easy to imagine the whipping that must have caused the marks beneath. "Oh, Jodith," I breathe. I struggle to keep my voice even. "I can Heal this, or at least begin to, without taking your dress off, all right? But I'll need to touch you. I promise, I won't hurt you."

Her head moves in a barely-perceptible nod, and, wincing on her behalf, I set my hands lightly on her back. The sharp bones of her shoulders jut out against my palms, and her skin is hot and stiff. I close my eyes and try to calm myself, to connect with Jodith, with my Healing power.

I sense it beckoning, pulling me, and I stretch for it.

A sharp knife seems to score my palms, and Jodith shrieks in agony even as I cry out and stumble backward, trying to shake the pain out of my hands.

"Ellin! What did you do to her?" Freya demands, but I can only look from my hands to Jodith, who's now trembling violently, and shake my head.

"I—I'm sorry!" I drag my gaze to Freya's face when she comes to stand next to me, and at her touch, Jodith lies still. "I didn't mean to hurt her!" I continue, feeling terrible. "I reached for my power, and it burned, and…"

"It burned? And you were out with Mathias and them." Freya closes her eyes, as if reaching for patience. "Child, tell me you didn't attempt a Healing after you did violence. Surely you know better."

My stricken face must be answer enough, and she sighs. "It's plain you didn't know. I suppose it's my fault, in a way, for expecting more than you've been trained for." She touches my arm to take the sting out of her words, but it hardly helps. "You can assist me, and do what you can without using your power. But leave the Healing to me, all right?"

Assist her like any novice could, I think, humiliated, but I nod anyway. I spend the next few hours doing what little I can, feeling wretched. I can't bear to meet Jodith's eyes, while Freya treats her or afterward. Her scream still echoes in my ears, and when I manage to tear my mind away from her, I think about the Guardian I fought instead. I wonder if anyone is healing him now.

It's evening by the time all of the newcomers have been tended to and fed. My back aches as I carry an empty tray to the kitchen, but instead of getting some dinner for myself, I fix a mug of tea and take it to Freya's tent.

She looks even more worn than I feel, bent, when I enter, with her hand on Jodith's forehead. Seeing Jodith embarrasses me again, but Freya smiles, the corners of her eyes crinkling, when I hold out the mug. "Is that for me? Bless you." She nods at the tent flap. "Come, let's talk outside, where we won't wake her."

"I'm sorry," I say, again, when she's seated herself on one of the stools and I've taken a place on the ground beside her. I poke at the dirt with my fingertip. "I've never had that happen before. I didn't know..."

"Of course you didn't," she interrupts, but she doesn't sound angry. "Ellin, have you received any formal training?"

"I helped my father." But I know that's not what she means. The truth is, the first time I used my healing power, it was on King Allard, and I knew I was taking a chance, doing something I wasn't supposed to yet. But that first time seemed so simple. I swallow, suddenly feeling very young. "I—no. I've never been taught to use my power," I admit. The next words are even more difficult, but I owe Freya the truth, since she is everything I've claimed to be. "In the Northlands, they called me Healer. Sometimes even Mistress, and it doesn't mean quite the same thing there that it does here, but...I didn't correct them."

Her fingers tighten around the cup before she takes a sip. "You are a Healer," she says at last. "Untrained, yes, but you clearly have the gift, and a knack for using it. And I wouldn't worry overmuch about what they called you in the Northlands," she adds. "It's a true name there, if not here. Or not yet. As they sometimes are."

When I look up in confusion, she smiles. "Names and titles are transitory things," she says, and her eyes sparkle as she leans closer. "After all, my name is Freya Goldenhaired, but you certainly wouldn't guess it, would you?"

I stare at her wonderingly. With her white hair and greenish eyes, a Healer, I'd simply assumed... "You're a Northlander?"

She laughs at me. "Half, yes. My da is. In fact, you might well know him—Josef the Apothecary?"

"He's your father? But—he must be so old!"

"As is anyone past thirty, at your age, hmm?"

"I didn't mean..." But since I did, I clear my throat and fish for another subject. "Your mother's a Southling, then? Is that why you have the Healing gift? Why you're with the True Southlings?"

She lifts a graceful hand. "I'm with the True Southlings because I believe their cause is good. Because Healers are needed here, as much as fighters. And, as you've seen, you can't be both."

"You can't? But my friend Finn says..."

"If you're speaking of Prince Finnlay, he's a physician, not a Healer. There's a difference, of course," she says, leaning forward slightly. "Ellin, has it not occurred to you that there's a cost for our gifts? A balance?"

I can feel my forehead wrinkling. "I don't understand."

"Of course you do. Surely you've noticed that those who can compel others—like you, from what I've heard—are the ones who can't feel anyone else's emotions in the least? And empaths, like Aiddan and, for that matter, like me, are unable to compel."

"Because they're opposites?" I ask after a moment, trying to take this in. "Because compelling is mean, while people like Aiddan—empaths?—are kind and understanding?"

She laughs. "That's simplifying it a great deal, my dear. An empath could manipulate someone just as easily, and far more subtly, than a compeller. No power is more or less evil than another."

"Are there any other pairings like that?" I ask, fascinated. My exhaustion is gone entirely; learning the things I most wanted to know, about myself, about these abilities, is too exciting.

"Only two, that we're sure of," Freya replies, after taking a sip of tea. "The first is so well-known that it's taught at the Healers' College, and that is simply: a Healer must be sworn to peace. The more often one bears a weapon, the more violence one does, the less their healing power will work. The second also concerns the Healing gift. It seems to be a bit stricter than other powers," she adds with a wry smile, "more's the pity. Did you ever hear of Seers in the Northlands?"

I shake my head.

"Seers are those who dream true. Strangely, it's an ability that seems to be more common in the Northlands than here, though they call it good magic there, instead of witchcraft. But Seers can no longer use Healing gifts once they begin to have the dreams. Marilee was a Healer, before." She makes a quiet, sympathetic sound. "It's why she couldn't help me, today. It breaks her heart that she can't reach the power anymore."

"Doesn't she like being a Seer?" I hope that if I hold myself very still, and don't breathe much, the overwhelming fear and despair I'm holding at bay won't reach me.

"Like it?" Freya echoes, shaking her head. "She didn't want it, can't control it, and it makes her ill every time. But is it not fitting, that the most powerful gift should also have the highest price?"

I have to clear my throat before I can speak. "It doesn't seem very fair to me."

"Tch," she says dismissively, "nothing's fair, child. Least of all the choice you have to make now."

When I look a question at her, she gestures, regarding me levelly. "Are you a warrior, Ellin, or are you a healer? I'd wager you haven't long to choose."

I clasp my hands over my drawn-up knee and look at them, running the pad of one thumb against the side of my other hand. The fear is still there, a dark, hulking thing behind my shoulder, making my skin cold and shivery.

The truth that I can't possibly tell her yet, that I don't even want to admit to myself, is that I'm afraid this choice has been taken from me. I dreamed of Aiddan in this clearing, and then I found him here, so I must be a Seer. There's no denying it.

It's strange how realizing this makes everything so much clearer. How easy it is to remember, now, the revulsion I felt when I cut the Guardian's hand off, and how heartsick I've been every time I've failed to heal someone.

I sigh and look up at Freya, whose hair gleams in the growing dark. They've built the fire up in the center of the clearing, and the others are gathered around it, silhouettes of every size and shape. Garreth is sitting beside the fire with Mathias, and Rose and Brek are laughing together. These are my people, as much as the Northlanders ever were. This is my home, just as the Northlands are.

I stand and brush off my skirt. "I want to be a Healer," I say, meaning it so sincerely my heart aches. And perhaps I can be, if only for a little while. Marilee's much older than me, and if she was a true Healer before she lost her powers, maybe it will be the same for me. On impulse, but an impulse I deeply feel is right, I bow. "Will you teach me, Mistress?"

"You are requesting to be my apprentice, Ellin Fisher?" Though her words are formal, the smile she gives me is anything but.

I smile back, as much as I can, and try not to wonder if I have enough time left to become a Master Healer. I try not to remember that I was supposed to be my father's apprentice. "I am, Mistress. If you will have me."

At her nod, I go to fetch Garreth as the witness, then kneel in the scrubby grass and bow my head as she rests a hand on my shorn hair and speaks the oath.

It's nothing like the important ceremony in the formal hall of the College, me in my dirty dress instead of fancy robes, Freya's hands still smelling of mint salve, but I doubt any apprentice in Whiteriver has ever wanted this more.

———ooo-)◊(-ooo———

With everyone gathered around the fire, the center of the clearing is crowded, at least two people to every bench, with others sitting on the ground or milling about. Wood smoke fills the air, along with the mouthwatering aroma of meat and vegetables from the big pot of stew. I helped myself to a bowl and a piece of hard bread when Freya and Garreth and I joined the others, and now I sit contentedly beside Garreth, mopping up the last of the gravy with a crust.

He turns to me. "You want to stay, don't you."

"For now, at least. I can't go back, and wouldn't anyway, not when things are so bad here. Besides," I add, setting my bowl on the ground, "it seems that Freya and Aiddan—and maybe others—know more about the powers than we'd be likely to find in Whiteriver."

"Oh?" But before I have a chance to answer, Aiddan steps in front of the fire and raises his hand for silence.

"My friends, the newcomers have news," he says. His beautiful voice is pitched to carry, and though I've yet to hear him sing, I have a glimpse of what it must be like when he does. The hush, the weight of his words, like stones into a pond. At a gesture from Aiddan, a man rises to join him, and I recognize him as Simon, one of the ones Freya healed earlier.

"My name is Simon Tanner," he says, into the waiting quiet. His voice is a little hoarse, but he looks better than he did earlier. "My companions and I owe all of you a great debt. We have been held, here in Harpersfall, as the Guardians' prisoners. My sister Jodith and I were the first ones taken, over a month ago, from Dunbarthon. After us, they brought others. We were..." he spreads his hands, sharp shadows on his face twitching. "Well. Know that the Guardians do not treat their prisoners kindly. They were waiting until they had a dozen of us, and the last, Kieran, was captured last night." He nods to a boy about my age.

"Were they planning a group execution?" Mathias calls. "That's..."

"We were to be hounds," Simon replies, practically spitting the word. "Or used for some other purpose, but they were careful to keep us alive. Two of them came near to killing my sister, and were punished for it. There were...lessons, daily, and I don't doubt they planned worse."

Garreth looks as puzzled as I feel, though all of the True Southlings seem to know what Simon's on about. I stand, lifting my hand to speak. "What are hounds? I don't understand."

It's Aiddan who answers, his features unusually stern. "Haven't you wondered how the Guardians know when someone uses their abilities?" he asks. "Their hounds are those with gifts, like us. They sniff powers out like dogs for their masters, and shield them from our attacks."

"But why?"

Simon makes a brittle sound that might be a laugh. "If all of you hadn't come, today, I would have become one, and gladly. They are...very persuasive." Something in the way he says it makes me remember Jodith's back, the marks of a gag by her mouth, and I know what other healing she required. Simon only had a few broken ribs.

Sickened, I nod my understanding. "There's more," Simon continues. "They indicated that they had other plans for us. Something more important than being hounds. They planned to move us tomorrow."

"Where?" Aiddan asks, and the expression on Simon's face chills me even before he speaks.

"To Whiteriver. The Healers' College."

CHAPTER TWENTY-THREE

I WAKE TO THE SOUNDS of birds chirping, surprised at how light it is, how late it must be. I'm not sure what woke me. Rose is still asleep, curled on the cot next to mine, and I expected everyone to sleep later than this, since the entire camp was up half the night arguing. At the sound of groaning behind me, I turn to see Marilee sitting with her head in her hands. I wince at the sight of her shiny skin and too-pale cheeks when she looks up.

"Do you need a bucket?" I whisper, but she shakes her head, rubbing her palms on the skirt of her shift.

"I'm all right," she says. "But thank you." She smoothes her hair back to braid it, and I marvel at her composure. After a true dream, I feel terrible, but her fingers begin to plait her hair deftly, not shaking a bit. I begin to dress, and I'm shocked when I happen to glance over again and see her pull on a pair of trousers before shedding her nightshift and reaching for a shirt.

Marilee's eyes meet mine, and the corner of her mouth quirks upward. "Come, now, did you think you were the first?" she teases, doing up the buttons. "I'll be riding today."

There's something in the way she says it makes my fingers still on the laces of my dress. "Your dream? Is something going to happen?"

Her thick braid sways, brushing against her shoulders. "Freya said she told you. Did she mention that it's rude to ask about a Seer's dreams?"

"I'm sorry. I didn't know."

She waves my apology aside. "Besides, I tell Aiddan before anyone else."

After she goes out, I put on my boots and do the same. I spot Garreth having breakfast and join him after fetching some tea. "Any news?"

He grimaces. "Nothing good. Mat and Brendin were still arguing when I went to bed. I haven't seen Aiddan yet."

I nod glumly into my cup. Things haven't changed overnight, then. The debate carried on for hours, with half the camp wanting to set out for Whiteriver to find out what the Guardians are up to, and the rest wanting to stay.

"Have you heard anything?" Garreth asks, breaking off a piece of his biscuit and offering it to me.

"Not much. Freya wants to go, and I don't blame her. If the Guardians have done something to the Master Healers—or worse, if their leaders are Healers..."

"I know." He makes a face, then sighs. "I suppose it's lucky we didn't go to Whiteriver. If we had..." He breaks off and tilts his head, and I hear it, too. Hoofbeats, and the jingle of tack. Garreth jumps to his feet, reaching for his sword, and I follow, tea sloshing onto my hand.

I curse, annoyed, when I see Jaysen, the lookout, approaching with a mounted rider behind him. Talking and gesturing, but certainly not sounding the alarm. Garreth gives me a rueful look as he sheaths his blade. "Sorry."

Before I have a chance to reply, Aiddan's voice is in my head, and everyone else's, requesting all of us to gather at the fire.

"I heard that," Garreth breathes, but we don't have time to discuss it further since the others are coming, joining the circle. In a matter of moments, everyone is here. Even Rose, barefoot, still looking only half-awake. I feel a pang of guilt for dragging her into all of this. The True Southlings are good people, but a rowdy camp is no place for a twelve-year-old girl. She should be at school instead of staying up all night listening to talk of torture and fighting. But then again, I'm not the one who should be guilty. The Guardians should be. They're the ones who are tearing the Southland apart.

When Jaysen and the newcomer approach, I'm startled to recognize the rider, a man of middling height but with massive arms and shoulders, faded copper hair and a scarred, blunt face. Garreth sucks in a breath. "Isn't that..."

"Cedran," I whisper, "from last winter! But wasn't he in prison?"

"They escaped," Garreth hisses. "Didn't you know?"

Cedran ambles to the center of the circle, and if he recognizes Garreth and me, he doesn't seem to bear us any ill will. Aiddan bends so that Cedran can speak into his ear, then gives a curt nod.

"The Commander sent me," Cedran says, loudly and without preamble. "Anyone who wishes is to head for Whiteriver at once. Something big's going on."

I nudge Garreth. "I guess that settles it," I murmur, and he nods.

After the startled exclamations fade, Cedran points a thick finger at Marilee. "Marilee, you're to come with me, if you will."

She nods as if this is no surprise, her eyes on Jaysen's face. Watching them tugs at my heart and makes me think of Alaric. I wonder if I'll ever have someone with whom a glance is as good as a conversation, who will go wherever I go, without question. Someone I'd want to follow anywhere.

"I'll pack and ready the horses," Jaysen says, in his deep, quiet voice.

"Brendin," Cedran continues, "you're to escort any who don't want to go to Whiteriver up to the Northlands. They'll be safer there. And the rest of you...leave as soon as possible, and hurry."

Aiddan gives a few instructions, but I can see, when the crowd disperses, that everyone knows what to do. Almost everyone, that is. Simon and Jodith and the other former prisoners remain sitting, in a group, talking amongst themselves. I wonder if they'll go with us, or if they'd rather not see the Guardians ever again.

Next to me, Garreth's pale brows are pulled together with worry. He looks so out of place among the True Southlings. So out of place in the shabby clothes he's wearing. I remember how he looked in his coat and breeches and circlet, the night of Thalia's feast, a sharp contrast to how he is now, so much harder and scruffier, with injuries he doesn't complain about at all. I think about Erik and Coll and Finn and Alaric, and I know how much I miss all of them. Even Keeper Nan. How much more must he miss the Northlands and his family?

"Aiddan," I call softly, with my thoughts, and he meets my gaze, raising his eyebrows in inquiry. I beckon. *"Would you please come and speak with us?"*

Garreth, frowning at his lap, barely seems to notice when Aiddan approaches.

"I think Garreth should go to the Northlands with—or instead of—Brendin." I say it quickly, so it will hurt less, and don't look at Garreth while I do. "I think Alaric should know what's happening here. And it's time you went home, anyway," I add, feeling rather than seeing Garreth's piercing blue glower. I look at Aiddan instead. "They'd be safer with Garreth. He could take them to the castle, perhaps find some employment..."

"And what do you think of this plan, Garreth?" Aiddan asks mildly.

"You're mad if you think I'm going anywhere!" he splutters. "What sort of a guard would I be if I left..."

"A Northlander one," I interrupt. "Garreth, what if something happened to you? Do you realize the position that would put Alaric in?"

"What does it matter?" Stone-faced, he frowns at Aiddan, and his hair falls across his forehead, catching the sun. "I'm not leaving."

Aiddan's brows lift again, and the corner of his mouth twitches. "Get your things ready, then. Both of you. We'll leave by sundown."

When he has gone, I look down at my hands, clenching them so hard my knuckles hurt. Garreth reaches over, covering both of mine with one of his, his skin warm. I still don't look at him. "You're an idiot."

"What am I going to do at home? Tend the horses with Coll? Guard the city from untaxed cows and runaway pigs?" He snorts, and I smile a little, reluctantly, remembering that argument. It seems like a lifetime ago. "Ellin, what's happening here is important. Far more than we realized, when we left." He stands, tugging at me until I follow. "I'm going to help Mat with the wagons, and perhaps write a letter home, to send with Brendin. D'you want to say anything?"

I turn away, aching, and watch a flame-colored leaf waft off a nearby maple and tumble lazily to the ground. The foliage of another, smaller tree is golden-tipped, gilding its branches like a crown. "Give them my love, please," I say, watching the leaves ripple like water in the breeze. "All of them."

Chapter Twenty-Four

TWO MESSENGERS ARRIVE on the same morning, when the sun is pale yellow in a cloudless blue sky, and the air is cool. The first messenger is a Southling, hair the color of autumn leaves, riding a nondescript brown nag. The second, riding into the yard on the Southling's heels, wears a deep blue coat with rose sleeves, is tall and white-blond, astride a mare whose coat gleams like polished silver. Finn, watching Erik and Thalia spar with quarterstaffs, sees Erik's weapon fall to the stones and roll as the color drains from his brother's face. Erik says something to Thalia, and she turns to watch them enter the castle, flushed cheeks at odds with her grave expression.

Heart heavy, Finn stoops to pick up the fallen weapon. Clutches it so that the smooth wood presses into his palms. The weight of it is strangely steadying. Thalia touches his wrist, and her eyes are troubled when he looks at her in inquiry. "Erik says those are Diedrick's colors," she says. Her lips press together when he nods. "You don't think...?"

Finn shrugs, handing the staff to Erik. *"I can't imagine it's good news,"* he says, and Erik translates. *"I'm going to fetch Coll."* Without waiting for an answer, he heads for the stables, reluctant to go inside and find out.

Coll seems no more pleased about the news than Finn, and they barely speak on the walk back to the castle. When they enter the throne room, they find the Southling gone already and Diedrick's man just leaving. Erik says, when Finn goes to stand beside him, that Diedrick's messenger will be staying until Alaric has an answer. Which tells Finn all he needs to know, even before the door has closed, leaving the four of them and Thalia alone.

"Well?" Coll asks.

Alaric's face is blank, hands immobile on the parchments in his lap. "Diedrick has challenged me for the throne," he says. "An honor-match, in seven days' time."

Coll's shoulders hunch in a shrug. "So, we'll prepare for battle and ride north within the week. We thought it might come to this, and Diedrick's army isn't…"

"No, Coll." Alaric stands. His eyes look strange, too dark, like he's not really seeing any of them. "I mean to accept."

"Why?" Erik demands, signing the word with such vehemence that Finn is certain he shouts it. But it's Thalia Alaric turns to, and she looks stricken, and angry, and must have asked the same thing. The parchment, when Alaric lifts it, trembles slightly.

"Because," he says, "our people already think I'm failing them, and Diedrick has threatened to attack if I don't accept. He will curse me publicly as a coward, unfit to be king, and declare himself the rightful ruler with the Northlands' best interests in mind. He has already won, if I refuse."

"At least appoint a proxy," Coll says, and spreads his hands before curling one of them into a fist. "Hells, Alaric, I'd be glad to beat him within an inch of his life, and spit in his smarmy face!"

"As would I," Erik adds, but Alaric shakes his head at both of them.

"The challenge specifies it must be me. Besides," he adds, mouth twisting, "perhaps I should thank him. This may be the only way to prove myself to our people."

There's a desperate flicker of hope on his face, a determination that Finn can almost feel. He sighs. *There's nothing we can say to dissuade you, is there.*

"Tell me there's another way," Alaric says, shrugging. "A way to prove myself, with every other person—at least—cursing my name, and more Southlings arriving daily, seeking refuge. We're balanced on the edge of a knife, Finn. But if I can best Diedrick, show them all that I *am* willing to risk everything, to fight for change, for my crown..."

The messages wrinkle as his fingers clench, and Finn looks away, grimacing. His gaze falls on Thalia, who stands very still, troubled eyes huge in a mask-like face. For a moment, he pities her, and almost wishes she were free to choose Erik instead. Alaric's disregard for her has never been clearer, and it's obvious, as she stares at him, that she knows it. Alaric could at least offer her a kind word, some sort of reassurance, Finn thinks. But he doesn't, and it's not Finn's place, or Erik's, or Coll's, to do so in his stead. Thalia bows her head in acceptance and leaves, shoulders stiff as boards, and no one follows her.

After a moment, Erik tears his eyes away from the door. "What's the other?" he asks, gesturing to the missive the Southling brought.

Alaric extends it. "A letter from Garreth, though I've barely skimmed it. It seems things are worse in the Southland than they are here. He and Ellin are fine."

"Well, Alaric," Coll says, out of nowhere, after they've read it over Erik's shoulder, "you'd best win."

The smile Alaric gives him is sharp and somehow wild, reminding Finn unsettlingly of his brother's temper, of late. "I intend to."

Chapter Twenty-Five

IT TAKES US MORE than a week to travel to the coast, slowed by the wagons and the fact that we travel mostly at night. The wagons are full, since only six of the ones we rescued in Harpersfall, and none of the other True Southlings, chose to go with Brendin to the Northlands. Garreth and I ride in Aiddan's wagon, with Freya, Rose, and Brek. This journey is nothing like the last time I traveled with the True Southlings, when laugher and snatches of music flew from one wagon to the next. This time, tension hovers over us like the canopy of changing leaves, and, while the forest prevents the worst of the rain from reaching us, the oppressive weather, cooler every day, doesn't help. Even when it stops raining, the flat, overcast sky glowers down at us.

I learn a great deal from Freya, but as I listen to her, I can't forget that learning to be a Healer is pointless. The thought is a weight dragging at my heart, all the worse because now I know, with certainty, that becoming a Healer is what I want to do.

Eventually, the trees thin, and the countryside grows greener, with rock cliffs standing out sharp-edged against the grass, like bleached bones. The air is wetter here, and though we are still far yet from the sea, I would swear that sometimes I can smell it. Big white birds circle overhead, almost lost against the gray sky. We pass whitewashed houses with red tiled roofs, scrubby trees bent and gnarled from the winds.

We stop periodically to make camp, but there are no songs or stories afterward. Everyone seems subdued, as if, like the pregnant sky, we're waiting. I notice that conversations about the Healers' College trail off when Freya approaches, and sometimes when I do. I try not to think about what it might mean.

I sleep, and eat, and I listen to Freya, and sometimes I drive the wagon after Brek teaches me how, and sometimes I sit with the hard bench bouncing beneath my rear and talk to Garreth. Rose and I sleep on one side of the wagon, our heads together, and sometimes she asks me about Lev. Sometimes, I answer.

I'm almost asleep one morning, after we've stopped to camp in the woods again. I sit bolt upright when I hear a commotion outside, clawing my way out of the narrow bunk. When I poke my head out, I nearly sag with relief to see Marilee dismounting from a dark horse with Mathias and Aiddan already at her side. Though I'm sore and tired, I climb out of the wagon, with a rumpled-looking Garreth not far behind.

"They're nearby," Aiddan says, when we approach. "Go back to sleep, if you can, for a little while. We'll meet when everyone has rested and the commander is here."

"Who is the commander?" Garreth asks around a yawn.

"Go back to sleep," Aiddan repeats, waving him toward the wagon as if Garreth is Brek's age. "No doubt many of your questions—and mine—will be answered later."

Lying in my warm bunk a moment later, knowing it's morning outside and hearing the others breathing, I don't think I'll be able to go back to sleep. But I close my eyes, and the next thing I know, I see bright sunlight out the front of the wagon, and hear voices, and a quick glance around the wagon tells me that, other than Brek, lying sprawled with one arm hanging off his bunk and snoring, I'm the only one still in bed. With a muffled curse, I comb my fingers through my hair and tighten the laces on my dress, then do my boots up in a hurry.

When I jump down from the wagon and brush off my skirt, my hand freezes, and I'm not sure which startles me more: the sight of Garreth deep in conversation with a girl...or the fact that, from the back, her bushy tail of ginger hair looks eerily familiar. It can't possibly be. The last time I saw her, Kethrinn Brewer was being taken away to prison in the Northlands, glaring daggers at me. I never expected to see her again, and certainly not here. Even though Garreth said that Keth and the others escaped, I never would have expected her to rejoin the True Southlings.

But when I move closer, tensing with every step, I see the side of her face, the tip of her sharp nose, and hear her voice. Mathias jogs up and asks her something, then gives her a nod of respect when she answers. Oh, surely not.

Ducking my head, I veer off course and head for Aiddan, where he sits with a plate balanced on his lap. "Aiddan, of all people, tell me she's not the commander," I snap.

He sets down a half-eaten piece of cheese; wipes his fingers on his trousers. "You haven't spoken with her?"

"I just woke up." I rub my forehead hard, trying to scrub the idea out of my mind. "Why didn't you tell me?"

He shrugs, mouth full. "It wasn't my place," he says when he's swallowed, "and I didn't want you to leave. As I've said, we have need of someone with your gifts."

"For what?"

His dark eyes seem to look right through me. "Have you considered that, had you been with us last winter instead of fighting against us, we would have won?"

The thought makes me flinch, perhaps because I can't deny the truth of it. Perhaps because I hate the thought of trying to compel any of my friends. Aiddan hastens to add, "You know my feelings about that mission, Ellin. Would it surprise you so much to know that Keth is likewise glad we did not succeed?"

"Why?" I ask bitterly. "Is the new man she's sweet on less ambitious than Lev?" It's a cheap thing to say, but I don't care. Aiddan doesn't dignify it with a reply, and I think I'm grateful for that. He finishes the last of his meal, and stands, and makes a small gesture with the empty plate.

"Talk with her," he says at last. "That's all I ask."

"Watch her try and kill me." He doesn't respond to that, either, beyond the arching of one auburn eyebrow. I sigh, throwing up my hands. "Fine."

———◦◦◦◦)◦(◦◦◦———

As it happens, I don't have a chance to speak with Keth before she calls for everyone to gather and hear her news. I purposely hang back, not wanting to be at the front. Garreth doesn't join me, and sits instead between Mathias and Simon on the other side of the fire. I consider joining Freya and Aiddan, but then I see the look they exchange, the way he touches her wrist, her answering smile. So, I stand alone, arms folded, near some women I don't know well.

Keth doesn't even need to raise a hand for silence. She simply goes to the center of the circle. I notice that there's something different about her. She looks the same as ever, short and small with generous curves, a face that's vivacious rather than beautiful. I note with surprise that she's not wearing her usual amount of cosmetics, and her pale red curls are tied back tightly, and simply, at the base of her neck. But it's the way she moves that's most different, and the way she speaks.

"The Guardians are forming an army in Whiteriver," she says without preamble. In the stunned silence that follows this announcement, the wind ruffles the flame, sends a few fallen leaves skittering past Keth's feet. "As some of you know, I have been working in Whiteriver for weeks, gathering information. And I know this, now: the Guardians and the College are connected. I think the Guardians have control over the Healers Council, and may have for some time. It'd make sense, wouldn't it?" she asks, lifting a hand. "Why else would Healing be the one gift not only permitted but respected?"

I grip my elbows tighter as she tells us that the Guardians' army is comprised mostly of gifted Southlings, prisoners forced to do their bidding. Most of the dorms at the college have been turned into cells and barracks.

Keth doesn't know their plans, doesn't know what the army is for, and when we all discuss it, everyone has a different guess. I'd wager at least a few are right. No doubt the Guardians want to use their army to attack and overpower us. With an army of "tainted" people to terrorize everyone, the Guardians could then establish an iron rule over the Southland, or even invade the Northlands, since even Alaric's soldiers would be no match for those with mental gifts.

The meeting stretches on and grows to include dinner. There's so much to wonder, so many terrible things they might be planning, and we, unfortunately, know so little.

I remain quiet, shaken perhaps more than anyone here—except Freya—at the thought of the Healers Council being involved in this. I'm glad to see Garreth jump in, though. Were it not for his hair, and his accent, I would swear he belongs here. Strange how he seems to care so much about the True Southlings. Or perhaps not so strange, I amend, remembering what Freya said about our powers. Perhaps love and friendship and loyalty don't end at the border. I look at Freya and see, now that I know to look, how the hair at her temples is silver threaded with gold, how her eyes change from blue to green in the light. Perhaps who someone is, and where their home is, isn't so easily labeled, either.

Deep in thought, I hardly notice when someone sits next to me. "I never thought I'd see you again," Keth says at last, in a tone I can't quite decipher.

"I never thought I'd see you here, like this," I reply carefully, still on edge.

She snorts quietly and looks at her hands. They're not as smooth as they used to be, and her nails are nibbled short. I remember when she stopped doing that. Remember her mother scolding her for it. I've braided her hair and diapered her sister, and she would have gladly killed me last winter. If she instead of Lev had been compelling the king, I would have killed her.

"Things have changed, Ellie," she says, and the name I haven't heard or used for so many years tells me she remembers, too. The smile that curves her lips is as tentative as I feel. "I've changed."

"Not too much, I hope," I reply. "I have, too."

At that, she laughs, though there's a hitch in it. "Well, I can see that, you goose. What did you do to your *hair*?"

I laugh, too, until I'm not sure I'm not crying. But even if I am, I don't mind.

CHAPTER TWENTY-SIX

THE WEEK AFTER Alaric sends his letter of acceptance passes too quickly, with the entire city in an uproar. Preparations begin the moment word is out, and, several days before the match, every inn in town is full to bursting, the streets brightly lit, strung with colored lanterns. The mood is festive as a carnival, and Finn knows it will only be worse at the match itself.

There's no chance of Alaric changing his mind, and Finn doesn't bother trying to talk him out of it, especially since he's still likely to take someone's head off for nothing. Coll spends the week training with Alaric, and the two of them circle one another in the yard with their sleeves rolled up, red-faced, neither giving an inch if they can help it. Erik spends the week entertaining Thalia, now as indifferent to Alaric as he is to her and not bothering to hide it.

Finn spends more time than usual at the college with Master Thorvald the Physician, avoiding all of them. The evening before the fight, the doors of every tavern are open wide, ale and whiskey flowing freely. Finn goes to bed early, hoping for rain, and isn't at all surprised, as he lies awake in the sleepless dark, that Erik doesn't return until just before dawn.

The morning sky is clear and brilliant, warm as spring, with a pleasant breeze. After breakfast, they ride out in procession: young Sven and some of the other stable boys walking before, carrying the standards: blue and white of the royal house, and Alaric's crimson and gold. After them comes Alaric, with Coll at his side. Finn and Erik follow, and Finn hopes that Erik looks better from a distance than he does up close, red-eyed and grimacing. Most of the Guard joins them when they approach the gates, falling in behind Erik and Finn, the Riders first and then those on foot. They've attracted a crowd, men and women and children trailing behind them like a tail. Finn spends most of the ride staring at the back of Alaric's head.

The appointed meadow is not far outside the city walls, and the vendors start just past the gate, selling flowers, wands with long ribbons, sweets, and meat roasted on sticks and every other kind of treat imaginable. The scents are overpowering, and Finn feels a pang of sympathy when Erik turns green, even if he deserves it.

Wooden stands have been erected at the meadow, tents for each of the fighters. More banners, in Alaric's colors as well as Diedrick's deep blue and rose. The combat square has been paced by both Lord Thomas and one of Diedrick's men, its edges marked with stakes and rope.

A crowd has already gathered when they arrive, farmers and merchants and seemingly everyone else come out to watch their king do battle. To cheer for him, or against. Diedrick's people are here, of course, and Diedrick himself, across the square. Tall and yellow-haired, already stripped of his coat, he makes an impressive figure as he practices forms, loosening his muscles. The edge of his blade catches the light, and Finn averts his eyes.

When they dismount, Alaric draws the three of them aside. They pass Thalia, arriving with Nan, and Finn expects him to stop and say a few words to her, but Alaric strides past quickly, offering his betrothed only the barest of nods. Her face remains impassive, but when she bows her head to walk on, she reaches up with a harsh gesture to brush tears away.

Alaric orders everyone else out of his tent before turning to his brothers. His face might well be carved out of stone for all the expression it betrays, lines chiseled deep. Coll takes Alaric's coat and folds it over his arm. They stand in a knot, and of course, it's Erik who speaks first, looking more wretched than ever. "Alaric..."

Alaric smiles a little, but without mirth. "Stop acting as if you're at my funeral. I'm going to win."

Coll's face is as hard as Alaric's, his eyes anguished. "Diedrick's known for his skill," he says, "more than either of us, and I'm not sure even Garreth will match him. You've seen him at the tournaments, Alaric. Don't underestimate him. Don't..."

Letting out a long breath, Alaric takes one of Coll's hands between both of his. He looks at Coll, for a moment, before turning so that Finn can see his lips, to include him and Erik in this moment. Alaric's throat bobs, and he closes his eyes, as if gathering strength.

"If Diedrick bests me, if my blood instead of his is spilled today," he says, slowly, "then I will die fighting for something that I believe in. For the honor of our family, and the crown, and the belief that all in the Northlands deserve to live free and equal. I am not Da," he continues, "and perhaps I am not the king he was, but I am king, now, and I believe—I know—that what I have done is right." He smiles again, and this time it reaches his eyes, which are clearer and more peaceful than they have been in weeks. "The sun is shining," Alaric says, gesturing to the tent flap, "and I will fight well, and you're with me. It's a good day."

He squeezes Coll's hand again and lets go only to step forward and embrace him, saying something next to Coll's ear that Finn can't see. Then, he moves to Erik and does the same, after which Erik turns away, face contorted.

Alaric comes to Finn, and takes his hand as he did Coll's, for a moment, before raising them to speak. *"Know that I love you,"* Alaric says simply. He adds a few things more, words Finn can't dwell on now but knows he will never forget, should he need to remember. And then Alaric embraces him, and his breath brushes Finn's hair, perhaps saying more, for himself, perhaps only breathing.

"We'll see you when it's over," Finn says, when Alaric releases him. *"Fight well."*

When they leave the tent, as the sun climbs and the hour of the match approaches, Finn doesn't look back.

Chapter Twenty-Seven

I'M NOT SURE THAT bringing out a cask of whiskey after dinner was a good idea. Though everyone still has their wits about them—it's too dangerous not to—the arguments have grown steadily louder and more impassioned. I'm sure I'm not the only one feeling utterly frustrated.

The few days we've been camped outside Whiteriver have been a strange mixture of dull and terrifying. I know everyone is unsettled, having the Guardians' mysterious army so close. Having the Guardians themselves so close. It doesn't help that there's so little we can do.

We've made several clandestine trips into the city, to gather what information we can. Keth divided some of us into teams, the first night she was here, according to ability and experience, each group comprised of at least one strong compeller and two fighters. Keth went into Whiteriver once with Marilee and Jaysen. Garreth and I went, too, under Mathias' lead. To my surprise, softspoken Simon is as skilled at compelling as anyone I've met, and he was more than willing to take a turn spying, with Alma and Cedran to guard him. The good thing about Whiteriver is that, on the crowded streets, in a city housing an army of gifted Southlings, we've been free to use our abilities without fear that the hounds will notice us. The bad thing is that none of us discovered anything useful.

Not, at least, until Simon's group returned and told us just how large the Guardians' army is. And we knew, with heartsick certainty, that we're hopelessly overmatched. It only got worse on Keth's group's second trip, when Marilee saw some members of the Healers Council in one of the college courtyards, helping to drill the soldiers. And Keth, dressed as a maid again, sneaked inside and found that the cellars have been turned into dungeons.

They returned early this evening, hollow-eyed, and the debates haven't stopped since they told the rest of us what they saw.

Across the fire, Marilee shakes her head at Alma and stands, face troubled. "Before anything else, we should plan a rescue," she states, loud enough to carry. "How can we consider an attack when we'd be fighting our own?"

Several others, including Simon, nod their agreement, but Mathias gestures sharply sideways, then takes a drink. "A rescue mission isn't an option, and you well know it," he says. "Into the College itself, where who knows what they're doing? You'd have to be mad."

"He's right," Keth interjects, looking tired. There are violet shadows beneath her eyes, and, like me, I don't think she's had anything but tea to drink tonight. She spreads her hands. "You're both right, in a way. I don't think we can act at all yet," she says, and waits for the babble to fade before she continues. "There aren't enough of us, and we don't know enough, yet. This may well be the most important blow we ever strike against the Guardians. May, perhaps, be the definitive blow. We can't afford to make a mistake."

Beside me, Garreth drains his cup and stands. His eyes are bright; his cheeks flushed, though I don't think he's had much to drink. His gaze settles on Keth, and one of his sinewy hands curls into a fist at his side. "I would propose a solution," he announces, sounding so like Alaric that I start. "Most of you know that my brother is Alaric the Golden, king of the Northlands. His army is large, and they—we, I mean—are well-trained. We have Riders, and horses to spare, and archers, and skilled swordsmen. They could help, and I think Alaric would recognize this cause as a good one." He gestures as if this should all be obvious. "Why don't some of us ride north and ask him for aid? If we returned with a contingent of Northlanders, the Guardians wouldn't..."

He trails off as murmurs chase one another around the fire, along with more than a few snorts. Someone laughs. Freya doesn't, I notice, but instead watches him with a curiously soft expression. But it's Aiddan who rises to face him and speaks, in a tone as serious as Garreth's offer. "It isn't our place to ask such a favor of your king, Garreth," he says. "It's clear that the Guardians' power is far greater than we knew, and if the Healers Council is with them, who knows what other leaders and elders are under their influence, or working with them? If King Alaric sent his men, he would, effectively, be declaring war not on the Guardians, but on the Southland itself. And that..." he shakes his head, and his hair, tied back with a leather thong, sways slightly. "...that, I think, is not something any of us wants."

"But..." Garreth begins. He stops abruptly when Keth pushes herself to her feet. She tucks a loose curl behind her ear.

"We have no choice but to lie low," she says firmly. "For now, at least. Aiddan's right, we don't want to start a war. Not yet. We will retreat into the Greatwood and continue to find out what we can about the Guardians' plans. And Garreth is right," she adds, smiling up at him. The expression transforms her face, making her look lovelier than I remember her ever being, even with the rouge and tight dresses she used to wear. "We do need reinforcements, and in the morning, I would like volunteers to ride out with messages to our friends. Donnal Marthen should know, and Mistress Blackwood, at least. They know others who might help us. Fight with us, if it comes to that."

Looking at my friends, their faces somber, I think it will, indeed, come to that. With all this talk of fighting, I might despair that I can't, that I won't be useful, were it not for the fact that all of these people have become dear to me. I meet Freya's eyes, and she nods as if to say that there will be a place for us. For Healers. There will be work to do.

A little later, when many are still trying to find courage, or solace, from the whiskey and each other's company, Aiddan sings for us, with Brek accompanying him, for the first time since I've known him. I look up into the dark, watching sparks chase each other, half-listening to Garreth and Keth talking nearby, their voices low. I realize that this, too, is a kind of healing. Another gift, just as important as compelling, or true healing, or skill with a weapon. I realize how much we're all needed, with all of our different skills.

CHAPTER TWENTY-EIGHT

BY THE TIME Alaric and Diedrick take their places in the square, the sun shines down white and fierce, more like midsummer than autumn. Coll shrugs out of his coat and puts it over his arm, on top of Alaric's. The back of his shirt is damp. On Finn's other side, Erik's face is parchment-pale and covered with a sheen of sweat, and Finn wonders—but doesn't ask—just how much he had to drink last night. The three of them stand at the front of the crowd, near the square's boundary. There are seats for them next to Nan and Thalia, but, by unspoken agreement, they remain here. The crowd presses close, so loud Finn can feel the air and earth vibrating with their shouting and stomping and clapping. On all sides of the square, people are waving ribbon streamers, scarlet and yellow and green and blue, trailing them in the wind. Waving pennants, scraps of cloth tied to sticks. Children run everywhere, little girls with flowers in their hair, boys and girls both with their mouths stained from sweets.

Someone walks past with a garlicky meat pie, and Erik presses the back of his hand against his mouth. Any other time, in other circumstances, Finn and Coll would doubtless bet on the likelihood of him puking. They'd laugh, and joke, and buy some food and enjoy the day. Any other time, Alaric would be with them. As it is, they don't speak. The caller, Master Philip, Head of the College, steps out into the middle of the square with measured strides. His white robes draw everyone's gaze, and there is a bugler beside him, presumably blowing for silence.

Coll still seems rooted to the ground, Erik still fighting sickness, so Finn doesn't turn to either of them and instead watches Master Philip as he gestures to the square, to Alaric, and to Diedrick. It's easy to imagine the formal words he's speaking, for the matches have been the same for generations.

Those who paced the square are named, its size described, the combatants cautioned not to leave it until the match is called, lest their honor and lives be forfeit. No one may enter the square to assist one of the fighters before the match is called, or they will bring shame upon their name and upon the one they would aid. This match will be fought with longswords, and each combatant has inspected the other's blade. At first blood, they may have the option of a recess, should the one who drew it request it as a courtesy.

This match, with the throne of the Northlands at stake, will be to the death. Should one's death be at his own hand, intentionally, he will be declared nameless.

Master Philip bows, first to Alaric as he enters the square, and then to Diedrick, in the opposite corner. The combatants walk to the middle, slowly, and the crowd roars again, shaking the earth. They return one another's blades. Retreat, five paces, and nod to one another.

The bugler's horn glints as he raises it to his lips. Finn's hands tense at his sides, tight fists, thumbs digging into his fingers.

In the center of the square, the fight begins.

CHAPTER TWENTY-NINE

AFTER BREAKFAST, Jaysen, Alma, and Cedran ride out, bearing messages from Keth, and the rest of us pack the wagons and ride deeper into the wood in search of a better campsite. The clearing we find at last is smaller than the one near Harnon, with a beautiful pool nearby, fed by an icy spring. We spend the day setting up camp, and I'm sure, judging by the quiet, that I'm not the only one whose mind is far from her work. Even Brek seems subdued, though he spends part of the afternoon teaching Rose to whistle like different songbirds, and I'm glad to see her smiling. I watch Garreth and Mathias and Simon, stripped of their shirts and sweating as they pitch the tents, and I wonder if Garreth misses being with his brothers. He's made friends here, but there was a note in his voice last night, when he spoke of the Northlands, that makes me wonder.

I miss the Northlands. I find myself wondering what Finn is doing at any given moment, or Erik. I want to tell Coll that he was right, after all, about me using a weapon. I wonder if Alaric and Thalia have wed yet, and, to my surprise, my heart aches less at the thought than I would have expected. It still hurts, a dull, secret throb I'm not sure will ever go away. I don't know if I'll ever be able to forgive him entirely. Don't know if I want to.

By the time the camp is set up with a fire built and dinner cooking, it's almost evening. Sunlight slants through the trees, liquid, honey-amber, casting long shadows. When I go to wash my grimy hands in the pool, I find Keth already there, an empty bucket beside her. Sitting at the water's edge, green skirt pooled around her, a shaft of light turns her ginger hair to gold. Her fingers look white, dangling in the dark water.

"I didn't know you were here," I say as I join her. Kneeling, I rinse my hands, savoring the cold.

"I needed a moment. It's so beautiful here."

"I can leave you alone." I start to stand, but Keth shakes her head.

"No, stay." She lifts her hand, watching the sparkling droplets fall. "I was just thinking. Ellin, do you think I'm doing the right thing?"

I settle myself in the grass. Smooth my hands over my skirt. "I think so," I reply at last. "I don't see that we have another choice. Attacking the Guardians would be beyond foolish."

"I know." But it's said in a small, quiet voice, and she sounds very young. She reaches for a fallen leaf, orange with yellow blotches, and leans forward to float it on the pool's surface. "I keep wondering what Lev would do. Keep thinking that he would have a better plan." Her fingers find another leaf, this one brownish, and begin to shred it.

I don't know what to say, and after a long moment, she looks at me. Her eyes are as green as the leaves overhead, and as shadowed. "Where is he?" she asks. "Is he still…?"

Stricken, I can't believe I haven't told anyone yet that he died. I meant to, I'm sure I meant to, but it hurts so badly, even now, and…

I find a leaf to pick at, too. It seems impossibly long ago that Keth and I used to collect them, searching for hours for the prettiest ones. There's a red one, perfectly shaped and brilliant scarlet, beside my knee. I drop it on the pool; watch it float away.

"He—Keth, he died," I manage, strangled. I try to say it gently, but I don't think I succeed.

I think she must have at least suspected, because she doesn't cry out, or gasp, or even move, for a moment. Very slowly, her face crumples, and her hand falters up to cover her mouth. "How?" she whispers, muffled, shaking.

I tell her, and by the time the first words leave my lips, I'm in tears, too. After I'm finished, we sit by the pool until the light fades, mourning him. On the black surface, smooth as glass, the leaves float lazily, circling one another but never touching.

CHAPTER THIRTY

PREDICTABLY, DIEDRICK MAKES the first move, a vicious downward slice that Alaric meets and disengages from in one smooth motion. They circle, both hands clenching the hilts, boots darting, lunging as their blades cross and separate with raptors' speed. And now, Finn knows, they are only testing one another. Alaric's brows are drawn together, a tense line between them. Diedrick is shorter, and fairer, with a sunburnt nose and hard eyes. He throws off Alaric's blows seemingly effortlessly, quick as a cat, and as graceful. Alaric's style is harder-edged, less flashy, subtler and brutally effective.

The blades reflect a thousand suns. Their feet kick up dust in the short grass. The noise of the throng presses like a wall; Coll and Erik press against Finn on either side. Colored ribbons snake in the wind.

The contest goes on, and there seems to be a rhythm to it, the pounding earth and their pounding feet and the measured strokes of steel. The fighters' faces are red in a matter of moments, their hair damp with sweat. Sweat trickles down Finn's neck, too, and he can smell it from everyone. Salty taste on his lips and bitter fear in his mouth. Coll moves slightly, almost imperceptibly tensing and shifting his weight, mirroring Alaric's motions—no doubt without realizing he's doing it at all.

Finn turns to Erik; finds him riveted to the fight. Erik glances over, and there's fear in his eyes, though his lips twitch in an attempted smile. *"He's doing well,"* Erik says, and gives a small nod meant to indicate the people. *"They're cheering louder for him. A lot of them are."*

In the square, they've moved in closer, with shorter, tighter strokes. Faster, too. Finn looks away, shoving hair out of his eyes. *"I hate this. Erik..."*

Erik jerks as if burned and whirls to face the field, and Finn does too, and sees Alaric down. Can't see more than that, can't see any blood, but his heart has stopped and it's too bright and he grabs Erik's arm. *"What happened?"*

Erik shakes his head tersely. *"I didn't see."*

"Diedrick kicked Alaric's feet from under him," Coll says. Finn has never seen him so furious, red-faced, his eyes wild, jaw flexing. *"Then jabbed him while he was down to get first blood. I'd like to break his frigging neck, the cheating bastard."*

"He's granted the recess, though," Erik points out, and Finn wonders why they aren't speaking aloud until he realizes it must be too loud to hear. Most of those in the stands are on their feet, now, to get refreshments and gossip, the better to see as Alaric climbs to his feet and brushes himself off while Diedrick watches, smirking.

Alaric raises a hand to them but doesn't come over. He accepts water and drinks; checks his wound, briefly, and dismisses it with a shrug. All too soon, they prepare to resume, and Alaric, holding his sword in one hand, pushes his fingers through his sweat-darkened hair. Finn's heart twists.

They begin again, and this time, Diedrick clearly has the upper hand. He moves faster than ever, striking quick with uncanny precision, while Alaric lags. Coll grips Finn's arm, just above his elbow, hard enough to bruise. Finn glances over, but Coll doesn't meet his eyes, watching the fight with a face like stone.

Alaric and Diedrick have eyes only for one another. One of them will not leave the square alive. The ground is shaking, tiny shocks traveling up Finn's bones.

Seeking escape, he looks upward and finds peace, for a moment, in the hot blue sky. Breathes deep, and it isn't hard to remember another day, another time. He remembers, vividly, sitting on the wall eating an apple, not quite ripe and pleasantly sour, watching his Da and Alaric sparring in the yard. It was a morning like this one, and Alaric was perhaps fourteen, and they were laughing as they jibed one another. Their strokes were graceful until Alaric started pressing his luck, looking cocky, and Da disarmed him with a trick that sent his sword spinning and landed him on his rear.

Finn remembers laughing at the look on Alaric's face, the wink Da turned and gave him. Erik came running into the middle of the yard, then, shirtless and skinny, and demanded to learn the trick along with his oldest brother.

It said something, Finn thinks, about both Da and Alaric, that they switched to wooden blades and taught him.

He remembers other times, as well: the mock-tournaments the five of them used to have out in the meadow, Alaric and Coll practicing mounted combat as boys, bruising one another until Nan forbade it. Alaric joining the Guard at sixteen; coming home in his blue coat and lording it over the rest of them until they couldn't stand it.

Coll's hand tenses, and Finn jerks his gaze back to the square. He's not the swordsman his brothers are, but it's easy to see that Diedrick is pressing his advantages, focusing his attacks on Alaric's wounded side. Blood stains the arm of Alaric's shirt, spreading, and his face has gone pale.

They continue, blades meeting high, then low. Up. Down. Pivot. Back and forth, and the grass is trampled beneath their feet, and Finn can see their chests rising and falling as they breathe hard. He's breathing shallowly himself, each rapid heartbeat seeming to thrum along his skin. Alaric's face contorts with concentration, and the sinews on his neck stand out.

But he's being pushed back, defending more than attacking, and it's obvious, from Diedrick's feral sneer, that he knows it. Coll might snap his arm, in a moment, but Finn doesn't care. It might be the only thing keeping Coll from charging into the square. Might be the only thing keeping Finn from doing the same, come to that.

Then Coll leans forward, as if he can see something no one else can, and, a moment later, the air and earth throb with noise. Something subtly shifts, and somehow, somehow, Alaric's blade quickens. Teeth bared in a ferocious grimace, he bursts from the corner Diedrick has backed him into and rains a flurry of blows on his cousin. His feet scarcely seem to touch the ground, and he moves with grace and speed that are stunning and unexpected, even for Alaric, brilliant and best as he is.

In this moment, he is the best, better by far than Diedrick. And it's clear that both of them know it. Diedrick falters, tension creeping into his face, his motions becoming jerky, desperate...

Alaric, in the center of the square, suddenly throws his arms open wide, clumsily, sword in one hand and his middle defenseless. Finn's heart leaps, and he clutches Erik's wrist blindly even as Coll lets go of his arm and pounds him on the back with joy...

And Diedrick, valiant, ambitious, *stupid* Diedrick falls for it and lunges.

Alaric's blade sweeps inward; makes an intricate twist almost too fast for the eye to follow...

Everyone is on their feet, doubtless screaming their throats raw, as Finn is, at the sight of Diedrick sprawled on his backside, his sword halfway across the square, impaled in the dirt, still swaying.

Alaric strides forward to deliver the killing blow. Finn doesn't breathe. Doesn't think anyone else does, either. And Alaric walks past Diedrick. Bends and picks up the other man's blade, then holds both swords aloft, one in each hand, facing the crowd. Even at this distance, even though Alaric's face is somber, Finn can see that he's doing all he can to suppress a triumphant grin. Alaric turns his head, shouting something, and Erik shakes Finn's hand off.

"*He told them to call it!*" Erik exclaims. "*And—wait a minute...*"

In the square, Master Philip, the bugler, and several members of the Guard approach Diedrick, who lets himself be hauled to his feet, seemingly resigned to his fate. Alaric speaks near Master Philip's ear, and the Master gestures at the bugler to sound for silence.

When Master Philip begins to speak, Erik turns to Finn again, eyes wide, something like awe on his face. *"Alaric's going to let him live. And stay in the Northlands, and keep his properties—everything. He'll be blinded, but that's all."*

"That's generous." And wise, Finn sees, noticing how many people are nodding, looking as impressed as Erik, throwing ribbons and flowers into the square to show their approval. Even Diedrick's formal bow seems more than perfunctory before he is led from the square.

Finally, it is finished. The instant Alaric steps out of the square, Coll rushes him, lifting him off his feet in a bone-crushing embrace. When Coll finally releases him, beaming and near tears, all at once, Alaric is laughing, gasping for breath as he clutches both Erik and Finn to him.

Alaric steps back at last, and a change comes over his face. His smile becomes softer, and he half-runs to Thalia as she approaches. He clasps both of her hands in his, then embraces her, pressing his cheek against her curls. Thalia looks shocked, but then her arms curve around him. When they separate a moment later, her smile is tentative at first, but then widens, bright as the sun.

—ooo-}◎{-ooo—

By the time they return to the city, it is late afternoon, with light gilding the edges of buildings. Fitting, Finn thinks; Erik says the people lining the streets are cheering the name of Alaric the Golden, the rightful king. Their horses' hooves crush flowers of every color thrown before them, and petals fall like rain from second-story windows.

Even battle-worn and exhausted, Alaric has never looked more like a king. Somehow, sometime between entering the combat square and leaving it again, the weight seems to have been lifted from his shoulders. His smile comes quicker, more genuine, and the lines between his eyes have faded. He looks like himself again, and Finn's heart feels lighter at the sight.

The victory feast is a magnificent affair. The great hall is crowded, tables strewn with flowers, laden with food. A truly impressive cake graces the high table, towering and golden, sugared and dripping with candied fruit, crowned with a wreath of violets.

It's the atmosphere that makes the evening wonderful, a sharp contrast to meals of late. Alaric is jubilant, more carefree than he's been in months, and his mood affects everyone. Finn can't remember the last time he laughed so hard, or Coll did, or Erik's eyes weren't haunted. Thalia seems like a different person, as she was when she arrived, vivacious and confident and charming. This time, however, Alaric seems to appreciate her. He sets a piece of bread down now and looks at all of them, smiling. "I think it's time," he says when he has their attention, and turns to Thalia. "Will you choose a date for the wedding, Princess? Whenever you would like, and it will be so."

Her lips curve into a smile as dusky color stains her cheeks. She looks at the table, lashes lowered, and then back at him. "The middle of autumn, so my family may return home before the weather turns bad. And..." she hesitates, but only for an instant, "...and so that your brother Garreth and Ellin Fisher Healer will have time to return before the ceremony. I'd like for them to be here."

Alaric looks startled before he laughs, teeth white against his beard. "Do you know," he says, "I'd thought of sending a messenger tomorrow, anyway." He places his hand over hers, and for the first time, there seems to be something between them. "A fine match this will be, Nathalia. I'll send someone in the morning. It's time."

"If I may, your highness," Lord Tomas interrupts, from his seat next to Erik. He leans forward, bushy brows twitching. "Perhaps it is too soon for the Fisher girl to return. Your brother, certainly, but I'm concerned that the people will..."

But Alaric cuts him off with a small, sideways motion. He takes a drink. "No, Tomas. I have done great wrong, I admit, but my error was not permitting the Southlings to live here in peace, nor would it be one to welcome Ellin back now. The mistake," he says, "...the mistake I made was not stepping in sooner. Not speaking to the people, explaining why I changed the laws. I asked for peace but gave no one any reason to uphold it or desire it." He shakes his head and looks around the table—at Erik and Thalia, nodding their agreement, and Coll, looking thoughtful. At Finn, watching him closely in order not to miss a word.

Alaric's eyes are clear, his features somber, but determined. He looks strikingly different from this morning, from yesterday, lit from within rather than all harsh lines and haggard shadows. As if, rather than fighting the weight of kingship, he has accepted it and wears it like a crown. It suits him.

"Things will be different, now," Alaric promises. "It's time— past time—for me to rectify the mistakes I've made. To change!" He lifts his glass.

"And a mighty victory," Coll adds, raising his.

Erik gives a half-hearted smile. "And the happy couple."

Their eyes fall on Finn, who shrugs. "*To peace*," he says, and they drink together.

CHAPTER THIRTY-ONE

I SEE A VAST HALL. *By moonlight, long shadows stretch thin on the marble floor. Booted footsteps echo, slow, measured treads. Wind whispers in the corners.*

The smooth pillars gleam like the bones of trees, ghosts captured in stone and frozen. By day, they are beautiful, but in this mix of grays, they are the eerie ghosts of a forgotten forest, all long-fingered, grasping branches, pedestals like gravestones.

Despite the moonlight spilling through the tall, arched windows, the Council's dais is blanketed in yawning darkness. A black-cloaked figure rises from one of the chairs and steps forward.

The dream shifts, and now I see a stone table, rough-hewn, upon which something shines like a star. The one in the black cloak and the booted man are in front of me. The booted man's cape is a middling gray that, in proper light, might be green or blue or brown. He is of average height and build, and could be anyone. He reaches for the shining thing, and light glints sharp on the blade.

"Tch. Careful," the hooded one whispers, voice creaking like old wood. "Cut yourself with that, and you'll regret it in a week."

He sets the knife down. Wipes his hand on his thigh. "A week?"

A nod, and one white finger reaches out to caress the hilt. "Two days before it starts, and a week before it kills. You'll be long gone by the time they start looking for a murderer."

The bell tolls once, twice, three times. Low, liquid booming, as the hooded one sheathes the dagger, then holds it out to the other. The booted man hides it away near his breast.

I wake, shaking and sweating on my cot in the tent, and I hear Marilee shifting restlessly behind me. I climb out of bed and tiptoe outdoors, where the forest is still, dappled silver by the circle moon, every leaf and blade of grass shadowed, knife-edged.

The camp is very quiet, and even at this distance, I can hear the bell at Whiteriver College tolling the hour. One. Two. Three.

CHAPTER THIRTY-TWO

NAN'S EYEBROWS LIFT in surprise when Finn enters the kitchen, and she wipes floury hands on her blue-checked apron. *"What are you doing here?"* she asks. *"I thought all of you were going to the market."*

Finn shakes his head and helps himself to one of the round sweetbiscuits cooling on the table, still warm from the oven. Its aroma is pungent with spices, and he takes a bite before replying. *"Erik and Coll went to hear his speech. And Thalia."* He pops the rest of the sweet into his mouth. *"I've read it already."*

And it's good, the speech Alaric has written, to be given today in the market square. It's brave, too, detailing Alaric's thoughts on Northlanders and Southlings, declaring no one is innately better than anyone else, that their actions define them rather than the color of their hair, or their abilities. Alaric wants the Northlands to be united, not divided by biases and prejudice. He wants the Northlands to be a bastion of strength as well as a place of peace, where everyone lives in freedom.

"Those are for dinner," Nan scolds, when Finn reaches for a second biscuit. She purses her lips as he eats it. "You know, I read it, too," she says, beginning to roll out another lump of dough. She doesn't press, but Finn sighs at the shrewd glance she gives him and lifts his hand in a shrug.

"All right, I'll admit, I didn't care much for being used as an example," he says, with a wry twist of his lips. *"I told Alaric he could leave it in, but I didn't want to be standing there while he said it."*

She rolls her eyes and hands him another sweet. *"Then you've missed the point, love. Your brother's simply pointing out that our differences don't matter."*

But then she turns her back to him and pulls a tray of biscuits from the oven, effectively ending the conversation. If he'd gone to the market, it would have been no different, standing too far away to see Alaric's lips, unsure from the vibrating street whether the crowd was cheering or booing. He smiles at Nan as he goes out, but he thinks that sometimes differences do matter, indeed, when they isolate people from the ones they love. Perhaps Northlanders and Southlings are not so different, but the powers some of them possess are another matter entirely. He suspects Ellin has secrets she keeps even from him and Erik, and he knows he has his own.

---ooo-)◯(-ooo---

Finn has no sooner stepped into the main corridor than the doors burst open and a crowd lurches through, dispersing in all directions. There's an air of panic, and Finn pushes past guards and a few lords to get to Erik, whose face is red with anger. *"What is it? What happened?"*

"Alaric," Erik signs distractedly, looking at the doors. Finn follows his gaze and lets out a breath when Alaric comes through, flanked by Coll and Davor. Erik starts to go to them, but Finn grabs his sleeve.

"What happened?"

"Just after the speech, some bastard threw a knife, and..."

"...And it's nothing," Alaric interrupts. He touches his left arm, where a patch of blood has stained his white shirt just below the shoulder. *"You'll bind it up for me, won't you, Finn?"*

"Of course," he replies, and Alaric follows him to the workroom. They leave the others to join the rest of the entourage in planning an investigation.

Warm sunlight bathes the workroom, the air heady with the scents of herbs. It's a peaceful place, and when the door is closed, Alaric sinks into one of the chairs with a grimace, reaching for the buttons of his shirt. *"It hurts worse than you let on?"* Finn asks, and Alaric makes a face as he struggles out of the sleeve.

"Bad enough. I think it went deep. It stings."

"Let me see." But after he has washed away the blood, he looks at Alaric and shrugs. *"It is deep, but it's a clean cut, and it should heal nicely. It doesn't need to be stitched."*

Alaric nods, seeming distracted, and turns his face away while Finn cleanses the wound. Finn frowns. It's not like Alaric to be squeamish at the sight of blood.

"Here, hold this," he says, instructing him to press a pad of cloth against it. He ties a bandage, then sits back and lifts his brows. *"Other than that, how was the speech?"*

Alaric laughs. *"Until I was pulling a dagger out of my arm, it went well,"* he says dryly. *"Most of them seemed to like it."*

Finn helps him put his shirt back on. The drying stain is a sharp contrast to the white cloth, and it's horrifying to see how close the blade came to burying itself in his brother's chest. A handspan, perhaps less. He touches Alaric's forearm. *"You were lucky."*

A shadow passes over Alaric's face, and he looks at the scarred tabletop as he does his top button. But when he looks up again, he smiles, brushing his fingers over the wound. "I know," Alaric replies, leaving Finn wondering if he imagined that fleeting sadness.

CHAPTER THIRTY-THREE

*B*ANNERS DANCE IN THE *wind, bright against the blue, blue sky. The breeze is sharp, the sun dazzling, midmorning. I watch fallen leaves skitter across the barren earth at my feet, scarlet and orange and dull, dry brown.*

Sunlight gleams on armor, helms and bracers and breastplates, horsetail plumes billowing, the hilts of swords at hips. Four of them carry the bier.

The sun glints upon the helm at his booted feet, caressing the curve of it. Silver on the sword beneath his hands, folded on his chest. Golden on his head. His face is still, eyes closed, but they were blue.

I would scream, but I have no words, no breath left, no tears. I can't move. I stare as they pass, and their faces are carved from stone, too...

Now someone is singing, and someone is sobbing, and there are stones at my feet. White ones, gray ones, round and piled into a cairn, and I know the fire has burned.

Droplets splash down on the rocks, and thunder rolls in the distance. I close my eyes, and when I look again, flowers are growing from the stones themselves. A scarlet one falls slowly, twirling, and I know that when it comes to rest I will die, too...

I find my voice and scream...

"GARRETH!" I fall out of bed and land hard on my knees, clutching my head and choking back a sob. I know, now, why I chose to become a healer. I know, now, what my destiny is. "GARRETH!"

―――――oooo-)◯(-ooo―――――

Hoofbeats pound, jarring my bones, their rhythm drumming into my skull. We've been riding for days, stopping only to eat and sleep and rest the horses. I put on my trousers, the night we left, and my thighs are rubbed raw. I'm grateful that Coll and Garreth forced me to learn to ride, as much as I can be grateful for anything, right now. I feel like I can't breathe. I remember being afraid of horses, but that seems long ago, and it pales in comparison to the terror that grips me now.

We stop at dusk in a nondescript field. Garreth tends to the horses, then rummages in his pack while I fumble with shaking hands to unroll our blankets. He presses a wedge of cheese and a pear into my hands, and we sit to eat. The pear is juicy, but I can barely swallow it, and it tastes like nothing. We don't speak. He reaches for his flask and drinks; hands it to me, and I do the same.

We lie down, side-by-side, and I think I sleep for a few moments. I try not to, because I don't want to dream. It's even darker when we roll up the blankets and mount up again and ride on. North. It's fortunate that he knows the way. To me, it all looks the same. Featureless grass and road and trees.

The sky turns violet, then pink, and when he looks back at me, his face is as pale as his hair. I don't know how long we've been traveling. The days blur into one another, hours measured from one ride to the next. I wonder, every time we rest, if we will be there in time.

When I woke at the camp, I knew, and I called for Garreth and told him about my dream. We woke Keth and Aiddan at once, and they said that of course we had to go to the Northlands, as fast as possible, in hopes of preventing what I saw. There was no time for goodbyes, though we promised to return, with help, if we can. I felt bad for leaving, but even Keth agreed, readily, that my place is elsewhere.

Garreth and I ride, and the sun is warm on our backs. His hair turns gold, and I try not to weep.

I am Ellin Fisher, and I have chosen to be a Healer. Now, I know why. I am to save King Alaric the Golden of the Northlands from death. And perhaps, in return, he will help the True Southlings who taught me.

Hours pass. Days. We eat, and we sleep, and we ride. And the fate of both my countries rides with us.

———ooo-)◯(-ooo———

Rain pours down in sheets in the Northlands when Garreth and I ride into the castle yard, soaked to the skin and shivering. He half-climbs, half-stumbles down from his mount, but I can't move. My aching muscles and bones have frozen, and I can't even pry my clenched fingers off the stiff, cold reins. When the door opens and light spills out, I turn, and Coll is there, with Erik behind him. Erik goes to support Garreth, and Coll lifts me down, and I cling to him and start crying, for the first time in days, as my knees give out.

He holds me close, and his hand is warm when he cups it to my cheek. I grab his wrist and dare to look up, afraid this is a dream. Afraid it isn't. It takes a moment of croaking to find my shriveled voice. "Coll, is he…"

I hope with every bit of my heart that he won't know what I'm talking about. But I can see it on his face even before he answers. "Not yet. But soon. Come on, girl," he says, voice rasping as though he hasn't slept in days, either. "Let's go inside."

The warmth is almost unbearable after so long out in the wet, and I sway on my feet, clutching Coll for support. "Where is he?"

He shakes his head at me, looking stern. "Dry off and warm up, first. There's time. Can you make it to your room?"

At my nod, he goes to Garreth and I head for the stairs, lurching on legs that don't want to hold my weight. I would go to Alaric anyway, except I don't know where he is. And I know, clutching the wall as I climb the stairs, that Coll is right. I'll be useless until I've thawed out.

My dark room is colder than the hallway, but I barely take stock of my surroundings. It takes forever for my trembling hands to unbutton my shirt, and my sodden clothing clings to my skin.

Gooseflesh prickles all over when I've stripped, and, for lack of anything better, I use the quilt from my bed as a towel. That helps, and dressing in clean, dry clothes is even better. It's been so long since I've worn my own clothing that it feels almost strange to have a shift and dress that fit. By the time I've pulled on thick socks, my teeth are chattering far less violently.

I'm using the blanket to dry my hair when a knock sounds at the door. "Yes?" I call, and it opens to reveal Erik, holding a steaming mug of tea. He sets it down when he steps inside, but even that seems like too long a wait before I can throw my arms around him. He squeezes me back tightly, and my face presses against his chest.

We don't speak. At last, I step back and look at his face, and I see at once that this isn't the Erik I left. This new one is haggard, harder, older. He reaches for the cup. "Drink some of this, and then you'd better come with me. He's..." He breaks off with a choked sound, and I gulp a few hot, steadying mouthfuls. I love tea, but this, like everything else I've had lately, is tasteless.

I follow Erik down the corridor, padding silently in my socks. To my surprise, we go to Coll's rooms instead of Alaric's. A fire blazes in the hearth, with Coll pacing in front of it; Garreth and Finn are perched on the bed. The sight of Finn's face almost breaks me, but we only have time for a quick, fierce embrace. Erik and I join the others, sitting in a row like schoolchildren. Coll faces us, eyes bleak, thumbs hooked into his belt. "You know," he begins, before his face contorts. He scowls and tries again. "You know Alaric is dying." Hearing the words spoken aloud, so bluntly, is like a knife in my heart, but somehow I manage not to cry out. I fumble for Finn's hand and squeeze it hard. His slender fingers grip mine, and somehow, I find strength to listen.

"He's been poisoned," Coll continues, the words falling heavy as stones from his lips. His hair is dull, unwashed, and his clothes look no better. "Getting steadily worse, quickly, for five days, now. At first, we all thought it was a touch of sickness, but..." He swallows and lifts a hand. "There's nothing to be done. He won't even let the physicians see him, today."

"But that's ridiculous!" I burst out. "We don't know it's incurable! I'd wager he hasn't seen a Southling Healer. That's why I came!" I jump to my feet, but Coll steps forward and takes hold of my upper arms.

"You won't, girl." His fingers tighten. "He specifically wanted you not to see him."

"What?" I breathe.

"He said…"

"No!" I try to twist free. "Coll, I have to see him! I can save him, I know it!"

He looks at me, anguished. "Ellin…"

"Let me *go!*" I shout, and whether he's surprised or because Finn comes to my side, I'm not sure, but he releases me. The others rise, too, looking stunned. "Please," I beg, much quieter, feeling as though my heart is being wrung out with every word, "I love him. Please let me go to him."

"Coll," Garreth begins, but Coll silences him with a gesture, sighing.

"Come, then. All of you."

He leads us to Alaric's suite, that used to be their father's. For a moment, I'm disoriented. This could easily be another night, not even a year ago, when Garreth and I hurried down this hallway, and he told me to pull up my hood to cover my telltale Southling hair. I remember the hushed voices, the smells, the sense of inevitability.

I have been in these rooms since then, once, with Erik, when he had to borrow something of his brother's. Early spring, and the windows were open, curtains pulled back to let the sunlight in. A mighty tree stands just outside the window, and its branches were budded and green. I remember, as Erik rummaged in Alaric's bureau, a redbreast lit on one of the boughs and whistled.

That day seems impossibly long ago, or perhaps as if it never happened. The rooms are back to the way they were my first night in the castle, except there are no lords and physicians crowded about the bed, and rain is drumming on the window instead of heavy, muffled snow. It's no different, except that the man on the bed is not a king I fear and despise, but one I love.

His eyes were closed when we entered the bedchamber, but he rouses now, blinking. I draw in a breath at the sight of him, and, next to me, Garreth swears in a whisper. If I didn't know the man lying there is Alaric, I wouldn't recognize him. His skin has a grayish cast, tight and stretched in places and drooping in others, like wax hastily smoothed over bone. His hands on top of the thick blanket are too thin, with their veins standing out. His left arm, where the sleeve of his nightshirt has been pushed up to bare it, is bruised and mottled, black and violet and red, and I shudder at the sight.

My horrified gaze travels back to his face, noting the dark smudges beneath his eyes, the gaunt hollowness of his cheeks. He looks like someone who has been deathly ill for months, not days.

But his eyes, at least, I recognize. Bloodshot and fever-glazed, they meet mine, and my heart flutters sideways, as if it doesn't remember what happened, doesn't realize I've been gone. He wets his cracked lips and turns his head, slowly, to take in all of us. "Garreth," he whispers, thin and brittle. "And Ellin. You're all here."

My feet move forward of their own accord, and I stop abruptly at the edge of the bed, desperate to reach out but just as afraid. "Coll said you didn't want me," I say in a rush, surprised I'm able to form words at all, "but even if you're still angry, please let me Heal you. I can save you, and then I'll go again, but let me..."

His hand twitches, as if he wants to gesture but can't, and his fingers curl instead, the tips of them pressing into his palm. He looks at my face, and then past me, at the others. "Let me speak with Ellin, now," he asks them. "She must be first, before..." he breaks off, coughing, and reaches up his right hand to press a cloth against his mouth. It comes away dotted with blood, and the fit leaves him gasping, but Coll shakes his head as if to say it's all right, it has happened before, as he shepherds the others out. He puts his arm around Garreth's shoulders, and Garreth's face, with the tip of his nose suspiciously pink, tells me he's going to start bawling the moment the door is shut.

I wish I could do the same. But I'm a Healer, so I turn back to the bed and try to remain strong.

Chapter Thirty-Four

THE ONLY SOUNDS in the room are his labored breathing and the rain on the window and the crackling of the fire. My chest feels tight with grief and panic barely held in check. I don't have the slightest idea where to begin, or what to say. Alaric makes a tiny motion, beckoning. "Come, sit," he rasps, eyes never leaving my face. His lips twitch. "I promise, it isn't catching."

The joke makes me want to cry, but I try to smile as I sit on the edge of the mattress, facing him. "Be better if it was," I reply, striving desperately for lightness. "That would be easier to heal. As it is, it might…"

"Ellin, you can't heal me. I won't let you try."

"But why?" I demand. "I've been training in the Southland, learning more about how to use my power, and I'm better now! Mistress Freya taught me how to do deeper healing, on things like your arm, and…"

"No!" His ruined hand reaches out to grip mine. His touch burns, as does his gaze. "Listen to me. Please. My time is short." Then his thumb caresses the back of my hand, and his eyes soften. I lay my other hand on top of his as my heart twists. "Please," he says again, more quietly, "there are things I must say to you."

At my nod, he lets out a rattling breath and inhales with a wheeze. He closes his eyes, and I know he must be gathering strength. "Ellin," he says at last, "do you remember what I told you, about my da dreaming the truth?"

Suspicion prickles like ice along my skin. "Yes?"

He nods against the pillow, still with his eyes shut. I've never noticed before how dark his lashes are. "If he hadn't been born a prince, he would have likely become a Seer. But he *was* the prince, and then the king, and he kept his ability secret, except from those closest to him." He swallows. "As I have, but I've told no one at all. Until now."

My lips tremble, and I press them together, hard, before I can speak. "Alaric, I…"

"Let me finish," he says, squeezing my hand. When he opens his eyes again, it's as if I'm seeing their beauty for the first time. No one else in the world has eyes such deep, sincere blue. "I've known for a long time about this, since months before you left. I've seen my death a hundred times. There have been other dreams, as well, and they all came to pass." He hesitates, breathing shallowly. "I saw you, sometimes. And Thalia, and my brothers. You and a harp, in a forest, and a woman with white hair."

I realize only when I lick my lips and taste salt that tears are running down my cheeks. "I—I saw it too," I stammer. "I thought I was the Seer, because you have to have the healing ability, and—and you healed me, once," I realize, wonderingly. "It was you all along! You did have the gift!"

He looks stricken, at that. "I didn't know," he says, shaking his head against the pillow. His hair is shockingly faded. "If I'd known you shared my dreams, I would have told you more. As it was…" He swallows painfully and blinks, his eyes too bright. "I had to send you away, so you wouldn't try to heal me. So you wouldn't want to. I knew you would fail, and I knew, too, what the people would say if you did."

A gaping hole has been torn in my chest, and it will hurt, very badly, in a moment. I press my free hand between my breasts, as if to staunch the wound. "They'd say I murdered you, like I did King

Allard." I search his face when I realize I missed the important part of what he said. "You didn't really want me to leave?"

He smiles at that, and blinks again, and swears, quietly, when a tear escapes the corner of his eye. His mouth works, and the sight of him struggling not to cry makes my tears fall faster, until I can hardly see. He might look like an old man, like a corpse already, but he is only twenty-six, and he is never going to marry, never going to have children, never...

"Of course I didn't want you to," he whispers. "What I said that day was said in anger, and because I wanted you to be angry with me, so you would go. You have been a great and good friend, Ellin Fisher Healer. You're a part of our family. My sister."

Somehow, the word doesn't chafe as much as it did before. It doesn't matter now; what might have been is unimportant compared to what is. What is important is that I love him, and he loves me, and there is not enough time left.

His free hand lifts, painstakingly, to cup my cheek. I lean into his touch, and his fingertips brush the shorn edges of my hair. "Grow it back," he says, and his voice is weaker, now, and very soft. "For me. Grow it back."

"I will."

He smiles at me and closes his eyes again. "Now, go, and make sure you're somewhere you'll be seen. I don't want anyone to think..."

"I know. I will."

"Send Thalia in, please."

I swallow hard. "I will."

Alaric's eyes remain shut, and I know he's building up strength again, clinging to life with the single-minded determination he's always used for everything else. I don't want to go. His blackened hand is still in mine, and even without using my abilities, I can almost see the poison spreading, and surely, surely there must be something I can do.

His eyes flutter open, and he looks at me, wordless, and I know he knows what I'm thinking. The bone-deep anguish I feel is written on my face, in the trembling of my hands, and I am a Healer, and I can't just leave him to die, and...

"Go," he commands, but gently.

I nod, silent because if I speak I will sob. Before I go, I lean down and press my lips to his. And then I stand, hands limp and useless at my sides. "I love you, Alaric," I tell him. "I've loved you since the moment I saw you."

I hurry for the door before he can see my face crumple, but before I've reached it, I hear his voice behind me, one last time. "Thank you. And farewell."

CHAPTER THIRTY-FIVE

THEY'VE BEEN WAITING in the hall for some time, not speaking,. Garreth started crying as soon as he stepped through the doorway, bending to put his head on Coll's shoulder. Finn looked down and realized he and Erik had taken one another's hands, but he couldn't remember doing so. They joined the others, and the four of them have stood since, shifting slightly but never out of arm's reach.

Years ago, in the autumn, a bard came to stay at the castle. A terrible storm raged one night, rain blowing in sideways and the wind whipping branches into a frenzy. Lightning streaked across the sky, and thunder shook the floors. The bard sang the most frightening songs he knew, about great beasts and angry spirits of trees, nameless horrors stalking the mountains' icy peaks. They all sat raptly, hanging onto his every word, but at bedtime, Finn and Erik lasted only a few moments alone, even with a candle lit. They were six years old, and they raced, jumping at shadows, into Coll's room, only to find that he'd already fetched Garreth from the nursery and had his dog and Garreth in bed with him. Finn and Erik crowded in. A little later, Alaric poked his head in the door and laughed at all of them. But he stayed, and he and Coll made shadow-animals on the wall, and none of them were afraid because they were together.

Finn sighs and stares at the floor, unable to reconcile the Alaric in his memory with the way his brother looks now. A curious numbness surrounds him, and he knows Erik and Coll feel it as well, and Garreth, perhaps, will soon. There's a sense of urgency, a need to keep busy, along with the terrible certainty that there will be time to grieve later. For now, there are more important things.

Erik nudges him, and he looks up to see Ellin coming out of Alaric's room. She buries her blotchy, tearstained face in her hands and stands in the middle of the hallway, sobbing. She must say something, because Erik nods. "*Thalia,*" he translates, before sprinting for the stairs.

When they return, and Thalia has gone in to Alaric, Ellin wipes her face on her sleeve and comes to stand near them. She crosses her arms blankly over her chest and stares at nothing.

After several moments, Thalia rejoins them, on the verge of tears as well. She takes a visible breath and looks at Coll with hollow eyes. "He wants to see you now. Garreth first, and then all of you, together."

Finn swallows as the nebulous terror becomes sharp, and very real.

When Garreth goes in, Coll puts a hand on Ellin's shoulder and one on Thalia's. "Go," he says. "Both of you. Nan is waiting in the kitchen to make sure you're seen, tonight."

Ellin and Thalia share a glance. It's strange, Finn thinks distantly, how two such different women can wear such similar expressions as they nod, almost as one. When they, too, have gone, it isn't long before Garreth pokes his head out and gestures. And they go in, so that the five of them can be together.

CHAPTER THIRTY-SIX

I N THE KITCHEN, Keeper Nan embraces both of us, her face tear-streaked and red. "They've gathered in the Hall," she says thickly. "We'll sit there, my dears."

She forces fresh mugs of tea on both of us, which I don't want and suspect Thalia doesn't either, but the warm cup does help still my shaking hands. The great hall is crowded with lords and ladies, Masters and Mistresses, all sorts of important people from the city and the college. And messengers, of course. All waiting, no one daring to speak above a whisper.

Nan leads us to the end of a long table, and nearby, I spot Master Thorvald the Physician, as well as Davor, sitting with some other members of the Guard. Thalia sits first, and I take a seat next to her. We sip our tea in silence until she sniffles, and I realize that she's crying. Hesitantly, I edge closer and put my hand on her shoulder. "I wish things had been better for you." I mean it sincerely, despite everything.

"I wish…" She breaks off with a ragged sob and shakes her head and puts her arm around my waist. And we sit, clinging to one another for a long time. The soft whispers around us fade to silence as the hours stretch thin.

In the quiet, the booted footsteps out in the hallway seem to echo, and Thalia and I both stiffen. We don't let go of one another's hands. Her fingernails dig into my skin. When Erik appears in the doorway, I bite my lip and taste blood.

"The king is dead," he says flatly, but loud enough to carry. I wonder if anyone else notices his white-knuckled grip on the doorframe. "Honor to Alaric the Golden, mighty and fallen. Honor to Coll Horse Master, the king."

In the wailing and exclaiming that follows, Erik beckons to us. "Coll wants to see all of us," he says when we go to him. "Come on."

He leads us to Alaric's study, where Garreth is feeding a newly-lit fire with shaking hands, and Coll and Finn are standing, looking blank.

"Sit," Erik says, pushing Coll toward the chair behind the desk. "And Thalia..." he gestures to one of the seats before it. "Ellin, you take the other."

"No," I say, picking my way on unsteady feet to fetch liquor from the cabinet, and glasses. "You can have it." I pour for all of us, sloshing a little, then sit with my legs folded in front of the hearth, next to Garreth. I shudder at the warmth on my back, and when Finn sits beside me, I lace my fingers with his.

To my surprise, it's Coll who breaks the silence, after he has drained half his glass in one swig. "I never wanted this," he says hoarsely, splaying a hand on a wrinkled map. His mouth works. "I was never supposed to be..."

"None of us were," Erik says bitterly. "Not without him."

"The best of all of us," Finn adds. We raise our glasses, at that, and drink to him.

His body is growing cold and stiff. Still upstairs in bed, I think, unless they've already begun to prepare him, and I did nothing to prevent this. I call myself Healer, and yet...

I drink deeply, welcoming the burn in my throat, since it distracts me from the crushing grief threatening to overwhelm me if I let it. If only I let this sink in.

"I wish I'd had the chance to know him better," Thalia murmurs, and I close my eyes.

"Then tell me," I said. We were in the kitchen, and there was a different dead king, and Alaric looked as stunned as I feel now. *"Remember what you loved best about him."*

But Thalia doesn't ask, and I don't think anyone wants to speak his name aloud, just yet. We sit in silence and wipe our faces when we think the others aren't looking, holding back the worst of our tears.

After awhile, Garreth turns to poke the fire, and Finn refills our cups. "Strange," Coll says at last, in an odd tone, "how something so small could do this."

I look up, stunned to realize I don't know. "How did it happen?"

Coll grimaces, and it's Erik who answers. "He was giving a speech, and someone threw a knife. The blade was poisoned."

My fingers spasm around my cup as ice slithers down my back. "And, two days later, he was ill."

"Yes," Erik replies. "That's why we didn't—what's wrong?"

The room spins as I stand and stumble to the desk. "Coll." My tongue feels thick, and I know it has more to do with shock than the drink. I clutch his hand urgently. "Was the hilt plain, dark wood, with a circle burnt onto the top?" He raises his eyes to mine, obviously startled, all the answer I need. "I know who did it," I gasp. "The Guardians in the Southland, at the college in Whiteriver. I saw it in a dream."

Behind me, softly, Garreth begins to speak. "Remember?" he asks. "Alaric told us in this very room. Da had a dream in which the Southland was a beast with no name. It rose up and caught the wolf that was the Northlands unaware, and swallowed it whole."

"The beast has sharp teeth," Finn says, obviously furious, *"and a long reach."*

"We didn't prevent it? I thought…" Erik shakes his head, draining his glass.

"No," Coll says, and he rises, fists balled on the desk. Though his face is still haggard with grief, there's a difference in his tone, his eyes, in the way he stands. He looks like a king. "Its teeth may be sharp, but we have swords, and can slay it. We're going to war."

———◦◦◦-◗◎◖-◦◦◦———

After Alaric is laid out for three days, like his father, the funeral happens as I had seen it. The day is cool and pleasant, and colored banners line the streets as his brothers, clad in armor, carry his bier through town and out the gates, to the place where their father was burned, and his father before him, and all the kings and queens of the Northlands back through time.

Thalia and I stand together, wearing black, and watch them light the pyre.

Afterward, the procession moves to the cairn that has been built to honor him. Laments are sung and words spoken, and everyone files past, some touching the stones, others leaving flowers or tokens upon them. Thalia and I are last, save for his brothers, and when my turn comes, I kneel and bow my head. The stone I touch is cool and smooth beneath my palm, and I remember him. And I miss him.

When I open my eyes, I find that tears have dripped from my chin, making dark, wet spots on the pale stones. Next to me, Thalia's breath hitches, and when I look, I find her lips moving, whispered words I cannot hear. She tosses the scarlet chrysanthemum she's brought for him, and it twirls as it falls, landing silently beside my hand.

I lay my gift next to it, a bundle of healing herbs bound with a few strands of my hair. And then I stand, and brush off my skirt. I tilt my face to the morning sun, which shines down warm and golden in a cloudless blue sky.

CHAPTER THIRTY-SEVEN

IT IS SEVERAL WEEKS before the numbness begins to fade, and most of autumn passes us by in a glorious blur of color. Barrels are filled with apples and root vegetables, and the aromas from the kitchen become warm and spicy, but for days upon days, everything I eat tastes like parchment, like nothing. I go about my work, harvesting and drying herbs, preparing medicines for the coming winter, but at the end of each day, I can barely remember doing any of it. I sleep dreamlessly but never wake rested, and I know it is the same for the others. We're very quiet when we're together, as if we're all afraid of speaking, lest someone's wounds be opened.

Then it begins to rain as autumn settles in, and winter's bony fingers start to reach. The leaves lay scattered, sodden and brown, blown off balding trees by cold and blustering winds. I think the chill wakes all of us.

I go downstairs early, planning to take my breakfast at the small table in the kitchen, alone. To my surprise, Coll is there ahead of me, staring into a mug of tea with an empty porridge bowl beside him.

"Morning," I say, hushed because the hour calls for it, and touch his shoulder in passing. "How are you?"

The king of the Northlands waits for me to get my own tea and join him. "I've set a date for the coronation," he says, which answers my question well enough. "In ten days' time."

"That's enough time to send messengers out?"

"It's usually within two weeks of…" He swallows. "Besides, the fewer that come, the better by me. I don't want a big affair."

"No," I agree, and smile a little. "If you had your way, it'd be held in the barn, with no guests but horses and your brothers and the guards, and nothing but ale, would it not?"

Coll chuckles. "Foolish girl, you're forgetting that I'd have beef and bread, cheese and soup, and I'd let dogs and cats come. And a few women, good ones, with brains in their heads."

"Dogs, cats, and a *few* good women?" I say archly. "Truly, you have a way with words. And women, for that matter."

"Don't get your back up," he replies, spreading his hands. "I've no friends in the guard who are idiot brutes or sly cowards, either. A man's got the right to choose his friends wisely, and I doubt you'll fault me for valuing a woman's mind over her face."

"'As your friend, I'm not sure I should be flattered by that."

"Hmph," he replies, but he winks at me over the rim of his mug before sobering. "But it's not to be. It'll be an affair, and I suppose we'll all get through it."

I take a sip of my tea, avoiding his eyes. "I hate to be the one to say it, but maybe we should try to enjoy it, at least a little. I don't like big celebrations either, but we all need to remember how, Coll. I know he wouldn't have wanted us to…"

I'm very conscious that I've just told the king it's time to stop grieving the brother who held more than half his heart. I expect anger, or silence, but instead he gives me the ghost of a smile when I dare to look up. "I know," he says simply. "That's why I've set the date."

———∞∞-)◦(-∞∞———

By midmorning, the drizzling rain has stopped, leaving fog and a dull sky in its wake. Indoor weather, as far as I'm concerned, a day for holing up in my workroom and doing some small, cozy job. I'm settling in to do just that, with a stack of labels to be written and tied to bottles, when I hear shouting and pounding from the yard below. Leaning out the window, I'm startled to see Erik and

Finn sparring with quarterstaffs. I grin and hurry out, grabbing my shawl on the way.

"What in the world are they doing?" I call above the din, joining Thalia on the wall that borders the paved yard.

She smiles in welcome, cheeks flushed from the cold. "They got it into their heads at breakfast to train together. And I'm glad. I have not heard Erik's laugh in too long."

I glance sideways at her, wondering yet again if there is truth to what Finn told me he suspects, that she might have chosen a different brother, had she been free to choose. But I don't ask. Thalia and I have become friends since I returned to the Northlands, brought together by our sorrow about Alaric and our desire to help his brothers heal. Even so, I'm not quite comfortable discussing love and men with her. Or anyone, really.

"Have you seen Coll today?" I ask instead, and she nods.

"The coronation, yes. I'm glad of that, too."

There's something odd in her voice, and my eyebrows lift as I turn to her. "What's wrong?"

Thalia shakes her head, looking at her clasped hands. "It's nothing. But I wonder if Coll will declare his intent to marry me in Alaric's place, or to send me home. I can't say either option would please me."

I take a deep breath. Obviously I'm going to have to discuss men sooner than I would have liked. "Oh. Well. You could ask him, I suppose. Or ask Erik to speak with him, if you and Erik have discussed..."

Her eyes widen, and I silently curse myself for sticking my nose in it. "Is it so obvious?"

"Oh, Thalia, no. It's only that you and Erik seem to get along well, and I assumed..."

Blushing a little, she shakes her head. "Erik and I haven't discussed anything, though his heart is in his eyes when he speaks to me, and I'm certain we both feel it. But it's far too soon for me to consider—I *did* care for Alaric—and I will marry Coll, if he asks it, to strengthen the alliance between our peoples."

"If many of your people are like you, they must be very strong already," I say, feeling a swell of renewed respect for her. "I don't know how you can bear to be told who to marry."

"It's not what I would wish, but it is my duty." She lifts a hand, palm up. "But I am fortunate. I would have been happy with Alaric, and truly, any of his brothers would make a good husband. In their own ways, they are all kind, and honorable. I like them all very much."

"But liking someone isn't the same as loving them."

"No," Thalia agrees, and with a small sigh, she turns to watch Erik and Finn, still circling, blocking each other's attacks. "I envy you your freedom to choose."

"But I don't have..." I begin, and then I realize, from her pointed nod and arched eyebrow, who she means. I must be gaping at her, because after a moment, her amused look turns to one of alarm.

"Surely you knew. Oh, no. Ellin, I didn't mean..."

It takes an enormous effort to breathe. "I—I knew," I reply at last, when I can speak. Strangely, I realize it's true. I've never thought about it before, never acknowledged it, but I think I've always known, deep down. Even if I haven't wanted to admit it. I close my eyes. "What am I going to do?"

I don't mean for Thalia to answer the whispered question, but she does anyway. "You should talk with him."

I'm far from ready for that, but before I have a chance to say so, the boys laughingly break apart. "Thalia! Want to go a round?" Erik shouts as Finn comes toward us. She rolls her eyes at my warning glare and stands to accept the staff from Finn with a smile.

"I'd love to put you in your place!" she calls back in challenge, and twirls the staff as she goes, leaving me and Finn alone.

He smiles down at me, cheeks flushed, and pushes sweat-darkened hair out of his eyes. *"Ten points to his twelve. Not bad, though I used to beat him every time."*

"I didn't know you liked fighting with the staff."

He shrugs. *"Rather not use a weapon at all because I see the damage they cause. But a bruise or broken bone's better than a gash, or a severed arm or leg."*

"True enough," I sign, then square my shoulders and stand. Behind Finn, Thalia and Erik are calling jibes to one another above the dull pounding of wood, both light as cats on their feet. And yet Thalia is a princess, a woman grown, older than Erik and perhaps destined to wed Coll. She doesn't shirk from any of it. That shames me for wanting to. "Would you like to walk with me?" I ask.

Most of the grass and weeds are limp and brown; the hay meadows long since shorn. Last night's raindrops have puckered the road, and wet leaves lay clumped at its edges. *"You're quiet today,"* Finn observes, after awhile, and I nod.

"I'm thinking." But I veer off the path to clamber up a wooden horse fence, perching on the top rung. I'm sure the damp from the wood will seep through my skirt, but I don't mind. If we must have this talk, I suppose it's better to do it sitting down.

He comes to stand beside me, the fence tall enough that he has to look up to meet my eyes. I avoid his and try not to blush when he touches my knee with concern. I can't help thinking of all the times I've reached for his hand, or ruffled his hair. Remembering that he kissed me. At the time, I was so angry at Alaric, so blinded by hurt, the gesture seemed like simple kindness, and I was grateful for it. But now it seems like I've been treating him as my sweetheart without thinking of him so. I've wronged him.

"What is it?" he asks, when I look up.

I catch the inside of my cheek between my teeth, bracing myself, before I can speak. "Before I left with Garreth, what was it you wanted to tell me?"

His eyes widen, and he tenses for an instant before his expression shifts to one of thoughtfulness. *"If you're asking me now, this nervous, you must know. Did Erik finally tell you?"*

I shake my head. "Thalia. But she thought I already knew."

"Well. It's been no great secret."

"*I know,*" I reply, because I can't trust myself to speak aloud. "*And I think I've always known, in a way. But I didn't want...*"

"*To disappoint me?*" he finishes, and even smiles a little. "*I love you as a friend as well, Ellin, and nothing will change that. I've accepted that you don't feel the same as I do.*"

"*Damn it, Finn, that's not what I was going to say!*" At his questioning look, I press my trembling lips together and continue. "*I didn't want to acknowledge you because I didn't want things to change between us. I was—I would have given my heart to Alaric. I loved him. But he didn't feel the same, and I understand that, now. He thought of me as a younger sister, and anyway, he was never free to choose. And he wouldn't have chosen me if he had been.*" It hurts to admit it, and hurts even more deeply to speak of Alaric, but Finn doesn't look surprised by any of this. He looks at me, serious and considering, before offering his hand to help me down. His fingers tighten around mine briefly.

"*Things needn't change between us,*" he says at last. "*It's like a seed just planted. If it's meant to grow, it will.*"

It begins to rain again, tiny light droplets more like mist than anything. His eyes meet mine, the color of stormclouds moving in, and I smile despite myself. This isn't at all what I pictured, when I imagined Alaric declaring his love for me. That was like something out of a tale, all bright and glorious, and this moment is cold and damp, with rain in my eyes and my heart and words tangled. But then, this is real, and I suppose that makes all the difference.

CHAPTER THIRTY-EIGHT

THE NEXT DAYS pass in a flurry of preparations for the coronation. Messengers ride out, food and drink are brought in, and Nan oversees the scrubbing and decorating of the hall. Guest quarters are aired and tidied as maids bustle about with their arms full of fresh linens. They don't speak of it, but Finn is certain that the preparations must also remind his brothers of other, happier times. Alaric's victory celebration; Thalia's welcome. Even Alaric's coronation, because they were all together, and Alaric becoming king was something they had all expected.

Finn is glad that at least Coll no longer looks ill when his kingship is mentioned. He looks resigned, instead, and seems stronger now than he has in weeks. Coll and Erik spend much time together, discussing policy and strategy, and Finn is glad of that, too. It's good to see Erik up late and clear-eyed with a pen in his hand, marking over Coll's writing, smoothing blunt edges. He will make a good advisor, a good second, as Coll was to Alaric.

On the sixth day, some of the guests begin to arrive, and Garreth, as one of the newest captains of the Guard, escorts them from the gate. They're all gathered in the courtyard still, greeting the latest arrivals, when Davor rides up on his gray dappled gelding with another group trailing behind. But if the newcomers are unexpected, Garreth's reaction is even more startling. His eyes widen, and then the broadest grin Finn has ever seen splits his cheeks.

He's across the yard in a few running strides, catching the reins of a brown pony in order to help the curly-haired Southling girl astride it climb down. She tugs him down by the hair and kisses him thoroughly as soon as her feet touch ground, and Finn laughs at Garreth's stunned expression.

"Well! Did you know about that?" Erik asks, nudging him.

He shakes his head, still smiling. *"I'm not sure even Garreth knew. Look at him."*

Cheeks bright red above his blue collar, Garreth seems both delighted and awkward as he struts about importantly, speaking with most of the Southlings as they dismount. Inside, he presents them formally to Coll and gives introductions all around. The pretty curly-haired girl is Keth Brewer, the True Southlings' commander, and the tall youth who claps Garreth on the back like a comrade is Mathias Oakenfold. There are a man and two women whose names Finn doesn't catch, and then the one-handed harpist, the famed Aiddan Innys, and his apprentice, Brek Marthen.

Finn's not surprised to recognize a few faces from the group who came before, though it's jarring to remember that some of them—including Keth, the girl Garreth kissed—were prisoners not so long ago. But allies now, or close to it, from what Ellin and Garreth have said.

CHAPTER THIRTY-NINE

A T DINNER, NO ONE talks about anything of great importance, and I'm sure I can guess why. It's startling enough, and enough of a statement, for Coll to welcome the True Southlings and seat Keth and Aiddan at the high table with us. The last thing anyone needs is to have a political talk with half the castle and Coll's coronation guests listening. But I don't mind. I'm glad of the chance to simply catch up on news of the Southland, of my friends there, and I'm delighted to sit quietly and watch Keth and Garreth beam at each other. I thought there might be something between them, back in the Southland, and I'm very glad I was right.

"And what are you smirking at, Ellin?" Keth asks across the table, eyes sparkling.

"I'm glad to see you. All of you," I add, turning to Aiddan beside me. "I only wish Freya could have come, too."

He smiles. "She wanted to, but our people have need of her, especially with the rest of us gone. She sends her love, and said to remind you of your oath. She means to collect your service, someday."

"She'll have it," I promise, nodding. "My true home might be here, now, but I'm sure I'll be back to the Southland soon."

"Not too soon," Keth adds, giving me a mysterious smile. "We'll have need of you here before then, I hope."

"What do you mean?"

But she only shakes her head, leaving me to pick at my food in frustration. Luckily, I don't have to wait long to find out. Near the end of the meal, Coll leaves the table in order to go and speak with some of the coronation guests, no doubt making them feel welcome (and, no doubt, at Erik or Finn's suggestion), and Erik leans forward, lowering his voice. "Coll would like to speak with us in his study," he says, and nods to Keth and Aiddan. "Including both of you, if you're not too tired from your travel."

Keth shakes her head. "We're used to late nights and quiet meetings. We would be grateful."

"Good," Erik says, and gives her a quick grin. "Because I'm curious."

Entering the study gives me a quick, sharp pang, and I expect it always will. I'm glad that Coll has moved the furniture, placing the desk further from the hearth and the chairs closer, along with adding a new bench along one wall. The little cabinet where King Allard and later Alaric kept a bottle of good liquor has been moved from one corner to another. And where Alaric's desk was always comfortably messy, heaped with maps and stacks of parchments, half-read books and ledgers, now that it is Coll's, it's almost painfully spare and neat.

Coll is already seated at his desk when Erik leads the rest of us in, and he gestures politely for Keth and Aiddan to take the chairs. The rest of us find places for ourselves on the floor or the bench, though I note with some amusement that Garreth chooses to stand beside Keth, with one hand possessively on the back of her chair. She gives him a quick smile before turning to Coll, sitting up a little straighter. "Thank you for agreeing to speak with us, Your Majesty. I hope we haven't come at an inopportune time."

Coll shakes his head, though I'm sure he's thinking of the coronation in only a few days. "Now's as good as any other, Commander Brewer. And as you're friends of my family, you're welcome to call me Coll. We don't insist on formality."

"Coll, then," Keth agrees, "and please, call me Keth." She hesitates for just a moment before leaning forward, including all of the brothers. "I want you to know how sorry I was—all of the True Southlings were—to hear about King Alaric. I know how much Garreth and Ellin cared for him, and I only wish we could have sent them back sooner."

Coll gives a curt nod of thanks, looking at her sharply. "How much do you know?"

"Only what was in the message Ellin and Garreth sent, after they returned. Ellin said she suspected the Guardians. Do you still?"

"Keth, I don't suspect them; I *know* it was them," I interrupt. "I saw the murderers discussing the knife in my dreams, and they were at the Whiteriver College. It has to be the Guardians."

"We've been able to discover nothing about this plot," Aiddan says, "but it makes sense. The army they're building is far too large if they plan only to conquer the True Southlings, or even the entire Southland."

"You think they've set their sights on us," Coll says, sounding unsurprised, and Aiddan nods.

"I do. You know that rumors of unrest here in the Northlands have spread to the Southland, and perhaps even beyond. It's no secret that the changes your brother made were not popular. My guess is that the Guardians wished to stir things up further, perhaps even incite civil war."

"And do the same in the Southland, between your people and those without the mental powers," Coll finishes, nodding slowly. "Create further distrust between the Northlands and the Southland, chaos in both countries, and swoop down on all of us when we're distracted and weakened."

"Exactly." Keth leans forward, gesturing. "Ending up with a united country that the Guardians rule, with an unstoppable army of people with gifts."

The words are chilling, and I try not to shiver. After a moment, Garreth breaks the tense silence. "But what do they want? Just power and importance?"

"No doubt," Coll says with a shrug. "Riches, probably. The ability to control those they consider a threat. From what I've heard, they really seem to believe there's something wrong with all of you. As my da did. That it's witchcraft. Evil."

"What do you propose?" Erik asks, translating for Finn. "You must have something in mind, or you wouldn't have come."

Keth takes a deep breath, visibly bracing herself, and looks straight at Coll, chin high. "We want to be sworn allies, the True Southlings and the Northlands. We want to attack the Guardians before they attack us, and defeat them before they have a chance to implement their plans. We want to free the gifted Southlings of their army and offer them a place with us if they want it. For all of this, we'll need your soldiers and weapons and skills. We have some trained fighters, but we're no army."

"And in return?" Erik asks, when Coll doesn't say anything, quietly considering all of this.

"In return, we will train you and any other Northlanders who possess the mental gifts to use them. We'll combine our True Southlings with your army to create a force to match the Guardians'. Because you couldn't win against them on your own, with swords alone."

"She's right," I add. "Not if you had ten times as many men."

Coll gives me a slow nod, then turns to Keth again, a short crease appearing between his brows. "Would you have my people go to your camps for training, as Ellin did?"

"Oh, no," Keth replies, curls bobbing as she shakes her head. "All we'd ask now is for a contingent of soldiers to accompany one or two of us home, to help protect our people and train them throughout the winter."

"With the rest of us staying here, if we may," Aiddan adds. "If you would put out a call for any Northlanders with abilities to come forward, we could train them here."

I think it sounds like a fine plan, and I can tell that Coll does, too. But instead of agreeing immediately, he sits back, crossing his arms. "I'll give you an answer in the morning," he says at last. "In the meantime, be welcome. Garreth, show them back to the hall, and their companions."

---ooo-)◯(-ooo---

The rest of us gather closer together when they leave, and when Garreth returns a little later, he perches on the edge of the desk, dangling his hands between his knees. "Well?" he demands. "If you want to know what I think…"

Erik snorts. "You don't get a say, Youngest. You're besotted."

"I'm not!" Garreth retorts, pink-cheeked. "So what if I…"

"Enough," Coll says mildly. He leans forward, resting his forearms on the edge of the desk. "I mean to agree, unless any of you object."

The firelight plays on Garreth's face, casting long shadows and glinting gold on his hair when he shakes his head. "I don't object. The True Southlings are good people—they're my friends—and they need our help. I suggested an alliance before. I'm for it."

I nod. "I'm for it, for the same reasons as Garreth. And I think it's what Alaric would have wanted—for Northlanders and Southlings to work together. Isn't that what he was trying to accomplish here?"

"He would've hesitated," Erik counters, jiggling the foot that's crossed over his knee. "I'm not sure which path he would've chosen, in the end." He looks at Coll, eyes serious. "You know it won't be a popular choice, sending men down there and having Southlings here, especially Southlings encouraging people to admit to having powers, let alone using them."

"But it's not only about the Southlings! Don't forget the Guardians, and the fact that you were ready to declare war a few weeks ago," Garreth says.

Coll exhales, scratching his beard. "Finn? What do you think?"

Finn shrugs, brows drawing together, seeming to consider his words carefully. "It won't endear you to everyone, but then, what would? You care less about such things than Alaric, and that's good, for this. A king at war does what's right, not what is popular. I think you should do it. I know you have the strength for it." A small smile curves his lips. "And the stubbornness."

"I agree," Erik says. "It's not an ideal choice, but it's the best option we have."

"That's all of you, then, except Thalia." Coll turns to her expectantly, and she spreads her hands.

"Clearly, it's the right thing to do, for now," she says, looking at her skirt, "but I wonder that no one has mentioned what might happen after." She raises her eyes to Coll. "These True Southlings are, in effect, asking you to conquer their land, are they not? They are but a small faction, and they did not mention a desire to rule, once the Guardians have been overthrown. I wonder…"

"I've no wish to rule the Southland," Coll says flatly.

"Besides, the Southland has never had a king," I add. "It's not their way."

"Maybe not," Erik replies, darting a speculative look at Garreth, "but if the True Southlings' commander were to wed a Northlander prince, maybe they wouldn't be king and queen, but close enough. Enough to guide the Southland through this change, and to cement the alliance."

"I'm not…" Garreth begins, indignant, but Coll raises a hand.

"All of this is premature," he says. "For now, it's enough that we're in agreement, and we'll give the True Southlings our decision tomorrow. From now on, they will be our allies." With a decisive nod, he pushes his chair back and stands. "Now, I'm off to the stables to look in on Marigold."

———◦◦◦⟡◦◦◦———

I find him still there a little later, after shivering my way through the dark, wet night with only the soft light from the stable to guide me. For a moment, I stand in the doorway silently, just watching him. Perhaps it should seem strange to see the king with his sleeves rolled up and dirt on his shirtfront, tenderly brushing a mare due soon to foal, but because it's Coll, it seems only natural. He's humming to her, too, something soft and low. I smile to myself, then clear my throat as I approach.

Coll turns, his scowl at being interrupted relaxing a bit when he sees me. "What're you doing here so late, girl?"

"Just thought I'd make sure everything is all right," I reply, leaning my elbows over the door of Marigold's large stall. "She's not having trouble, is she?"

"Oh, no. Everything's fine." He smiles proudly, stroking her broad side. "She says not tonight, I think. Within the week, but not yet."

"Good girl," I murmur, as she tilts her head to look at me. "Pretty girl." And she is. Pale blond, dustier than Sunrise's vivid gold, with dark eyes and a white star on her forehead. She's a younger half-sister to Snowflower, Coll's favorite, and the family resemblance is clear.

I watch while Coll finishes up, then takes the brush and metal comb back to the tack room. He returns a moment later with the flask he keeps there and comes to stand beside me. "Drink?" he asks, uncapping it.

I nod and take a sip, then pass it back. Coll takes a deeper drink, watching Marigold pick at her hay. Outside, I can hear the wind picking up, rain pattering harder on the roof, but it's warm and dry in here, and very peaceful.

"I wanted you to know, I think you're doing the right thing," I say after a moment, quietly. "And I know this had no bearing on your decision, but it means a great deal to me. A year ago, I hated the Northlands so much, and now..." I take a deep breath. "Now, I truly can't think of anyone better to save the Southland. And if Thalia's right and the countries somehow unite, I'll be glad."

"Hmm," Coll murmurs, but he looks pleased. "As I said, all of that's a long way off, girl," he says after a moment. "But we'll see."

CHAPTER FORTY

B Y THE DAY OF Coll's coronation, all the guests have arrived, and the castle is full to bursting. Thalia and I spend the afternoon getting ready together, along with Keth, since she and the other True Southlings have been invited. Of course, Keth didn't bring a fine dress, but Thalia offered to lend her the green one she wore to her welcome feast, and, once hemmed, it looks almost as beautiful against Keth's red-gold hair as it did on its owner. I wear my yellow dress again, since it's the only nice one I have. Of course, Keth teases me about my shorn hair—not as short as a boy's anymore, but not far from it—but she helps me curl it. Once it's tied back with a pretty ribbon, I look as feminine as I could wish.

Both of us pale in comparison to Thalia, though. Of course, as a princess from a wealthy country, she has more fancy dresses than I've ever seen, and the one she chooses is truly breathtaking: scarlet silk, with gold embroidery on the bodice and a wide, full skirt. She wears her hair tied back, with strands of gold thread twined in, and rouges her lips with scarlet, too. She looks more like a princess than ever, and I'm proud of her for making herself up even though she must be nervous, wondering if Coll wants to marry her or not. I'm not sure I would be so composed, and I'm very glad I'm not a princess. It makes me nervous enough that I've agreed to let Finn be my escort to the festivities.

The coronation ceremony itself, before dinner, is short and a little boring, much as Alaric's was. The lords make speeches, and then Coll kneels and swears the oath, and then Erik places the crown on his head, just as Coll did for Alaric. It's all very somber, and I spend the entire time trying not to think about Alaric. My throat feels tight when I think of how few times he wore the crown for ceremony, how little time he had to sit on the throne. King for less than a year, and someday, in the histories of the Northlands, maybe children will only remember King Alaric as a note, in passing, a monarch they always forget because his reign was so short. No one will ever know him as we did, those of us who loved him, and not even we will ever know what great things he might have done, if he'd had more time.

By the time the ceremony is over, I'm crying, and I'm glad that some of the other women are, too. Better for everyone to think I'm simply overcome with emotion than for anyone to guess the truth, that I'm mourning the old king rather than celebrating the new. I duck out quickly and try to compose myself, and by the time Finn finds me and offers his arm, I'm almost able to smile, though it feels jagged at the edges.

"I meant to tell you before, you look beautiful," he says with his mind as he leads me to the hall. Even at a distance, the scents of food are thick in the air.

"You look very nice, too." And he does, dressed in his coat and high boots and breeches, with a gold circlet glinting on his brow.

The hall itself is decorated beautifully, with colored runners on the tables and bright paper lanterns, and the tables themselves are laden with all kinds of food. Finn leads me to the high table, with his brothers, Thalia, and a few lords and other important people. I'm not surprised to see Keth as well, partly because she's Coll's newest ally, and partly because she's being escorted by Garreth this evening. Before we eat, Coll stands, and the room falls still.

"I'm honored to be your king," he says, voice gruff and deep as always. "I am grateful for your trust. And while I cannot promise peace, or prosperity, I pledge that I will stop at nothing to protect this great land, her people, and her friends." He stops for a moment, swallowing. "I will do my best. This I swear to you."

There's silence again, for a moment, before the applause begins. "Hear, hear!" someone shouts, at another table, and then everyone joins in, raising their glasses and calling honor to Coll Horse Master. I catch Erik's eye and smile, knowing he had nothing to do with this speech, at least. Alaric always said the right thing, and beautifully, and I know Erik has at least a bit of that knack. But this was all Coll, simple and to the point, and I'm glad for his sake that everyone seems to approve.

I surprise myself by enjoying the meal. The food is delicious, and unlike the last feast I attended, I'm at ease here, among friends. It's strange to look at Thalia's smiling face and think I ever disliked her, or to laugh with Keth and Garreth across the table and remember a time when Keth and I were sworn enemies or, further back, a time when Garreth and I didn't like one another. Things are better now in so many ways, and I'm grateful.

And yet. When the meal ends and the true celebrating and dancing begin, I find myself alone for a little while. Finn pulls out his book and pencil and goes to talk with some cousins, and my other friends disperse as well, to drink or dance or both. I refill my wineglass and find a seat apart at the edge of the crowd, watching the dancers. It's easy to remember Alaric dancing with me here, not so long ago, and I close my eyes. I wish, now, that I'd been more pleasant to him then. That I'd enjoyed that one dance more. But it was Finn I danced with twice that night, and I did enjoy it. It was Finn I talked with, shared a moment that should have been romantic out in the garden. I'm not sure whether I was more a fool then, for not realizing it, or if I am now, for moping.

With a determined nod, I drain my glass and stand, intending to look for him. But I've only gone a few steps before Garreth grabs my hand. "Dance with me...Eland, lad," he says, grinning wickedly. I roll my eyes at the teasing, which is nothing new, but take his hands anyway and follow his lead. I dance next with Mat, until we spin and change partners, and I find myself clutching

Erik's hands and laughing. The room seems a little brighter, a little louder, and the floor might be tilting a bit beneath my feet from the wine, but I don't mind.

"Where's Finn?" I ask, speaking loudly to be heard over the music, and his shoulder lifts beneath my palm.

"Not sure. He was talking with our cousins, Diedrick and Moira," he replies, nodding to the stocky man with the blindfold and his tall, pale-haired sister, "but I haven't seen him in awhile. He might be with Coll."

"Maybe!" I agree, feeling pleasantly carefree. It's no matter. Wherever Finn is, I'm sure he'll wait for me.

CHAPTER FORTY-ONE

THE LITTLE GARDEN is cold, but the shock of it is refreshing after the warm, crowded room. For a moment, Finn breathes deeply, savoring the cool air on his cheeks, admiring the colored lanterns strung against the dark sky. A movement at the far corner draws his eye, and he smiles to see that he isn't alone.

"Shouldn't you be entertaining your subjects?" he asks once he's crossed the garden, and Coll grimaces.

"Needed a moment. There's too many people and, at this point, not enough wits to go around."

"They're only happy for you," Finn replies, and plucks a sprig off the hedge to drop in the fountain. *"I liked your speech."*

Coll shrugs. *"I meant it."*

"That's why I liked it." Finn joins him on the carved wooden bench, and they sit companionably for a few moments, watching the revelers dance past the open door. Inside is a bustle of color and movement and undoubtedly plenty of noise, but this corner of the garden is removed from all of that. Peaceful.

Thalia and Erik dance past the door, waltzing in a slow circle, and she looks more stunningly regal than Finn has ever seen her. Erik looks purely, overwhelmingly delighted, and Finn takes a deep breath before turning to Coll. He's not very surprised when Coll beats him to it. *"He loves her, doesn't he."* It's not a question, but Finn nods anyway.

"He does, but you know he'll do what's right. He never would have vied with Alaric for her attention, and he won't now, if you plan to…"

"I don't." It's said so bluntly that Finn blinks. Coll shifts slightly on the bench and shrugs. "If they wed, and I don't, I'll name Erik my heir, and his son or daughter will be king or queen. Thalia's people will be pleased; she and Erik will be pleased. And I'll be pleased, as well, because I won't feel that I'm taking something that isn't rightfully mine."

"Thalia, you mean?"

But Coll shakes his head. "The throne. It was supposed to be Alaric's, and then his son's. Certainly not mine alone. Let Erik and his sons share it, someday."

Finn nods slowly, feeling the future spreading out like the threads of a tapestry, like a tangible thing. It's past generous, what Coll is doing, and he swallows hard. "It's a wise plan, you and Erik here, with the Northlands between you. And Garreth in the Southland, whether to rule or simply to lead."

Coll pushes himself to his feet and gives Finn a sharp look. "And you, Finn?"

"I think my path lies elsewhere," he begins to say, but stops abruptly and smiles at the sight of Ellin coming to the door, looking flushed and happy and a little unsteady on her feet. Coll follows his gaze and chuckles.

"I'd best get back inside, boyo. Don't be too long out here." He stops in the doorway and speaks to Ellin briefly before leaving the two of them alone. Finn rises to meet her by the fountain, and Ellin beams. With her shining eyes and pink cheeks and her short curls coming undone from their ribbon, she's never looked more beautiful.

"So, I've found you," Ellin says, very deliberately, and Finn laughs.

"So you have. Are you having a good time?"

"Better now," she replies, and Finn's blood seems to stop in his veins when she reaches up to touch his cheek, trailing fingertips over his suddenly too-warm skin. "Come dance with me," she says with her mind, but he shakes his head.

"Not yet. I want to talk with you about…"

"No," she says aloud, lips round on the word, and curls her hand behind his neck, raising gooseflesh. It takes everything he has not to pull her against him, but then she does that, instead. *"Finn, I'm tired of talking. Tired of thinking too much about this. Let's just..."* Then she's on tiptoe, tugging him down, and her lips are against his, and his hand finds hers. The fingers of her other hand thread through his hair, and he can taste wine, waxy rouge, and he closes his eyes and could drown in the darkness.

But he also hears her thoughts, feeling them in the odd sideways gift he has, and if there are plenty of flattering things there, there are snatches of Erik and Thalia, Garreth and Keth, and, of course, Alaric, too. And for all this moment is his heart's desire, he can feel that she's kissing him like she's drowning in truth, like she's trying to make a point. He loves her stubbornness, but not for this. He steps back with more than a little regret to find her stumbling back as well, looking stunned. Her hand flutters to her lips before dropping limply to her side, and he could kick himself for hurting her. "Finn," she says aloud, looking shaky, "I—I'm sorry. I don't know what came over..."

"You have nothing to be sorry for," he says, and takes a deep, slow breath. *"But I need to know. Was that—is this—what you want, or is it because you think you should? I love you, Ellin. I'm certain. Are you?"*

She looks indignant, but then her mouth closes abruptly, and she shakes her head, taking another step back. *"I wish I knew."*

He nods, expecting this. *"Then I'll wait,"* he says, and gestures to the door. *"But in the meantime, we can still dance, if you want to."*

Ellin smiles, looking more like herself again, as she takes his proffered arm. *"Always,"* she says. *"That, I'm sure of."*

CHAPTER FORTY-TWO

THE FIRST SNOW falls a few weeks later, and I wake to its brightness out my window, coating the land all white and pristine. I admire the view as I pull on my warmest socks, even though the sight of it makes my heart twist, because I know what this first breath of winter means.

My friends and the Northlander soldiers traveling to the Southland have been delaying as long as possible, but the snow means that they can't wait any longer. The day is spent preparing for their departure, and the next morning, we gather in the hall after breakfast to say goodbye.

"I can't believe you're going back. And without me!" I exclaim, pulling Garreth close for another tight embrace. "How will we ever get along without you here?"

He laughs, startlingly deep, sounding so like Alaric that I swallow with difficulty. The short beard he's trying to grow doesn't help, and as I look up at him, it strikes me that, all of a sudden, he's far closer to a man than the boy I first met. He's still Garreth, though, and his eyes twinkle at me with the mischief I know so well. "You're only jealous because I'll be in the Southland while you're weathering blizzards here," he says, then tilts up his chin. "Besides, they need military expertise, someone who gets along with both Northlanders and Southlings, and who better?"

"Who better to herd their pigs," I mutter, but I smile. "You'll do fine. They've made a good choice."

"'Course we have," Keth says, coming up beside us. She looks at Garreth with pride, and, as always, I marvel at the change in her. She used to be so silly around boys she fancied, but with Garreth, there's nothing but true warmth and respect between them. When she turns back to me, we embrace as well, and I'm momentarily overwhelmed by the scent of her perfume. It almost makes me giggle, and I'm glad that some things, at least, never change.

"Good luck," I say simply, and she nods, hair brushing against my cheek.

"To you, too. I hope there are as many Northlanders with gifts as we suspect."

After more goodbyes and last-minute advice, the rest of us stand in the yard and watch them go, Keth on her brown pony, Garreth with his blue coat and a bright green scarf, his pale hair shining like a beacon in the sun. I wave until they've turned the corner and are out of sight, heading toward the gate and the contingent of Guards waiting for them there.

——ooo)◯(ooo——

In truth, I don't expect many Northlanders to come forward and admit to having mental gifts when Coll and Erik begin to put out the word. But I'm surprised twice over: first, when Coll gives his speech explaining the situation and the alliance with the True Southlings, I expect resistance. But what resistance there is is quiet, a few murmurs against a tide of support, as if Alaric's deeds in life paved the way for this, and his death at the Southling Guardians' hands was fuel to the fire of change. And things do change, rapidly. Every few days, new Northlanders come to the city, to the castle, shyly admitting to having healing ability, or the gift of reading thoughts, or the Sight, or any number of other powers. Erik sends messengers out to the villages and towns, bearing signs and letters of explanation for the lords and ladies.

And still they come, all these Northlanders with the "witch-craft," to learn to use their gifts and embrace them after hiding and fearing them for so long. Out in the city, people are more likely to call a greeting to me than to sneer at my red hair, and for the first time since coming to the Northlands, I feel truly at peace, and proud to be myself. Ellin Fisher, called Healer, with abilities others admire instead of hate.

"Will you look at all of these?" Erik exclaims, sprawled in a chair in the tower with a sheaf of parchments in his hand. The snow swirls against the windows, but with a fire blazing in the hearth and a pot of tea, we're all snug and warm. "How are we going to do this?"

"Give me those for a moment." I lean over to pluck the pages out of his hand and spread them out on the table, nudging my cup aside to make room. "Well, I suppose it's like any other school," I say at last. "We'll divide them up by ability and give each group the tutor best suited to teaching them to use their gift."

"So, I would teach people how to speak with their minds—as I taught you, for that matter—and you'd teach healing." Erik nods over the rim of his mug. "That might work."

"I'm not so certain," Aiddan says. "There are basic skills they all need to learn first, such as controlling their abilities and shielding. Not to mention, some might already possess two gifts, or a latent ability alongside their primary one. Most of us have at least two abilities, after all. We should test them early on."

"Anyway," I add, "I think you'd be better suited to teaching people to read others' thoughts stealthily, Erik. Finn could teach them how to speak to one another. And Brek can teach illusion, Mat can teach compelling now that he's learned how, and…"

"*Actually,*" Finn interrupts, meeting my gaze across the table, "*I won't be teaching anything. At least, not for awhile. I'm leaving in the morning, going to stay with Moira and Diedrick in the Northwatch.*"

For an announcement that's silent, the reaction it receives is anything but, with everyone exclaiming and asking questions at once, since Finn has been a member of this project from the start, and we were all counting on him. Everyone speaks, that is, except for Erik, who looks miserable, as if he already knew, and me, because I can't seem to find any words at all.

"Why?" I ask at last, hands trembling as much as my voice would. Is it because of me? I wonder. But then, I don't think I want to know.

With Erik translating, Finn tells everyone about the talk he had with Moira and Diedrick, when they came for Alaric's coronation. They're cousins of the royal family, and Diedrick is the one who challenged Alaric for the throne, though apparently, since being blinded and especially since Alaric's death, he's a changed man, less concerned about power and more focused on honor and doing right. And Moira and the twins have always been close. That's why she urged Diedrick to tell Finn about an ancient power waking in the Northwatch, in the rugged, frigid heart of the Northlands.

Long ago, before the city and its guards and even before the crown, there were protectors of the Northlands, men and women filled with the spirit of the land herself, who could change into animals and defend her. They were a secret clan, living far from settlements, and everyone thought they had died out, or perhaps never had existed except in tales and legends. And yet, in recent months, there have been rumors of wolves and bears turning into men, snowcats who come upon travelers and look at them with intelligent eyes and don't attack.

"They defended the Northlands once," Finn says, leaning forward, *"and we think that perhaps they will again. And…"* he hesitates, *"…for months, I've dreamed of flying, and I woke recently with my window open and an owl's feather on my pillow. If anyone is meant for this, it's me."*

When he leaves, a few days later, I kiss him again. Clear-eyed, this time, with a nose red from tears and the stinging wind and hope in my heart. *"I'll miss you,"* I say, and tug his blue scarf tighter against the cold. My smile wobbles at the corners, but his doesn't falter.

"It's not for long," he replies. *"I'll be back by spring at the latest."*

And I'll make up my mind by then, I think. It's a promise I don't speak, saying instead, *"Don't forget me."*

Finn must remember, too, because he laughs. *"As if I ever could."*

When he rides out, since Erik has already turned away with Thalia, his eyes bright and his nose suspiciously red, I go to Coll, who puts his arm around my shoulders. He clears his throat, but even so, his voice is rougher than usual. "C'mon, girl," he says, steering me down the path. "Let's go look in on Marigold and her little filly."

"Are horses your answer to everything?" I ask tartly, half-smiling and halfway still in tears.

"Fixed things between us once, didn't they?" he replies, and tugs my hair. "But no, it's not the horses themselves as much as the peace. You take it where you can find it. That's what I say, and the horses know it, too."

So says the king of the Northlands, I think, and smile as I follow him in.

CHAPTER FORTY-THREE

ON MIDWINTER'S NIGHT, a blizzard rages in the Northlands, with snow heaped on the streets and blindingly thick outside the windows, with wind shrieking and knifing against the glass. In the hall of the castle, a fire roars in the hearth, warming the room, and candles and lanterns glow warm and golden, illuminating tapestries and banners. The remains of a special meal have been cleared away and mulled wine brought out, and everyone in the castle has gathered round the hearth to hear the renowned bard Aiddan Innys sing.

As always, his voice is like honey, like warmth itself, and I close my eyes and allow myself to be carried away in the songs, familiar ones from the Southland and tales of far away, of Rhodanath and the high seas, ships with bright sails and the corsairs who man them, princesses in towers and great magical beasts. After many songs, Aiddan holds up his hand and allows Brek, who has been playing the harp for him, to take the center seat while he comes to sit beside me, accepting a glass of wine when Erik offers it.

"That was beautiful," I whisper, and he acknowledges the compliment with a smile, nodding to Brek.

"You'll want to hear this," he says softly. "He wrote it himself."

Delighted, I turn back to the hearth in time to hear Brek introducing his song. "An' this one is better than most," he finishes grandly, "because it's true."

There's a smattering of applause, and then he begins, picking out a simple, haunting melody, the rhythm used in the Southland for heroic tales. "In the Southland, they used to say that the Northlands could chill the skin right off your bones, and Northlanders themselves were colder still," he says over the music, and when he starts to sing the tale itself, my hand falters up to cover my mouth. I can't believe it.

"But this tale doesn't end!" I protest to Aiddan with my thoughts, thrilled and embarrassed all at once. *"The war hasn't even begun, and there's so much left unfinished. I don't understand."*

Aiddan smiles again and gestures with his cup to the scene around us. A Southling boy playing the harp in the Northlands castle. Erik and Mat sprawled on the floor like two companionable puppies, with Thalia of Rhodanath behind them, her hand on Erik's shoulder. There's Coll, the Northlander king but like a brother to me, and Aiddan, on my other side, embodying the peace and wisdom of the Southland. Then there's Finn, away north, finding the magic of the Northwatch even as Garreth and Keth are deep in the woods of the Southland, with soldiers and healers training side-by-side. *"Look at how much has changed, in so little time,"* Aiddan says. *"It may be only the beginning, but it's enough for a tale."*

I think of my family, my people, Northlanders and Southlings together, and I agree. We know that we're not at all different, and for now, that's enough.

Northlander: Tales of the Borderlands Book One

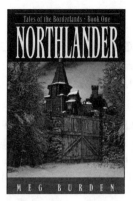

When 16-year-old Ellin Fisher and her father travel to the Northlands on a secret mission to heal the ailing king, she longs to go home to the Southland, where the practice of healing isn't called witchcraft, punishable by death. A fugitive in the Northlands and hunted at home by the mysterious Guardians, she must choose between her homeland and the Northlands, thus setting in motion events that will shape the future of two kingdoms.

WINNER, GOLD AWARD, YOUNG ADULT FICTION, FOREWORD MAGAZINE BOOK OF THE YEAR, 2007. INTERNATIONAL READING ASSOCIATION, NOTABLE Y-A FICTION.

Northlander · Tales of the Borderlands · Book One

ISBN: 978-0-9768126-8-5
Trade soft cover 280 pages
$8.95

Brown Barn Books
119 Kettle Creek Road
Weston, CT 06883

SCHOOL LIBRARY JOURNAL, February, 2008

...The author's careful attention to everyday details builds a richly believable fantasy world with a medieval flair. A strong heroine, Ellin matures as the narrative progresses. There is plenty of action, danger, and page-turning suspense, and issues of prejudice and persecution are well handled. Science fiction fans will appreciate the threat of mind control as a weapon. A satisfying ending with a hint of future romance will have readers eagerly awaiting the sequel.

BOOKLIST, January 1, 2008

...Giving Ellin a lively character and the resilience to survive physical dangers and devastating personal losses, Burden places here in a conventional, well-ordered setting, supplies a surdy supporting cast and—an unusual touch—replaces the customary sorts of villains with people who resort to violent deeds out of innocence or good intentions. Although billed as the series opener for Tales of the Borderlands, this stands alone so well that it's hard to see what's coming next.

WANDS AND WORLDS: Fantasy and science fiction for children and teens, January 06, 2008

Northlander is a book that continues to surprise the reader. At first it seems a standard, cliched us vs. them: the evil Northlanders are prejudiced against the good Southlanders. But it turns out to be so much more than that. I can't say too much without giving away some of the surprises, but this is a book painted in a rich palette of many shades of gray, not just black and white. It's a book that shows how prejudice and hatred can exist anywhere there is ignorance and fear, and goodness can be found in the most unexpected of places.

ABOUT THE AUTHOR

MEG BURDEN has been reading fantasy and science fiction since sometime around kindergarten. She graduated with a B.A. in music from Mary Baldwin College at 18 and shortly afterward, began writing when she wasn't waitressing, tending parrots (really), and teaching as a graduate student at the University of Virginia.

Nowadays she lives in a small Nebraska town with more cows than people and divides her time between writing and raising Siamese cats. She's actively involved in online science fiction fandom, which she credits with teaching her to write and keeping her sanity intact.

She is currently co-writing a six-book series of tie-in novels for the television show *Stargate Atlantis*.

Her last book, *Northlander*, received the Foreword Magazine Book of the Year award and was an International Reading Association Notable Book.

If you'd like to write to Meg, her email address is meg@megburden.com.